Dr. Beckett

A Novel

by:
Grace Maxwell

Brothers Paradise: Dr. Beckett/Grace Maxwell—1st edition

One

Sadie

R ain pelts down relentlessly, as if the heavens themselves are weeping for my plight. I stand at Beckett Paradise's door, shivering, feeling cold droplets seeping through my jacket to touch my skin with icy fingers. My luggage is piled at my feet, a sad testament to my current life, packed in haste when I stormed out of Alex's place, a chaotic collection of everything I own.

I hesitate, my finger hovering over the doorbell. *Am I really this desperate?* Desperate enough to ask Beckett for help, the grown-up boy who spent our childhood finding new and creative ways to terrorize me? The boy who once locked me in the treehouse for an entire afternoon just because he could? Beckett is measured and controlled while I am impulsive and messy. It's no wonder we've never particularly gotten along.

I take a step back, my breath coming fast and uneven. *Maybe this is a mistake.* Maybe I should turn around and figure something else out. A homeless shelter doesn't seem so bad. At least it doesn't come with the added humiliation of asking Beckett for a favor. But this is also the Beckett who has long been my brother Caleb's best friend. Since our parents are gone and my brother lives overseas, he's always told me I could go to Beckett if I were ever in trouble.

Another gust of wind howls through the night, sending a shiver straight to my bones and making the reality of my situation clear. I have nowhere else to go. My pride is the only thing standing between me and warmth, and at this point, it's already in tatters.

Before I can talk myself out of it, I press the doorbell. The chime echoes behind the heavy wood barrier, the sound nearly swallowed by the storm. My heart thumps, and I brace myself for the inevitable scowl that awaits me. When the door creaks open, that's exactly what I get.

Beckett looks like he's been dragged out of bed — no shirt, messy hair, and clearly not thrilled to see me. His face goes from annoyed to shocked, his blue eyes narrowing. He takes up the whole doorway, tall and strong, with a presence that would make most people step back. But I'm not going anywhere.

A muscle in Beckett's jaw ticks. "What the hell are you doing here, Sadie Calloway?"

"I had nowhere else to go," I inform him.

I didn't leave because Alex hit me; he would never dare. But the people he'd started hanging out with? The way they whispered when I walked into the room or shut up entirely like I didn't belong? That told me everything. Add in how little he seemed to notice I existed anymore, and suddenly, staying felt more dangerous than leaving.

Beckett exhales, rubbing a hand down his face. I see the moment he resigns himself to this situation — the subtle shift in his shoulders, the flicker of irritation that turns into something more resigned.

"Get in before you drown on my doorstep," he mutters, stepping aside.

I want to say something, anything that might explain why I'm here, drenched and disheveled, but the words lodge in my throat, stubborn as stones. Instead, I meet his gaze squarely, letting the suitcases speak where my voice fails.

With a muttered curse, Beckett steps aside as I shuffle past him, my soaked sneakers squeaking against the hardwood floor. I try desperately to ignore that his scrub pants are hanging low on his hips, and his chest is a washboard. Instead, I drag my bags into his house, water pooling beneath them.

"Are you serious?"

I swallow hard. "No, I'm just testing how waterproof my luggage is."

His scowl deepens. "Jesus, Sadie."

A clap of thunder cracks through the night, and I flinch. I won't beg. If he wants to kick me right back out, fine.

But he doesn't.

"Make yourself scarce," he mumbles, scratching the stubble on his cheek. "You know where the guest room is. And don't think this is a sleepover that turns into a weekender."

I roll my eyes. "Please, like I'm thrilled about being here."

"You seem to be moving right in."

My fingers curl into fists. "I'll be gone soon enough."

"Good."

But neither of us moves, we just stand there staring, the tension thick.

Beckett sighs, shaking his head as if trying to dislodge reality. He glances at the mess my suitcases are making. I'm sure it's making his skin crawl. "Towels are in the closet. Try not to flood the place."

He turns on his heel and disappears, likely already counting the seconds until he can call my brother, Caleb, and wash his hands of me.

I head down the hallway to the guest room and drop onto

the bed, my wet clothes clinging to me uncomfortably. I've never stayed here before, and the scent of Beckett is everywhere — clean, crisp, and a little like cedarwood. I rub my hands up and down my arms, trying to will warmth back into my bones, but it's useless. My fingers are stiff, my body aching from the cold.

I should move, get up and take a shower. Or at least change into something dry. But exhaustion weighs me down, my mind spiraling as I think about Caleb, my only family, half a world away as usual and completely unable to help me. Even if he wanted to fix this, there's nothing he can do from the other side of the globe. I'm stuck for the foreseeable future.

Eventually, I force myself to my feet, my body protesting. The bathroom is small but spotless, of course, and I peel off my wet clothes with shaking hands. The hot water stings at first, sharp pinpricks against my chilled skin, but soon enough, the warmth seeps into my muscles, loosening the knots of tension.

I press my forehead against the cool tile, my breaths coming fast as I try to keep my thoughts from running wild. *This is temporary.* It has to be. Beckett doesn't want me here, and I don't want to be here any longer than necessary.

But as the water rushes over me, washing away the grime and the worst of the night, I can't ignore the truth. Temporary or not, for now, I have nowhere else to go.

Sunlight peeks through the blinds, its soft intrusion a huge shift from the storm that raged last night. I'm perched at Beckett's kitchen counter, one leg swinging idly as I cradle a mug of coffee between my hands. The oversized T-shirt I borrowed — or commandeered from the dryer, depending on who you ask — hangs off one shoulder, the fabric warm and smelling faintly of Beckett's cologne.

Footsteps shuffle behind me, and Beckett's grumble of irritation is my greeting. He makes a beeline for the coffeemaker, pouring himself a cup with an air of desperation.

"Morning." I sip my coffee.

He doesn't answer right away, but his gaze travels over me, more specifically, to the oversized shirt hanging off my frame.

His shirt.

His scowl deepens. "You're really making yourself at home, huh?"

I sip my coffee, feigning indifference. "It was either this or dripping all over."

Yes, I have bags with me. No, I did not pack effectively.

His eyes narrow, like he wants to argue, but instead, he focuses on his coffee, taking a slow sip as he watches me over the rim.

His phone rings, and Beckett glances at the caller ID, mutters another curse, and answers. "Caleb," he says.

I tense, curling my toes against the cold tile floor. This is it — the moment Caleb tells him to kick me out. I texted Caleb last night to tell him where I was. He sent back a slew of curse words, and I turned my phone off.

Beckett's expression shifts from annoyed to stunned. His eyes flicker to mine, and I straighten up, suddenly self-conscious.

"Yeah, she's here," he says, his tone cautious. I watch Beckett's jaw tighten as he listens, his grip on the phone tightening until his knuckles turn white. "Are you serious?" His voice rises. There's a long pause, and then he sighs heavily. "All right, all right, I'll keep her away from Alex. Yeah, I get it. Do whatever it takes."

I freeze, coffee forgotten. The room feels smaller somehow, the walls inching closer. Beckett ends the call and slams the phone on the counter. He rubs a hand over his face, clearly at a loss.

"What did Caleb say?" I ask.

"Damn it, Sadie." He groans, meeting my gaze. There's

something—concern, maybe even fear—before his eyes harden again. "What is Alex up to, and how deep are you in it?"

"I don't want to talk about it." I turn away from him, racing through how I can explain what happened and why I left in the middle of the night. I can't even describe it myself. "It's none of your business."

Beckett breathes in and out noisily, like a bull ready to charge. "Your brother wants you to stay here until—"

"Oh, I'll be out of your hair as soon as I can."

"No." Beckett has a no-nonsense vibe now. "You will do as Caleb and I say."

"You're not my keeper."

"According to Caleb, I am."

I shut my eyes in frustration. I knew I shouldn't have come here.

"Your brother has given me specific instructions to make sure I do whatever it takes to keep you safe from Alex. Do you know what that means?"

I swallow, my throat suddenly dry. "Trouble," I whisper. Here I am, wearing his T-shirt, sipping his coffee, and now bound to him by a promise he never wanted to make.

Two

Beckett

Sadie storms out of the room, leaving me standing here after her brother called in a big favor. A door slams.

"Great," I mutter.

I like living alone. The quiet. The space. I grew up in a busy household with four brothers and a sister. I enjoy things being different these days. I enjoy things being exactly the way I want them. But now Sadie's here, sleeping in my guest room, and I'm pretty sure that means a tornado has been unleashed in my house. I already know I'm going to regret saying yes. But it wasn't like I could turn her down, and I definitely can't turn Caleb down.

I run a hand through my messy hair and glance at the mirror. I look terrible. *Good*. Maybe she'll realize how annoying this whole situation is. I'm not doing this for her. I'm doing it for her brother. And Caleb better know how much he owes me for this.

My stomach growls. I need more coffee. Badly. I start the espresso maker and prepare a double shot. I don't want to deal with Sadie's troubles or her excuses. But I can't stop thinking about her.

Last night, she looked so sad—like a puppy left out in the rain. She said she had nowhere else to go, and that made me feel like a jerk for even thinking about saying no. But how long is she staying? A couple of days? A few weeks? I don't have time for this. Caleb wants me to be sure Alex is out of the picture. I'm not even sure what that means.

The smell of coffee fills the kitchen, but it doesn't help. When my drink is ready, I take a quick sip—too fast. I burn my tongue. At least the pain helps me wake up.

Then I hear a door creak behind me. She's back. This should be fun.

Sadie walks into the kitchen, yawning. Her hair's a mess, her eyes still sleepy. She's changed into jeans and the T-shirt she arrived in last night.

"I'm sorry," she says. "I wouldn't be here if I had somewhere else to go."

"What happened to all your friends?" I grumble, keeping my eyes on my coffee.

She rubs her eyes and frowns. "My best friend lives at the hospital, and most everyone else I know would tell Alex where I am. Frankly, I'd prefer not to see or talk to him again."

I stand, ready to defend her. "Did he hurt you?"

She rolls her eyes. "Hilarious."

I don't laugh. I just wait, hoping she'll tell me what's going on. Growing up, Alex's older brother, Simon, was behind me a year in school. He was a bully then, and I can't imagine he and Alex aren't still the same.

"No. He never touched me." She clears her throat. "Anyway, I've got stuff to do today. Errands and things."

14

Errands. Sure. I almost believe her. "What kind of errands?" I ask.

She pauses. I can tell she's making something up. "Just stuff I need to handle. Do you think I could borrow your Jeep? I'll fill it with gas. I promise."

I was planning to drive it to work, but it's supposed to be nice today. I guess I can take the Porsche. My jaw tightens, but I don't have a good reason to say no. Not one that doesn't make me sound like a total asshole.

"Fine. Just don't crash it."

She grins, and it's the first time she's looked even a little happy since she arrived last night. "Thanks, Beckett."

I let out a grunt. "What about work? Do you have a job?"

Sadie's smile disappears. "I'm trying. It's just... I was working at Della's Coffee Hut, but then..."

"But then what?" I push.

"The bank took the hut. So now...I'm kind of unemployed."

I want to feel like I was right, like I've known since we were little she'd end up a mess. But instead, something in me softens. She looks so tired and sad. I want to make it better, almost as much as I want to make her go away.

She pulls at the hem of her shirt, and I notice how old and worn it is. She looks just as worn down. "I'll figure it out," she says. "I'll get a job and be out of your way soon."

I want to believe her. But this can't be that easy to solve. And even if I don't want to admit it, I care. We grew up together, for God's sake. And now she has hardly any family left.

I reach into my pocket and toss the Jeep's fob to her. "Don't scratch it," I say, trying to sound annoyed. Like I don't care. Like she's not getting to me.

"I won't," she says softly. I can tell she thinks I'm not as tough as I pretend to be. And maybe she's right.

"I've got a long day at the hospital," I tell her as I pick up my bag and head for the door. I need to leave before things get too chummy here. "There's a spare house key on the hook by the phone. Don't trash the place."

"Like I would," she calls after me. Her voice is playful, but I hear something else too. Relief. She really did need somewhere safe to go.

I shut the door behind me and get into the car. That's when I realize I forgot my coffee. Too late now. I'm not going back in there.

I drive to the hospital, hoping work will help me forget about this. But I can't shake the feeling that this is just the beginning. Sadie is going to turn everything upside down.

I walk through the hospital's main doors, and right away, the smell of cleaner hits me. It's sharp, but it's familiar. It reminds me why I'm here. Just like every day, I carry a lot on my shoulders. I'm the lead cardiothoracic surgeon at Paradise General Hospital and the best in the valley.

I get to the locker room and change out of my regular clothes and put on scrubs — the soft, clean uniform that helps me feel ready. Then I grab my white coat. It feels like a superhero cape. I stuff the pockets with pens, a notepad, and gloves. Swinging my stethoscope over my head, I'm set for the day. My office is across the street, but I'm here at the hospital today.

The hallway is busy. Nurses walk quickly past me, laughing and chatting. I hear patients talking, machines beeping in the background, and phones ringing. It's loud, but it's the heartbeat of the hospital. I nod and smile at a few people I know. Even though I'm tired, I'm glad to be here. This is where I belong.

My first stop is Rosemary Kennedy. She was born with a septal defect — a hole in her heart. It was repaired when she was an infant, but her heart has always been weak and is slowly giving up on her. She's on the transplant list, and she's fighting, but I need to find a way to get her a heart soon. Every day we wait, I get more and more nervous.

When I reach her door, I stop. I always do this. It's my little moment to breathe and get ready. I can't show her how worried I am. I take a deep breath, letting it fill my lungs and calm my nerves. Then I knock.

"Come in, Dr. Beckett!" she calls.

I smile and walk in. She's been living in the hospital for over a year, yet she's almost always cheerful. Her room is cozy and colorful, the walls covered with drawings and postcards. It doesn't feel like a hospital room. It feels like home.

In the midst of it all, wrapped in blankets, is Rosemary. Her eyes light up when she sees me. "Hey, you're late!" she teases.

"Traffic," I say, trying to sound casual, though I feel my cheeks turn red. "You know how it is."

She raises an eyebrow. "I can tell when you're lying. I bet it was a woman who made you late."

I laugh a little and shrug. If only she knew which woman. Soon enough, she probably will. "I hate being so transparent."

She looks down at some papers in her lap.

"What are you working on?" I ask, hoping to change the subject.

"Bucket list," she says. "I'm doing all the research now so I'll be ready to hit the road once I have a new heart. I cut out pictures and put them here in my planner. The first stop? Paris! I want to see the Eiffel Tower and eat every pastry I can find."

"Paris sounds amazing," I say, feeling a spark of hope. "You'll get there. I know it."

Just then, my pager buzzes. I look at it and sigh. "I have to go. The emergency department needs me," I tell her, frowning.

"Don't worry about me," she says, still smiling. "I'll be here tomorrow, and the day after, and the day after that. Go save someone's life!"

"I'll come check on you later," I tell her. "We'll talk more about Paris then."

I leave her room and head down the hallway. I push open the door to the emergency department and spot my older brother, Greyson. "Whatcha got?" I ask.

He tells me about his patient. "Kurt Cole's a fifty-six-year-old male who was bussed in this morning with chest pains. His BP is one-sixty over ninety-five. His EKG shows Q waves in leads II, III, and aVF, and the cardiac enzymes show very high troponin, but they're falling."

I skim the notes in his records. "Looks like he needs a bypass."

"I thought you might say that." Greyson nods. "We've got theater four prepping for you."

"Thanks. And his family?"

"They're with him in bay one."

I head off to meet Kurt Cole and explain to him and his family what my plan is. They're worried, but this is a routine surgery for me.

After that, I walk up to the operating room and begin my scrub as the team moves Mr. Cole into position. I hold my arms up and Margo Martindale, my head surgical nurse, is ready with gloves.

"Okay, Mr. Cole, we're going to get you taken care of," I tell him as I enter the room. "As I told your family, this is a four-to six-hour surgery. Do you have any questions before we put you under?"

"I want to be at my daughter's wedding in June."

"I'll do my best to make it happen."

I wink at Dana Camp, my anesthesiologist, so she can start her process. She injects into his IV. "Mr. Cole, start counting down from one hundred."

He lasts to ninety-five, and he's out. She's an expert with the endotracheal tube, and he's soon placed on the ventilator.

"Okay, team, let's get started," I tell them, checking that everything is in place.

Margo turns the music on, and Depeche Mode's *Music for the Masses* fills the room.

I do this surgery often, but every patient is different. Every case matters. I go over his history in my head — test results, scans, and reports all flash through my mind. I take a deep breath and focus.

"Scalpel," I say, and my assistant places it in my hand.

The surgery begins. My hands move with care and practice. With every cut, I remember the reason I became a surgeon. It's not just about fixing hearts. It's about giving people a chance at life.

We move him onto a bypass machine so I can stop his heart and repair the damage. There are three clogged arteries.

The surgery is long. I guide the graft and make sure it connects just right to the aorta and the blocked artery. As we work, a few things go wrong — some bleeding, a couple of problems that need quick thinking. But my team works together like a well-oiled machine. We stay calm. We fix what needs fixing. Every second brings us closer to saving a life.

Finally, it's time to see if our efforts paid off. "Okay, ladies and gentleman, let's see how we did."

Dana turns off the bypass machine, and we all hold our breath. The room goes quiet. So quiet, it's like time has stopped. I press my hands to the patient's heart. It's cool. I close my eyes and take a breath. This is the moment that counts. *Come on. You can do this. Don't give up on me now.*

Then I feel it — a little twitch. A pulse.

"There it is," I say, smiling. "Come on, buddy."

I rub the heart gently, helping it along. Slowly, the rhythm gets stronger. The monitors beep faster, steadier. It's working. We did it.

My team lets out quiet cheers, smiling behind their masks. "Great job, everyone," I say, feeling a wave of relief. "Let's close him up."

We finish the surgery and get the patient ready for recovery. His heart is beating. He should be able to go to his daughter's wedding. I feel ten feet tall every time I do this. That's why I do this job, why I keep going even when it's hard.

I pull off my bloody gown and mask and step out into the waiting room. His family looks exhausted. I try to smile early when it's positive. "Kurt did great," I tell them.

The resulting celebration drowns out everything we did, but that doesn't matter. They'll hear it again. His wife pulls me into a big hug, followed by his daughter and several others.

"Okay, he'll be in the ICU all night, and we'll give his body some time to rest, so he probably won't be conscious for a few days."

"When can I see him?" his wife asks.

"It could be a while."

"I'll be here," she says.

I thank them for being such great supports, encourage them to take care of themselves, and answer a few more questions before stepping away. I do a bit of follow up with other patients, but I don't have a lot of energy left after all those hours in the OR. After tackling a small pile of paperwork, I give up and head for home.

When I walk through my front door that evening, the first thing I notice? The living room is a disaster. Immediately everything feels off. There's a takeout bag with ketchup on it. A glass rests on its side, and I can only hope it's water spilled on my glass-top table and not something else. Dishes fill the sink, and there's a pile of shoes inside the doorway.

My head starts to ache. Dear God, she's been here less than twenty-four hours. I knew it would be a tornado. *Where is she?* I look all around the house and finally spot her in a tiny yellow bikini out by the pool. *Sweet Jesus, I am not going to be able to do this.*

Three

Sadie

I sink farther into the lounge chair, letting the warm sunshine soak into my skin with my sketch pad in hand. I'm working on a drawing of the view. The sun will be setting soon, but I'm chasing it on this late day in May. Donna Summer plays through my earbuds, her music thumping in my ears. It's a disco kind of afternoon. The kind that makes me feel alive. Summer is getting closer, even though there's still a little chill in the air. I've covered myself in baby oil, hoping to get a base tan and chase away my pale winter skin.

The music pulses, and I smile. It's happy music. The kind that makes you want to spin around in the sun without a care. I stretch out a little more, arching my back, soaking in the warmth. Beckett's backyard feels like a secret hideout. No one asking for anything. No problems. Just me, the sunshine, the pool, and a beautiful sunset to sketch.

Still, deep down, worry lingers. I can't forget how I ended up here, knocking on Beckett's door with nothing but a suitcase and a mess of problems. But I couldn't take it anymore. I know Alex is up to something shady. Or maybe I'm still that girl who acts without thinking, chasing trouble just to feel something.

But not right now. This moment is mine. Outside this yard, the world is full of hard things. But inside? I feel like maybe things can get better. I close my eyes and let the music carry me away.

Then a cool breeze hits me, and I'm in the shade. I open one eye.

Beckett.

He's standing above me, waving his arms around like he's on fire. My peace disappears in a snap. I groan and pull out one earbud, the music fading as I sit up, squinting at him in the light. "What are you doing?" I ask, already annoyed. My calm is officially over. "What's going on?"

But instead of a real answer, he yells a string of random words: "Jeep! Water! Ketchup! Disaster!"

I blink. That makes no sense.

I sit up, dropping my feet to the tile. Ketchup? A Jeep? What kind of problem mixes those things?

Beckett looks even more worked up now. I raise an eyebrow, trying to figure out if this is just more of his drama or if it's something serious.

I stand and scan the yard, my heart picking up speed. "Do I need to call someone? An ambulance maybe?" I ask, only half-joking.

His face turns bright red. He takes a breath, shakes his head, and yells again, less wild this time, but still firm. "Just come inside!"

I roll my eyes. Great. There goes my disco daydream. "Seriously, what is your problem?" I mutter, following him toward the house.

When we get inside, he points to the living room.

Really? This? "Oh, sorry. I'll get that all picked up. But right now I'm trying to get what's left of the vitamin D and finish my sketch before it starts to rain again tonight."

"I can't live like this," Beckett snaps. "And you can't either, not in my house. I like order, and you're..." He waves his hands around.

Then he spins on his heel and storms toward the guest room. I follow him, as that's where all my stuff is currently located. His face darkens. I peek inside, and yep, my things are everywhere. Clothes, shoes, makeup, bags — half of it is still in my suitcase, the other half spread across the room like I plan to stay forever.

"I couldn't find my swimsuit. I'll get it all picked up," I assure him. "You just got home before I had the chance."

"Sadie." He lets out a long breath, shaking his head as he looks at the mess. "I said you could stay here. That didn't mean turn the house upside down. Just...be respectful."

I quickly gather my things and dump them back in my suitcase. It's not really better. When I walk back out to the living room, he's still glaring at me.

I cross my arms. "Okay, okay. I'll keep the common areas clean. I promise."

I leave him standing there and walk back outside to the pool, pulled by the sun like it's calling my name. I can feel Beckett's eyes on me, but I don't turn around. I just want to sink into the sunlight and forget everything for a little while longer.

I lie back in the chair, put my earbuds in, and Donna is singing "Last Dance." I close my eyes and try to relax again, like I'm floating in a perfect pre-summer bubble.

I make it through maybe four songs before the sun sets and it's too cold outside. I gather my stuff and head in. But when I step back into the living room, I stop cold.

Everything is clean.

The mess on the coffee table? Gone. No wrappers, no spilled water, no ketchup stains. It's spotless, like someone hit a reset button. It doesn't even feel like the same room.

"What the heck?" I whisper, blinking at the sparkling table. Did he do this all by himself? In, like, twenty minutes?

Beckett walks in, arms crossed, his eyebrows pulled tight. "You finally done pretending you live at a beach resort?"

I almost laugh. "You could've warned me. I was planning to clean after I finished outside."

"Sure," he says, raising an eyebrow. "You looked really busy out there."

"It was an important appointment — with Vitamin D," I say with a shrug.

He shakes his head and grabs a water bottle. "I ordered from Paradise Grill, and I thought we could talk."

That gets my attention. I start to sit down on his leather couch.

"What are you doing?" he asks.

"I'm waiting for dinner to arrive. What did you get?"

"You can't sit on the couch. You're covered in sunscreen."

"Actually, it's baby oil."

Beckett narrows his eyes. "You know that lying in the sun with baby oil can lead to skin cancer, right?"

I laugh, feeling playful. "I'll take my chances, thanks! I want a good base tan to start the season. I promise I'm not always irresponsible. I'll try to cut back on the baby oil."

"Just take a shower. Dinner should be here in about twenty minutes."

I hold up my hands. It's not worth the fight. Back in my room, I take off my bathing suit and inspect myself. I don't think I got enough sun to consider this a base. I shower and pull on a pair of joggers and a T-shirt.

I pile my hair into a messy bun and walk out.

Beckett immediately zeroes in on my chest. "You need to wear a bra."

"You're lucky I'm wearing a shirt."

He inhales loudly. "Dinner's here."

"Oh goodie." I walk over to the table, which he's set, and peek into the paper bag. "What did you order?"

"I got you a roasted chicken salad," he says. "Figured it'd be a healthy choice."

I raise one eyebrow. "Oh, I see. You looked at me and thought—salad? Wow."

"No. It's that every woman I know seems to order salad. I just figured that's what you wanted."

"What did you get yourself?"

"A pot roast dinner."

I grab it before he can stop me. "Not everyone lives on leaves. And Paradise Grill has the best pot roast in town."

He gives me a look, but I see the tiny smile tugging at his mouth. "Yes. I know that. That's why I ordered it for myself."

"This body needs real food, not rabbit snacks."

He laughs under his breath, and for a second, everything feels easy.

"Good. That's a start."

He rolls his eyes. "Careful, Sadie. You're lucky I'm feeding you tonight."

I smirk. "And I'm very thankful. Truly."

As we eat, the mood starts to shift. It's not so tense anymore. It almost feels...normal.

Then Beckett leans in a little. "So, how did your errands go?"

"I stopped in to see Rosie and applied for a new job."

"Oh yeah?"

I sit up straighter, proud of myself. "I've filled out four applications. One at the bookstore in the mall, one at another coffee shop, one at a fruit stand, and one at a convenience store."

His eyebrows rise. "That's a start. But why not try for an office job? Don't you have a degree?"

I make a face. "An office job sounds boring. I like having a little freedom. Sitting at a desk all day? No thanks."

His face tightens. I can feel the change in his mood. "But how are you going to pay rent or bills? Caleb can't cover everything forever."

I look down at my plate, feeling worry sneak in. "Caleb

doesn't help me. I paid my half of the rent with Alex."

Beckett's voice is low. "Caleb wants you to stay here until Alex is fully out of the picture. How long do you think that will be?"

I shake my head. "Trust me. Alex is fully out of the picture. I'm just here temporarily. I'll figure it out."

He studies me for a moment, and I see a softer look in his eyes. "You need to start thinking long term. Maybe we can come up with some ideas together."

"As long as none of those ideas involve a nine-to-five office job," I say, giving him a small grin.

He doesn't smile, but he doesn't argue either.

We keep talking as we finish dinner, joking one minute and getting serious the next. It's nice — different. There's something new between us. It's not like when we were kids and he'd tease me just to get a rise. If we can manage not to drive each other crazy, perhaps we could get along.

As Beckett leans back in his chair, he brings up his weekend plans. "What about working at Paradise Grill?" he asks. "Or maybe Tarryn can help you find a job at the winery."

I freeze for a second. The idea of his sister, Tarryn, helping me? That feels like a long shot. "Hmm, I don't know about that," I say, looking down at my plate. "You do remember that Genevieve Dempsey was one of my best friends in high school?"

"And that matters how?"

"Ginny and Tarryn were archrivals."

Ginny is a Dempsey, and Tarryn is a Paradise. The rivalry between those families runs deep, fueled by eight generations of competition, land disputes, and betrayals. Each family claims the other crossed the line first, and while the newer generation might not fully understand how it began, they've inherited the tension all the same. In the town of Paradise, loyalty is everything, and siding with the wrong name can turn you into an outsider overnight. We've all known each other forever, but that doesn't make it easy.

He raises an eyebrow. "I know. But people grow up. She

might surprise you."

I roll my eyes. "She didn't like me back in high school. I doubt she's waiting around to hand me a job now."

"You never know," Beckett says with a shrug. "It doesn't hurt to ask. Knowing the right people is important when you're looking for work."

"Easy for you to say. Your family owns this town," I tease. But his words stick in my head. Maybe it wouldn't be the worst idea to try. "Fine." I sigh. "I'll think about it."

Beckett nods. "Just keep an open mind. It might not be as bad as you think. It's a new chance. A fresh start. Just be yourself."

I nod, taking in his words. "I'll try. It's just…hard. I don't want to put myself out there if the past has already ruined a chance for something good."

He gives me a warm smile. "Don't think of it as a problem. Think of it as a challenge. Face it. You've got skills to offer, and you might surprise yourself with how strong you are."

I stand up to clear the table, still feeling unsure, but not as scared as before. There's something solid under my feet now, a bit of confidence I didn't have earlier. And surprisingly, part of that is because of Beckett.

Four

Sadie

With the dishes done, I step into the guest room. It's cluttered with my clothes, but it doesn't feel like home. It feels temporary, just a place to stay for now. The walls are painted light blue, a color I used to love. Now, it just feels cold. I drop onto the bed and let my thoughts drift…straight to him.

Beckett Paradise.

I haven't thought about him like this in years, not since we were kids. Back then, I thought he was cool and funny. But the more I remember, the more my feelings get mixed up. I used to like the way he smiled at me, even when he was being annoying. Like the time he tossed me into the lake and laughed as I struggled to come up for air. He thought it was hilarious. I didn't, but I still liked his attention.

There was a time when I had a huge crush on him. I was young and didn't know any better. He and Caleb were at university in Toronto. My parents had died, and his parents had taken me in. I was thankful, but when Ryker, Beckett's youngest brother, said I couldn't be friends with Ginny and stay with them, I left. I spent the last year and a half of high school couch surfing, and then I got an apartment with Ginny.

One memory still makes me cringe. It was summer, and I had just eaten a bowl of rice I'd found in the fridge. Beckett went to the fridge and asked if I'd seen the mealworms he fed his bearded dragon. He said they'd been right here and described the rice container. I threw up immediately, and he couldn't stop laughing. That moment ended my crush for good.

Now, I'm living in his house. And not because I want to. Yet for the most part, Beckett is not as bad as I feared. Being in his space, breathing the scent of cedar and faint cologne — it brings something back. A feeling I don't want. I try to push it away.

My phone buzzes on the nightstand.

unknown number: Canada Post has a package to deliver to you. It has $2 in duties. Please follow this link to pay for your package.

Spam. I wish there was a way to block those. I delete it and report it as junk. Then I continue to search my phone, hoping for something to cheer me up. I check my email — nothing back from the job applications I sent. My heart sinks.

I think about all my old jobs — bagging groceries at the IGH, folding underwear at Victoria's Secret, working at the Paradise mini-golf course. Most ended badly. And then there was the lawyer, the one who didn't know how to keep his hands to himself. That job was the worst. When he pulled out his micro-wiener and asked if I wanted to taste it, I ran out the door. That's why I don't ever want to work in an office where I can't get away.

Would working at Paradise Vineyard be any better?

My phone buzzes again, and my heart drops. It's Alex. I don't want to read it. But I do.

Alex: Where are you? When are you coming home?

I stare at the words, and after a moment, I type a response.

Me: I'm not coming back.

His reply comes fast.

Alex: You better get your butt home and cook me some dinner, if you know what's good for you.

Fury boils in my stomach. But I don't reply. I toss my phone into my backpack. Today, I closed my bank account because he had access to it. He'd already taken most of my savings. I gathered what was left and opened a new account at a new bank where he can't get to it. He's not taking anything else from me. Not money. Not time. Not power. I'm done.

Still, adrenaline zings through my veins. I close my eyes and think of Caleb, working hard across the ocean. He would want me to stay strong. "One step at a time," I whisper.

But I can't relax. I can feel Alex's threat. I know he's not done with me. Fear is what he uses. And he won't just stop.

I can't keep reading Alex's texts, so I fire off a message to Caleb.

Me: I'm exhausted and going to bed. I hope we can talk tomorrow.

I shut my phone down and switch off the light. Darkness surrounds me, but it doesn't feel peaceful. I lie on my back, eyes open, listening to the silence, trying to figure out what comes next. Tomorrow, I'll look harder for a job. One that's stable. One that gives me a fresh start.

Paradise Vineyard would be a dream. I loved it when I lived in the main house for a while. The idea feels warm and bright. I imagine the sun shining on rows of vines, the smell of the earth, and the quiet peace of a good day's work. It sounds like something real. Something I could love.

What if Tarryn won't hire me? What if she's worried about Ginny Dempsey being my friend? I haven't talked to her in years, but she doesn't know that. She doesn't know me.

But I have to believe I can do this. Even if it's scary. Even if it doesn't work out right away. It will still be better than the life I had with Alex. I don't ever want to feel trapped again. I remember night after night of watching him get high on weed and fall asleep in the recliner. What a waste of time and money.

I see that now.

I close my eyes and take another deep breath, letting the strength I found yesterday flow through me again. I took back a piece of my life. I took a step forward. Tomorrow, I'll keep going. I'll find a way to stand on my own.

Five

Sadie

I linger in my room after I wake up because I can't face Beckett right away this morning. He showed up in my dreams, and we weren't dressed. He did all sorts of naughty things to me. And I liked them a lot.

Once I feel like he's gone, I pad to the kitchen and use his espresso machine. I make a nice leaf design in the foam of my cappuccino. I plan my day a bit as I sip. I need to follow up on a few jobs, maybe find a few more, and I'd like to get over and visit Rosie at the hospital. That's not a very full day. I need work. Mostly because I need to get out of Beckett's house.

I look over into the living room. His taste is typical male — black leather couch and loveseat, glass-top coffee table and end table, and giant television. But scattered around are tons of framed photos of his family and mementos from his life. The place feels full of stories. It smells warm and clean, and soft morning light fills the room. I don't belong here.

In the corner he has a Paisley Martin from her driftwood series. It's a piece of gray driftwood dipped in silver, as if it's submerged in water. It's gorgeous. I wish I had some real art talent. I definitely don't.

There's also a framed photo of him with a bunch of kids, from India maybe. They're all smiles. His skin is tanned, his hair messy, and his blue eyes shine with something kind. There's a gentle pull I can't ignore. Maybe I never knew him at all. There has to be more to him than the guy who teased me on the playground. He wasn't that guy last night when he urged me to speak to Tarryn.

A wave of memories hits me, and I feel a little sad. I used to think I had him all figured out. But this Beckett is different. He's full of stories, full of life. He's getting things done. I start to feel something new, something like respect.

I wander through the living room, letting these thoughts swirl in my mind. I shouldn't focus on who Beckett used to be. It's about who he is now and what that might mean. Our connection is complicated, but it's real.

I think I have to let those old memories go. I'll carry this new understanding with me as I figure out what comes next.

I cringe as I notice that my shoes are by the couch, my sweater's tossed over the back of a chair, and my half-finished cappuccino is making a ring on the coffee table. I need to be more respectful of his house — and not just because he said so. I need to stay here for a bit. He and Caleb have made me into a squatter with emotional baggage.

I fold the sweater and deposit my shoes neatly by the door. It's a small gesture, but it's a quiet promise to try harder. To be better. Not just for Beckett, but for myself.

When I walk back to my room, I'm hit with the aftermath of what can only be described as a clothing tornado. My suitcase is still open on the floor, clothes spilling out like it exploded in protest. I shake my head and sigh, then start picking things up, folding, sorting. I spot a pair of jeans draped over the end of the bed and reach for them automatically, thinking I'll wear them today.

But when I hold them up, my stomach tightens. These aren't mine. They're Alex's. I turn them over in my hands, surprised by how unfamiliar they seem. They're not worn in enough to be his favorite pair. I remember them, though. He used to wear them with a smug grin and a shirt that he claimed made him *"look put together."*

I toss them into the closet and head for the shower. I have things to do. And none of them include looking backward.

A little while later, the hospital stands tall in front of me, clean and cold, but full of life. Rosie is here, and that reminds me that even when things feel scary, there's hope. I used to hate this place. This is where they brought us after the accident, and this is where my parents died. But now I come here for Rosie. She's too important to me to stay away.

I take a deep breath and go inside. The hallways twist and turn, filled with machine beeps and quiet conversations. People move around me — patients, families, nurses — all busy with their own problems and things to do.

When I reach Rosie's room, I stop just outside the door and take another deep breath. I need a second to be strong. Then I walk in, and everything changes. The bed is neat, the sheets white, but it's Rosie who shines the most. Even though she looks weak, she somehow seems full of light.

"Sadie!" she says, her face glowing with joy. She's sitting up with pillows behind her, her dark curls wild.

When I was working at the coffee hut, I never got here this early. This is a nice change. "Hey, Rosie," I say. "What's up, tater tot?"

"Same old, same old. Just waiting for my golden ticket," she jokes, patting the bed for me to sit down.

I smile. Her good mood helps me forget my troubles, even if just for a minute. "Did you have any fun dreams last night?" I ask as I sit beside her.

"Of course! I was in the jungle, dodging crocodiles," she says, laughing. "I'm ready for a real adventure as soon as they spring me!"

"I'm up for going wherever you want. You will be the cruise director of our travel itinerary."

She nods. "I'm getting all the research done so we don't waste any time."

We talk about fun stuff, skipping the scary parts of her illness — for now. But the light moment doesn't last. There's a knock, and when I look toward the door, Beckett is standing there. My heart jumps. I usually avoid being around when Rosie's doctor visits.

He looks professional and calm, wearing comfy clothes. His scruffy face gives him a rugged look I didn't expect. The way he walks into the room, gentle and quiet, makes me stop and stare. This is not how he usually is at home. He's in professional mode for sure.

"Hey, Rosemary," he says quietly, approaching her bed.

"Dr. Beckett!" Rosie says with a smile.

For a moment, I forget to be nervous as I watch the way they talk to each other. Beckett nods to me and makes a few jokes as he listens to her heart and looks at the EKG machine. Only if you're really paying attention do you realize he's putting her through a battery of tests. His smile is pleasant, and the way he talks puts her at ease. Who knew he had that in him?

I mean, I guess I kind of did, after the last couple days. He used to scare me, but now I want to know more. Beyond the gruff exterior, grown-up Beckett seems real and kind, as long as I keep my mess reasonably under control. And that makes my heart beat faster. Rosie laughs at something he says, and they joke back and forth. I feel so many things at once. I'm proud of Rosie for staying strong, but I'm also drawn to this new Beckett I never realized was in there.

Then he looks over at me again, just a quick glance, but it feels like time stops. His eyes are soft, and it makes something inside me flutter. For a second, everything else disappears — my fears, our past, my worries.

I'm thankful that Rosie has someone like Beckett who can make her smile, even as she gets the care she needs. I can't see Beckett as my childhood bully anymore. I see a man who's been shaped by life. And I start to understand him a little better.

After a while, I stand and tell them I'm going for coffee. I need a minute to clear my head.

Rosie's been on the heart transplant list for years, but an episode last year left her too weak to live on her own. I offered to move in and help, but the doctors said she needed round-the-clock care, so they admitted her to the hospital. Beckett has been managing her case ever since. I need her to get that heart. I need her to live. Because we have plans — real, wild, beautiful plans. We're going to run away the second she's strong enough. Paris, Rome, Tokyo — every place she's dreamed of, I'm going with her. We'll eat croissants on cobbled streets, ride trains through vineyards, and swim in oceans we've only seen on postcards. She keeps saying there's still so much she wants to do, and I keep nodding like I'm not terrified. Like I'm not silently begging the universe to give her a chance.

The smell of fresh coffee fills the air when I step into the cafeteria. My head is spinning, and I realize I need to get serious. I need to be reliable — for myself and for Rosie. She's depending on me. I don't have time for anything other than a decent job and working on a bucket list with Rosie. Alex was clearly a mistake, and one I don't intend to make again. So for now, I should just take men out of the equation.

Six

Beckett

When I get home after a long day at the hospital, the house is picked up and silent. It's clean enough that I worry for a moment that Sadie has moved out, but then I find her sitting by the pool. The setting sun makes her look like a shadow against the golden sky. It feels strange to see her here, in my private space. Even stranger is the heavy look in her eyes when she looks up at me.

"Beckett," she says, her voice a little unsure.

"Sadie." The serious feeling in the air catches me off guard. "What's going on?"

She looks out at the sunset, the sky turning darker by the second. "Thanks for helping Rosie today. You treat her like she's not sick, and I know that means a lot to her."

I nod. "She's living in the hospital, waiting for a heart. It's the least I can do."

Sadie looks out at the lake as the sun disappears. "Is it terrible to hope someone dies so she can live?"

"I think the better way to think about it is that *if* someone dies, it will give her a chance to live," I say, trying to sound optimistic. "But that needs to happen pretty soon."

Sadie nods. "We have so many plans for after she gets her heart. I'm sure you see this all the time, but why does someone like Joey Madero get a liver transplant without issue and Rosie, who likes everyone and is always so positive, doesn't?"

I sigh. Joey is a guy from town who's in jail in Alberta for killing someone on the oil fields.

"At least she has people visiting her," I say with a shrug. "She's not alone."

"Yeah," Sadie says, but she doesn't seem convinced. "It's just...unfair."

I nod, feeling the same way.

"Why don't you call her Rosie like everyone else?" she asks after a moment.

I shrug. I can't tell her I crossed a professional boundary with Rosie by thinking of her as a friend. We went to high school together, for God's sake. But I'm her doctor now, so I'm trying to correct that. "She's my patient, and her name is Rosemary."

Sadie rolls her eyes, and it makes me smile. There are more layers to her than I realized.

"What about you?" I ask after a moment. "How's the job search going?"

Sadie offers a small smile, but I catch frustration in her eyes. "Slow. Very slow," she says, looking away. "But summer is coming. When the tourists show up, I'll have plenty of jobs to choose from."

Long shadows stretch across the patio. "Why not find a job that lasts all year?" I ask.

Sadie's face changes. "I did once," she says quietly. "It made me feel trapped."

I want to ask more, but I hold back. I can tell she doesn't

want to talk about it.

The evening air turns cool. In the distance, I hear neighbors laughing, but it sounds small compared to the quiet between us. "It's okay to feel lost sometimes," I tell her. "Especially when the world feels like it's asking too much."

Sadie looks at me, and for a second, it seems we understand each other without saying anything. "I suppose you're right," she says. "But sometimes, it feels like I'm just waiting. Waiting for everything."

"Me too," I whisper. Her worry for Rosie mixes with my own frustration about finding a viable heart. Somehow, it pulls us closer.

"Let's go inside," I suggest after a moment. The cold is sinking into my bones. "I'm hungry."

She nods. "Me too."

The warmth of the house wraps around us, and I lead Sadie toward the kitchen. I can't stop thinking about the soft smile she gave me outside.

I open the fridge and look in. It's pretty empty—just some takeout boxes and a bottle of ketchup. "Looks like I need to go grocery shopping," I note.

Sadie leans against the counter, her fingers sliding over the cool surface. "Or you could just get someone to cook for you."

I laugh. "I'll get right on that. But for now, how about I order Paradise Grill? You interested in a salad?" I tease.

She lifts an eyebrow, and a playful spark returns to her eyes. "I didn't know you had a rabbit."

I grin. "What do you feel like eating?"

"I think the roasted chicken," she says. "What about you?"

"A ribeye, medium rare," I say as I send the order.

Just then, Sadie's phone pings. She stiffens.

"Everything okay?" I ask. "Is it Alex?"

"No. It's nothing," she says quickly, but I can hear the tightness in her voice. The easy feeling between us fades.

I try to lighten the mood. "We don't need to stand around in the kitchen. Let's go sit in the living room. It won't be long."

"Right," she says, but her voice is far away, like her mind is somewhere else.

As I follow her into the living room, she pauses, seeming lost in her thoughts. "I'll just grab some drinks," I say, going back to the fridge.

"Sure," she murmurs. Her eyes stay glued to her phone, like she's waiting for something.

After a minute, Sadie clears her throat. "I'll be right back." She walks toward the bedroom.

I'm left alone in the living room, surprised by how easy it was to talk to her. I hear her phone ping again and wonder who keeps messaging her. Despite what she said, my guess is Alex.

I sit down on the couch, and my mind spins with questions. What is she hiding?

I'm left waiting, wondering if she'll come back...and if she'll ever let me see the things she's hidden.

Seven

Sadie

I sit down on the edge of the bed. My room gives me a little space to breathe. I'm not used to that much interaction, and I can't let Beckett know Alex has been texting me. I don't want him looking at me like I'm some helpless kid Caleb handed off as a project. I need them to see me as capable, strong enough to stand on my own, not just the girl who ran from a mess, but the woman choosing how to handle it.

Anyway, if Alex figures out where I am, I worry he might show up. He didn't seem to care all that much about me when we lived together, but he's certainly spiteful and not happy that I'm gone.

The screen lights up, and for a second, I just stare at it. My heart beats faster.

Alex: Where are you?

My heart sinks. His words are too normal, like I didn't move out, just went to the store or something. I can almost hear his voice, sharp and annoyed. My stomach twists.

Alex: Do you really think you can just walk away?

I don't answer. I can't. I made the right choice. I left him. I took back control. Still, my hands shake as I read the next text.

Alex: I need what you took.

I grip the phone tighter. Is he talking about his jeans? That doesn't make sense. I picture Alex, red with anger, yelling and throwing things. I remember what it felt like when he got mad. It's a memory I wish I could erase.

The messages continue.

Alex: You know what happens if you don't return it.

My heart races. He can't hurt me if he can't find me. He's never touched me before. But it can't be the jeans. He wouldn't be this worked up over a pair of pants. So what is it? That's the part that gets under my skin, the way he's dancing around it, like naming it gives me power. Or like putting it in writing might be dangerous. He's never cared about privacy before. So why now?

Me: I only took what's mine. What are you talking about?

Alex: Bullshit. You know what you took. And if you think you can get away with it, you are very mistaken.

Alex: Do you know what I'm capable of?

I chuckle. If he could stay sober long enough, maybe. Maybe someone swiped his favorite bong. That would get him pissed. But it wasn't me. I never touched it. It was nasty.

I drop the phone into my lap and shut my eyes tight. I have to hold it together, at least for now. I don't want to ruin whatever friendship I'm establishing with Beckett. No matter what Caleb says, this isn't his problem. It's mine.

The phone keeps pinging, lighting up with more of Alex's angry words. Each message reminds me why I left him. I want to be brave, but right now, it's hard. He's just relentless. Who knew he had this sort of focus?

Beckett knocks on my door. "Dinner's here!"

I open my eyes and take a deep breath. I can't think about Alex right now. I just have to get through dinner. Then I can figure out what to do.

Suddenly, even my clothes feel too constricting. I'm trapped. I have to change into something more comfortable. I pull out a sleep shirt and a pair of shorts. With a quick move, I unhook my bra and toss it aside. Instantly, I feel lighter, like I can breathe again. It's a small, silly win, but I'll take it. Bras are something I can't live without, but *hate* isn't a strong enough word. Why must they be perpetually uncomfortable?

I glance in the mirror and try to fix my messy hair. It's no use. It just sticks up in weird places. It doesn't really matter.

After a deep breath, I return to the kitchen, Beckett is bent over the takeout food, moving his dinner from a box and plating it like it's a fancy meal. Why dirty a dish when you don't have to?

Our eyes meet, and his cheeks turn a little pink, which surprises me. I fidget with my sleeve, feeling nervous. I don't know what to do with myself right now. "Uh, hey."

He gives me the onceover. "Are you going to wear that?"

I roll my eyes. "Sorry, I didn't realize this was a black-tie event."

He shakes his head. "You can't wear that around here."

"What?"

He points at me with a dinner fork. "You're practically naked. You can't…"

I realize the high beams are on and cover my chest. "Jeez, you're a doctor, and from what I remember, you're also a bit of a man-whore. It's not like you haven't seen nipples up close and in person."

He storms into the living room. "No! This is not what I agreed to." He reaches the couch and throws a blanket at me. "Cover up."

"Oh my God. Are you serious?" I laugh. "It's takeout. I'm not asking you to eat your meal off my body."

Beckett groans, and now I'm ready to have a little fun with this. Though I should know better. "Try to respect my boundaries," he says.

I hold up my hands. "Fine. I'll eat in my room."

"No," he says again. "I don't want food in the bedrooms."

I open my mouth and then close it. There is no pleasing him. And I'm completely covered. I'm not going to bend to his weirdness. He walks around here without a shirt on…

I pick up the roasted chicken in its takeout container, collect a fork and knife, and return to my bedroom. I don't need to put up with this.

I set the box on the dresser and flip it open. Mashed potatoes and some green beans flank the chicken, but suddenly my heart isn't in it. I don't fit anywhere.

I glance over at my phone, and my heart pounds. There are twenty-nine unread messages now. That's more than Alex sent me during the entire year plus of our relationship.

A new notification lights up. My hands shake as I grab the phone.

Alex: I know you're there. I will find you if I have to. I need to know what you did with my stuff.

A cold sweat breaks out on the back of my neck. He's threatening me. I can almost see him — angry, dangerous, just like before.

"Calm down," I whisper to myself.

Another message pops up.

Alex: I can make this very difficult for you.

I shiver. *How did I get here?*

I left. We got in a fight, and I realized how unhappy we both were. I packed my things. At the time, it felt like freedom. Now, it feels like I threw gasoline on a fire. But I certainly don't want to go back.

Panic bubbles inside me. I squeeze my eyes shut and breathe deeply, trying to push it back down.

What can I do? Run away? Buy a bus ticket and disappear? Would that even work? Alex would still chase me down. If I leave, I'll need a real plan. Not just dreams. Plus, I can't go without Rosie.

For now, I stay here, in this room, in this safe place.

I pick up a piece of chicken and chew slowly, focusing on the taste. My heart feels heavy, but a small fire lights inside me. I won't let Alex control me. I'm stronger than that.

I know I didn't take anything that belongs to him, at least not on purpose.

Unless he planted something?

I drag my suitcase out of the closet and tear through every pocket, every seam.

Nothing.

So what the hell is he talking about?

I go back to my dinner and try to figure out how I'm going to get myself out of this mess. And the more I think about what Beckett said about my clothes, the more it gets me all riled up. He can do whatever he wants, but I have the decency police after me?

Alex's texts continue to ping in the back of my mind like a warning I can't shut off. The threats, the manipulation — it's all so familiar. But tonight, it lands differently. Because I'm not alone anymore. I'm not curled up on a couch pretending everything's fine. I'm in Beckett's house—his space—because he allowed me to be here. Maybe it's just loyalty to my brother, but I'd like to think we're making progress with each other. Despite the gruff exterior, and the ridiculous argument we just had, I've seen something different in him than I expected. A softness buried beneath the growl. A man who's scared to care but already does.

And when he doesn't wear his shirt? God help me, it does something to my insides. Something warm and dizzying and a little dangerous.

I throw myself onto the bed, exasperated. Why can't I stop thinking about him? What kind of voodoo has seeped into my veins? The need—the want—overwhelms me. I reach over to my side table and pull out my vibrator. At least I remembered this.

My thoughts move to Beckett and the dream I had last night. I wish he was in here. Between my legs. Doing all sorts of dirty things.

I lock my bedroom door, pull my sleep shorts off, and turn on my toy. I lose myself in his crooked smile that tells me he's up to no good. His soft surgeon hands running over my skin.

I pinch my nipples as the soft vibrations pulse through my sensitive clit. Memories of Beckett's heated stare arouse me even more. Closing my eyes, I can almost feel his strong hands caressing my body, sending shivers down my spine.

Unable to resist any longer, I insert the vibrator as the familiar sensations course through me. In my mind's eye, it's Beckett inside me, filling me up, claiming me as his own. With each thrust, it's him pleasing me, making me moan and beg for more. The fantasy intensifies, a storm I can't outrun, nor do I want to.

Lost in the fantasy, my back arches off the bed as I edge closer to climax. The thought of surrendering to him is both exhilarating and terrifying, but in this moment, none of it matters. It's pure, consuming need. How can something feel so right yet so dangerous? It goes against every instinct—the peril of wanting someone like Beckett—but still, I want more. I want everything.

With one final thrust, I pull my pillow over my face as I shatter, crying out his name. Panting heavily, I open my eyes after a moment and stare at the ceiling above me. What has happened to me?

Eight

Beckett

I put my rinsed plate in the dishwasher. I can't believe she just picked up and went to her room. This is my house. She doesn't need to be flashing her nips around.

Why is that so hard to understand? Yesterday she was in a bikini, though at least that was because of the pool. I dreamed about her last night, for God's sakes, and I had an actual wet dream. The last time I had one of those I was fourteen.

I consider calling Caleb and telling him this isn't going to work. Sadie and I are oil and water, and we don't mix. But I can't stress him out like that. He's an ocean away. I can do this.

I walk down the hall and stop outside Sadie's door.

"Yesssssssss!" she cries out, low and breathy.

No way.

No freaking way.

Heat rushes straight to my groin. My soldier snaps to attention so fast it hurts. I jerk back from the door, heart pounding like I just ran a mile.

I stand there frozen, not sure what to do. I've already heard too much.

This is private, and it isn't for me.

I scrub my hands over my face, feeling like the worst kind of jerk, and force myself to walk away. I've invaded her privacy, not long after giving her a lecture about boundaries. Good grief.

Back out in the living room, I pace. I need to talk to her about the messages. I can hear her phone continue to ping. I never knew my walls were so thin.

A minute later, the shower turns on. I stop pacing, standing here like an idiot.

Should I check on her? Should I just leave her alone? Maybe she needs space. Maybe she needs someone to care enough to ask.

Ping.

Her phone cuts through the silence again.

Ping.

Ping.

Each one hits me like a slap. Someone's trying to reach her. Someone who won't stop. If it isn't Alex begging her to come back, maybe it's Caleb? We talked last night, but maybe I should assure him Sadie is okay. I won't tell him that I heard her moan my name. He would castrate me.

My stomach tightens.

This isn't just about boundaries or feeling awkward.

I turn the television on and look at the scores of the day. But I can't even pay attention because I'm listening for her.

I wait until the shower shuts off and give her enough time to get dressed. Then I knock on her door.

"Yeah?" Sadie says, her voice small. "You can come in."

I step inside.

She's wearing a thin silk robe, and my soldier is once again about to break my zipper. I can still see her nipples. Why doesn't she understand I don't want to do that?

I look away from her and realize every surface in my guest room is covered. Makeup. Nail polish. Her half-eaten dinner on the dresser. I take a deep breath. My fingers itch to pick stuff up, to make it neat again. But I shove my hands into my pockets. *This isn't my space right now. This isn't my problem.*

Sadie stands by the dresser, brushing her wet hair. The scent of her shampoo — something sweet and flowery — lingers in the air. She won't look at me. "What do you want?" she asks, her voice tight.

I shift on my feet, uncomfortable. And the last thing I want is for her to notice. "I'm sorry," I say, my voice rough.

Sadie turns toward me, confused.

"I was out of line earlier," I add. "About what you wore to dinner. About...everything." I rub the back of my neck, heat crawling up my face. "I don't even know why I said it. I want you to be comfortable here. I guess I'm just not used to... I guess I just..."

I trail off. I can't tell her the truth, that I find myself attracted to her in a way I shouldn't be. That she's a much more interesting person than I realized, even if her mess makes me nuts.

She's a complication, but Caleb is trusting me to take care of her. Yet every part of me wants to pull her close. This makes no sense. Sadie would not even remotely be a good match for me. And she's been through so much — losing her parents... She doesn't need me messing with her head.

Her phone pings again.

I glance at it. "Who keeps texting you?"

Sadie shrugs, trying to play it cool. "It's just a group chat. I'll turn it off."

Ping.

This time the screen lights up before she can hide it.

I can tell it's Alex, and I see the preview of her message on her home screen.

Alex: If you don't come home right now, you're gonna regret it.

The words slam into me like a punch. *I should have seen that coming.* My fists ball up at my sides. "Is he —" I ask.

Sadie flips her phone over so fast it nearly falls out of her hand. "No," she says quickly. But her voice shakes. And that's all the answer I need.

I step closer, lowering my voice. "Sadie, has he ever hit you?"

She freezes. Then slowly, she shakes her head.

I give her a look because I'm not sure I believe her.

Her shoulders fall. "No. He's threatened. But he never... He was always too stoned to be any threat. He never did anything. That's why I left."

I nod, though I want to explode. Threats are bad enough. But threats can turn into actions before you know it. I've seen what some men do to women and children in our emergency department. I don't want that for Sadie. She's had a tough life already.

"You should file a restraining order," I say quietly. "Go to the police. Don't wait for it to get worse."

Sadie wraps her arms around herself, squeezing tight. "I'm fine. He doesn't know where I am, and once he sobers up, he'll let this go."

"You're not going back to him..." I try to phrase it as a statement rather than a question. I want to tell her stories of women I've seen, but I can't.

"I don't want that..." she confirms. Her eyes fill with hurt. "I don't think I need a restraining order."

"Do you want to call Caleb?" I offer. "Get his opinion? He knows you both better than I do."

Sadie lets out a sharp, bitter laugh. "Definitely not."

I almost smile. There's some fight left in her yet. "Okay," I say. "Just...sleep on it. Please."

She nods, but it's small and unsure. I leave her room and

head straight to mine. My hands shake as I pull out my phone. I can't let Alex think he can do this.

I open the group chat with my brothers — Ryker, Greyson, and Kingston — and fire off a message.

Me: Sadie Calloway is staying with me. She left her boyfriend — Alex Tremblay. He's now threatening her.

The replies come almost instantly.

Greyson: We'll back you up if you need us.

Kingston: Name the time and place.

Ryker: Alex's mom's a Dempsey. Makes me want to go even more.

I sit on the edge of my bed and crack a smile. I knew they'd be there for me — and for her. Sadie might not realize it yet, but she's not alone anymore. Not while she's got me.

Nine

Beckett

S adie's been at my place just over a week now, and I can tell it's driving her nuts not to be working. I've offered to make a few calls, pull a few strings at the vineyard, but she keeps turning me down. At least Alex has been quiet lately, nothing like the barrage she was getting those first few days.

I pull into the rec center parking lot just as the sun slips behind the trees, casting long shadows across the pavement. And, of course, I'm late for the weekly game with my brothers. Again.

I grab my gym bag from the passenger seat and jog toward the doors, the strap bouncing against my shoulder. Inside, the air smells like sweat, rubber, and whatever fast food someone snuck in earlier. The squeak of sneakers and the rhythmic slap of a basketball echo off the gym walls. They're still warming up.

As soon as I step onto the court, Ryker fires a pass at me like he's trying to dislocate a finger.

I catch it—barely—and shoot him a glare.

"You're late, princess," he notes, grinning like the overgrown menace he is.

Kingston jogs over, lazily dribbling a second ball. "Thought maybe you got lost. Or tied up with your new roommate."

Greyson whistles low. "Maybe he likes being tied up. You never know with Beckett."

I roll my eyes, tucking the ball under my arm. "You guys done?"

"Not even close," Kingston says.

They're like bloodhounds on a scent. They can smell a good story from a mile away, and apparently, I'm the story tonight.

"So," Greyson starts, leaning back against the padded wall, "you gonna tell us how Sadie Calloway ended up under your roof?"

Ryker crosses his arms and raises a brow. "And don't leave out the juicy parts."

I snort under my breath. There are no juicy parts, just the kind that tie your stomach in knots and keep you up at night.

I remind them how she has no family in Paradise anymore and, currently, no job, so she showed up after she'd left Alex, who's now texting her nonstop and being a real jerk.

Their jokes dry up fast.

"She didn't have anywhere else to go," I add, looking down at the ball in my hands. "And Caleb trusts me."

Kingston's jaw tightens. "She's lucky she found you."

Greyson nods. "You did the right thing, Beck."

I shrug. I know it's right. That doesn't make it easy.

"She okay?" Ryker asks, his tone finally serious.

"She's tough," I tell him, and it's the truth. "But you know she's been through hell, so she's not on the strongest footing to start with. It's gonna take time."

They all nod.

Kingston claps a heavy hand on my shoulder. "We got your back. You know that."

"Always," Greyson echoes.

Ryker grins. "And if that idiot Alex tries to cause trouble, he's got the four of us to deal with."

I nod. It means more than I can say.

"Okay," Ryker says, stealing the ball from under my arm. "Enough soap-opera crap. First to ten wins. Loser buys post-game beers."

"Hope you brought your wallet, old man," Kingston tosses the ball at Greyson with a smirk.

I laugh and fall into line with them, feeling grateful.

We start a quick two-on-two scrimmage. It feels good to move. To sweat. To not think about Sadie for five whole minutes.

But with my brothers, nothing ever stays off-limits for long.

Ryker jogs up beside me, casually bouncing the ball. "You remember Sadie back when she was a freshman?"

I glance over. "Maybe. Braces. Wild hair. Always tagging along with Caleb and me. She's...changed."

Ryker nods. "She was in Tarryn's class. Kinda quiet at first. Skinny. Then boom—around seventeen, she blossomed."

Greyson chuckles from across the court. "Yeah, I remember that. Suddenly every guy in town noticed her."

Kingston elbows Ryker. "Especially you, if I remember right."

Ryker shrugs like it's no big deal. "She was cute. Still is."

The twist in my gut comes fast and unexpected. Sadie isn't just some pretty face. Not to me.

"But then," Ryker says, "was the accident, in the middle of grade eleven."

Just like that, the air goes heavy.

We all remember.

Caleb and Sadie's parents were killed on impact in a

drunk driving accident. Caleb and I were at university. Sadie was in the car, still a teenager. Nobody really knew how she survived.

"Our folks tried to step in," Kingston muses quietly. "Tried to help them hold it together."

Ryker nods. "Didn't help that Sadie's best friend was Ginny Dempsey."

Greyson groans. "Ginny's life was a goddamn disaster. Her parents made public screaming matches look like theater. Divorce was like a sport to them."

"Sadie and Ginny moved into an apartment while they were still in high school, right?" Ryker adds. "Started throwing wild parties."

Kingston grins. "Half the county showed up for those things."

I can picture it. I wasn't here, but Paradise is a small town. I can see Sadie laughing too loud. Masking the pain. Pretending none of it mattered. I feel a stab of sadness.

Kingston glances over. "Where's Ginny now?"

Ryker catches the ball and smirks. "Last I heard, she was living in Vancouver or maybe Toronto."

That answer says enough. Whatever Ginny's doing, she's not doing it here. I file that away for later. Right now, I just want to focus on the game.

We again split into teams—me and Ryker vs. Greyson and Kingston.

Ryker claps me on the back. "Youth versus fossils. Let's go."

"Keep dreaming, kid," Kingston retorts.

And with that, the ball's in play.

Greyson sets a pick, and Kingston drives in, but Ryker's already there, stealing the ball with a speed that shouldn't be possible.

"Move those old-man hips!" Ryker yells, laughing so hard he nearly trips.

I chase after him, grinning like an idiot. Greyson and Kingston are behind us, wheezing like we're back in PE class.

"Careful," Ryker calls over his shoulder. "I don't wanna see you blow out a knee, Grandpa!"

"Smart mouth's gonna get flattened," Greyson warns.

Ryker lays the shot in with ease. "Two points for Team Young and Handsome!" he crows.

Kingston wipes his forehead. "Enjoy it while you can. After thirty, the knees go. It's science."

"Maybe for you dinosaurs," Ryker fires back. "I'm in my prime." He flexes dramatically and kisses his bicep.

I laugh so hard I have to stop, bracing my hands on my knees.

We play hard. Fast. Sloppy. But it's good.

It's needed.

Ryker keeps the trash talk flowing. I get in a few jabs of my own. Greyson mutters about ibuprofen and retirement. Kingston claims he's pacing himself.

By the end, we're all soaked, muscles aching, but souls lighter.

Ryker leans against me, pretending to limp. "Think we can get Kingston one of those little scooters?"

Kingston smirks. "You'll be in traction before that happens."

We grab our towels and collapse onto the benches. The laughter lingers for a second longer.

Then Ryker speaks, quieter this time. "Speaking of stretching our legs..." He tosses his towel over his shoulder. "Maybe we should pay Alex a little visit."

Kingston looks at me. Greyson flexes his knuckles. Ryker just smiles, but it's not friendly.

I nod. Nobody threatens Sadie. Not while she's under my roof.

I pull out my phone, scroll, and find what I'm looking for. I show them Alex's address.

Ryker whistles low. "Crappy side of town."

Kingston leans in. "Of course."

Ryker heads for his gym bag and pulls out his baseball bat.

Kingston and I exchange a look.

"You planning to swing that?" Kingston asks, one brow raised.

"Nah," Ryker says, twirling it casually. "Just for intimidation. Unless he makes it necessary."

I'm not sure this is the best idea. But I'm not about to talk Ryker down when it comes to Sadie. Watching over her is part of him having my back. Arguing with him won't get me anywhere.

Outside, we pile into one car, and Kingston drives.

The sun dips lower, the leather seats sticky against our backs, tension thick in the silence. The longer we drive, the worse the neighborhood gets. Houses lean like they've given up. Porches sag under their own weight. Lawns are nothing but weeds and dry patches littered with garbage and forgotten toys. Fences are broken, gates hanging by rusted hinges.

Kingston slows as we approach a house behind an automotive repair shop that Alex's brother owns, and for a second, I'm not sure how it's even standing.

The windows are boarded up with rotting plywood, some of it peeling away like paper. A giant blue tarp stretches across the roof, weighed down with bricks, tires, and a few cinder blocks. It's sagging in the middle, like it's soaked through. That tarp's been up for years. Maybe decades.

The yard is worse. A busted porcelain sink leans crookedly against a dying tree. There are at least four cars scattered across the grass—or what's left of it—each rusted to hell, some missing doors, others propped on cinder blocks with no wheels at all.

"Home sweet home," Ryker mutters, gripping the bat in one hand.

We get out of the Escalade. The air is thick with the smell of damp earth, old oil, and something else. Something sour and rotten that sticks in your throat.

Kingston leads the way to the door and knocks. Hard.

We wait.

And wait.

For a second, I think no one's coming. Then the door creaks open an inch, hinges groaning like they're about to snap.

Alex appears in the gap, barefoot and swaying, like the floor underneath him is moving. His eyes are bloodshot, glassy. His T-shirt is stained, his jeans crusted with something I don't want to identify. He smells like booze, stale pot smoke, and rot.

How the hell did Sadie ever give this guy the time of day?

"You Alex?" Kingston asks, though he doesn't really need to.

"What's it to you?" Alex slurs, blinking slowly as he tries to focus.

I step forward, keeping my tone neutral, steady. "Do you need to go to the hospital?"

He squints at me like I just offered him a math test.

Then he laughs. It's a harsh, wet sound—bitter and broken.

Ryker steps up beside me, tapping the bat lightly against his palm. Just enough to make a sound. A warning. "Listen up, Alex," he says, his voice low and dangerous. "You're gonna leave Sadie Calloway alone. For good. If you don't..." He pauses, gaze dark. "...you'll be dealing with the four of us."

The smirk slides off Alex's face.

But not for long.

He sneers, defiant. "She stole from me," he spits, his lip curling. "She's no prize. I just want my stuff back."

Every muscle in my body locks up. My vision narrows to him and him alone. "What stuff?" I ask. "Is she using?"

Alex barks out a laugh that makes my skin crawl. "She's too prissy for that." He sways in the doorway, voice rising as the venom builds. "Sadie's a goddamn prude. Sucked in bed too. Wouldn't even—"

He doesn't finish.

Because Kingston is suddenly there, grabbing the doorframe, eyes like ice.

"You ever say her name again," he growls, "and you'll wish you hadn't."

His voice is like a loaded gun.

Alex stumbles back, hands in the air like we're the ones with the problem. "Fine, fine," he mutters. "Whatever. I'm done. Just...just tell her to return what she took."

He slams the door hard enough to rattle the house.

We wait.

One second.

Two.

Nothing.

Kingston turns to us, tension rippling through his shoulders. "That guy's not going to touch her."

"Yeah," Ryker says, bouncing the bat off his thigh. "He got the message."

I hope to God he did.

Ten

Sadie

I had a second interview for a job at Steaming Mugs this morning. It took almost two weeks of applying for work all over town to get to this point. It's the worst shift—five in the morning until nine and back again at five at night until they close at nine. But at least it's a job. They also don't care so much about the artistry of making a good espresso drink. It's about getting orders in and getting them out. I should be able to do that. Hopefully, they'll call me later with the good news that they agree.

With the interview finished, I walk to the hospital and into Rosie's room with a cribbage board and a deck of cards tucked under my arm. Beckett's not there when I arrive, and even though I tell myself that doesn't matter, it does. It really does.

Rosie's sitting up in bed, her face bright as she talks a mile a minute about her favorite TV show. It's some Korean drama I've never seen, but I smile and nod, throwing in the occasional, "Really?" "No way!" and "You've got to be kidding me," like I'm totally following along.

I shuffle the cards, trying to focus, but my eyes keep drifting to the door, just in case he walks through.

Rosie doesn't miss a thing. "Who are you looking for?" she asks, tilting her head. He hair falls into her eyes, and she brushes it away with a smirk.

"No one," I say way too fast.

"Sadie..." she says in that singsong, I-know-something-you-don't voice.

I sigh and set the deck down. "Fine. Dr. Paradise."

"Ohhh," she says, eyes sparkling. "Which one? Your roommate, maybe?"

I can't even admit it aloud. It's embarrassing.

Her grin stretches ear to ear. "Ah-ha! I knew it!"

I roll my eyes, trying to laugh it off. "Don't get yourself too excited."

"Have you moved out of the guest room and into his room?"

"No, of course not. We barely see each other. It's not like that."

Her mouth drops open. "What? Why are we talking about Korean love triangles when you should be telling me how you finally got rid of that walking dumpster fire, Alex, and on to something better?"

"I told you, I got tired of Alex's crap and the mediocre sex. Caleb insisted I stay with Beckett until I get things sorted out. That's it."

"I can't believe you're *still* staying with him. Are you sure you're sticking to your own room?" Her voice goes high with disbelief. She shuffles the cards like a Vegas pro. "The nurses say he has a huge dick and knows exactly what to do with it."

"I wouldn't know."

She shakes her head. "You should climb that man like a

tree. You're single. He's single. You don't have to marry the guy. Just enjoy the ride!"

"I'm not going to sleep with him." I glance at the door again, this time hoping he *doesn't* walk in.

"Don't you like him?"

"I will admit that there's more to him than the bully he was as a kid, but he's my brother's best friend. And also, he's ridiculous, and he drives me crazy. He ordered me a salad for takeout the other night because, and I quote, 'the women he dates only eat salads.'"

Rosie gasps. "Is he dating rabbits?"

"Exactly! That's what I said. Then I took his dinner and left him with the salad."

She grins. "You like him."

I laugh, but my face is on fire. "It's not like that. Besides, if anything were to happen, Caleb would chop off his dick, and he'd be known as Stubby Paradise for the rest of his life."

Rosie howls. "Screw the Korean drama. This is better! What's your next move? How are you going to seduce him?"

"I'm not! Are you listening to anything I say?" I roll my eyes dramatically. "I need a place to live until I find a job. Then I'll disappear and, hopefully, never run into him again."

"Paradise is way too small for that." She lays down the first card and gives me a sly look. "If only he wasn't my doctor, right? And also, that's not a no," she sings.

I shake my head, but inside, my heart's racing. I picture Beckett leaning in, brushing my hair behind my ear, his hand warm on my cheek. Would he kiss me soft and slow? Would it feel like I actually mattered?

The thought makes my stomach flip, and I drop my gaze to my cards.

Rosie taps her fingers on the cribbage board. "Beckett's one of the good ones, you know." She winks. "But don't worry. I'm only here for a new heart, not a boyfriend."

I laugh, shaking my head. "I wouldn't fight you. You can have him."

She plays her two cards for two points on the board. "I'd win."

"In your dreams," I say, grinning as I play mine.

We dive into the game, tossing insults and snark back and forth like it's part of the rules.

"Are you even trying?" Rosie teases, racking up two points. "Or are you daydreaming about Beckett making you breakfast shirtless?"

I nearly drop my cards. "He doesn't walk around shirtless!" I lie, my face burning.

"Mmm-hmm," she hums. "Bet he's bossy in the kitchen. Bet he gets all serious when you don't load the dishwasher just so."

I snort. "He's bossy about everything. It's like a compulsion."

Rosie deals the next hand, still grinning. "I bet you like it when he gets all grumpy."

I groan and cover my face with my cards. "I'm not talking to you anymore."

"You love it," she sing-songs. "You love grumpy Beckett!"

Laughing, I play a five of hearts without thinking.

Her eyes gleam. "Thank you for that," she says, slapping down a run and pumping her fist. "Skunked you!"

I toss my cards on the board in defeat. "You're evil. You totally distracted me."

She winks. "What? Where's my dying-patient pity?"

I sit back and smile at her. "No way. Besides, you're not dying, Rosie. You're just getting warmed up."

Her smile softens. "You know what? I think you're right."

She sits up a little straighter, and for a moment, everything feels almost normal. We're just two girls hanging out, laughing about boys and playing cards. The world outside this room doesn't exist. Nothing bad can touch us here.

But the illusion fades when Rosie's energy dips, her bright expression faltering. A little while later she looks pale, her eyelids heavy as they fight to stay open.

"I'll stop by again tomorrow," I assure her, gathering the cribbage board and cards. "I'll bring nail polish, and we can do manicures."

Her eyes flutter. "Are you implying my nails look bad?"

"I didn't want to say anything," I tease with a grin.

"See you tomorrow," she murmurs, her voice soft and sleepy, the weight of the day settling over her.

I give her hand a squeeze — light, careful — and slip out of the room.

Outside, the air smells like rain, even though the sky hasn't cracked yet. That sharp, earthy scent clings to the pavement, carried on a breeze that feels colder than it should. I take a deep breath, then make my way to Beckett's Jeep, which, yes, I'm still driving.

Instead of heading straight home to Beckett's, I take the long way, winding around the edge of the lake. The water is still and glassy. Clouds hang low, thick and gray, and there's something beautiful about the sadness in the sky, like it understands me.

I open the window, letting the wind brush across my face. One hand on the wheel, the other drifting outside, fingers skimming the air.

For a minute, I imagine Beckett beside me — quiet, solid. The kind of presence you don't realize you need until it's gone. He'd probably grumble that I shouldn't have the window open if I'm cold, and I'd roll my eyes at him. But secretly? I'd like it.

That's the thing about Beckett. He drives me crazy and still manages to make me feel safer than anyone ever has. And I hate that I want him around.

I can't believe I kept glancing toward the door with Rosie today, hoping he'd show up, like it was a social call instead of a doctor visit. I still wish he had.

And now, I can't stop wondering what he's going to say when he finds out what a mess I'm truly in. My grip tightens on the steering wheel. I'm not sure if I'm heading toward comfort or walking straight into a storm.

When I pull into the driveway, everything looks calm. Quiet. I slip into the house and drop my bag by the door, kicking off my shoes with a sigh. Once I've settled in, I grab my favorite book from the coffee table — a contemporary romance — and curl up on the couch, pulling a blanket over my legs. I want to disappear into someone else's love story for a little while.

I flip to the last page I read. The hero is strong and sweet. He always knows exactly what to say. He fights *for* the girl, not with her. He touches her like she's a treasure and makes her feel seen.

I try to read. But the words blur.

When I refocus, it's a sex scene. The hero is bossy and huge and somehow gets her off with barely a touch — no direction, no awkward fumbling. Just magic.

It's never like that in real life. Not for me.

I did everything short of drawing a map for Alex, and he still never figured it out. I wasted too much time with that guy. Time I'll never get back.

And now I'm thinking about the hero's abs — his perfectly sculpted, totally unrealistic six-pack — and how just once I'd like to read about a guy with a beer belly and a little performance anxiety. Just to feel seen.

But instead, my mind drifts again…to Beckett.

Beckett does have a six-pack. I've seen it. It takes all my will power not to stop and run my hands over those hard plains.

But it's not just that. It's the way he checks on Rosie, the way he fights for her to get a heart. The way he encourages me, puts up with my disruption. The way he carries everything like it's his job to protect the whole damn world.

I wonder what it would feel like if he touched me the way the hero touches the heroine in this book. If he brushed the hair from my face with his fingers. If he leaned in, so close I could smell the soap on his skin and the coffee on his breath.

Would I pull away? Or would I lean in too? The question lodges deep in me. It's stupid. But it's there. Quiet. Persistent. Impossible to ignore.

I turn another page, trying to escape again. In the story, the guy knows how to kiss her until her toes curl, until she forgets everything but the feel of his hands and the sound of his voice. *What if that could be real*? What if, for once, I didn't have to pretend? Somehow, the hero makes her feel beautiful, safe, and wanted — all at once. Like she matters. Like she's someone worth protecting.

I wish real guys were even half that good.

The men I've known? They didn't look at me like I was someone to treasure. They looked at me like I was a puzzle they didn't have time to solve. Or worse, something broken they needed to control.

I think about Alex. How many nights I tried. All the times I told myself if I just waited...if I just loved him harder, it would get better. That eventually he'd see me. Hear me. Care enough to ask what I needed.

But the last month? I gave up. I stopped asking and hoping. I found it hurt less that way. Expecting nothing meant I couldn't be disappointed.

I close the book and hold it against me. But a tiny voice whispers from the shadows of my mind. *Maybe it's not just them.* Maybe the real problem is me. Maybe I'm too much. Too needy. Too broken. Too whatever it is that makes men pull away. Maybe men like the ones in these books don't exist for me. And maybe I'm foolish for wishing they did.

I squeeze my eyes shut as the weight of it all presses down — the loneliness, the silence, the aching fear that I'll never find the kind of love that doesn't come with conditions or power plays.

My parents had it, though. Before they died, they had something soft. Something steady. And I know Caleb loves me, but it's from halfway around the world. His care feels more like obligation than presence.

Sometimes, being strong feels a lot like being isolated.

I breathe in. Try to settle the ache. Try to remind myself I've made it this far without needing anyone.

But deep down, I know the truth.

I don't want to just survive anymore. I want more. I want connection.

I'm still hugging the book when my phone pings beside me on the couch.

Alex: If you think sending all the Paradise brothers over will make me forget you stole from me, you're wrong. You must've forgotten who my brother is.

I stare at the message, a chill settling over my skin like frostbite.

What is he talking about? What did Beckett do?

My thoughts scramble. I shove the blanket aside and rush to my suitcase, heart pounding so hard I can feel it in my throat.

I rummage through my clothes again, hands shaking, until I've examined them all. Nothing — not even in the pockets. I don't know what I have that's so important to him. This is my suitcase. My clothes.

Me: What did I take? I have nothing that belongs to you. I've checked. Tell me what I'm looking for. I will get it to you.

Alex: Don't play dumb with me. You know very well what you took. I want it back yesterday.

I walk out to the pool and sit on a chaise lounge, under an umbrella, and stare out at Black Bear Lake. Through the all the noise in my head, I hear my mother's voice — clear and steady. The way it always was when she taught me how to ride my bike.

"You're stronger than you think."

That memory anchors me.

I look up to the heavens and tears roll down my cheeks. I miss my mom so much. I turn back toward the still water of the lake. The sky's turning that soft gold that makes everything beautiful, even when it shouldn't be. I swallow the ache that's rising in my throat. It's been years, almost ten, to be exact. But tonight, it feels like the accident happened yesterday.

"I don't understand," I whisper, my voice barely audible. Maybe if I keep it small enough, it won't crack. "Why did you save me?"

I wait. Like I always do when I talk to God. Like there might be an answer this time. Tears burn behind my eyes, and I bite the inside of my cheek. "Why did you leave me to figure it all out alone?"

The memories hit me hard. The crunch of metal. The sound of my mother's voice, so calm, even when she was scared. The sudden silence that followed, heavier than anything I've ever carried.

I made it out with a broken collarbone and a lifetime of questions. Mom didn't make it. Dad either. Just…gone. And all I got was a second chance I never asked for.

"Caleb was away at school," I say, as if God forgot. "He didn't see what I saw. He didn't feel the blood soaking through the seat. He didn't hear Mom's last breath."

The tears come faster now, spilling down my cheeks unchecked. "I was seventeen. Grade eleven. I didn't even finish school properly. I couldn't. I just—couldn't."

Everyone expected me to bounce back. To dust myself off and get on with it. Finish school. Apply for university. Be normal.

But I wasn't normal. I was broken. Still am.

"I didn't just lose them that night," I whisper. "I lost myself too."

I lean my head against the chair, the cool air grounding me.

"I needed my mom. I still do. She was everything. My anchor. My compass. And you took her. You took them both— and left me."

The words echo in the silence, and then I hear the distant call of a loon across the water. Grief pulses through me, sharp and unshakable. Like the dreams I buried the day they died.

"I don't know who I am without my parents."

The quiet stretches, long and empty. I don't expect an answer. I never do.

But tonight, I needed to ask.

As I walk back into the house, everything feels heavier than ever. I flip on the television and find a rerun of *NCIS*. I start a bag of microwave popcorn. It'll be my dinner tonight.

I hear the garage door creak open, and voices drift toward me — low, muffled, familiar. Who is Beckett with? Does he have a date? I don't know if I can manage this.

Then I realize he's on a call.

The microwave beeps, and I carefully dump the bag into a large bowl and return to the living room, settling on the couch like I've been here the whole time. I grab the remote control and adjust the volume. My palms are damp. My heart is a drumbeat in my throat.

I tell myself it's just nerves.

But I know better.

It's not just fear pulsing through me. It's tension, guilt, the weight of everything I haven't said about the situation with Alex…and something else I still can't name.

Then Beckett walks in.

He stops in the doorway, eyes scanning the room with precision. Eventually, they land on me.

And I know, instantly, that he feels it too.

It seems his mood mirrors mine — tight, restrained, raw. He looks like a man trying to hold himself together by sheer force of will.

His jaw is locked. His shoulders rigid. His body radiates tension.

Our eyes meet. And suddenly, everything inside me stills.

We don't say a word. We just stare at each other across the room, two storms on a collision course, bracing for impact.

But there's heat in the air too.

The kind that starts low and spreads outward, slow and dangerous.

And it's getting harder to pretend it isn't there.

It makes my skin hum when he's near. It curls low in my belly when he looks at me like this — tight and searching and way too serious.

I push it down. Hard.

"I got a message from Alex," I say, breaking the silence. "It was threatening. He said something about you and your brothers showing up to scare him." I take a breath. "What did you do, Beckett?"

His face stays still, unreadable. But I see the twitch in his jaw. The only crack in his armor. "You weren't supposed to know about that," he says after a moment.

I rise to my feet, folding my arms across my chest. It's not a power pose. It's a defense. I need something — anything — to keep from shaking. "I figured as much," I say. "But I do, so talk."

He steps closer. Just one step, slow and deliberate. And even though I know — I know he'd never hurt me — my breath catches anyway.

Not from fear. But because he's too close.

"I was trying to protect you," he says. His voice is rough, like gravel dragged over steel. "Alex could be dangerous. I saw what he was doing to you, and I thought my brothers and I could get him to leave you alone."

I shake my head, jaw clenched. There's a burning rising in my throat. "So instead of telling me about your concerns, you went behind my back?"

He doesn't flinch or retreat. "Would you have let me help if I'd asked?" he says.

The question lands like a stone between us.

I don't answer.

Because we both know the truth.

I wouldn't have.

He exhales hard, dragging a hand over his face. He looks tired, like this day has cost him something. "Look," he says. "He said you took something from him. I didn't believe it. Not at first. But I need to ask you…" His eyes lift to mine. "Did you?"

I close my eyes a moment. "I've searched everything and

still have no idea what he's talking about. When I ask, he just snaps that I should already know." My mouth goes dry. "I didn't take anything that wasn't mine."

His eyes stay on me. Watching. Reading. I can see it in the way his gaze flickers over my face, looking for cracks in my story, in my voice, in me. His mouth parts slightly, like he wants to push, to press, but he doesn't.

My skin prickles under the weight of his stare. It's not judgment. It's perception. And I hate how much I want to be seen.

He's too close now. I can smell the clean edge of his cologne, the hint of soap. Part of me wants to reach out. To eliminate the space. To press my hand to his heart and remind myself that something solid exists in the middle of all this mess.

But I don't.

Instead, I do the only thing I can think to do. I break the moment. I turn away, fast and awkward, my legs trembling as I move down the hall. My hands are clenched so tightly they ache.

I reach my bedroom door and push it open, then shut it harder than I mean to. The slam echoes down the hallway. I press my back against the door, breathing like I've just run a mile.

Eleven

Beckett

I t's maddening how one person can take over your thoughts. And right now, that person is Sadie Calloway. Since she confronted me about my brothers and me visiting Alex on Friday night, she's made herself scarce. And maybe I'm avoiding her, too. I want to spend time with her, but I can't. Or at least I shouldn't. It would be too easy to confuse things between us.

I keep my eyes focused on the coffeemaker as I prepare my steaming mug. But I think about the way her hair tumbles over her shoulder in soft waves, and for a moment, I forget myself. She's beautiful. Radiant in that quiet, natural way that sneaks up on you. For a split second, I let myself feel it, that pull toward her. The warmth. The ache.

Then guilt rushes in like a cold wave.

She's Caleb's little sister. She's got enough going on right now. And also, she drives me crazy. We are in no way compatible.

"I'm off to the hospital," I call, not sure if she's listening. I'm in the emergency room this morning with a long list of patient appointments this afternoon before I can make my evening rounds.

She doesn't come out of her room or acknowledge my declaration. I don't know if that bothers me or is a relief. I head out, trying to shake off the tension clinging to me like static.

The hospital is where I go to feel steady. In control. But as I enter the building, even that feels off today.

After my morning in the ER and my stint in the office, I return to the hospital and check on two patients I operated on earlier this week—routine post-ops. Both are healing well and ready to be discharged. Normally, that would give me a sense of satisfaction. Today, it barely registers.

Because I'm already thinking about Rosemary. She's my youngest patient, and she's barely hanging on. Her heart is failing faster than we expected, and if a donor match doesn't come soon, I'm terrified she won't make it. I can't let that happen. I won't.

As I walk down the hallway toward her room, a heavy feeling settles in my gut. The air feels wrong, like something's waiting for me just around the corner. My footsteps slow as I hear laughter—light and familiar—drifting out of Rosemary's room.

My stomach tightens.

I pause in the doorway.

Sadie is there. In fact she's perched on Scott Porter's lap, laughing at something he said. It's like a high school reunion in here. Scott was Tarryn's year, and he's not my favorite guy. He's a little too slick for my taste. They look like they're in their own little world, and it punches the air out of my lungs. Her head tilted back, cheeks pink from laughter, hair spilling over her shoulders—and Scott with his arm slung casually around her waist like it's his right.

That image hits me in a place I didn't know was still vulnerable.

"Beckett!" Scott calls, grinning like a jackass. "You're just in time to join the party!"

I don't know what grates more—his voice or the way Sadie flushes, suddenly aware of how it looks.

"Not a chance," I snap, letting the edge in my voice land where it needs to. "I'm at work."

Sadie jumps off his lap like she's been burned, eyes wide. "I'm sorry," she says, like she's been caught doing something wrong.

Scott leans back, smug as ever. "We were just catching up with Rosie. Having a little fun."

Rosemary giggles beside him, clearly enjoying the show. Her soft laugh should warm my heart—it usually does—but right now it only reminds me why I've always hated Scott Porter. He's been a problem since high school, the kind of guy who leaves a trail of broken hearts and grinning apologies behind him. He did it to my sister, and he'll do it to Sadie if she gives him the chance.

I place my laptop on the rolling stand, eyes on Sadie. She looks back at me, unsure. Scott, on the other hand, is busy checking her out, eyes dropping to her ass like he owns it.

My jaw tightens.

"Rosemary, I'll come back," I say, my voice clipped. "I know how much you enjoy your visitors."

She frowns slightly, catching the shift in my tone. "Scott, tell your mom she's welcome to visit anytime. And I'd love more of her scones and strawberry jam."

Scott stretches like he's in no rush. "Guess that's my cue."

He leans down to hug Rosemary, then turns to Sadie. "You too, sweetheart."

He wraps her up in a hug that lingers too long. One hand lands low on her back, drifting lower, and he has the nerve to look me dead in the eye as he does it. Like it's a challenge.

Sadie pushes him off — politely, but firmly. "Go on, Scott. Dr. Beckett needs to check on Rosie."

He smirks all the way to the door, like he's won something. Once he's gone, Sadie reaches for Rosemary's hand and gives it a squeeze.

"I'll head to the cafeteria, give you two a minute," she offers.

But Rosie doesn't let go.

"No. Stay," she says, turning to look at me. "Is that okay, Dr. Beckett?"

I look between the two of them — Rosemary's hopeful eyes, Sadie's uncertain ones — and I don't know what to say. Nothing about this feels simple anymore.

"Of course," I tell her with a shrug, trying to sound casual.

Sadie's smile falters for a second, but she recovers quickly.

I check Rosemary's chart and review her latest labs. Everything looks steady. Stable. It's the best kind of update I can give, but the tension inside me hasn't eased. Not with Scott's smug expression burned in my mind.

"I'll be back tomorrow," I tell Rosemary when everything is done.

"Bring Sadie with you," she replies without missing a beat. "And don't forget your sense of humor."

I give her a nod and a tight smile, then head out. My rounds are complete for the evening, so I trade my scrubs for jeans and a button-down in the locker room. The drive out to the family estate for dinner is quiet — too quiet. My thoughts chase themselves in circles. Why am I so bothered by Porter putting his hands on Sadie? She's not mine.

By the time I pull into the driveway, the sun's starting to dip behind the hills, casting long shadows over the vineyard rows.

Inside, the house smells like chicken and lemon. The table is already set — for eight people, which must mean Uncle Max is joining us. I follow the voices to the kitchen.

I step in just as Mom turns with a glass in hand. Her smile warms the space like it always does, but then her eyes narrow. "Where's Sadie?" she asks.

My jaw tightens before I can stop it. "I don't know," I tell her. "I assume she has plans."

Mom lifts a brow, not buying it for a second. "Mm-hmm."

"She's not family," I add, heading for the wine.

"Yes, she is. Maybe not by blood, but she and Caleb are family. And I hear she's staying with you." Mom winks at me.

I don't answer. I take my seat at the kitchen table, hoping no one else brings her up.

Of course, that's wishful thinking.

Kingston walks in from the back patio, sunglasses perched on his head even though the sun's nearly down. He makes a beeline for the counter, lifting a lid to sniff what's inside. "Please tell me this is lemon chicken," he says, sounding like he hasn't eaten in days.

"Touch anything before we sit and you lose a hand," Dad calls from behind him as he comes in with a bottle of cabernet under one arm.

Ryker trails after him, barefoot, shirt untucked, and with Pinot, our spaniel mix, bouncing at his heels like a shadow.

When I snicker, he turns to look. "Did she pee again?" He groans. "Nooooo."

"She missed you," I deadpan. "She always pees for her favorite."

"That's a messed-up compliment," he mutters, rubbing his temples as he goes to find a rag.

Greyson walks in last, looking put-together in that effortless way he always does, like he didn't just spend twelve hours in an ER. Trinity slips in beside him, her hand brushing his as he passes.

"Look at this," Mom says. "All my boys under one roof. It's a miracle."

"It's a weekly family dinner," Ryker mutters, but his grin gives him away.

"You should call Sadie." Mom dries her hands on a towel and gives me a look. "She needs to be here. She's all alone with Caleb in the UK. She's very welcome."

"Mom—" I start, then stop. She won't understand. She doesn't know how complicated things are, how tangled my feelings have gotten.

"She's staying with you," she says firmly. "It's just dinner. Call her."

Before I can say another word, she thrusts the phone into my hands.

I sigh, then pull my phone from my pocket instead, avoiding a debate I won't win. I tap out a quick message.

Me: Hey, you want to come by the vineyard for dinner? My family would love to see you.

The dots appear almost immediately, bouncing like the nerves rattling around in my ribcage. Then her reply pops up.

Sadie: Sure! In the main house or the restaurant?

Me: Main house. You know how to get here, right?

Sadie: Yep. Just leaving the hospital now. I'll be there in ten.

Me: Great. See you then.

I stare at the screen for a second, then tuck the phone away and try to settle the strange flutter in my chest.

"You called her?" my mom asks.

"I texted her. She's on her way," I mutter, moving to the

counter where she's prepping dinner.

"Good," she says, turning back to her chopping board.

She hands me a massive salad bowl and a pile of ingredients, and I get to work, grateful for the distraction. She starts in on the town gossip, telling me how the Dempseys are claiming that several acres up by the ridge belong to them, and now both families have deeds to the same land. The legal mess sounds like a nightmare.

"Remind me why I didn't go into law?" I ask, peeling a cucumber.

"You like fixing people, not arguing with them," she replies. "And you hate paperwork."

Fair point.

After a pause, I ask, "Do you think Sadie will be okay?"

"What do you mean?" My mother glances at me, narrowing her eyes.

"Just...being around the family," I hedge.

Her brow lifts. "Why wouldn't she be?"

"She and Tarryn didn't get along in high school."

"Who didn't I get along with?" Tarryn asks, breezing into the room. She pops a cherry tomato into her mouth and grabs another.

"Sadie Calloway is coming for dinner," I say.

Tarryn's eyes widen. "Here? At the house?"

"She's living with Beckett," Mom adds casually, as though that clears everything up.

"You two are dating?" Tarryn's voice jumps three octaves.

"No," I answer. "She left her boyfriend and didn't have anywhere to go. I'm just helping Caleb out."

Tarryn shrugs. "It'll be good to see her. She always had a sharp sense of humor." Another tomato disappears.

"But didn't you hate her in high school?"

"She was best friends with Ginny Dempsey," she says, waving a hand. "That was a long time ago."

I roll my eyes, slicing a pepper a little too aggressively.

As dinner comes together, the room fills with the scent of

roasted vegetables, garlic, and fresh herbs. The conversation rolls on, casual and chaotic, exactly the way it's always been. But I keep glancing at the clock, pulse ticking faster every time a minute passes.

Then, just as I'm starting to wonder if she's coming, the front door swings open.

"Hello? Beckett?" Sadie calls.

I turn, and there she is, framed by the evening light. She's changed out of the jeans she was wearing at the hospital into a sundress that brushes her knees, soft and simple, and her hair falls loose over her shoulders, slightly windblown from the drive.

She looks like summer, like something I wasn't ready for.

"Hey," I say, trying to hide the way my heartbeat skips.

She smiles. "Wow. Smells amazing in here."

Then she spots my mother and walks straight over, pulling a bouquet from behind her back.

"These are for you," she says, handing over a vibrant arrangement.

My mother pulls her into a hug. "You didn't have to bring anything, sweetheart. I'm just glad you're here."

When they pull apart, I fumble for something to say. "Mom made dinner," I blurt.

Sadie laughs softly. "Thank you for inviting me. Beckett's been ordering from the Grill most nights."

Mom eyes me. "You're a heart doctor. You know better. You should be cooking healthy meals, not dodging the stove."

Before I can defend myself, Greyson and Trinity walk into the kitchen hand in hand.

I turn to Sadie. "You already know my family. Trinity is the newest member." I turn to Trinity. "This is Sadie Calloway. She's the younger sister to my best friend, Caleb, who is currently living in London. She's staying at my place."

Trinity beams. "Hi! It's very nice to meet you."

Sadie nods, glancing my way. "Thanks."

The night unfolds in a blur of laughter, wine, and the kind of warmth that can only come from being surrounded by family.

80

Sadie fits right in, her charm effortless. She's telling my mom a story about visiting Rosemary and a confused patient who thought she was a nurse and insisted she find him pudding, gesturing with her hands and keeping everyone laughing.

Every time her eyes find mine across the table, I feel a little jolt. We're not together. We shouldn't be anything. But I can't stop watching her.

"What are you doing for work, sweetheart?" my mom asks, passing her the wine.

Sadie shrugs. "I've applied all over town, but nothing's panned out yet. I figure once the tourist season hits full swing, I'll start getting some calls."

"Well, you just let me know if you need anything," my mom says. "We take care of our own."

Sadie gives her a soft smile. "Thank you. That means a lot."

I should be relieved she's fitting in so well, yet I can't help but feel it—that low hum of tension beneath everything. I'm not sure what I'll do if she becomes part of this family...but not with me.

"Where have you worked before?" Tarryn asks, curiosity lifting her brows.

"I've done a little of everything," Sadie replies. "Retail, waiting tables—I don't want to sit at a desk. Coffee shops. I've worked in a lot of places."

"Why'd you leave those jobs?" Tarryn presses, tone still casual but her gaze assessing.

Sadie doesn't flinch. "Some of it was me—being young, showing up late. But I spent the last three years working at Della's Coffee Hut."

"Hey!" Ryker cuts in. "They shut down the one near the hospital."

Sadie nods. "Yeah. Della stopped paying her taxes, and the CRA shut the whole business down."

"You worked there for three years?" Tarryn asks, with a hint of surprise. "At a coffee hut?"

"I loved it," Sadie says with a smile. "There were regulars I saw every day. And I had fun when people gave me those ridiculously complicated orders."

"Like what?" I ask, leaning in before I can stop myself.

She grins. "An extra-large salted caramel mocha blended iced coffee with five dark roast espresso shots, four pumps of caramel sauce, four pumps of caramel syrup, three pumps of mocha, three pumps of toffee nut syrup, double blended, with extra whipped cream."

Greyson stares. "That's...real?"

"It's more common than you'd think," Sadie laughs. "Some people want their caffeine with a side of sugar coma."

"How does that person ever sleep again?" Kingston mutters.

She shrugs, still smiling. "I wasn't in charge of their sleep. Just their drinks. My goal was to keep the line moving and make the best possible cup."

"You worked full time in one of those huts?" Tarryn asks, clearly impressed despite herself. "Those places get brutally hot in the summer."

Sadie nods. "I did what I needed to."

Tarryn studies her for a second, tapping her nail on the rim of her glass. "I need someone in the tasting room. Any interest?"

Sadie tilts her head, intrigued. "What would that involve?"

"Pouring tastings, helping guests, learning about our wines," Tarryn says. "We host private events and tours, so there's some prep work. But it's fun and steady. You'd be working with our cousin, Zach, but he's harmless. Mostly."

"You meet all sorts of interesting people," Trinity adds helpfully.

Sadie's eyes brighten. "That sounds kind of amazing. I miss being around people who enjoy what they do. And wine tastings? Count me in."

I watch them, my sister and the woman who's been living

in my house, forming an unexpected connection. Something about Sadie changes. She seems more vibrant, energized. Like she's been holding her breath for weeks and finally let it out.

"Perfect." Tarryn beams. "Zach might try to dump everything on you, so take what you want and push back on the rest. We've been looking for someone with a backbone."

"Is Zach getting promoted?" Sadie asks.

Tarryn snorts. "If I can prove the tasting room's been underperforming, Zach's next promotion might be to the unemployment line."

"Well..." Sadie grins. "I'm here to help however you need."

"Great. Swing by my office tomorrow morning, and I'll get you set up. Wear comfortable shoes. You'll be on your feet all day. And bring a notepad. I'm giving you a crash course in our wines."

"Thanks, Tarryn," Sadie says warmly. "Really."

As dessert arrives—a dense chocolate torte drizzled with ganache—Sadie leans across the table toward me, her eyes gleaming with mischief.

"You planning to share that, or do I need to wrestle you for it?"

It takes me a second to recover from the jolt of unexpected heat in her tone. "You might want to think twice before challenging a cardiologist."

Her laugh is low and playful, and something about the way she looks at me makes the air in my lungs feel thinner.

After dinner, Mom shoos us all out of the kitchen, insisting she doesn't want help—just "clear space." The group scatters. Sadie tells Tarryn she'll see her in the morning, and I find myself walking out with her.

"Thanks for inviting me tonight," she says. "Your family has always been so good to me. Tonight, they made me feel...included."

I glance over, surprised by her honesty. "They're good at that," I reply. "As you know, it can be a lot at once, but it comes from a good place."

She stops on the porch, leaning against the railing. The moonlight casts a soft glow over her face as she looks out toward the trees lining the edge of the property.

"It felt good to laugh again," she says, voice quieter now. "It's been a long time since I've done that."

I want to step closer, to reach for her hand or say something that might ease that ache, but I don't. I can't.

"I'm glad," I say instead.

Silence stretches between us, not uncomfortable, but heavy. Charged.

Eventually, I clear my throat. "Well, we should get going so you can get some sleep. You've got your clothes ready for tomorrow?"

She nods. "I think I can pull something together with what I have at your place."

"Good." I start down the steps, then glance back. "'Night, Sadie. In case I don't see you at home."

"Goodnight, Beck."

She heads for the Jeep, and I settle in my car. When I close the door behind me, I don't move. I lean against the seat for a second, closing my eyes.

She was perfect tonight. Warm, open, funny.

It's good that she's feeling more comfortable, getting back on her feet. But, I remind myself, that doesn't have anything to do with me.

Twelve

Sadie

I'm wiping down the kitchen counter at Beckett's, trying hard to keep the house as clean as I can. I've been working at the tasting room for over a week now, and I wipe down counters there all day. I can't stop myself. Suddenly, the front door creaks open.

The sound cuts through the quiet like a warning bell. I glance at the clock. 10:47 p.m. My stomach tightens instinctively. *Alex?*

The name hits me like ice, but a second later I hear the steady thump of heavy footfalls down the hall, confident and unhurried. No way that would be Alex. And it's dumb to think he could have found me. There's a squeak of rubber soles against the hardwood.

That's Beckett.

He hasn't been around much since I started my new job in the tasting room. I wonder if he was out with a woman? It shouldn't be any of my concern, but that green monster is ready to roar. I grit my teeth and keep wiping, pretending my pulse isn't doing something weird.

He pushes through the door — hair mussed, shadows dark under his eyes, a hospital badge still clipped to the neckline of his green scrubs. In the three weeks I've lived here, I've never seen him at home in scrubs.

"I didn't realize this place came with full-time staff," he mutters. He leans heavily against the edge of the kitchen counter, like he can't hold up his own weight. "You're doing dishes?" he adds, a dry smirk tugging at his mouth.

I don't flinch, though I do realize this is a distinct change from the way I did things when I first arrived. "I was cleaning up." I shoot him a pointed look and toss the towel over my shoulder. "But since you're here, feel free to make yourself useful. Trash needs taking out."

He lets out a tired snort and shakes his head. "Charming as ever."

"I aim to please."

Our eyes meet — his bloodshot and exhausted, mine probably a little sharper than they need to be. I shouldn't care. I don't care.

But something in his eyes gives me pause.

It's not just exhaustion. It's weight. A pressure bearing down on him, making it hard to breathe.

Before I can stop myself, I blurt, "Did you eat today?"

He blinks like I've just spoken a foreign language. "Excuse me?"

"You heard me," I say, already turning away. "You look like death warmed over. I figure you've been running on caffeine and sarcasm since noon."

"I had a granola bar," he counters, trailing after me like it's involuntary.

I glance over my shoulder. "That's not a meal. That's a cry

for help."

I open the fridge and pull out what I stashed earlier — a roasted veggie flatbread and half a salad I didn't touch during lunch. I slide the flatbread onto a cookie sheet and pop it into the oven, ignoring the way his eyes follow every movement.

"I didn't ask you to feed me."

"Good," I snap. "Because I'm not doing it for you. I'm doing it because if you pass out and crack your skull, I'll have to explain it to paramedics. And to Caleb. And frankly, I've had enough drama for one week."

"What did Zach do?" he asks after a moment.

I look across the dark living room. "I haven't told Tarryn, so keep this between us, please."

He doesn't respond and looks at me, waiting for me to continue.

I pour a glass of water and place it in front of him, like I'm not shaking inside. "I'm not a hundred-percent sure, but I put a fifty and a hundred-dollar bill in the till this morning, and after he left, it was gone."

"Did he take it to accounting for change?"

I shrug. "I never got the change, and my till didn't balance at the end of my shift."

"Did you take it, and you're blaming Zach? I mean, getting him in trouble wouldn't bother me, but —"

"No!" My voice comes out sharp. My heart's pounding now, tight with panic. "I actually covered it with my tips this week." This is exactly what I was afraid of. He doesn't believe me. "If this turns into a thing," I say, trying to catch my breath, "it'll blow back on me. And I really like my job."

I hate how desperate I sound. But it's true.

"He was only in the tasting room for maybe fifteen minutes," I continue. "I noted it on my till sheet, but the whole thing was drama from the second he showed up. I mean, of course, I don't want to get blamed. I don't want to lose this. But stealing is not okay. That money belongs to the vineyard."

Beckett doesn't answer right away. He just looks at me,

and then when he speaks, it's so low I almost miss it. "You used your own money?"

"I just know what's right. But I'm not explaining how this happened to Tarryn."

"Why did you replace the money?"

"Because I don't want there to be a problem. But there's something going on. I can feel it."

Beckett snorts. "You could say that." He glances over at me, and something in his posture shifts. He's less guarded, more open. "The land's been in our family for eight generations," he says quietly. "Passed from the firstborn son to the next. Only once did it skip. My great-aunt was the oldest in her generation, but they gave it to her younger brother instead."

I move to the table and sit. He's not just talking to fill the air. He's offering me something.

"My dad fell in love with my mom while she was doing her residency at Paradise General. When she finished her residency, she got a job out on the island."

"Vancouver Island?" I ask, just to make sure.

He nods. "Yeah. He didn't want to live without her, so he left the vineyard for a year and moved there. My grandfather was still running it then, but Max—my uncle—started preparing to take over."

"And then your parents moved back."

"Right. They missed Black Bear Valley too much. Once they came home, my grandfather passed the vineyard to my dad. And my dad hired Max to stay on. Which, in hindsight, might've been a mistake."

I nod slowly. "I've heard bits of this from Tarryn."

Beckett lets out a humorless chuckle. "Yeah, well, Max has always had a chip on his shoulder. When all four of us boys decided we didn't want the vineyard and Tarryn stepped up to run it instead, Max and Zach didn't take it well."

"They were pissed she got named as the heir." So much makes sense now.

"Understatement of the year," he mutters. "My sister's

damn good at what she does. But Zach—he's been bitter ever since Dad said he was considering retiring. Pulling little power plays. Undermining her. Making her life harder. And when she hired you, that may have pushed him over the edge. She brought someone into his part of the operation. He knows full well that Tarryn keeps an eye on the numbers."

I feel my stomach twist. "So I was set up."

He shakes his head. "No. But you were used."

I hate how much that makes sense. "Do you want me to tell her about the money?"

He nods. "Yeah. First thing tomorrow. She owes you. Covering the till isn't your job. That's a good day of tips."

I nod, because that was going to buy me a new outfit to wear to work.

"He won't know what to do about the money not being missing. It will drive him crazy when he tells Tarryn about it."

My shoulders slump. "Everyone's going to think I stole it and then put it back."

For a moment, he just watches me. Then something soft flickers across his face. Empathy. It's quick, but it's there. "No," he says. "I don't think they will."

The oven dings, cutting through the silence. I pull the flatbread out and place it in front of him, shoving the fork toward him like it's a dare.

He doesn't touch it right away. Just studies the plate. Then he lifts his eyes to mine. "This your way of apologizing after the note I left yesterday?" he asks.

I blink. "You mean because you lost your mind over one plate, one fork, and a single glass left in the sink?"

That earns the smallest ghost of a smile.

I roll my eyes and turn back to the counter, feigning interest in tidying something that's already spotless.

But then—quietly, sincerely—he says, "Thanks."

And for once, I don't say anything sarcastic. I just keep my hands moving, pretending it didn't mean more than it should.

Beckett eats in silence, and I keep pretending to be busy,

straightening a stack of napkins that didn't need fixing, drying the sink. I don't know why the sound of his chewing feels so loud, or why I keep glancing at him from the corner of my eye like I'm afraid to look directly.

He devours the flatbread like it's the first real food he's had in days.

Maybe it is.

After a few minutes, he speaks. "I forgot how quiet it is here at night."

"That's because you're never here to notice."

He lets out a grunt. Not quite agreement, not quite a laugh. "Didn't think you'd still be around."

"I live here."

"Right." He nods and takes another sip of water. The glass clinks faintly as he sets it down. "Hard to forget with your stuff everywhere."

I raise an eyebrow, still turned slightly away. "Is that your way of saying I'm a slob?"

He smirks. "You are a slob."

"Your house doesn't need to be as sterile as an operating room." My hand stills on the counter, fingers curling around the edge of the sink. He's not wrong. I am a slob. I don't mean to be.

"I get it," he says. "You want to be able to pack up fast. Keep everything visible in case you need to bolt."

His words land hard. Because as soon as he says it, I know that's the truth.

I turn toward him, bracing. "What made you so smart?"

"I just figured it out." His voice isn't harsh. Just tired. Honest.

"I'll try harder. Keep things clean. Stay out of your way."

His gaze doesn't waver. "I've known you most of your life, Sadie. But I don't really know you."

I fold my arms across my chest, a defense. "And what? Now you suddenly care?"

He leans back on the stool, shoulders heavy. "I don't know," he admits. "Maybe I do."

The room goes quiet again. Just the faint hum of the fridge and the whisper of wind against the windows.

He's looking at me — really looking. Like he's peeling back every layer I've built. And I hate that part of me wants to let him.

I need to shift the weight. "Why medicine?"

His eyes soften. "My mom. I grew up watching her take care of people. I guess I followed the path."

"And you never wanted the vineyard?"

He shakes his head. "I love the business from a distance. But there are too many things you can't control — weather, vine age, fires, water issues. In medicine, the variables are different. I like knowing the outcome, at least most of the time."

"What about Rosie's outcome?"

His expression tightens. "If we can get her a heart in the next month or two, she'll live a full life. If we can't... I don't want to think about that."

"I get that," I say.

His eyes meet mine again, searching. "What about you?" he asks. "Do you like the vineyard?"

"I do. I like the people. And you can't grow up in this town and not know wine."

With a faint smile, he looks me up and down. Then he sighs and walks away, leaving me standing in the kitchen. "Goodnight," he calls faintly.

God help me, I want him so badly it hurts, especially because he doesn't seem interested.

I will him to return and kiss me until my toes curl, but he doesn't. So I turn the lights off, head to my room, and try to go to sleep. I lie there for what seems like hours, but the clock only shows twenty minutes.

I groan and shove the blankets off, swinging my legs over the side of the bed. Bare feet on cool floorboards. I pad into the kitchen, hoping water will fix the heat still simmering under my skin.

Something cold. Something simple.

I flip on the dim light — and nearly scream.

Beckett is sitting at the counter.

Shirtless.

He's hunched slightly, reading something on his phone, looking perfectly casual, like he isn't the cause of my sleepless night. His hair is messy, damp at the ends from a shower, and he's wearing soft gray pajama pants slung indecently low on his hips. It takes all my self-control not to reach out and trace my fingers over the lines of his corded muscles.

He glances up when he hears me. "Couldn't sleep either?"

His voice is rough, and it scrapes against something inside me.

I blink, scrambling for composure. "I—uh, yeah. Just need some water."

He sets his phone aside and rests his forearms on the counter. "This place is too quiet."

I nod, filling a glass at the tap, grateful for the distraction. "That's the idea."

He watches me, his gaze steady. I can feel it like static against my skin.

"Why did you come here?" he asks.

"I told you, I needed some water."

"No. I mean, why did you knock on my door?"

I grip the glass. "I didn't want Alex to find me." I hesitate, then add softly, "I wanted to be somewhere I knew I'd be safe and no place anyone would suspect."

He tilts his head slightly. "Except Caleb."

"Caleb's my brother."

He stands, and I feel it immediately. The shift in the air. The charge.

Like lightning before a storm.

"He told me to look out for you," Beckett says.

I turn to face him, folding my arms like armor. "Is that what this is? You playing bodyguard?"

He doesn't hesitate. "No. That's how it started." He takes a step closer. "Now it's something else."

My throat tightens. I don't step back. I can't.

His hand lifts, slow and steady, giving me time to stop him, but I don't. His fingers graze my cheek, and it sends an ache straight through me. He drags his knuckles along my jaw, and I forget how to breathe.

"You drive me crazy," he murmurs, his voice a rasp. "You're stubborn and sharp and impossible to ignore."

"You're arrogant," I shoot back, my voice catching. "And bossy. And a total pain in my ass."

His mouth curves slightly, but his eyes don't leave mine. Something flickers there. Then he leans in, just enough that I can feel the whisper of his breath across my lips.

I stop breathing.

The air thickens. My heart slams against my ribs. My lips part on instinct.

But then, he freezes. Pulls back an inch. Maybe less. His gaze searches mine, like he's reading a truth I'm afraid to say out loud.

"Not yet," he says, barely above a whisper.

Those two words are both a promise and a punishment. I nod, though it feels like I've been split wide open.

He brushes his thumb across my cheek. "Goodnight, Sadie." He turns and disappears into the hallway, leaving me alone.

Glass in hand. Heart in pieces. And the echo of something I never expected to want still buzzing against my skin.

I return to my room and lie in bed, eyes wide open, staring into the dark like it might offer clarity.

It doesn't.

My pulse still hasn't settled. My skin still burns where he touched me. Just a brush of his thumb, and I'm completely undone.

Not because of the almost-kiss, but because he stopped.

Beckett Paradise. Smug cardiologist. Local royalty. The man who argues just to hear himself win — he stopped.

He looked at me like I mattered. Like he didn't want to screw this up.

And that's worse than if he'd actually kissed me. What made him stop? I'm confused. *"Not yet"*? He seems to have a plan.

I roll to my side and punch the pillow, like it'll knock loose the knot in my stomach.

This was meant to be a clean slate. A break from men — or at least from those who take and take until there's nothing left. Beckett wasn't supposed to see me. He wasn't supposed to make me feel safe. He wasn't supposed to be kind.

I drag the blanket over my head like it can block out his voice, that low whisper of *"not yet,"* like he's giving me time. Like he knows I'm scared and he's willing to wait.

My heart squeezes.

That wasn't part of the plan. Not even close.

Thirteen

Beckett

I blink my eyes to clear them, still wondering why I almost kissed my best friend's little sister last night. Why I essentially told her I would.

Sadie Calloway. The girl I promised to look out for, not get involved with. It was so bad, I showed up at the hospital at five o'clock this morning and walked into a double bypass. Thank God I can do those in my sleep.

Rather than go home now that the surgery is done, I shuffle down the hall and find a spot in the sleep room. There are three other people already in there, but I dive into an empty bunk, pull up the light blanket, and stare at the ceiling.

I drag a hand down my face. *What the hell is wrong with me?*

She was just standing there — barefoot, soft-eyed, a glass of water in her hand, that silk robe barely hanging on. And I forgot everything, every reason I was supposed to keep my distance, every line I swore I wouldn't cross.

And she didn't pull away. She looked up like she was hoping I wouldn't stop.

After a restless few minutes, I throw off the blanket and sit on the edge of the bed, elbows on my knees. My scrub top still smells like antiseptic and stress. I should shower. I should eat. I should do literally anything other than replay the way she looked at me.

But I can't.

This was never supposed to be complicated. She showed up at my door, and Caleb asked me to keep her safe, give her space, not daydream about how her mouth would feel against mine.

I pull out my phone. The screen is black, but I know what's coming. Eventually, Caleb will check in, ask how she's doing, ask if everything's okay.

And I'll either lie to my best friend…or admit I can't be trusted.

I grab the phone and open our message thread. My fingers hover.

Me: Hey, man. Everything's fine here. Sadie's doing great.

Backspace.

Me: I may have fallen for your sister. Don't kill me.

Delete.
God, I'm an idiot.

Nothing happened. I didn't kiss her. I didn't touch her, at least not in any way that counts.

But I wanted to. I said I might.

And that's just as dangerous.

It's Sadie. And it's Caleb. Two people I care about. Two

96

people I can't afford to hurt. Two people who have been hurt enough already.

I drop the phone on the bunk and press my palms to my eyes. Eventually, I'll have to tell him. I'll have to make a choice. But not today.

Today, I exit quietly from the sleep room, pull on a clean shirt in the locker room, splash cold water on my face, and pretend I haven't already crossed the line with Sadie a hundred times in my head. Because right now, there's something else I need to deal with — Tarryn.

Sadie trusted me with what happened in the tasting room yesterday. I need to make sure my sister hears it accurately before someone else twists it.

Out in the parking lot, I slam the car door harder than I mean to, gripping the steering wheel like it's the only thing holding me together. The air is crisp, but sweat clings to the back of my neck. Guilt. Anger. I almost kissed Sadie last night, and now I'm heading for a meeting where I have to protect her again. This time from my own damn family. Sadie's caught in the middle, and she's an easy target.

Not this time. Not while I'm able to look out for her.

When I arrive, I step into the vineyard's main office, the air thick with the scent of oak barrels and the low, earthy tang of fermentation.

Tarryn's perched behind her desk with a stack of invoices in front of her. "You look like shit," she says, eyes flicking to mine before going back to her screen.

"Didn't sleep."

"Sadie?" she asks.

I don't answer that. "We've got a problem. Zach stopped by the tasting room yesterday, and after he left, the till was short a hundred and fifty bucks."

That gets her attention. She sets her pen down. "Sadie told you this?"

"Yeah. She didn't want you to know, used her own tip money to cover the gap. Noted the shortage. My guess? Zach's going to pin it on her."

Tarryn leans back in her chair, crossing her arms. She looks out the window at the syrah vines. "I knew it."

"You think he's stealing?"

"I know he is. This isn't the first time something hasn't added up. He knows I track the income, but he doesn't seem to realize I look at the sales figures as well. I've been tracking small inconsistencies since last quarter." She shakes her head. "This was more than usual, but unfortunately, it doesn't surprise me."

"Then why haven't you done anything?"

"Because every time I bring it up, Dad tells me I'm being paranoid. Says I'm too hard on Zach, that calling out his brother's 'perfect son' is just another way of insulting the sacred Paradise name and Uncle Max." She stands, frustration vibrating off her as she starts pacing. "I wanted cameras installed, just above the registers. Basic coverage. Nothing invasive. But no. Everyone said it was 'too much.' Accused me of spying."

"Maybe because you were about to catch him red-handed."

She spins to face me. "I don't care anymore. I want the cameras up by Friday."

I nod. "I know a guy. Discreet. We can get them in after hours, keep them so small Zach won't even see them."

Her jaw tightens. "Do it. And Beckett, thank you." She sighs. "Sadie doesn't deserve this." She goes over and counts money from the petty cash box. She hands it to me. "Make sure Sadie gets this. She's killing it out there. Sales are up when she's working. Customers love her. And Zach hates having her around."

I shrug. "She belongs here. He doesn't."

"I know. But I don't get the final say — yet."

"Sadie's a thousand times better than him."

Tarryn tilts her head, studying me. "You're not just talking about the money, are you?"

I look away.

"You going to tell Caleb?"

I rake a hand through my hair. "Eventually."

Her mouth twitches, almost a smile. "Better it come from you than Zach blabbing to him. You know this is a small town."

That's Tarryn—blunt, sharp-edged, and never wrong.

I leave her with the logistics of setting up the cameras and go to find Sadie.

The tasting room is buzzing when I step inside. Glass clinks, laughter rises from the bar, and the rich scent of pinot and oak fills the air.

Sadie's behind the counter, laughing with a couple as she pours their flight. Her smile is warm, but I can see the tension in her shoulders. The way her eyes flick toward the register every time someone pays. The way she double-checks every entry, even when no one's watching. Except me.

She doesn't see me. She's in her rhythm, uncorking the next bottle with confident grace. Capable. Focused. Beautiful.

God help me.

Then her eyes find mine. Her smile falters, just slightly. Like she's not sure which version of me she's about to get.

"Hey," she says as I approach. Quiet. Guarded.

"Hey." I nod to the couple at the bar. "Hope she's treating you well."

They chuckle and raise their glasses.

"She's great," the woman says. "Knows her stuff."

When the couple moves toward the patio, I step in close enough to speak low, just for her.

"I told Tarryn about Zach," I tell her. "She wasn't surprised. We're going to install cameras above the till. Catch him in the act."

Her lips part slightly, but her voice stays low. "Are you sure she believes me? I mean, blood's thicker than water."

"You've given her no reason not to trust you, and you're doing a great job. Zach's not exactly beloved. Tarryn just can't fire him without proof."

Sadie swallows hard. "I replaced the money," she whispers.

"I know." I offer her the cash Tarryn gave me.

She blinks, surprised. Her fingers hover before she takes the bills, like she's not sure if she should thank me or argue. "I just..." Her voice catches. "I like this job, Beckett."

"I know you do." My voice softens. "And you're good at it. Tarryn sees it. We all do."

She exhales. "Is the rest of the family okay with this?"

"They don't know yet. My brothers won't care. My dad will say we should cut Zach some slack. And Max? He'll lose it, especially if Zach's caught."

Her mouth quirks. "That tracks."

I shrug. "Unfortunately, it does."

There's a pause. She glances toward the patio, then back at me. "Thank you."

"You don't have to thank me."

"I do," she says. "Because this isn't your fight."

"We're all on Tarryn's side, and I don't like that you got put in the middle."

She looks away, blinking quickly, and I know if I stay any longer, I'm going to say something I shouldn't. Like how I haven't stopped thinking about last night. Or how I wonder what would've happened if I hadn't pulled away.

I clear my throat. "I should get back to the hospital."

She nods. "Okay. If you see Rosie, tell her I'll come by tonight."

I head for the door but glance back. She's already serving another group.

Outside, the late-morning sun beats down as I walk toward the edge of the property. I spot Tarryn talking with Mitch and Elise, our head vintners. They're the ones who turn our fruit into magic, the people who care about the vines like they're family.

I walk over to join them, offering a quick hello. But before I can ask about the new plantings, Zach shows up, unannounced, of course.

He struts around us like he owns the place in a vineyard-branded polo, designer shades, and smugness dialed to ten. He looks every bit the image of competence — if you didn't know better.

Mitch and Elise depart for the barrel room, leaving me and Tarryn alone with the guy none of us trust.

"You might want to hear this," Zach says, like he's about to deliver an earthquake instead of whatever self-serving speech he's rehearsed.

I cross my arms and wait.

"I just wanted to give you a heads-up," he says. "After Sadie's shift yesterday, I did a quick check on the till. Looked like it was a couple hundred short. Probably just a mistake, but, you know…figured you'd want to know."

He says this like he's doing us a favor. Like he's being responsible.

Tarryn's voice is flat. "Thanks for the info."

Zach frowns slightly, like he expected a pat on the back. "I mean, I'm not saying it was her. Just weird, you know?"

I don't blink. "And you didn't notice any discrepancies before she started working?"

He shrugs. "Could've happened before, I guess. But I wasn't looking for it then."

Convenient.

Too convenient.

Tarryn looks away and then back at Zach. "We'll handle it. Thanks for bringing it to our attention."

Zach shrugs, all false humility. "No problem. She's new. Maybe doesn't know how the system works."

"It wasn't short when accounting got it," Tarryn says evenly, her voice cool and calm like she's reading a weather report. Not a hint of the storm behind her eyes.

He pauses. Just a second. But I see the flicker — the misstep.

Then he recovers with a cocky grin. "Right, well, she must've seen me count it and covered her tracks. Smart girl."

I bite back the heat rising in my body. "We'll look into it," I say again.

Zach gives a lazy salute, like this is some kind of game. "Just doing my job." He turns and strolls off, whistling like he's already won.

As soon as he disappears around the corner, I let out a sharp breath and rake a hand through my hair. "We're calling the security company today."

Tarryn's already scrolling through her phone, eyes narrowed with purpose. "After hours. I don't want him catching wind. The minute he knows, he'll find a new way to cover his ass."

I nod. "And we're not letting him pin this on her."

Tarryn doesn't look up. "No. We're not."

Because this isn't just about missing money anymore. It's about respect. It's about a girl who's trying to start over and Zach, who thinks he can use her as a scapegoat and walk away clean. But he won't. Not this time.

Fourteen

Sadie

Last night at the family dinner, Beckett's mom, Vicky — who absolutely refuses for me to call her anything else — roped me into her latest project. She's chairing a fundraiser for kids who need medical care in rural Canada. Despite our medical care being free, rural areas are always short on doctors, and the money raised will help bring medical professionals to remote communities all over the province.

Thankfully, it's already mostly put together. My job is just to pick up the donations local businesses have promised for the silent auction. Easy enough.

At least, that's what I told myself.

Now I'm juggling a paper checklist and a trunk already half-full of wine baskets and gift cards. The people in this town are generous — chefs handing over dinner vouchers, shop owners packaging candles, trinkets, and handwoven throws. But there are a few things missing, so I also stop by some of my own contacts and get additional donations.

I'm in a groove by the time I pull up to the last stop at Black Bear Vineyard.

I haven't been here in years, almost a whole decade, not since Ginny left for Vancouver when we were nineteen. She headed for university with a vow never to return. Her grandmother is a true matriarch, and a bit scary, if you ask me. She is strong, and it's her way or the highway. Ginny had had enough.

Ginny really saved me after my parents died, and we had an apartment together while we finished high school. We stayed in touch for a while after she left, but we were headed in different directions. I didn't want to move to Vancouver, and she didn't want to look back. Now it's been a long time. I'd love to see her again, but don't even know where she is. I guess I could ask someone while I'm here.

But then when I enter the gift shop, I see her immediately. For a moment, I'm not sure it can be real. She vowed never to come back here, let alone go to work for her family's business. But I guess people change.

I've managed to close my gaping mouth by the time she turns, her braid tucked over one shoulder. She smiles the second she recognizes me. "Sadie!" she says. "How are you? What brings you here?"

"It's so good to see you," I tell her, engulfing her in a hug. When I step back, I hold up my clipboard. "Vicky Paradise roped me into helping with her fundraiser. I'm the errand girl today, picking things up."

Ginny nods, wiping her hands on her apron. "She's been working on that forever. Our donation is right here."

She walks over to the counter and hands me a gorgeous basket — six bottles of wine, a collection of gifts. It's thoughtful and generous.

"Wow. Thank you." I lift it carefully. "How long have you been back in town?"

"Not long. I'm sorry I didn't call. I've been —"

I wave her off. "Don't worry. I get it. I just can't believe you're here."

She chuckles. "Yeah, I know. I'd love to catch up sometime. Maybe hang out?"

"Have you seen Rosie yet?"

She shakes her head. "No, but Mom told me she's in the hospital. Waiting on a heart."

"She'd love to see you."

"I'm not so sure." She looks away. "I didn't do a good job keeping in touch."

"We don't care about all that. We're just glad you're back. I can go with you if it helps. I visit almost every day."

"Really?"

"Yeah, she's sick of sudoku and daytime TV. Sometimes we talk, sometimes we play games, and sometimes we plan what we'll do when she gets her new heart."

Ginny nods. "I'd love to visit. Maybe I can come with you next week."

"Great." There's a pause. I want to say something that matters, but all I can manage is, "She deserves a heart."

"She's a fighter," Ginny says. "But even fighters get tired." Then she straightens. "After you're done with the fundraiser…maybe we could get coffee? Just us."

I nod before I even think. "Yeah. I'd like that."

We exchange numbers, and she tells me she's living in the old caretaker's cottage on the vineyard.

"Other than fundraising duties, what are you doing these days?" Ginny asks.

I exhale. "Not much different from when you left. I just got out of a bad relationship, the kind you run from or end up in jail over." I roll my eyes. "I'm crashing at Beckett's place until I can get on my feet."

Her brows lift. "Where's Caleb?"

"His company has him working in London — in the UK, not Ontario."

"Nice. Have you visited?"

I shake my head. "I want to. But I feel like I should manage my own life before I couch-surf internationally."

"Are you working?"

"I am. Tarryn hired me in the Paradise tasting room."

"You're with the enemy," she teases.

"They've been good to me."

She holds up her hand. "No judgment here."

Just then a customer walks in. Ginny smiles and excuses herself, and I heft the basket and head back to Beckett's Jeep. I now have a back full of donations to drop off, and Beckett's backyard pool is calling my name.

I drive away from Black Bear Vineyard with the windows cracked, letting the early summer breeze curl around me. It smells like wet earth and something blooming.

I sort through my feelings about Ginny being back in town. She seems to have that same ache I sometimes see in my own reflection, the one that comes from running hard and fast, only to end up right back where you started. She left Paradise on fire. Big city dreams. Fresh start. Now she's back. In her family's gift shop. Wearing her dad's apron.

I wonder if she came back because she had to — or if she realized what I'm just starting to understand. Sometimes, the place that hurt you most is still the only place that feels like home.

I can't shake the look on her face when she talked about Rosie, the sadness and hesitation. And she seemed a little scared and tired. But that's something Rosie and I can fix. Ginny's part of the sisterhood, and she's back for a reason. Despite the time apart, she's still my best friend.

I take the lakefront road for the scenery. I've lived here my whole life, and for a while, I forgot how beautiful Paradise is. But not these days.

My phone buzzes.

Beckett: Pizza at Tarryn's at 6. Don't be late or she'll give you the passive-aggressive side-eye.

I smile. A real one. I want to tell him about Ginny. About visiting Rosie together. About how strange and beautiful it is to feel connected again. But I don't. Maybe later. When I stop at an intersection, I dash off a text.

Me: Sounds great. See you then.

No pool time tonight, but that's okay. When I was living with Alex, I felt completely alone in Paradise. I don't feel that way anymore.

I weave through town to the hospital. Things are starting to pick up with all the summer visitors. I love it here when it's jam packed. I really do live in paradise.

When I reach the hospital, I park near the administration building and haul two tote bags stuffed with whiskey, gift cards, and a handwoven throw blanket through the automatic doors.

The receptionist brightens as I approach.

"I'm here to drop off fundraiser donations," I tell her. "With the head of development?"

"That'd be Christine. Second door on the right."

Christine's office is buried in folders and color-coded spreadsheets, but she lights up when I enter.

"Sadie! Beckett's Sadie?"

I smile tightly. "Just Sadie's fine."

She doesn't push. I appreciate that. She helps me find a big cart, and we head back out to load it with the remaining donations.

"I stopped by a few other places and picked up some additional things." I hand her a piece of paper listing all the extra donors. "And I put in an ask with my dad's best friend. I'll let you know when I hear from him."

We stack everything in her office, and after a few quick thank yous, I'm back in the hallway. But I don't leave. Instead, I take the elevator to Cardiology. Room 304 — Rosie's room.

She's sitting up, puzzle book in her lap, headband holding her curls back. She looks tired. But her eyes light up when I walk in. "Sadie!"

"Hey, superstar. Thought I'd check in before I go to pizza night at Tarryn's. Their mom had me playing errand girl for her fundraiser." I give her a hug. "I stopped by Candi's store, and she put together the most spectacular sweets basket. And I talked Daniel into a year of free oil changes. I ended up visiting a lot of my old customers from Della's, and I got a nice batch of extra loot."

"Oooh. Nice work. That dinner is always so fun and fancy," she says. "Will Beckett be there?"

I smirk. "Probably. Avoiding eye contact and feelings. His specialty."

She laughs, but then she looks more closely at me. "What's wrong?"

"Did you know Ginny's back?"

Her eyes widen. "She is?"

"She's working at the Black Bear gift shop. We talked when I stopped by for their donation. She said she might come visit next week. I think she's nervous."

"You told her we don't care about anything in the past, right?"

My throat tightens. "Of course."

"She didn't say why she came back?"

I shake my head. "Nope."

Rosie shrugs, flipping her puzzle page. "I need to get out of here. Maybe you could put in a good word and let me know what Beckett says about springing me for a road trip."

"Promise." I pause. "You okay?"

She looks at me, eyes suddenly sharp. "I need to breathe fresh air."

"I have to go to Appleton tomorrow to pick up some of the silent auction items. Maybe I can talk Beckett into giving you a hall pass for the afternoon?"

"I'd love that. Speaking of Dr. Perfectly Handsome, what's going on with you two?"

I laugh. "I have no idea."

"That bad?"

"He avoids me. And when he doesn't, he looks at me like I'm glass. Or lava." I decide not to go into further detail. This is her doctor, after all.

"Maybe he's scared," she muses.

"Of me?" I force a laugh.

"Of himself."

Maybe he just wants me to move out. I squeeze her hand. "You're too wise."

"Chronic heart failure does that to a girl."

We fall into an easy silence. I scoot in next to her and rest my head on her shoulder as she works her puzzle.

Eventually, I glance at the clock. "I should go. You need to rest."

She grins. "Tell Beckett he's an idiot."

"I'll make that my opening line." I wave as I leave.

That heart better come soon.

I park in front of Tarryn's house just as the sky shifts from gold to lavender over Black Bear Lake. The scent of woodsmoke and roasted garlic winds through the breeze makes my stomach grumble.

The big stone pizza oven on the patio is already lit, flames flickering behind the blackened iron door. Tarryn waves from the prep table, flour smudged across her cheek and a bottle of rosé chilling in a bucket beside her.

"You beat Beckett," she calls, her grin wide and teasing. "Extra points for punctuality."

I smile as I walk up. "I figured I'd earn my slice before the cardiologist shows up and tries to steal all the good toppings."

Tarryn pulls me into a warm hug, one of those Paradise-family hugs that seems to say more than words. They really are amazing. "I'm glad you're here," she says.

The prep table is a mosaic of color—red sauces, golden cheese, green basil, glistening peppers, marinated artichokes, and enough mushrooms to start a forest.

As I reach for a dough ball, she lifts an eyebrow. "So...what's going on with you and Beckett?"

I freeze mid-roll. "Nothing."

"Uh-huh." She doesn't even blink.

"We're roommates."

Tarryn gives me a look that could cut through steel. "Not just that, based on the way he watches you when you're not looking."

I huff and return to flattening the dough. "He avoids me half the time and glares the other half."

She giggles. "That's Beckett's love language."

"I thought his love language was clinical detachment and cardiac emergencies."

She laughs again. "Nope. Grumpiness and deep, unresolved feelings."

I layer on toppings—olives, sausage, roasted garlic, a little bit of everything. A small reminder that I'm allowed to take up space, even if I don't always know how.

"Everything but pineapple," I murmur as I finish.

Tarryn chuckles. "Funny, that's exactly how Beckett makes his. Down to the spicy honey drizzle."

"I know pineapple is supposed to be a Canadian thing, but I stand by it. Pineapple does not belong on pizza."

"Amen to that," Beckett's voice rumbles from behind me.

I turn, startled, and there he is—jeans, black T-shirt, tired eyes, and a six-pack of vodka cranberry slushies dripping condensation over his fingers.

He holds one out to me. "In honor of your excellent taste

in pizza?"

I take it. "Only if you didn't spike this with pineapple."

He cracks a grin and opens his own. "Wouldn't dream of it."

We toast — plastic cups clinking beneath the warm haze of string lights — and settle into the Adirondack chairs overlooking the lake. The scent of baking pizza rises into the air, and I let myself sink into these surroundings.

This isn't just pizza. It's a moment I thought I'd never get back — safety, warmth, family without blood.

"I saw Rosie today," I say softly, staring out over the water. "She was in good spirits."

"She always lights up when you visit," Beckett replies.

"She asked if she could come with me to Appleton tomorrow to pick up fundraiser donations."

Tarryn turns to her brother. "You know she'd love it —"

Beckett cuts in, his tone gentle but firm. "It's not safe. If a heart becomes available, we'd need to prep her immediately. Plus, we can't risk her getting sick."

"I know." But it still sucks. "She just wants to get outside and breathe fresh air — to do something normal and not be hooked up to a thousand machines. Be somewhere besides that hospital bed."

"She's lucky to have you," Tarryn murmurs.

I look down at my drink, swirling the slush.

"She's not the only one," Beckett adds, his voice quiet.

"I know," Tarryn agrees. "The tasting room would be a mess without you."

I look up and find Beckett watching me, and for one breathless second, everything goes still.

Tarryn, blissfully unaware of the emotional grenade between us, shifts the subject. "Oh, and Sadie, you should know, we installed cameras. One over the register, one outside Zach's office, and one by the back door."

I blink. "Beckett mentioned that."

"I'm really sorry you felt you had to cover for Zach. You're

111

doing a great job," she says. "And you deserve to know we're protecting you."

"Zach's probably going to try again," Beckett adds. "And this time, we'll be ready."

I nod, swallowing past the knot in my throat. "Thanks. For believing me."

Tarryn shrugs like it's obvious. "You're smart. Kind. And our customers love you. You're valuable here. Don't let his crap make you think otherwise."

After dinner, as the sky deepens into twilight, we carry our plates back inside and trade one-liners about whose pizza reigned supreme. Spoiler, Tarryn insists hers always is the winner.

As we say goodnight, Beckett walks me out to his Jeep. The breeze has cooled, and somewhere nearby, crickets chirp like it's their job.

"I'll follow you home," he says.

I stop beside the driver's door. "You don't have to do that."

"I want to. And we're going the same place," he adds with a laugh.

Once I'm behind the wheel and headed toward the main road, my phone buzzes in the cupholder. I answer on Bluetooth, and Beckett's voice fills the Jeep. "Do you always drive like a granny?"

I laugh out loud. "Try to keep up, Paradise." I floor it, tires kicking up gravel as I pull onto the road, grinning when I see his headlights right behind me.

Fifteen

Sadie

I check the clock on the dash. I've been on time for everything this week. In addition to working thirty-eight hours in the tasting room, I coordinated auction items, followed up with businesses, and organized all the paperwork. But somehow, today, of all days, I'm nervous about being late. I steer the Jeep down the winding road toward Paradise Vineyard, my fingers tightening around the wheel as I approach the main house.

Not that anyone gave me a strict arrival time. But still.

The sun slips in and out of the clouds overhead as I make the final turn toward the family estate. The vineyard rolls out like something from a postcard — rows of vines stretching in neat lines toward the lake, its surface glinting in the late-afternoon light. It looks calm. Unlike me.

I exhale and try to focus on what I've accomplished. This week, I've been all-in on the silent auction for the fundraiser supporting rural medicine. Cold calls. Follow-ups. I picked up things every day and dropped them at the hospital. Vicky was there when I brought the last of it yesterday. The room was overflowing, and she was practically giddy as she reviewed the items.

"*I want you at my table,*" she told me, like it was the most natural thing in the world to invite me to a black-tie gala. "*You've earned it.*"

I'd thanked her, blushing like a kid caught playing dress-up. "*I don't even have a dress.*"

That's when she'd grinned and waved away my concerns. "*You'll borrow one of mine. Come to the house early on Saturday and spend the afternoon with us. Get ready with the girls.*"

The girls as in Tarryn, Elise, Trinity, and Vicky herself. Women who are stunning and polished and belong at a fundraiser. I still can't believe I managed to smile and accept. I'm an orphan who doesn't have a pot to pee in.

I park the Jeep in the gravel drive and stare up at the main house. Every window sparkles in the sunlight, like the whole place is waiting for something magical to happen—or someone more prepared to walk through the front door.

I smooth my hands over my jeans and reach for my bag, heart thudding. Fancy fundraisers aren't exactly my comfort zone. I'm more jeans and boots than cocktail dresses and champagne. But I promised Vicky. And honestly…a part of me wants to belong. Even if it's just for one night.

I step inside and immediately freeze. The house seems entirely different than when I've been here for dinner. The housekeeper leads me upstairs to the main bedroom suite, which has been transformed into a salon. Stylists bustle between women in chairs—curling hair, painting nails, and applying makeup with precise strokes. The air smells like hairspray and perfume and something floral.

"Sadie!" Vicky says. "Come with me. You're going to love

this."

The bedroom suite is bigger than most apartments I've lived in. The walls are a soft cream, and floor-to-ceiling windows frame the view of the vineyard and Black Bear Lake like a painting come to life.

I step toward the window, momentarily lost in the view. "This is…beautiful."

Vicky smiles. On the bed is a large box, and after looking at me a moment, she pulls out a sleek black dress. "What do you think of this one?"

It's a sheath dress with a lace overlay—form-fitting, strapless, with a high slit up one thigh. Classic and elegant and very feminine. Terrifying. And it has a price tag that's more money than I make in three months.

I narrow my eyes. "This isn't your dress."

"I couldn't resist. I had it brought in from Montreal. I saw it and thought it was perfect for you."

I press my palms together. "It's gorgeous. But you didn't have to do this."

"Of course I did. After all the work you've done, you should get the chance to enjoy the party."

I hold the dress up. "I just hope it fits."

She walks over and takes the dress from me. "It will. And if it doesn't, I have backups. But this one will look incredible on you."

I don't say it out loud, but dresses like this don't usually work for me. I've got hips and a bust that demand their own zip code, and the idea of stuffing them into something tight and unforgiving makes me want to hide under a blanket. Still, I nod and take the dress, whispering a silent prayer as I carry it to the adjoining bathroom to change.

It slips over my hips and after tucking the girls into the dress so I don't make the local papers for exposing myself, I look in the mirror and twirl. I feel like a real princess. The slit is nearly to my hip. *I hope I can wear a thong with this.* Jeez.

When I come out, Vicky gasps. "You're stunning." She

shows me the shoes — black, strappy stilettos that somehow look both delicate and powerful.

Tears prick the corners of my eyes, and I blink them away. "Thank you. This is so generous of you."

"You earned it." She gives me a hug. "Okay, change back into your shorts and the button-up shirt I asked you to bring. That way Darla and her team can get you ready."

I change, putting the dress back on its hanger for now, and we spend the rest of the afternoon getting primped, plucked, painted, polished, and preened. Trinity talks about vineyard tours gone wrong, including something about a goat getting loose during a bachelorette party. Elise tells a story about Beckett losing a bet and having to pick grapes barefoot for a week. He hates spiders, which love the vines. Tarryn laughs so hard at one point she smudges lipstick over her cheek.

I laugh, too — really laugh. The kind that bubbles up from somewhere deep inside and feels warm, whole, and real.

Vicky heads off early with a wave while the rest of us are still being prepared. "I'll see you there," she says.

When they're done with me, I barely recognize the woman in the mirror. Chestnut waves fall in soft curls over my shoulders, and my makeup — subtle smoky eyes, warm blush, lips the color of ripe berries — makes me look like someone else. Someone elegant. Effortless. Like the kind of woman who belongs at a black-tie fundraiser, sipping champagne without worrying about the price tag on her shoes.

But that's not me. It can't be. And yet...here I am. I slip into a dress that hugs every curve without apology. The slit up my thigh is bold, scandalous even, and the strappy stilettos make my legs look about a mile long. I should feel like an imposter. But instead I feel...fantastic.

"Ladies!" Greyson bellows from downstairs. "If we don't leave soon, Mom's going to donate me to the auction!"

Laughter erupts around me, but I smile politely and step into the bathroom one last time. It's silly, maybe, but I want to make sure I've done everything before we head out. The nerves are real now, coiled low in my stomach. Once we get to the vineyard ballroom, I won't have a second to myself. There'll be crowds. Champagne. Expectations.

And Beckett.

Oh God.

I take a deep breath, smooth my dress again, and step out. The others are already heading down the sweeping staircase, chatting and laughing, a swirl of silk and perfume.

I follow a few steps behind.

The staircase is long, and I'm the last one, white-knuckling the railing. One wrong step in these stilettos I barely know how to walk in, and I'll go down like a domino, taking out every perfectly polished woman ahead of me.

When I get to the bottom, I look up and there he is.

Standing near the base of the stairs, Beckett waits in a black Armani tuxedo, one hand in his pocket, the other holding a single cufflink as he talks to his brother Kingston. He looks every bit the headline — confident, powerful, devastating.

Everything else stops.

Beckett goes still.

So do I.

His gaze sweeps over me, slow and deliberate, like he's trying to make sense of what he's seeing. And then — like he forgets how to speak — his mouth parts, but nothing comes out.

I force a smile, nerves rattling. "Is that a full sentence, Dr. Beckett?"

The corner of his mouth lifts, but his eyes don't leave mine. "You're…"

A pause. A beat too long.

"Wow," he finishes, his voice low, almost stunned.

I arch a brow. "Still not a full sentence."

He huffs a quiet laugh and steps closer, his gaze dropping to the slit in my dress and then trailing back up, lingering on my mouth. "You look perfect," he says softly.

It hits harder than it should. Not because he's handsome or wearing a tux or because the words are nice. But because there's no smirk. No sarcasm. Just quiet awe, like he means it.

I suddenly forget how to breathe. "You clean up okay, too," I say, trying to lighten the moment, but my voice wavers. He's always handsome, but in a tuxedo he's drop-dead gorgeous.

He chuckles and smooths his hand down the front of his jacket. "I was coming to pick you up, but it looks like you're about to shut the whole event down."

I laugh despite the heat blooming in my cheeks. "Stop."

"I'm serious. You're going to cause a scene."

Behind him, Trinity appears, looking like a queen in sapphire silk. "You two ready?"

"Yeah," I say. "I think I am."

Beckett offers his arm, and I slide mine through it. His touch is warm, grounding. And just like that, I'm not afraid anymore.

As we walk out to the car, heels tapping in rhythm, the sky blushes pink above the vines, and Black Bear Lake shimmers in the distance. Under the portico of the main house, four black limousines wait in a neat row, their engines idling, headlights glowing in the dusky light.

Greyson and Trinity are the first to go.

He opens the door for her, but not before whispering something that makes her laugh and swat his arm. Her cheeks are flushed, her lipstick fresh, and her hair perfect, but there's something unguarded in her smile that surprises me after spending the afternoon with her. Trinity is guarded. Smart. Private. But around Greyson…she softens.

Ryker whistles low as the limo pulls away. "Ten bucks says they don't make it to the hotel without fogging up the windows."

My head jerks toward him. "What?"

He just smirks and shrugs. "You saw them."

Tarryn elbows him hard. "Gross. That's our brother, idiot."

Ryker grins like a man who lives for stirring the pot. "Still true."

Elise shakes her head, her lips twitching. "My date's meeting me there. You two coming?"

She nods toward her own limo, and the three of them— Elise, Ryker, and Tarryn—head off together, chattering about appetizers and dance cards like they've done this a hundred times.

That leaves Beckett and me.

Our limo door opens smoothly, and he gestures for me to go first. I slide in carefully, trying to keep the slit of my dress from showing too much thigh. Once I'm seated, Beckett follows, sealing us inside the quiet, dimly lit space.

The cabin smells faintly of leather and something earthy— probably Beckett's cologne—and I swear the temperature rises the second we're alone.

"You really do look stunning," he says.

I wave a hand like it's nothing, though my face instantly warms. "You've said that."

"Yeah, and you still didn't say thank you."

I glance at him, caught off guard.

"You should," he adds, eyes on mine. "It's the truth."

I hesitate, then murmur, "Thank you."

His lips twitch like he's holding back something more. "That blush…"

"What about it?"

He leans in just enough to make my skin prickle. "I'd love to see where it goes." He peeks down at my vast cleavage before winking at me.

I blink, speechless for a half second too long. "Behave."

He lifts both hands in surrender, his grin unapologetic. "Just an observation."

I exhale and shift slightly in my seat, trying to steer the conversation to safer territory. "So…they sent out a teaser about the silent auction. I've seen the goods, but do you have any idea what you're bidding on?"

He stretches one arm across the back of the seat, his fingers brushing the ends of my hair. "I haven't looked at the list yet."

"You should. There's a spa weekend at Whistler, a wine-and-dine helicopter tour around Vancouver Island, and a cooking class with a celebrity chef."

"That last one sounds like punishment."

I laugh. "There's a trip to New York City too. Includes a Broadway play and hotel near Times Square."

"That actually sounds fun."

"If I had money," I say wistfully, "that's the one I'd bid on."

Beckett studies me for a second. "I can picture you in New York."

"Really?"

"Yeah. Bold, brave, fast-talking—"

"I prefer being here in a small town. I only like to visit the city. It's too claustrophobic because there are so many people. Plus, I'm not fast-talking."

"You are when you're nervous."

I shove at his shoulder, and he chuckles, but his gaze drops again—to my leg, to where the slit of the dress parts slightly, showing smooth skin and the glint of my shoe.

I pull the fabric across my thigh, suddenly unsure. "Is this dress too much?"

His voice drops an octave. "It's not enough."

My breath catches.

Before I can form a reply, the limo slows, turning toward a circular drive.

The Grand Delta Hotel rises before us like something out of a movie—glittering windows, elegant arches, and staff lined up with tablets, earpieces, and practiced smiles.

The driver opens the door, and I glance across the seat.

Beckett smirks. "Ryker called it. Greyson and Trinity didn't beat us here."

I step out, my heels clicking against the polished stone. I'm still reeling from everything he said, but I lift my chin, square my shoulders, and let the confidence from earlier in the afternoon find its way back into my bloodstream. Hopefully I'll not be tripping over my own feet.

Let's do this.

A server offers us flutes of sparkling wine as soon as we check in. I take mine with a quiet "thank you," nerves fluttering as we step into the grand ballroom.

The lighting is golden and warm, and the hum of voices wraps around us like velvet. I make a beeline for the silent auction. When I left this morning, it was a large room with tables, and the plan was to place the Harley Davidson motorcycle my dad's best friend donated in the center. He threw in a Harley Davidson gift basket, which has a leather jacket, shirts, mugs, glasses, pens, and tons of other things, all with the Harley Davidson Paradise logo. I talked him into donating anything the items bring in over their cost. In return he offered me a job, though I'm not sure I'm ready to sell motorcycles.

We walk into the auction room, and I stop short.

It looks amazing.

The items I picked up all week — gift baskets, vouchers, bottles of rare wine, getaway packages — have been arranged on linen-draped tables with handwritten signs and soft lighting. Everything looks intentional. Elevated. Like it belongs in a glossy magazine spread.

Vicky appears beside me, smiling wide. "Isn't this great?"

I nod, still taking it in. "All these things were in the back of he the Jeep," I say with a laugh. "I can't believe what they look like now. I just hope people actually bid on them."

Her hand lands gently on my arm. "Wander through. I think you'll be surprised." She gives me a squeeze, then drifts away to greet someone.

I glance at Beckett, who lingers close, his eyes sweeping across the tables like he's casing a very elegant potential crime scene.

I walk through the displays, fingertips brushing the edge of a sign here and there. The bid sheets are already filling up. Every few steps, someone stops Beckett to say hello. He knows everyone — or they know him — and when they turn to me, curiosity in their eyes, he always says the same thing.

"This is my friend, Sadie Calloway."

Friend. I don't know why that makes me a little woozy, but it does. And not in a bad way. Just…it matters that I'm not only Caleb's sister.

At one point, a couple Beckett knows from the hospital stops to chat, and as I try not to fidget, his hand finds mine. It's warm and sure, and the moment his fingers wrap around mine, my breath steadies. I hold on.

He keeps moving through the auction like it's second nature, bidding on a Whistler spa weekend, a vineyard helicopter tour, and — because of course — an absurdly expensive week-long yacht charter.

I trail behind him until we stop in front of the New York trip. Four nights at the Plaza Hotel. Tickets to a Broadway play. Dinner at a swanky rooftop restaurant.

I stare at it a little too long.

"That one?" he asks quietly.

I shrug. "If I had the money."

He doesn't say anything, just studies me for a beat. I can feel the weight of his gaze, but I don't look up.

A moment later, the lights in the ballroom flicker, and someone calls for guests to move into the dining room.

Beckett sets his champagne flute down and offers his arm.

I take it.

Together we walk toward the next part of the evening with my hand tucked in his. I'm still not sure how I ended up here, but I'm grateful that I did.

Sixteen

Beckett

S adie is the most beautiful woman here.

I knew she was stunning before tonight. That wasn't new. But this—the way she moves in that black dress, the slit teasing just enough skin to drive me mad, the way her hair spills down her back in those soft curls—this is something else entirely.

Sultry. Sophisticated. Sexy.

And somehow still entirely Sadie.

Half the room can't stop staring. The other half is pretending they aren't. I've shaken more hands than I can count tonight, men who glanced at her twice before even saying hello. But she held her own, never once flinching. When people stopped to compliment her work on the auction, she smiled graciously and deflected with humor and ease. It's like she's used to being in the spotlight, even when I know she isn't.

I'm not an insecure man, but damn if I don't feel like I'm walking around with a crown jewel on my arm.

And the best part?

She has no idea what kind of power she holds.

Dinner's long over now, the wine has mostly disappeared, and the band has transitioned into a sultry version of an old jazz standard. The lights dim to shift the mood. The dance floor is filling.

I lean toward her. "Dance with me."

She looks up, the softest question in her eyes. "Now?"

"Yes. Now." I offer my hand. "Please."

She hesitates for half a heartbeat, and then slides her fingers into mine. They're warm and sure, and I swear my pulse jumps at the contact.

I lead her to the floor, anchoring a hand at the small of her back. Her body settles easily against mine, like this is where she's always belonged. Her eyes focus on my chest, then move up to my face, and everything inside me goes still.

"I'm the envy of every man in this room," I murmur near her ear.

She lets out a quiet laugh. "I wouldn't say that..."

"I mean it." I lean back to catch her eyes. "You blew me away tonight."

Her cheeks flush. That same blush that made me say things I'm still thinking about. *I'd love to see where it goes*. Still true. Maybe more so now.

We fall into a slow rhythm. One song blends into another. Her head tips closer, and for a few minutes the excitement of the event—the buzz, the noise, the pressure—fades out. It's just her, warm in my arms, glowing under the lights.

When the music winds down, my mother steps back up to the microphone with her signature charm and commanding presence.

"I want to thank everyone who made tonight possible," she says. "Our donors, our volunteers, and our auction coordinators…especially Sadie Calloway, who took a short list for the silent auction and tripled the donations." She gestures toward us, and Sadie stiffens slightly, then smiles as polite applause fills the room.

"Before you go, just a quick reminder," Mom continues. "We take cash, credit cards, and checks. Yes, those still exist. Don't let your silent auction winnings sit lonely and unclaimed!"

Everyone laughs, and soon the cashiers are doing a brisk business.

As we file out of the ballroom, it takes forever to reach the door. I have my auction confirmations in hand—several trips I probably won't take but bid on anyway.

Sadie glances at the paperwork. "You won more than a few of those."

"Yeah," I say, holding the door for her. "Looks like I did. I got it all paid for and told Mom to just get them to her house, and I'll go through them there."

When we get to the limo, the driver is already waiting. Sadie slides in, her dress shifting with the motion, and I follow, settling beside her as the door shuts and the hotel disappears behind us.

"So," she says cautiously, looking at the list in my lap. "When are you going to find time to go on all those trips?"

I glance over. "They're not for me."

She looks up sharply. "What do you mean?"

"I bought them for you and Rosie, so you can check some things off her bucket list."

Her eyes widen. "Beckett, no. I can't—"

"You can," I say simply.

She shakes her head. "That's—that's too much. I can't accept that."

I shrug. "We'll see."

Silence falls between us, but it's not awkward. It's charged. We're not touching, but I can feel her like a live wire, every shift of fabric, every breath. Her thigh is inches from mine, the slit in her dress still dangerously high. Her perfume encircles me — subtle, warm, something like vanilla and summer heat — making it nearly impossible to think straight.

The city races past the windows. The driver says nothing, and the hum of the engine is the only sound. I can't look away from her.

The car drops us at my house, and the door clicks shut, leaving the night outside. I feel every breath she takes, every movement.

"Beckett," she whispers, and her voice fills my ears like a melody I've forgotten but longed to hear. It's both a plea and a challenge.

"You are such a tease in this dress." I close the space between us and grip her waist, pulling her tight against me. Her body is hot, lighting up every part of me. I pause just long enough to take her in — hair a little messy and wild, eyes burning with nerves and something bold and hungry. The pull between us has always been strong, but right now, it's like a fuse ready to blow. And I want the spark.

Before I can think, my lips are on hers. The kiss starts rough — full of want — then slows, turning deep and hot, like it's been building for years. Our mouths move together like they already know the way, each touch electric. Her tongue slides against mine, and I lose myself in the way she tastes — sweet, with a hint of fire.

She pulls back, and I see mischief dancing in her eyes. She slides off my jacket, her fingers brushing my skin. It hits the floor with a soft thud, and I laugh, the tension breaking for a second. But it doesn't last. She moves to my shirt, unbuttoning slowly, each touch a jolt, a promise of everything we're about to become.

In one swift motion, I unzip the back of her dress, and the fabric piles at her feet. My breath hitches as I look over her body, clad only in a delicate thong and those incredible stiletto sandals that elongate her legs in the most breathtaking way. The sight before me is intoxicating, but the weight of this moment makes me hesitate.

"Are you sure about this?" I ask. I need to hear her say it, to know she's ready for this leap, to grasp the gravity of our choices.

She nods, steady and sure, and it sets my pulse racing. I lift her into my arms, and she laughs, light and breathless. She fits against me like she belongs there, and I take the stairs without thinking, my mind full of everything that could happen next.

When we reach her room, it feels different. I set her gently on the bed, my fingers brushing her soft skin as I fumble with my shirt. I need it off. I need nothing between us. The fabric clings, and I rush to pull it away.

When I finally get it off, my heart pounds. I meet her eyes, hoping she sees there's more than heat driving this. It's trust. "If it ever feels like too much," I tell her, "just say the word. I'll stop. I promise."

She holds my gaze. We're *choosing* to step into something real, no matter how messy it might be.

And I can't wait any longer.

I kneel on the bed, my eyes locked on hers as I kiss my way down her body. Reaching the waistband of her thong, I take my time teasing her, tracing patterns along her stomach before slipping my hands around her hips to remove the final barrier. I groan at the sight of her, soaked and swollen for me. "God," I breathe against her skin, "You're so wet."

Her cheeks flush scarlet, but she doesn't deny it. Instead, she tangles her fingers in the sheets above her head, gripping them tightly as I explore her folds with one hand, stroking and teasing each sensitive spot. She arches her back in response, a quiet moan escaping her full lips. Emboldened by her reaction, I slide two fingers inside of her, reveling in the heat and wetness that greets me. Her muscles clench around me, but instead of crying out, she moans, pushing herself against me.

"Beckett," she whimpers, a desperate edge in her voice. Using my free hand, I spank her swollen clit.

Every part of me craves her, and I can't resist any longer. I remove my boxers in record time, my dick at full attention. I give it a hard pull.

Sadie meets my gaze, her eyes glossy with pleasure. "Beckett..." she whispers, breathless and glowing, yet still draped in vulnerability that tugs at my heart. "I want you inside me."

I have no idea how I'm going to face her brother after this. But all I care about is being with her, over and over.

My body's shaking from how much I want her. I break long enough to race to my bedroom, my heart pounding as I grab a condom. Every nerve in me is lit up, and the feel of it sends a jolt through me.

Sadie watches, her eyes wide. "I've never seen anything like that before," she breathes, her cheeks flushing even deeper. "That's...definitely the biggest."

Her honesty is a lightning bolt, and a playful grin breaks across my face. I stroke my cock slowly, savoring the tension in the air, cradling my balls with my other hand. "Well," I say, voice low and teasing, "just wait until you see what it can do."

That playful look flashes in her eyes as she bites her lip.

"Are you sure?" I ask again, but my heart already knows the answer. The way she nods, resolute yet a bit shy, tells me everything I need to know.

I position myself at her entrance, and my breath hitches as I feel her warmth surround me. I push inside, and the feeling is unreal. Her body pulls me in like a warm, welcome embrace. It's everything. Every part of her surrounds me, causing sparks in places I didn't even know could burn.

Sadie's breath hitches, a soft gasp escaping her lips as I fill her completely. The way she moves with me, the way her body pulls me in drives me crazy. I both want to protect her and claim every inch. I can't believe this is real, that we're crossing a line we can't uncross, diving into something wild and deep.

"Beckett," she whispers. She wraps her legs around my waist, pulling me closer. The heat between us grows, and I start to move, slow at first as I savor every delicious moment, the pressure building within us like an impending storm.

With each thrust, I lose myself in the rhythm of our bodies

connecting. Her moans echo in the room, pulling me deeper. There's something so beautifully raw about this. It's more than just physical. It's an acknowledgment of all we've hidden from each other, the pain and longing that have lingered beneath the surface.

I lean down to capture her lips again, swallowing her gasps as I plunge deeper within her.

As I stare into her lust-filled eyes, a surge of desire courses through me. "When it becomes too much, just tell me," I growl, my voice hoarse with the effort it takes to maintain some semblance of control.

"Just don't stop," she pants, her nails digging into my back.

With her consent, I let go of all my remaining restraints. I grip her hips and jackhammer in and out of her. Her breasts bounce with each powerful thrust, and her moans fill the air between us. It's an erotic symphony that sends shivers down my spine. Pumping my hips even harder, I feel myself getting closer to the edge.

Sadie's breathing becomes more ragged, and I know she's close. "Beckett!" she cries out, arching her back as her orgasm washes over her. She grips me like a vise, spurring me on. My climax approaches like a freight train, and I can't hold back. With one final thrust, I explode inside the condom with a growl, my entire being consumed by the intensity of the release.

I get lost in the rush, the world shrinking to just us. With a deep groan, Sadie clenches around me, pulling every last bit from me. It's pure fire, so strong that everything else disappears.

Eventually, I pull out, still feeling her warmth, not ready to let go. She rolls to her side, breathless and glowing, her eyes full of heat that makes my heart pound. I'm trying to catch my breath, but the weight of what just happened lingers in the air.

I get up, still buzzing with want, and walk to the bathroom. The cool tile under my feet helps steady me. I spot a bit of blood on the condom as I throw it out. It's a small thing, but it feels big, like proof of everything that just happened. She wasn't a virgin, and it hits me that maybe we were too rough. I run warm water over a washcloth, then wring it out and head back to her.

Sadie looks up when I return, her eyes soft but fierce. I kneel beside her and gently clean her, each touch slow and careful.

"Beckett," she whispers, closing her eyes as I glide the cloth along her thighs. "This was...incredible."

I smile. "It takes two to be incredible."

"Beckett," she murmurs, "that was the first time I...you know." Her cheeks flush again, and a shy smile graces her lips. "I've never climaxed with anyone before."

I freeze, still holding the cloth, and look up at her. "Really?" I ask.

Sadie nods, her eyes shiny with emotion. "I lived with Alex for over a year," she says, staring down at the sheets. "He used to say I was bad at sex because he couldn't get hard. And when he did, it was quick. After he was done and asleep, I'd finish myself."

A rush of anger rises in me. I hate the thought of anyone making her feel that way — like she didn't matter. Those nights alone in the dark, left with nothing but disappointment. She deserved better. She deserves everything. "That's not true," I say, my voice firm as I cup her face in my hands, forcing her to meet my gaze. "You're not bad at anything. It was him."

Without thinking, I lie down beside her, sinking into the mattress. I'm not usually the type to stay close after sex. It gets messy, too personal. But with Sadie, it feels right. I pull her close, wrap my arm around her shoulders, and let my fingers drift over her warm skin.

"Beckett," she whispers, curling closer.

I breathe in the scent of her hair, vanilla and something that's just her. It calms me, even as my heart races. I've never liked this part, lying close, getting tangled in something that makes it harder to walk away. But this time, I don't want to pull back. I want this. I want her.

130

"You deserve so much better than what he gave you," I murmur into the quiet space between us, resting my chin atop her head.

Caleb's face flashes in my mind. My best friend. The guy who would do anything for me and who asked me to look out for his sister, not sleep with her, not want her like this. This wasn't supposed to happen. I was supposed to keep my distance. Be the safe place she needed, not the reason she runs again.

I spot dark marks forming where my fingers were. Small, faint bruises across her hips, her thighs. And one on her breast. If I can see them now, I know they'll take ages to fade. Christ. I didn't mean to leave them. She never said stop. Never pulled away. She met me beat for beat — wild and unafraid — and I'd be lying if I said that didn't light up something dark inside me.

But what if I misread her? What if I crossed a line she was too afraid to draw? I swallow hard, the back of my throat raw. After her breathing evens out, I ease out of bed, careful not to wake her. I stand there watching for a moment. She looks so damn peaceful, like I didn't just wreck her, leave marks. Like I haven't let guilt crawl in and twist something good.

I grab my shirt off the floor and walk out of the room, leaving my mistake behind.

Seventeen

Sadie

My old sweatpants might as well be a chastity belt. They hang off my hips, big and baggy, as I stretch out on the lounge chair by the pool. It's my day off, which means I have plenty of time to let Alex's insults and Beckett's disappearing act after I fell asleep run laps around my brain. I tried. I failed. Maybe I am bad at sex.

I push the thought away. It circles back anyway, taunting me.

My sunglasses shield my eyes, not from the sun, but from my own bruised pride. The real bitch of it? Beckett doesn't even seem to want to be my practice partner.

I roll onto my stomach, pressing my cheek against the rough towel. A breeze skims the water, and I try to let it carry the thoughts away. The day is warm, not a cloud in sight. It should be perfect for lying out here, soaking up sun. But I can't shake the feeling that something's wrong. That I'm wrong.

He told me I wasn't bad at sex, yet he left me right after. Why would he go sleep in his own bed?

If I'm bad at sex, does that mean I'll always be bad?

Was last night a huge mistake?

I groan and bury my face in the crook of my arm.

Of course Beckett would turn out to be incredible while I'm left floundering, second-guessing every move I made. I wish I could say it didn't matter. That I don't care.

But it does.

And I do.

The worst part is, it's not even about the sex. Not really.

I sigh. When Tarryn offered, a day off work sounded great. Between the fundraiser and the tasting room, I needed some time to rest. But now it just means more time to overthink. I roll onto my back and drag my fingers through my hair. It's a mess of tangles, but I leave it that way, too tired to fix it. Last night, it was messy for different reasons.

I wasn't expecting what happened between us, but now I know exactly what I'm missing.

This morning, I found Beckett in the kitchen, and he asked if I regretted it, like he already knew the answer. I told him it wouldn't happen again.

What else was I supposed to say? He wouldn't have left me if he didn't regret it.

I've never had a one-night stand. I guess I can check that off my bucket list.

I keep playing it over — the feel of him, the heat of his skin, the weight of him above me. The way he whispered my name.

I thought we were both feeling the same thing.

But apparently not. God, I hate him.

I let him in, just for a moment, and now I don't know how to shut the door again.

The pool glitters like it's mocking me. I wish I could dive in and wash the last twenty-four hours away. Hell, the whole of last year. Alex's voice creeps back in, sharp and cruel. *"You're too uptight. Stuck in your own head. No wonder you're bad at sex."*

He'd said it like a fact, not an insult. Like I should've already known.

But that doesn't make it hurt any less.

And now I'm sprawled out on this chair, trying to convince myself it doesn't matter what Beckett thinks, that I'll survive this the same way I survived Alex.

But it feels different.

Because this isn't just some guy I was biding my time with. It's *him*. Beckett. The one who took me in. The one who arranged a job for me and is encouraging me as I get on my feet.

And maybe that's the real problem.

Later that afternoon, I stare at myself in the mirror, trying to decide if I look casual or like I'm trying to look casual.

Crisp white capris, a T-shirt just fancy enough to say "I planned this," not "I gave up." A small pair of earrings, mascara, and a swipe of lip gloss round it out, like a little extra effort will somehow prepare me for what's ahead—coffee with Ginny and family dinner tonight with the Paradises.

I should be excited—and part of me is—but mostly I'm nervous. It's the kind of nerves that tighten the closer you get to something you're not sure you can handle.

Ginny and I were close once. Really close. Years ago there were whole months where Ginny was the only person I could talk to without falling apart. Her family was a mess. Her grandmother, Evelyn, ruled the Dempsey house like a dictator, and Ginny bore the brunt of it. There were screaming matches, slammed doors, and so many nights she'd sneak out just to breathe.

We held each other up while everything around us crumbled. How we finished school was a miracle. But we did it. We worked crappy jobs and lived in an apartment together and tried to forget about our families.

But her family wouldn't let her go. They called, begged, and threatened. And then she left.

She packed her bags and moved to Vancouver. She promised we'd stay in touch, and we tried. I visited once. But she already had a new rhythm — new friends, a new life. I felt like an afterthought, a shadow from a part of her past she didn't want to remember.

Eventually, the calls slowed. The texts stopped.

And I let it go because it hurt too much to hold on.

But now she's back. And I have no idea what that means.

When it's time, I slip into sandals, grab my bag, and drive across town with a stomach full of nerves and a heart full of things I haven't said out loud in years.

The café where we always used to meet is exactly the same — the same chipped blackboard menu outside, the same smell of espresso and sugar drifting out the front door. For a second, I'm sixteen again, waiting on the front patio for Ginny to show up in her battered blue hatchback with that reckless grin and a stolen six-pack of light beer in the trunk.

I take a breath and walk inside.

And there she is.

Sitting at a small table in the back corner, her long legs crossed, a half-empty mug of coffee cupped in her hands. Her hair's pulled into a messy bun, sunglasses perched on top like she just stepped off a plane. She hasn't seen me yet.

But I see her, and for a moment, I just watch.

She looks older. Sharper around the edges. But there's still something so familiar in the curve of her shoulders, the way she taps her fingers against the ceramic, like she's keeping time to a song no one else can hear. All the old memories rush in — late nights, whispered secrets, shared grief — and it makes my throat tighten.

Then she looks up, and our eyes lock.

Ginny Dempsey smiles like nothing's broken. Like no time has passed. "Sadie," she says, rising to her feet. There's something soft in her voice. Hopeful.

I walk toward her, heart thudding, unsure what to say. But before I can overthink it, she wraps her arms around me.

"God, it's good to see you," she murmurs.

"You too," I say, my voice rough.

We sit across from each other, a little hesitant now that the hug is over, now that there's no formal agenda to guide us. Her coffee's already half gone, and I haven't even ordered. I glance toward the counter, but she waves a hand.

"I got here early. Guess I wasn't sure you'd come."

I smile, a little wry. "I almost didn't."

"Why?"

"I wasn't sure if this would be awkward."

"And is it?"

I hesitate, then shake my head. "Not yet."

Ginny laughs, and it sounds like it used to — easy, unfiltered. "Give it time."

Something inside me loosens. I lean back in my chair, finally taking a breath. "I've missed you," I admit.

She nods. "Me too."

And just like that, we're not strangers anymore.

We ease into conversation the way you do with someone who used to know you by heart, carefully, testing the temperature. It's not like it was, not yet, but the rhythm is still there, buried under time and hurt and everything we never said.

Ginny wraps her hands around her mug, eyes dancing. "So..." she says, drawing out the word. "Imagine my surprise when I opened the *Black Bear News* yesterday and saw you in the social pages."

I blink. "What?"

"You didn't know?" Her grin widens, and she reaches into her bag, pulling out a folded copy of the local paper. She slides it across the table.

There we are. Me and Beckett. Frozen mid-laugh on the dance floor. My head tipped toward him, his hand on my back like it belongs there. The headline underneath reads, "Paradise's Newest Flame? Dr. Beckett and a Mystery Brunette Light Up Fundraiser."

"Oh my God." I press a hand over my face. "No."

Ginny laughs. "Yes. And look at you. Glamorous, glowing. That dress? The hair? You look like you two belong together."

"I look like I was holding on by a thread," I mutter. "That dress had a slit up to my soul."

Ginny snorts. "You're ridiculous." But she's smiling, soft and maybe a little wistful. "Well, it worked. You and Dr. Perfect looked cozy."

I lower the paper. "We live under the same roof, not in the same bed."

Her brows shoot up, and she gives me a look that says, *Okay, sure, and I was born yesterday.*

"Just the guest room," I add quickly. "I showed up on his doorstep after walking out of my ex's house."

"Ex-boyfriend?"

"Yeah. Alex Tremblay."

She nods slowly. "Let me guess. You walked in on him and someone else."

"No. I don't think he was seeing anyone else. He had pot dick."

Her sip of latte almost sprays me. She dabs at her mouth with a napkin. "What is pot dick?"

"It's a version of limp dick. You can't get it up because you get stoned too often." I take a sip of my drink. "But I left because the lies had stacked too high and I was always afraid. He and his brother were up to something, and I didn't want to find myself an accessory."

Ginny winces. "Oof. That's a good idea."

"Is walking in on your boyfriend with someone else what brought you back here?"

Her eyes pool with tears, and she takes a deep breath and nods.

My eyes widen. "Wait—really?"

She lifts a shoulder, casual but not unaffected. "Caught my fiancé in bed with his so-called business partner. In our sheets. Wedding was in six weeks."

"Oh, Ginny…"

"Yeah. I packed a bag and drove straight home. Didn't even stop to tell my family I was coming. Just…left."

I reach for her hand across the table. She lets me take it, her fingers warm in mine.

"I'm so sorry I didn't keep in touch," I whisper. "You needed me."

She shrugs again, but her eyes are still glassy. "Life got messy. But I'm glad we're here now."

I squeeze her hand before letting go. "So what are you going to do back in town, besides dodge future heartbreak?"

She perks up a bit, her smile returning. "You saw me doing it. I took over the gift shop from my mom."

"Really? That's great."

"I like it more than I thought I would. I put together the basket you picked up, since my mom was busy with Evelyn."

Ginny started calling her grandmother by her first name when we were in high school, mostly because it irritated her.

"That basket was fabulous. Clearly you have a gift for working in the gift shop." I complete my statement with a ridiculous face.

She giggles. "Yeah. I actually love it—organizing inventory, helping tourists find the perfect overpriced tea towel. It's weirdly satisfying."

I smile, because it sounds like Ginny—capable, creative, and determined to build something on her own terms.

"That's amazing," I say. "I feel the same way about the Paradise Hill tasting room. I love how with a few preference questions, I can find someone a wine they'll like enough to buy a few bottles."

Her eyes widen again. "Wait, I just put it together. You're living with Beckett *and* working for his family?"

"Temporarily. It just…happened."

Ginny leans back, crossing her arms with a knowing look. "You really are cozying up to the enemy."

I roll my eyes. "It's not like that."

She grins. "Sure it's not."

And somehow, just like that, we're back. Not completely or perfectly, but enough. Conversation falls into a lull, quiet but comfortable, and then I clear my throat again. "There's something else," I say softly.

Her gaze lifts to mine.

"I'm worried about Rosie," I continue. "She's been in the hospital for almost a year, and they still can't find a match."

Ginny freezes. The color drains from her face. "A year? Why is it so hard?"

"Her blood type is AB-negative. It's the rarest one. Then they have to match her size and some health factors. She's stable right now. But when they admitted her, she was in terrible shape. She lived alone and needed constant medical care. She's a real trooper, though. We've been working on a bucket list of things to do and places to go once she gets her heart transplant. You should check it out and go with us."

Tears fill Ginny's eyes so fast I almost reach for her again. Her lips tremble as she exhales the words. "Sadie, I've been a terrible friend."

"No, you haven't."

"I left her, and I didn't look back or call. I didn't even try."

"Rosie doesn't care about that," I say gently. "She just wants to see you. Honestly, she'll probably cry happy tears and then make some snarky comment about your outfit."

Ginny lets out a shaky laugh that breaks into a sniffle. "That sounds like her."

"I'm going to stop by there after this," I tell her, making a snap decision. I'm not a Paradise, so there's no reason I'm required to have dinner at their house. Beckett can handle that without me, like he does everything else. "You want to come with me?"

She hesitates. Swallows hard. Then nods. "Yeah. I do."

We head out to the Jeep, and I unlock the doors with a beep that echoes. Ginny climbs into the passenger seat while I toss my bag into the back. But as I round the front to the driver's side, I catch sight of someone across the street.

My stomach drops. It's one of Alex's friends—Dwayne, I think. One of Alex's shadows. Always lurking, always watching with those cold and calculating eyes. He's leaning against a truck, arms crossed like he's been waiting.

He sees me. Smiles. Then he lifts his hand. He forms a finger gun and aims it straight at me, pulling the imaginary trigger.

I freeze, breath caught in my throat.

Ginny's already inside, struggling with her seatbelt. She doesn't notice.

My skin prickles, heat rushing to my face, but I force myself to move. To act normal. I open the door and slide in, my hands trembling as I grip the steering wheel.

I try to tell myself it's nothing. A stupid gesture from a stupid man. But it doesn't feel harmless. No matter how hard I try, I can't pretend I'm not afraid.

Beckett

It's late when I come home on Sunday night, and the front door creaks like it knows I'm guilty.

I'm supposed to be the one in control. Steady. Unshakable. But for the past twenty-four hours, Sadie's been inescapable, lodged firmly in my mind and burrowed under my skin. I can't stop thinking about her. Turns out we both skipped dinner at my parents' tonight. I told them I had an emergency at the hospital, but that was a lie. I wasn't there either. I was out with an old high school buddy. And Sadie was with Rosemary and Ginny Dempsey. I saw them before I left the hospital.

Now I can't bear to be anywhere near her without crossing a line I'm pretty sure I shouldn't have crossed in the first place. The one time didn't get her out of my system. It only made the need worse.

The clock blinks past eleven as I lock the door, feeling damp from the summer humidity and sour from too many beers. I shake off my jacket and toss it on a chair, trying not to think about the minefield I'm walking into. Because Sadie Calloway, in all her inconvenient glory, is still here. And last night only made things worse.

I step into the living room, trying to avoid every creak and shadow, when my foot knocks a glass.

Clink.

Her voice cuts through the dark. "So nice of you to come home."

I stop cold. She's curled on the couch, arms folded, watching me like she's been waiting all night.

"A guy can't go out without an interrogation?" I try for casual. It lands somewhere near twitchy.

"Interrogation? Please. I don't care where you go." She stands, pulling her sleeves over her hands like armor. "But I would like to know why you snuck out of my room last night."

I look away. "Last night?"

Her scoff is sharp. "Really? You're going with that?"

"I thought we said everything there is to say this morning," I mutter, running a hand through my hair. "You said it was a mistake, never to be repeated."

"What did you expect me to say? Please come to my room again to ravish me and leave as soon as I fall asleep? I feel so good when you do that. Classic." She shakes her head.

"You're still here," I snap, shifting the subject in the shittiest way possible. "I've got a life, you know."

Her eyes harden. "If you want me gone, just say so."

"I'm not the one making this complicated." My mind threatens to spin out of control. There's so much going on here.

"You sure about that?" She steps closer. "Because this hot-and-cold act is exhausting. One second you're pushing me away, the next you're looking at me like —" She cuts herself off. "Then we do the deed, and you're out the door as soon as you're done."

"That's not what happened." I waited for her to fall asleep

first.

"No," she fires back. "You won't own it. You won't say what it was."

My throat tightens. "You're Caleb's sister." That's my excuse, but that's not the reason. I don't dare tell her the truth.

I don't know that I could handle this. The bruises I left were a slap in the face.

Caleb wasn't just my best friend in high school. He's the reason I'm a doctor. When my older brothers bailed on the vineyard, all the pressure landed on me. I was supposed to carry the legacy, keep the Paradise name rooted in the soil.

But that wasn't what I wanted. Medicine was.

And Caleb—he's the one who told me I didn't owe anyone my future. He said, "*Then be a doctor.*" Just like that, like it was that simple. It wasn't. Standing up to my father tore us apart for years.

But when Caleb lost his parents, something in me cracked open. He needed me like I needed him. He believed in me when I didn't know how to believe in myself.

And now, not only did I hook up with his little sister, I left marks. I know what the emergency room would do if she went in. This would not be good. It's not just complicated. It's wrong. It feels like a betrayal of everything he gave me.

Her voice drops. "And that makes me off-limits?"

"I don't know." I shake my head. "You said—"

"I said it was the best sex I'd ever had," she says, cheeks flushed but unflinching. "Then you bailed."

"It wasn't like that."

"Then tell me what it was," she demands.

I open my mouth, but nothing comes out.

"Exactly." She crosses her arms. "You shut down every time we get close to something real."

I hate how right she is. I hate how close she's standing. And I really hate that she can see the cracks I've spent years pretending don't exist.

"Why did you avoid me all day?"

The question isn't loud. It doesn't need to be.

It guts me just fine on its own.

When I don't respond, she shakes her head and stomps out of the living room. After a moment, she slams the door to her bedroom.

What am I doing?

I sit on the edge of the couch, elbows on my knees, hands locked behind my neck as if that'll keep me from unraveling. The silence is louder than the fight we just had. And I deserve it. Every second of her anger. Hell, I've been avoiding her like she's a threat to everything I've built...and maybe she is.

Because I want to go to her. Right now. I want to knock on that door, crawl into that bed, and lose myself in her until the rest of the world disappears. I want to apologize with my mouth on her skin, tell her without words how sorry I am. But that's the problem.

Sadie's my kryptonite. One look from her and I forget the rules. One touch and I'm ready to burn down the only boundaries keeping us safe. Caleb would never forgive me. She might not forgive me. And if we end up in that bed again, I don't know if I'll have the strength to walk away.

I drag a hand down my face and let out a breath. It's all too dangerous. Too fast. Too much. But damn it, my feet itch to move, and my heart aches like she's already gone. I want her. God, I want her. But I don't know how to have her without breaking everything else.

Then I'm standing in the hallway, and I knock on her door. "It's me," I call, forcing calm into my voice as I lean against the doorframe like I belong here. Like I didn't disappear last night without an answer.

"What do you want?" she asks.

I open the door, then say the only thing I can. "I thought we could try again."

Her brow lifts. "Try again—as in, another round of you getting weird and bolting?"

"Sadie." It's a warning, but it doesn't slow her down.

"We need to talk," she says. "And you can't keep dodging me."

"What's left to say?"

"I don't regret it," she says plainly. "Not one bit."

That takes my breath away. I didn't think she'd say it out loud. I nod. "Okay."

Her lips twitch into something like a smile. "Okay?"

"Yeah."

She studies me. "Then help me."

I blink. "With what?"

She hesitates. "Figure this out. Get better. I want you to teach me."

My pulse stutters. "Teach you?"

"If I really wasn't good, maybe you can give me some...pointers."

I stare at her. There are a thousand reasons to say no, and only one of them has anything to do with Caleb. "Sadie, I meant it when I said you're incredible. Our night together was amazing. There is nothing wrong with you—nothing. Whatever Alex said, that's his damage, not yours. He didn't deserve you. But you need to understand, I can't give you pointers."

"You can't or you won't?"

"Both."

"Why?" she pushes.

I look away, but she doesn't let up.

"Because Caleb would kill you? Or because you think I'll fall apart?"

"You said you don't regret it," I say.

"I don't."

"That was one night. You want to keep doing this and pretend it won't blow up?"

"Probably will," she admits. "But it'd be fun until it does."

God, she's killing me. "You should ask why I really won't do it."

"I did."

I step closer. "You told me not to go easy on you. So I

didn't. I saw the bruises. The hickey. You think I don't remember where I put my mouth?" My voice drops. "That was one night. And I hurt you."

Her eyes widen.

"I didn't mean to," I add. "But I did."

A flicker of shock crosses her face before it turns to anger. "And here I was thinking you were the fun one. Don't you think I know when I've been injured?"

"You asked for honesty."

"It was fun for me," she mutters. "Guess I read it wrong."

"You didn't. That's the problem."

We stand here in the thick of everything unsaid. I want to fix it. I want to pull her back in.

But instead, she shuts down. "Go ahead," she says. "Bail again. You're good at that."

So I do. I walk out of her room and into mine. One of us needs to be the adult here.

I lie awake all night, the argument playing on a loop in my head. Every word, every look, every breath we didn't take because we were too busy hurting each other. What she's asking for—it's impossible. She doesn't see it, doesn't get that she's already in my bloodstream. Letting her in even more? Giving myself free rein to touch her, want her, have her whenever I want? That won't fix anything. It'll just feed the obsession. And I'm already hooked.

I hear Sadie in the kitchen the next morning, banging around like she's daring me to show my face before I'm fully awake. But by the time I venture out, she's already gone.

Then she walks in from the deck, tossing a wet towel over a chair. "You've got a weird idea of a quick getaway," she says.

"I'm a glutton for punishment," I mutter, making a slice of toast.

After a moment, Sadie sits across from me, elbows on the table, eyes locked on mine. "So...where'd we leave off? Right. You were about to explain why you're acting like a coward."

I drop the spoon next to my coffee. Loud. Final. "We left off with you getting mad and me not giving in."

"Because you 'hurt' me." She rolls her eyes. "Seriously?"

"You think I made that up?"

"I think you're exaggerating. A few bruises don't scare me."

"I'm not doing it again." I try to make it sound like a decision, not a defense.

She shrugs. "Guess I'll find someone else, then."

Her casual tone makes something snap.

"This isn't a game."

"Maybe not to you," she fires back.

I try to hold the line. "It's not worth the risk."

"Funny. You're the only one who seems scared."

"I'm not scared."

"Then what is it?" she pushes. "Because I've taken worse in a pillow fight."

My jaw tightens. "It's a bad idea."

"That's a terrible excuse."

She leans in, and I know I'm seconds from breaking. "You really want me to believe this is about protecting me?"

"Isn't it?" I challenge. "Because I told you. Your skills in bed are not an issue." My voice drops. "That was about him."

"Alex?"

I nod. "Yes."

She goes still. "You left me right after you were done. How can I not believe him?"

I grit my teeth. "Because I told you he was wrong. Can't you believe me?"

"Believe you? The guy who won't touch me without apologizing?"

I stare at her, struggling to hold back what I really want to say. "You're not fragile, Sadie. And I don't care what Alex told you. He's a loser."

"He has a job, and he owns a business." Her voice is quieter now. Wounded.

I can't explain it to her.

"Why can't you tell me the truth?" she asks.

I try again to shift her focus. "If a guy can't get a woman like you to come, he's the one with the problem."

She blushes. "So you don't think I'm bad?"

How many times do I have to tell you? I slam my hand on the table. "I think you're incredible. And yeah, I held back. You want me to go all in? You'll wake up with more than bruises."

Her expression flickers — hurt, anger, disbelief — before it sets hard. "I didn't ask you to hold back."

"You didn't have to."

"Then who are you protecting?" she asks. "Me? Or yourself?"

I don't answer. I can't. I push away from the table, scraping the chair back with too much force. "You need someone who won't ruin your life."

Her eyes don't soften. "Ruin my life? You are awfully high and mighty."

"That's not what I meant."

"But it's what you said."

"Caleb wouldn't want it to be me," I admit.

She doesn't even blink. "Great. I'm fragile, Caleb's the boss, and there's a string of women out there whose lives you've ruined with good sex. Good to know where we stand."

Sadie rises so fast her chair tips over. She storms out, and I stay right where I am, alone with the smell of burned toast. What the hell am I supposed to do?

"Fine," I hear my voice saying. "I'll give you sex lessons."

I hear Sadie's door open, but then my phone pings with an emergency at the hospital. *Noooooooo.*

"I have to go," I call before she's even had a chance to say something.

Nineteen

Sadie

All day, I've been replaying the moment Beckett said yes, if not to me, then at least to giving me sex lessons.

Then he left, and I've been spiraling. My skin feels too tight, my nerves buzzing like they've been electrified. I've tried to distract myself, but nothing works.

Then my phone pings, and it's him. I hold my breath.

Beckett: I'm on my way, and practice starts tonight.

My heart skips, then stumbles. *Tonight?* Do I put on a robe? Stay in my shorts? Wait in my room or pretend I'm casually lounging on the couch? I want this—God, I want this—but excitement is tangled so tightly with anxiety that I'm not sure if

I'm going to kiss him or combust.

I can almost hear his voice — teasing, calm, commanding.

I bite my lip, my nerves stretching taut. I try to breathe, to settle the thrum in my veins, but anticipation only sharpens everything.

A few minutes later, the front door opens. I freeze. He enters quietly, kicking off his shoes like he owns the space, which he does. His frame fills the room, effortless and confident.

"Hey," he says. "You ready?"

I hesitate. "Should I, uh…wear clothes?"

He chuckles, stepping closer until he's right in front of me. His finger lifts my chin, directing my gaze to his.

"I look forward to undressing you," he murmurs. And then his lips are on mine.

The kiss is searing. His tongue teases, deepens, steals every breath I had left. He trails soft kisses down my neck, his breath hot against my ear.

"Relax," he whispers.

But when he pulls back, I'm trembling.

"I'll be upstairs," he says. "Give me a few minutes and come up when you're ready."

And just like that, he disappears, leaving me stunned, breathless, and aching.

Five agonizing minutes pass.

Then I move, slowly, one foot in front of the other. Each step up the stairs is a heartbeat. A question. A choice.

When I push open his bedroom door, the scent of floral candles filters toward me. The room glows, low light, warm air, intimacy pulsing through every corner. It's filled by a massive bed, soft linens, and shadows cast from the candlelight.

"Come in here," he calls from the bathroom.

The sound of running water mixes with candlelight, flickering against the floor-to-ceiling mirrors. When I see myself, my face seems cautious and unsure, but I really want this.

Beckett stands by the extra-large tub, shirtless, jeans unbuttoned, confidence radiating from every line of his body. He reaches for me.

I let him draw me closer, my skin electric.

He kisses the back of my neck, slow and reverent, and I feel the breath leave my lungs. His arms surround me, and he pops the button on my jeans.

"Relax," he whispers again.

When his hand slides under the waistband of my panties, I can barely stay upright.

"Are you looking forward to tonight?" he asks, his voice a hush of heat.

I nod, unable to find words.

He peels off my shirt and spins me to face him, eyes roaming my body with a mix of hunger and reverence. "You're beautiful," he says. "If anyone told you otherwise…that's on them."

His fingers slide down, tugging my panties to the floor. I can see glistening at my slit. His hands ghost over me, and my brain short circuits. He unhooks my bra, fingertips grazing my skin until my nipples tighten. A gasp slips out as he murmurs, "So responsive."

He presses himself against me, the hard line of his arousal unmistakable. His voice is rough against my ear. "This is what you do to me."

I'm dizzy with want.

He takes my hand, guiding me to the tub, dipping my fingers into the steaming water. "Too hot?"

I shake my head, and he helps me in. The water cradles me like a second skin. He strips off his jeans and slides in behind me, arms wrapping around my waist as he pulls me in close.

The water laps softly, the room full of steam and breath and tension.

"What do you like?" he murmurs.

"Everything," I breathe.

He runs his hands along my thighs, up my sides, mapping me slowly. Gently. Possessively. He doesn't feel like a teacher…

The steam rises around us, blurring the world as the

tension within me begins to melt away. His fingertips trace delicate arcs along my collarbone, sparking a fire that both confuses and excites me. It's an overwhelming feeling to be here with him — daring, reckless, and utterly alive.

I close my eyes, savoring every caress. He's surprisingly gentle, yet there's an underlying intensity to his touch that sends jolts through my body.

"Are you okay?" he murmurs, his voice deep and gravelly, threaded with concern. I can feel his breath ghosting over my ear, and I shiver. It's an absurd question. Of course, I'm not okay, but in this moment, I want to forget everything else. I want to drown in the warmth of him, in this shared space that feels so different from the noise outside.

"Yeah," I say. I tilt my head to catch his expression. His blue eyes have darkened — intense, focused — and my heart stutters.

Slowly, deliberately, his hand slides up and settles between my breasts. I lean back into his shoulder, every touch sending sparks across my skin. His breath hitches. I've stirred something in him.

Driven by impulse, I swing a leg over his and press against his thigh. The move surprises us both. His hand tightens on my hip, and the rush that follows is instant. Heat curls in my belly. He swallows. We're on the edge, caught between what we've been and everything we could be.

"Sadie, just feel and tell me what you like. Communication is key."

"Don't stop what you're doing." I groan, pressing back against him, driving my point home with a determined thrust of my hips.

I rise first, water sliding down my body as I reach for his hand. His fingers curl around mine, warm and certain, and together we step out, leaving the bath behind.

The tiles are cool underfoot as we move to the bedroom. When I glance back, his eyes are locked on me.

Twenty

Beckett

I sit down on the bed in front of her and take in her exquisite body. It's just soft enough, and she's not all bones.

Laying her back on the bed, I dry her, spending longer than is probably required with her pussy. Her folds are so wet and inviting, glistening with moisture. I can't help but lean in and gently brush my lips against them, savoring her sweet nectar. Sadie moans, arching her back, and I know she's enjoying this. I continue to tease her, sucking on her swollen clit before diving my tongue inside her heat, exploring her depths.

Her fingers tangle in my hair as she grasps for something solid, her other hand pressed against the headboard for support. She's panting now, gasping my name between ragged breaths, and it spurs me on. I want to make her feel good; I want to erase the memories of that asshole, Alex, and show her what it's like to be with someone who truly cares for her.

I increase the speed and pressure of my tongue, flicking against her G-spot as she writhes beneath me. Her legs tremble around my head. "Oh, God... I'm... I'm..." She pants, unable to finish her sentence as she climaxes.

Her body convulses around me as she rides out her orgasm. I look up at her, my face wet with her juices, and all I can think about is how gorgeous she looks in the aftermath, her eyes hazy with satisfaction and her cheeks flushed a pretty shade of pink.

Slowly, I stand and help her to her feet. She sways slightly, and I catch her in my arms, holding her until she's steady. Then I stand before her, my cock hard and dripping. "Show me how you like to give head."

Her eyes light up, and she kneels between my legs. She carefully strokes my cock.

"Harder," I command.

Sadie complies, her grip tightening around my shaft as she moves her hand in long, slow strokes. I close my eyes, savoring the sensation of her warm palm caressing my swollen length.

"Faster," I grunt.

She complies, picking up the pace until she's working my cock with vigor.

"Get it all wet with your tongue and put it in your mouth."

Sadie does as I say. She licks around the head before taking more of me into her mouth, bobbing her head up and down in time with her hand. Her tongue swirls around my shaft, finding my sensitive spot. I groan as pleasure shoots through my body. "Fuck," I roar, unable to keep my voice down. Her response is a muffled moan of pleasure.

"Pump it with your hand and look up at me."

She shifts so that her hand alone continues to pump my shaft, and our eyes meet as she reaches down to rub her clit. I can't believe this is happening. My best friend's little sister is sucking me off like an expert, and I'm about to lose my mind with desire. The thought only spurs me on; I grip her hair lightly, angling her head so she can take more of me into her mouth.

"Oh, God, I'm close," I warn, my hips bucking involuntarily as the edge of orgasm draws near. She simply moans in response, sucking harder and faster, seeming intent on bringing me over the edge. "This is your chance to let me come on your titties. Otherwise I'm going to lose my load down your throat."

She doesn't stop.

And then it happens. White-hot pleasure explodes from my core, and I release myself into her waiting mouth. "Fuck!" I cry again. The world goes dark for a moment as stars shine behind my eyes. I take a deep breath and lower myself to the edge of the bed. "That was..." I trail off, at a loss to describe the intensity of that experience. "You get an A-plus for oral skills."

Sadie smiles at me, a smug look on her face as she wipes her lips.

I reach for her, and she drapes herself across my chest, her skin still warm and slick. I trail my fingers lazily down her spine, still trying to convince myself that what just happened wasn't some fever dream cooked up after too many late nights and too much restraint.

"You were incredible," I murmur. "Every damn second of that."

She shifts to look up at me, her lips curling into a sleepy, satisfied smile. "Was it too much?"

"No," I say without hesitation, brushing her hair back from her face. "But I need to ask you that as well. I was rough. You didn't hesitate, but I need to hear it from you."

Her eyes flash with heat. "Not in the least," she says, fingers tracing my stomach. "If anything, I want to know how to make it better for you."

I chuckle. "You sure you want the honest answer?"

She grins. "Always."

I tilt my head toward her, dropping my mouth to her ear. "Any guy'll tell you—your mouth on his cock is great. You're never gonna go wrong with that." I feel her shiver, and it shoots straight through me. "If you want to take it deeper...when you hit your gag reflex, try to swallow. It helps."

She blinks slowly, her lips parting, and I swear I can feel her storing that away like it's gospel.

She curls into me, one leg thrown over mine, her hand resting low on my stomach. Neither of us says another word, and before long, her breath evens out and her body goes slack in my arms.

I stare up at the ceiling, my heart thudding in the quiet. This was supposed to be a lesson. A favor. But now she's wrapped around me like she belongs here, like this is normal, and I'm completely fucked. I don't know how I'm ever going to get out of this alive.

Twenty-one

Beckett

B y the time I wrap up rounds, my feet ache and my brain's fried. But all I can think about is Sadie curled up in my bed, hair messy from sleep, eyes half-lidded as she reaches for me. Every night this past week has ended with her in my arms, and I've started measuring my days by the moment I get to climb into bed beside her.

Tonight, though, before I can go home, I promised Tarryn I'd stop by the winery.

The sun's low over the hills as I drive up the long gravel road to the Paradise Hill tasting room. The vines stretch in every direction, early-summer green and humming with life. There's something about this place that settles me. Maybe it's the legacy. Maybe it's the land. Definitely helps that Sadie's here now.

I spot Tarryn walking a row near the production barn,

tablet in hand, ponytail swinging with each step.

"Hey," I call, stepping out of my car.

She looks up and smiles. "Well, if it isn't Dr. Beckett himself."

I roll my eyes but wait to speak until I'm closer. "Is Zach still up to his usual?" I ask softly.

Tarryn sighs and flips the tablet around so I can see the video footage—security cams from the tasting room. Zach's leaning on a barrel, phone in hand, while one of the interns is cleaning up from a tasting.

"Still working hard, I see," I mutter.

"Working his charm, maybe. Not much else." She tucks the tablet under her arm. "Elise's over at Black Bear. They've been having water issues, and she's trying to get ahead of it before we hit peak sun. Plus, she's trying to figure out which acre to recommend for the white wine vinegar this year."

Black Bear is our acreage on the east side of the lake and gets all the afternoon sun, which is perfect for white grape varietals. Kingston's home is over on that side, so someone is usually there.

I raise a brow. "We're in the condiment business now?"

She nods. "And after the disaster last season with that vat of white wine, we sold out every bottle of white wine vinegar within a week. It was a smaller bottle than the wine would have been, so we made more money per ounce. People have been asking about having it again this season, and there's no reason not to."

"How will that impact wine production?"

"It won't. We're only using a small section of our whites, and I'm buying more from the Thompson Farm and the local indigenous nation. They're really becoming a powerhouse grower."

"I can't believe how great you did, turning a bad event into something so successful."

"If it turns a profit, I'm not picky," she says, grinning. "Elise's got numbers. They work. If it pans out, we'll start a yearly batch. Small, but high-end."

It's good news. Smart. Strategic. But my mind's already drifting. "Sadie in the tasting room?" I ask.

"Mm-hmm." Tarryn's smile shifts — knowing, maybe. "She's got two couples in there right now. Charming the pants off them, last I checked."

I head toward the tasting room, the sound of laughter carrying before I even open the door. Inside, the space glows with warm wood, soft golden light, and Sadie's voice, weaving between her guests' delighted comments.

She's behind the counter, pouring with elegance, her eyes bright as she talks about flavor profiles and food pairings. The two couples she's helping hang on her every word, nodding, pointing at bottles, setting them aside in a neat cluster by the register.

And then — Zach.

He sees me but doesn't acknowledge me, strutting like he owns the place, all swagger and fake charm. He slides in beside Sadie and starts pouring without even glancing at her. One of the women giggles at something he says — something suggestive, no doubt — and then he turns to the men and says loudly, "Am I right?"

They chuckle awkwardly. It's forced. And when he claps one of them on the back, I see their expressions shift, polite but distant.

They finish their final sips, mutter something about having to get on the road, and leave. No bottles. No sale. Sadie's careful setup left behind on the counter like an afterthought.

Then Zach smirks, turns to her, and says, "You gonna clean up your mess or what?"

She doesn't argue. Doesn't even flinch. Just nods, quietly collects the glasses, and begins wiping down the bar.

I feel the burn of anger crawl up my spine. I step forward until I'm standing just behind her. She doesn't turn around, but I see the way her shoulders tense.

"Zach," I say, voice low. Controlled. Dangerous.

He looks at me with fake surprise. "Didn't see you there, Beck. Everything okay?"

"No. Not really."

He looks between me and Sadie, then shrugs. "Just having a little fun."

"Looks like you cost us a sale." I point out the obvious.

He scoffs. "They weren't serious buyers."

"They were until you opened your mouth."

He opens his hands like he's about to say something else, but I give him a look that shuts it down. He mutters something under his breath and heads for the back.

Sadie still hasn't looked up. Her hands are steady as she dries the glasses, but I can see the tightness around her mouth.

I lean in, lowering my voice. "You okay?"

She nods. Barely.

But I'm not. Not even close.

I wait until the last glass is dried and stacked before I speak again. "Sadie."

She finally looks up. Her smile is faint, polite. It doesn't reach her eyes.

"I'm fine," she says before I can ask.

"You're not," I say softly. "You don't have to lie."

She presses the towel to the counter a little harder than necessary, then straightens, squaring her shoulders. "It's not a big deal."

"It is to me."

Her mouth opens, then closes. I can see the tug-of-war playing out in her head. Pride, restraint, self-protection.

"I don't want to cause problems," she finally says. "I'm the new girl. He's family."

"So are you." The words come effortlessly. "Or at least you're starting to feel like it."

Her eyes flicker. That softens her for a second, but she shakes her head. "Beckett..."

"He embarrassed you. He disrespected you. And he cost you a sale you earned."

"It's just wine." Her voice is too light. "They'll come back."

"Maybe. But that's not the point."

She looks down, folding the towel, and then unfolding it. "Look, I've dealt with guys like Zach before. You smile, let it roll off, and move on."

"Why should you have to?"

"Because it's easier," she says. Her voice doesn't rise, but the honesty in it hits like a punch. "Because if I say something, I'm the difficult one. The drama. The problem."

I step closer, careful not to crowd her. "You think I'd ever see you that way?"

She finally meets my gaze. There's heat in her eyes now, not anger, just something tired and raw.

"Maybe not now. I've won you over." She cracks a faint smile. "But I also know this isn't your battle."

"Yes, it is," I say quietly. "Not because I want to fight it for you, but because I give a damn when someone treats you like that."

She swallows hard. For a second, I think she might tell me the truth. The whole thing. But instead, she just smiles again.

"I'll be okay," she says. "Just…don't make a thing of it with Zach. It will only make things harder when you're not here."

I nod, even though it kills me. "Okay," I say. "But if it happens again, I'm not pretending I didn't see it."

She sighs. "Fair enough."

I reach for her hand before she can turn away. Just a brush of my fingers against hers. She freezes at the contact, then lets her fingers slip between mine.

"I missed you today," I admit.

Her expression softens like sunlight on water. "I missed you too."

And even though I'm still angry — at Zach, at the way she's had to armor herself — I tuck that away for now. Because what I want more than anything is to take her home and remind her that not everyone in this family treats people like they're disposable.

Because she's not. Not to me.

I take her hand and lead her toward the main house. "You took a rideshare in this morning?"

She nods.

Sunday dinner is always a circus. Tonight should be no different.

As we reach the door, Sadie hangs back near the entrance to the kitchen. "You okay?" I ask.

She nods, giving me a tight smile. "Do I need a playbook for tonight?"

I lean in. "Just follow my lead. And don't let Max get to you. And whatever you do, don't let Zach bait you."

"Noted."

We enter the dining room just as Tarryn finishes placing a giant serving platter in the center of the table. Roast chicken, fingerling potatoes, heirloom carrots—all laid out like a food magazine spread. Mom's done her usual magic. Dad's already in his chair, wine glass in hand while Max lounges at the far end like he's the king of the estate. Zach is beside him, looking far too smug for someone who torpedoed a sale less than an hour ago.

"Ah, there he is," Max says as I pull out a chair for Sadie. "Dr. Beckett, gracing us with his presence."

"And not a minute too late," I mutter as I sit.

"Sadie," Mom says with a warm smile. "So good to see you again."

"Thanks for having me."

Max's eyes flick to her, assessing. "So, you're the one keeping our boy distracted these days."

Sadie's shoulders go rigid beside me, but she manages a smooth reply. "I don't think of myself as a distraction."

"She's got a point," Kingston says, not looking up from carving the chicken. "Let's eat before Max starts interviewing the guests."

The meal starts in relative peace. Plates fill, wine is poured—our merlot tonight, smooth and spicy. But it doesn't take long for the tension to crawl in.

"So," my dad says between bites, "we finally ran the

numbers on the pinot barrels."

All eyes turn to him.

"We're good to bottle," he continues. "And not a moment too soon. Grapes were crushed eighteen months ago. But there's a catch."

"There always is," Tarryn says.

"Glass costs are up," Dad says. "By a lot. If we go with traditional corks, it'll dig into the margins. We're looking at another twenty-five cents a bottle for closures alone."

Zach waves a hand. "So we eat it. It's a premium vintage. People expect corks."

"But do they?" Kingston leans forward. "Studies show screw caps preserve flavor better for whites and light reds. And they're easier to open."

"They're cheap," Max snaps. "And they look it."

"It's not about how it looks," I chime in. "It's about what's smart. We've got fewer bottles this year thanks to the frost. If we can cut costs without sacrificing quality, why wouldn't we?"

Sadie stays quiet beside me, but I feel her tense with every volley across the table.

Max scoffs. "This is the problem with your generation. Always chasing efficiency instead of heritage."

Tarryn sets down her fork. "Max, this isn't about tradition. It's about survival. We lost a third of the crop to the frost, and another quarter to smoke taint from the fire season. If we keep pretending we're invincible, we won't be around to argue about it next year."

Zach clears his throat. "We could cut the restaurant allocations. Keep it direct-to-consumer only."

"Or," Max says with a smirk, "we could stop wasting resources on vinegar and tasting room fluff."

Tarryn's eyes narrow. "The vinegar line made a twenty-two-percent profit last quarter."

"But it's not wine," he says with a shrug. "It's novelty."

Sadie leans over and whispers to me. "Sometimes novelty is what keeps the doors open."

The whole table goes still. Max's eyes lock on hers, and for a second, I'm ready to step in. But she doesn't flinch.

"Well," he says, lifting his glass, "if you've got something to say, why don't you tell all of us."

"Things like the tasting room and wine gifts are a great value," Sadie says. "People impulse buy all the time, so in my opinion, if the margins are good, why complain?"

"Miss..." He waves at me.

"Calloway," she says. "Sadie Calloway."

Max takes a sip. "Of course you are."

Whatever the hell that means.

Mom swiftly changes the subject, asking Kingston about Black Bear's irrigation around his house. The tension lifts slightly, but it lingers in the corners of the room like smoke that won't quite clear.

After dinner, while the others are helping clean up, I guide Sadie out to the back porch. "You okay?" I ask again.

"I held my own."

"You did," I say. "I'm sorry he's an ass."

She leans on the railing, looking out over the vineyard where the last of the light is bleeding into the hills. "I should have saved my comment for the ride home. It's my fault. But I see where Zach gets his attitude from."

I slide in behind her, wrapping an arm around her waist. "Everyone at that table except for the two of them agreed with you. You don't have to be quiet to belong here."

She exhales. "What is their problem?"

"Tarryn. She's a natural with this business. She's not afraid of trying new things or making changes when things need to be changed. They want her to fail so they can sweep in and fix it all."

I'd love to stay out here with Sadie all night, but eventually, I look at my watch. "We need to get going. I have an early morning."

We go back in to say our goodbyes, and it takes us almost fifteen minutes to get out of there.

I'm trying to put the family frustrations behind me once we leave, but I don't even make it to the end of the gravel drive before I let out a sharp breath and thump the steering wheel with the heel of my hand. "God, he's insufferable."

Sadie sits quietly in the passenger seat, hands tucked in her lap. The porch light from the main house fades behind us as I take the turn toward the road, tires crunching over loose rock.

"I know Tarryn can handle things," I mutter, "but Max bulldozes every damn conversation just to push his own agenda."

Sadie's voice is calm. "He doesn't respect her."

"No," I agree. "He doesn't. He respects control. Power. And in his mind, neither of those things belongs to Tarryn. Or to me, honestly."

I glance over. Sadie's watching me carefully, not with judgment, but like she's seeing something new. Something I don't show anyone else.

"He wanted Zach to run the winery," I say, jaw tight. "Always did. Said it outright at a family dinner once, when Zach was seventeen and could barely tie his shoes without help. He called him *the natural heir*. Like the rest of us were just squatting in his legacy."

"And you think he still believes that?"

I laugh once. "We've joked that he'd burn the place down before letting Tarryn take full control. But sometimes, I wonder if it's really a joke. And Zach—he's not really malicious, he's just...lazy. Entitled. He's not built for this."

Sadie's quiet for a few beats. "But you are."

I shake my head. "I'm not running the vineyard. That's never been my path. Tarryn's doing an incredible job. Max just refuses to see it because it doesn't fit his narrative."

There's a long pause as I pull onto the main road. The mood lightens a little, like just saying these things out loud drains some of the poison.

When we get home, I drop the keys in the bowl by the door and toe off my shoes. Sadie follows, wordless, but I can feel her gaze on my back.

We settle on the couch, not quite touching.

She's the one who breaks the silence.

"You always carry it like it's yours," she says.

"What?"

"The family," she says softly. "The winery. All of it. Even when it's not your responsibility."

I scrub a hand over my face. "Because it is mine. At least in the way it matters. I see the cracks before things fall apart. And what if no one else steps in until it's too late?"

Her voice is gentle. "That's a hard way to live."

I don't answer.

She shifts closer, tucking her feet beneath her on the couch. "Beckett…"

I glance over. Her eyes are soft.

"You take care of everyone else," she says. "Let me take care of you."

Something in me breaks open.

Not dramatically. Not loudly. Just…quietly. Like a hairline fracture letting in light.

I nod.

Sadie leans into my side, her head resting on my shoulder. I wrap an arm around her, pulling her closer. And for the first time all day, I let myself breathe.

We sit like that for a long time. No expectations. No performance. Just warmth and steady presence.

Eventually, I murmur, "You make it easy."

She looks up. "What?"

"Being still. Feeling seen."

She reaches up and touches my jaw, fingers feather light. "Maybe that's what we're both learning to do."

I tilt my head, pressing my mouth to her forehead, her temple, then finally her lips. It's not rushed. Not hungry.

Just honest.

And when we part, her eyes shine. "I like being here with you, Beckett."

I like it too.

Twenty-two

Sadie

The sun filters through the leafy canopy above the produce market on a Saturday afternoon. I pause beside a display of peaches, close my eyes, and let the warmth settle over me. It's been a little more than a week since things shifted between Beckett and me, and for once, everything seems to be falling into place.

A voice cuts through the air. "Sadie?"

I freeze, trying to place it. *Demi.* Demi Franklin is dating Alex's brother Simon's friend, but I think she dates Simon occasionally too.

I turn slowly to face her. She looks the same — bright-eyed, friendly, glowing with the effortless confidence I always envied. But my body reacts as if she's a threat. My shoulders stiffen. My smile is automatic and fake. "Hey," I say, trying to keep my voice steady. "It's been a while."

She steps closer, her eyes searching. "You look…different."

I shrug. "I'm still me." *How awkward is that?*

Her smile dims slightly. "Have you talked to Alex?"

I grip the peach in my hand. "No, I haven't."

Her eyes dart toward the entrance like she's worried someone might overhear. "He's been spiraling. Really upset you left."

"That's too bad. He must miss his housecleaner and cook." My voice is cool, but I can't help it. Just the sound of his name curls my stomach.

She drops her voice. "And Simon…he's not taking it well either. He said you took off with something."

The fruit slips from my hand and hits the bottom of the basket with a dull thud. "What did I take? I only have my clothes and belongings."

Demi shifts, uncomfortable. She won't meet my eyes. "He said if you're not already dead…he'll make sure you are."

Everything in me stills. My breath vanishes. The world narrows.

"I have to go," I whisper.

I drop the basket and bolt, ignoring the calls of vendors and the blur of curious faces. My vision tunnels. My thoughts splinter. My heart thunders as I burst into the parking lot, fumbling with my keys.

I don't even make it halfway down the row before my hands start shaking. *Simon wants me dead?*

Demi just casually dropped that like it wasn't the most terrifying thing I've heard in weeks. Simon once broke a pool cue in half because someone beat him at darts. He's huge and angry and unstable.

I grip my tote and try to swallow past the lump rising in my throat. Why would Simon want me dead?

It doesn't make sense. Alex and I are a mess, but I left clean. I barely even took what belonged to me. I know I left stuff behind in that house, but I don't regret it for a second.

I thought Alex's texts were trying to scare me. Get me to come back. That's what abusers do, right? Make it your fault. Twist until you start questioning your own memory.

But I didn't take anything. I know I didn't.

Except...

I pause mid-step, a chill crawling down my spine.

There was that one pair of jeans that were Alex's. I remember tossing them aside when I unpacked. But why would the jeans matter? They just got mixed in when I swept everything off the bedroom floor in a rush.

There is no way they're that upset about a pair of jeans. Even if they were designer or something—and trust me, they weren't—Simon wouldn't be angry over clothes.

If *Simon* thinks I took something valuable, this isn't just a misunderstanding anymore. It's dangerous.

Do I tell Beckett? I bite my lip. He's been so good to me, and we're just figuring things out. The last thing I want to do is drag him into the wreckage of my old life.

But Simon's unhinged. He's the kind of guy who doesn't make threats. He makes examples.

I suck in a shaky breath as I reach the Jeep and focus on remembering how to drive back to Beckett's. The scenery a blur.

Maybe it's nothing. Maybe Alex is bluffing, and Demi misheard something, and I'm just paranoid because that's what trauma does. Or maybe I'm sitting on a ticking time bomb, and I didn't even know I lit the fuse.

By the time I reach Beckett's house, I'm barely holding it together. My hands are shaking so hard I almost drop my keys. I shove the house key into the lock, step inside, and slam the door behind me. The noise echoes like a warning shot.

The house is quiet, but Beckett's scent lingers in the air—cedar and citrus—and I breathe it in like oxygen. But even here, I don't feel safe. Not really. Because Simon is still out there.

Beckett appears just as I round the corner into the living room. He's barefoot, hair a little tousled, holding a glass of water.

The sight of him, calm and ordinary, twists my gut.

"Sadie?" he says.

I manage a weak smile. "Hey."

He watches me closely. "What happened?"

I shake my head, my arms wrapping around my middle. "I just...picked up some fruit and did a few errands. To clear my head." I can't just dump this on him. What if he goes back over there? Simon could really hurt him.

He nods like he doesn't believe me but won't push. "Come on," he says, setting his glass down. "Let's go for a walk."

I take a deep breath and try to calm my frayed nerves. "It's a beautiful day. That sounds like a great idea."

We cross the pool deck and head out into the warm afternoon, picking up the lake trail behind the pool fence. It unfurls in front of us, lined with tall natural grass that rustles in the breeze. We walk in silence for a few minutes, our steps crunching softly on the gravel. My thoughts organize themselves a little better with every step.

But just as I've rehearsed what I want to tell Beckett, he reaches for my hand and the contact erases all my thoughts.

"I can't believe all the houses along the lake now. Remember when we used to come here as kids?" he asks.

I smile at the memory. "You dared me to jump off that big rock. I still can't believe I did it."

He laughs. "I really thought you'd chicken out."

"You made it sound like I'd be branded a coward if I didn't."

"Well, yeah," he says, bumping his shoulder against mine. "There were reputations at stake."

I laugh softly. "You always had that thing about you. Like people needed to rise to your level."

He shrugs. "Still do, I guess."

We reach a bench near the water and sit down. The ski boats are out across the lake, but their wakes are too far away to affect this side.

"I always felt invisible," he says after a moment. "Being in the middle—you get used to people talking around you, not to you."

I turn to him. "I never saw you that way. You always seemed so self-assured."

"I faked it," he admits. "Sometimes, it felt like I had to shout to be seen."

His words stir something inside me. "Caleb used to steal my dolls. Not because he wanted them, but just to upset me. It wasn't about the toy. It was about the power."

Beckett's brows knit. "That's awful."

"It was just…normal back then. I didn't know how to fight back. I just wanted peace."

He looks at me, his eyes softening. "We all want that. Peace. Safety. Someone to see us."

Silence falls between us again.

"At least I never had my dolls stolen," he teases.

I smirk. "You were too busy stealing hearts."

He grins. "Only because you made it look easy."

We sit together, laughter lingering in the air between us, and I let myself believe that maybe he can help me find my way out of this. I want to tell him what Demi said, but it's not the time. Maybe later.

Back home, in the comfort of Beckett's house, I settle on the couch, pulling my legs beneath me, trying to convince myself that the worst has passed.

Beckett moves through the kitchen, filling the kettle, the quiet sounds of domestic life grounding me. "Glass of wine?" he calls over his shoulder.

I open my mouth to answer, but something catches my eye through the window—a flicker of headlights, the shape of a vehicle parked just beyond the tree line out front.

"Beckett…" My voice is low, tight. "Can we close the curtains?"

He appears in the doorway, mug in hand, brow furrowed. "Why?"

"There's a car outside. It wasn't there earlier."

He sets the mug down and moves to the window, brushing the curtain aside.

"It could be someone lost," he says after a pause. "Or waiting for someone."

"No," I whisper, stepping closer. "It feels wrong. It's just sitting there."

He turns to look at me. "You think someone is watching us?"

I nod slowly, stomach churning. "I don't know. Maybe. But I've learned not to ignore this feeling."

He pulls on a hoodie and moves toward the door.

"Wait." I reach for him, grabbing his sleeve. "What if it's someone who has a gun?"

"I'll be careful," he says. "Stay inside."

He disappears outside.

The quiet swells around me, too loud and empty. I pace the living room, peering through the blinds, heart racing. Every shadow looks like a threat. Every creak in the floorboards winds me tighter.

Minutes crawl by. I count each one like a prayer. When the front door opens again, I practically jump out of my skin.

Beckett steps inside, face flushed. "It's empty," he says. "No plates. No one inside. Probably left by a hiker or a neighbor visiting someone down the road."

I sag with relief, but my hands are shaking. "You're sure?"

"Yes. But we'll be cautious from now on. No going anywhere alone. No late-night errands."

I nod, swallowing hard. "You can keep me safe?"

His gaze softens, something fierce burning in his eyes. "Absolutely."

There's no hesitation. No flinching.

Despite the fear still rattling in my bones, I believe him.

Then a sharp knock at the door jerks me upright. My heart leaps into my throat. Beckett's head snaps toward the sound, and he motions for me to stay back as he crosses the room. I follow anyway, anxiety a live wire under my skin. He cracks the door and peers out.

Two uniformed police officers stand on the porch, backlit by the porch light.

"Evening," one says. "Hi, Beckett."

"Elijah. Jonas. What brings you here?"

"We understand Sadie Calloway is living here," Elijah says.

Sometimes I cannot believe this small town. I went to school with both Elijah Fallwell and Jonas Goodwin.

Beckett glances back at me. I nod slowly and step forward. "I'm here, but how did you know that?"

"May we come in?" Jonas asks, his tone polite but firm.

Beckett hesitates, then opens the door wider. "Yeah. Sure."

They step inside, bringing the night air with them. Elijah removes his hat. They're not here to reminisce about school.

Jonas flips open a notebook. "We received a report of a domestic dispute at your former residence. Can you confirm whether you know an Alex Tremblay and Simon Tremblay?"

My stomach drops. I grip the back of the couch for balance. "Yes. Of course. We all went to school together."

"But you were in a relationship with Alex Tremblay and living in his home until recently, correct?"

Beckett moves to stand beside me. "She doesn't have to answer anything without a lawyer."

I place a hand on his arm. "It's okay. I want to answer. Yes, I used to live with Alex, and Simon is his brother. Alex and Simon own a garage."

"Why did you leave?" Elijah asks.

I inhale slowly. "The list is long, but really I left because I was tired of the lies, and I no longer felt safe."

Elijah and Jonas exchange a glance. "Why didn't you feel safe?"

I give a single-shoulder shrug. "Wow. Lots of reasons really. Scary guys would come over, which I assume were his dealers. We got robbed, but all they took was his old laptop and the television. And also, we didn't have much of a relationship anymore."

"With the break-in, do you know if they called the police?" Jonas asks.

"I assume so. I was on my way out for work, so I didn't stick around, and when I got home again, he had a new flat screen on the wall."

They look at each other, and Beckett puts his hand in mine.

"Were you aware that Simon Tremblay has a known history of violence?" Jonas asks. "Did you ever feel physically threatened?"

"I know he's big and often angry."

"Did he threaten you?" Jonas leans toward me.

Suddenly, I'm sure he knows, and I don't want to get arrested for lying. I hesitate. "Only recently."

Beckett turns and looks at me, seeming shocked.

I take a deep breath. "Earlier today, I ran into Demi Franklin. Her boyfriend hangs with Alex and Simon. We were at the fruit stand on Market Street, and she told me Simon was upset with me and had said that if I wasn't already dead, the next time he saw me, I would be."

"Why would he want you dead?" Beckett asks.

I shake my head. "I honestly have no idea."

"You're not involved in any ongoing activity related to either of the Tremblay brothers?" Jonas asks.

"No," I say, louder this time. "I left when I started to feel unsafe. I'm not part of whatever they're into."

Beckett's voice is calm but firm. "She's telling the truth. She's been living here in my guest room for the last two months. She works at the Paradise Hill tasting room. And when she's not there, she's visiting Rosemary Kennedy at the hospital."

Elijah nods. "My mom said she needs a heart transplant."

Sometimes, Paradise is way too small.

Jonas folds up his notebook. "Thank you. If for any reason you feel unsafe again, please reach out. We'll be following up on the report, but at this point, this is just a check-in."

I nod, my throat tight. "Thank you for coming."

They leave as quietly as they arrived. The door clicks shut behind them, and silence falls.

Beckett turns to me, his hand settling on the small of my back. "Why didn't you tell me about Simon's threat?"

I exhale. "I was going to, but after we went for the walk and started talking, I couldn't bring it up. I'm sorry. I'm not involved in anything they're doing."

"Do you think they're dealing drugs? You said you thought the guys that came over were drug dealers."

"Alex always had something, but mostly just pot, and he could get that from any BC cannabis retail store. I never saw him do anything more."

"You're safe," he promises. "He can't get to you here."

His words don't just comfort me. They steady me. And in that quiet, I realize something deeper than fear is growing inside me. *Resolve.* I'm done running. Whatever comes next, I don't have to face it alone.

We try to return to normal, but we can't quite get there. Beckett pours me a glass of wine and himself a carbonated water. He's trying to act like everything's fine, like this is just another night. But we both know it's not.

I take the glass he offers, our fingers brushing. "Are you on call?"

"Not exactly, but I'm hoping tonight's the night Rosie gets her heart. Someone was killed with an AB blood type in an accident up north. They're doing the surgery now."

I raise my glass. "Fingers crossed that you get the notification soon." Now we have two reasons to be alert.

We sit side by side, and I catch him watching the window more than once. Every time headlights pass on the road outside, we flinch, though neither of us says anything.

There's a weight between us now. Not tension exactly, but awareness. Something dark is following me. Whatever life I thought I could rebuild might still be out of reach. But Beckett doesn't pull away. If anything, he leans in, offering comfort without asking anything in return.

"I hate that I brought this to your doorstep," I say finally.

"You didn't," he replies. "They brought this. Not you."

His conviction calms me. I rest my head on his shoulder, grateful for the strength he offers. We talk quietly for a while about nothing important. Books he's reading. His shift next week. The vineyard fundraiser. Talking helps. It reminds me there's a world outside my fear. But deep down, I know we're just waiting for his beeper to sound.

Though it doesn't.

Finally he reaches for his phone and calls someone. "Any news?" I watch his shoulders fall. "Nope. That won't help us. Thanks, though."

"What happened?" I ask, knowing from his body language it was nothing good.

He sighs loudly. "The heart wasn't viable for transplant."

Tears prick at my eyes. "Why not?"

"The victim had an unknown heart condition that showed up during an echocardiogram."

I want to drink the rest of the wine in the house. "What are you going to tell Rosie?"

He shakes his head sadly. "Nothing. I didn't tell her there was a possibility. This happens more often than you think."

I roll my head back and look at the ceiling. "I hate that you can't go in and fix what's wrong. And if I'm being real honest, I wish someone with a good heart would just die."

"Me too on both counts. Let's go to bed," he adds softly after a moment. "I want to hold you."

So I go with him. The thought of sleeping alone feels impossible anyway.

He doesn't press me for more, doesn't ask again about Alex or Simon. He just holds me, one arm wrapped around my waist as I tuck myself into the familiar comfort of his bed.

Twenty-three

Sadie

A few days later, I'm halfway through drying the breakfast dishes when there's a knock at the front door. Not a polite tap. A firm, official knock.

Beckett looks up from the couch, frowning as he stands. I dry my hands on a dish towel, my stomach already turning.

When he opens the door, Jonas Goodwin and Elijah Fallwell are back, this time in casual clothes.

"Sorry to bother you again, Sadie," Jonas says. "Do you have a minute?"

Beckett looks my way, and I nod, even though everything in me wants to slam the door and pretend I'm not home.

Jonas pulls out his phone, swipes a few times, then holds it up to show me a photo. "Do you recognize this man?"

My breath stalls.

I think I do.

He looks like one who was at the house the night before I left. He showed up with a few other guys, all covered in tattoos, guns strapped to their sides like it was normal. They didn't talk to me. Alex made sure of that. He told me to go to my room, shut the door, and put my earbuds in. I did what I was told.

I don't know who the man is. I just know he made my skin crawl. And the fact that the police are interested can't mean anything good.

"I'm not sure," I say, my voice careful. "He looks...familiar. Maybe from around town?" I pull on my shirt sleeve.

Jonas watches me, expression unreadable. I feel like he knows I'm holding back.

"Let us know if anything comes to you," he says after a pause, slipping the phone back into his pocket. "Thanks for your time."

They leave without another word.

I close the door and lean against it, heart pounding. Beckett is watching me.

"Sadie?" he asks quietly.

But I can't speak yet. My past is getting too close again, and I don't know how much longer I can keep pretending it can't touch me here.

"I wish I knew what Alex and Simon are up to." I shake my head as I return to the kitchen.

Later on, I'm grateful to have work to distract me as the early-afternoon sun glints off the glass bottles lining the bar in the Paradise Vineyard tasting room. I've just finished pouring another tasting flight for a nice couple from San Francisco. The room is buzzing—light laughter, clinking glasses, and the scent of oak filling the air. It should feel familiar, normal. But the next time the door opens, all of that comfort drains away. First the police this morning and now this.

She walks in like she owns the place—Julia Tremblay. Alex and Simon's sister. I recognize her in an instant, though it's been months since I've seen her. She's a big-deal real estate agent in town. She has sleek dark hair, designer sunglasses perched on top of her head, and the kind of effortless confidence that used to make me feel like I didn't belong in the same room.

My throat goes dry. She shouldn't be here.

I glance around, hoping she's just a tourist with a passing resemblance, but no. It's her. She sees me and smiles—familiar, wide, and deliberate. My pulse spikes. If Julia's here, it means Alex and Simon know where I work and possibly where I live. The fragile peace I've been holding on to shatters.

"Hi," she says, gliding up to the counter like we're old friends. "Fancy seeing you here."

I force a smile. "Hi, Julia."

"I've been doing some work nearby," she says, her voice all sugar and varnish. "I have a dinner with friends and wanted to pick up a bottle of wine. I always go local. How's life been treating you since you left my brother? Truly the smartest thing you've ever done."

How's life? My palms sweat as I place wine glasses on a tray. "Busy. I'm really enjoying working in the tasting room."

She peers around like she's casing the place. She nods to the couple now looking at us. "Isn't the wine here spectacular? I grew up in Paradise, and I've always loved it. They're the best." She winks at me, and the couple goes back to their tastings and hushed conversation.

There's an edge to her compliment. But I busy myself with the guests, guiding them through the tasting notes—cabernet with hints of cherry and spice, Chardonnay kissed with pear. I keep my tone light and professional, even as every cell in my body screams.

After a minute, Julia takes a seat at the bar, orders a glass of wine, and listens as I talk, sipping thoughtfully. She laughs at the right moments, nods along, and even compliments the wine. On the surface, she's just another customer.

But I know better.

A little while later, I ring up the couple's purchase—just shy of a thousand dollars in wine and merch. I should be excited. This is a big win for the vineyard, but instead I'm moving into a full-blown anxiety attack.

I motion to Zach and give the sign we use to indicate needing the restroom before I slip out to the back hallway, past the private cellar and into the office. I close the door behind me, heart pounding so loud I can hear it in my ears.

I press my back against the wall, hands trembling. What the hell is she doing here? Did she follow me? Do they know I'm here? Do they know I'm living with Beckett? Is she here to lure me back or to warn me? To threaten me?

I try to breathe—four seconds in, hold, four out—but it doesn't help. A knock rattles the door before I can collect myself. I freeze.

"Sadie?" It's Julia.

Of course it is.

"I'm not here to make trouble," she says. "Can I come in?"

I don't answer, but the knob turns anyway. The door creaks open, and she steps inside, closing it behind her. Her expression is calm. Pleasant.

"I just want to talk," she says, leaning against the desk like we're having a casual chat. "You looked surprised to see me."

"That's because I was," I say, trying to keep my anxiety attack at bay. "How did you find me?"

She shrugs. "Like I said, I like to buy wine here, and I happened to see you."

I don't believe her for a second. But I keep my face neutral.

"Alex was upset when you left," she adds, like she's sharing a piece of family gossip.

My jaw tightens. "He doesn't get to be upset. I only took

what was mine."

Julia nods, almost like she agrees. "I told him that. I always liked you, Sadie. You were good for him. For a while, anyway."

My stomach turns. She says it like I was a failed investment. "If you're here to guilt me—"

"I'm not." She raises both hands in mock surrender. "Just...checking in. Offering an olive branch. Maybe we could grab a drink later? Just to talk. Public place, of course."

I study her, trying to read the real message beneath her perfect smile. Every instinct I have is screaming not to trust her. And yet...agreeing might be the only way to figure out what she's really doing here.

"Sure," I say coolly. "Let me know the place."

Her smile widens. "Wonderful. I'll text you. We've got a lot to catch up on."

Before I can respond, the office door opens again. Zach fills the doorway, arms folded.

"Sadie, your break's over," he says, eyes darting to Julia.

Julia straightens, brushing invisible lint from her blouse. "Don't let me keep you. I'll see you later."

She brushes past Zach, her perfume lingering like a warning.

Zach frowns after her. "How did she get back here? What are you doing?"

None of your damn business. "She's my ex's sister, and she wanted to catch up."

"Is she going to be a problem?"

"No. Just an old...acquaintance."

His eyes narrow. "Did you invite her back here? This is an employee-only area."

"Yes. She wanted to talk, but I didn't want to speak in the tasting room," I lie. "It's fine."

He doesn't press, but I can tell he's watching me closely as I return to the bar. I go through the motions—pour, smile, describe—but my hands won't stop shaking. My focus blurs. My smile feels glued on.

Julia's visit confirms what I guess I already knew, what's becoming more clear all the time. Paradise is too small, and I didn't disappear. I didn't escape. They found me. I'm not safe.

By the time I clock out, my nerves are shredded. I drive aimlessly for a while before pulling over near the cliffs, the vineyard stretching behind me like a golden sea. I rest my forehead against the steering wheel and breathe.

What if they come for me? What if Alex shows up?

What if Beckett gets dragged into this?

A gust of wind rocks the Jeep, and for a second, I imagine Julia's face again — smiling, pleasant, calculated. Maybe she's still loyal to Alex. Maybe she's testing me. Maybe she wants me to come back. Or maybe she wants to scare me into silence.

I rub my arms, suddenly chilled.

I did the right thing. I know that. Leaving Alex, taking my suitcase, vanishing. I had to. I saw what he was becoming. And if I'd stayed, I would've lost myself completely.

But now I've dragged the vineyard into it. Beckett's family. Rosie. The people who've taken me in and made me feel seen again. What if I've made them targets?

I don't have answers, just a million spinning thoughts and a rush of fear.

My phone buzzes.

Julia: Can't wait to catch up. 7 p.m. at the Blue Bird Lounge. See you soon. 📎

I stare at the screen. Every part of me wants to delete the message and block her number. But I need to know what she was doing here. What they want.

Me: See you there.

I toss the phone on the passenger seat and grip the wheel until my knuckles turn white. Whatever she's planning, I need to stay one step ahead. I've come too far to let them pull me back.

Never again.

Twenty-four

Sadie

The moment I step through the door, I know I'm not alone.

Beckett's jacket is hanging on the hook. His keys sit on the counter. And his presence—calm, quiet, and now suffocating—presses against me like a wall.

I let the door shut behind me with a soft click, sagging against it for a breath.

My arms ache. My back's a tight knot. My feet feel like I walked on broken glass, which isn't far from the truth. I actually did step on a shard today because the stupid dishwasher exploded mid-shift, and I had to haul racks of rinsed glasses down to the restaurant like a dishwasher mule. After cornering me when Julia visited, Zach ghosted the whole afternoon. Eight tastings. Most overlapped. I barely got a bathroom break.

And now I get to manage Beckett.

"Hey," he says, stepping out from the kitchen like he's been rehearsing this moment.

I freeze. The look in his eyes isn't casual. It's sharp. Intent.

I drop my bag on the bench and kick off my shoes. My socks are damp. One has a hole in the toe. I shake my head. "Not tonight."

"You talked to the police this morning."

I don't even look at him. "And? You were here."

"You told them you didn't know anything about that guy whose picture they showed you." His voice is level. Calm. Which somehow makes it worse.

"Because I don't," I snap.

"You smoothed your sleeve when you said it."

That gets my attention. I turn slowly. "I what?"

"You have a tell. When you lie, you mess with your clothes. You straightened your sleeve, just like you do when you're dodging something."

A small, bitter laugh escapes. "Wow. You keeping notes on me now?"

"I notice things." He crosses his arms, jaw tight. "You were lying."

"No," I say, dragging a hand through my hair. "I wasn't lying. I don't know anything for sure. I suspect. And suspicion doesn't mean anything without proof."

"You could've told them what you suspected."

"What would be the point?" My voice climbs. "So they can write it down and do nothing? So I can give them fuel for a 'he said, she said' they'll never pursue? So I can label myself a snitch?"

"You didn't even tell me." His voice softens.

"I didn't tell anyone."

"Bet you told Rosie."

I flinch, but I didn't tell her. I never want anyone to worry about me. No one knows the truth.

"I don't want to be part of this," I whisper. "I was hoping

it'd go away."

He takes a step closer. "That's not how things like this go away."

I meet his gaze, bracing for judgment. "God, you sound just like everyone else. My brother. Alex. Everyone who thinks I need to be told what to do, like they need to save me."

His brow furrows. "I don't think you need saving."

"Really?" I step back, the heat rising under my skin. "Because last I checked, you're the reason I'm not homeless right now."

"Seems I'm the reason you have a bed and a door you can slam when you're angry." He offers me a smile.

That does it. My stomach knots, tight and sick. "You didn't do that out of kindness. You did it so you could control the outcome."

He blinks. "Are you serious?"

I throw my hands up. "You're a fixer, Beckett. You see a mess, and you have to clean it. I'm just one more mess to fix. One more box to organize."

His voice is suddenly razor sharp. "You're a tornado, Sadie. You leave everything in your wake. You never put things back. You never close drawers. You've started five art projects and haven't finished one. You make smoothies and leave the blender out for days. You live like nothing has consequences."

"And you live like life's a sterile operating room where God forbid anything is out of place!" I pull in a shaky breath. "You're so focused on control that you don't even know how to feel unless it fits into your checklist!"

"At least I finish things," he growls. "You quit everything. You don't stick around. You didn't stick with your last job, your last city, your last relationship—"

My face burns. "Don't. You don't get to go there."

"Why not? You think you're the only one with baggage? With fear?"

"Fear?" I laugh, but it cracks. "You think I'm afraid? I've been surviving for more than ten years all on my own. You know my parents died inches away from me when I was seventeen. Sure, I have Caleb, but he's never here. As soon as he had me stashed with your parents, you both returned to school. He's never come back. Your parents were great, but I was a mess. I lived with Ginny, and then I had my own place until I lost a job and couldn't make rent. I've had that happen more times than I can count. But I've managed to feed and handle my own shit without anyone's help. I keep showing up."

His voice is low now. "Then why won't you tell the truth?"

"Because the truth makes it real," I say. "And if I make it real, I have to face it. All of it. I don't know if I can."

He softens, just a fraction. "You don't have to face it alone."

I shake my head. "You don't get it. You can't be my everything. You already took over my living situation. Now, you're monitoring what I tell the police?"

"I'm trying to help."

"It doesn't feel like help."

I turn and walk down the hallway, jittery with adrenaline. He doesn't follow. *Good.*

"Sadie," he calls.

At my bedroom door, I pause. "Just leave me alone. I mean it."

I slam the door. The echo rattles the frame.

And then I slide to the floor. My breath catches. Everything hits at once—the aching muscles, the fear I've been pretending isn't there, the way he looked at me like he knew every flaw I've ever tried to hide. And worse…the way he didn't leave when I pushed him.

I bury my face in my hands and let the tears come. Quiet, hot, and heavy.

He was right.

And that scares me more than anything.

A minute later, the front door slams so hard the windows rattle. Then I hear the squeal of tires ripping down the driveway.

I don't know if I want to scream, cry, or punch something.

No. I do know.

I'm done. I have to get out of here. It's too much.

I rise and yank my suitcase from under the bed. It scrapes against the hardwood, catching on the edge of the rug, but I don't care. I grab handfuls of clothes — clean, dirty, wrinkled. I don't even look. I stuff everything in without folding, without thinking. A pair of socks gets tangled in a T-shirt. A bra strap hangs out the side. I jam my sketchbook in on top, the edges already curled from the last time I had to pack in a rush.

I was supposed to be safe here. This was supposed to make things manageable. But everything feels overwhelming again. I slam the suitcase shut, the zipper catching on fabric. I yank it loose with a curse. My hands are shaking. Beckett is impossible. Condescending. Cold when it counts. Always right. Always fixing. Like I'm one more broken thing on his to-do list.

And still, when I walk out of the room, dragging the suitcase behind me, part of me doesn't want to go. As much as I hate his meddling, I know I'm throwing a tantrum right now. But I feel powerless to choose something different.

I call the rideshare from the porch. My phone is at fifteen percent, but it's enough to get me to the hospital. It has to be.

The car shows up five minutes later. I climb in, swallowing the lump in my throat and hugging my suitcase like a security blanket. The driver says nothing, just nods at me in the rearview mirror. I'm grateful for the silence. I couldn't speak if I tried.

Halfway there, I remember my shampoo and conditioner are still in the guest bathroom. The expensive kind I splurged on last month, bright citrus scent, sulfate-free, the one little luxury I allowed myself.

I close my eyes and let my head fall back against the seat. *Whatever*. I can buy more. Eventually.

Maybe.

The thought makes my stomach twist.

I've finally saved a few thousand dollars. A miracle. Enough to breathe. Enough to feel like I have a cushion for once in my life. But now I'm about to blow it all on rent. On another move. On first and last month's deposit, setting up utilities, scraping together a mattress because I can't carry one with me.

Again.

I watch my reflection in the window, distorted by streetlights flashing past. My face looks pale. Hollow. Like I'm disappearing, one crisis at a time.

I don't know where I'll sleep tomorrow.

But tonight I can go to the hospital. I can see Rosie. I can sit by her bed and pretend like something in my life makes sense. I can be there for her, focus on something besides myself.

When the car drops me off, the hospital is quiet. Fluorescent lights buzz overhead, casting everything in an over-sterilized glow. I roll my suitcase down the hall, the wheels wobbling over a crack in the tile. I smile weakly at the receptionist who's seen me a half dozen times already this week, and she nods without a word.

Rosie's hallway is dimmer, quieter still. I pause outside her room, her laugh catching me off guard. It's a raspy burst, followed by Ginny's sharper cackle and the unmistakable sound of shuffling cards. For just a second, I stay still, watching the light underneath the door, listening to the murmur of their voices.

Warmth. Connection. A little bubble of normal.

I could stand here forever, pretending everything in my life hasn't just blown apart. But I can't delay the inevitable.

I push open the door.

Ginny's curled up in the chair by the window, dealing cards. Rosie's propped up in bed, her cheeks pale but glowing from laughter. They both look over at the same time.

Ginny clocks the suitcase first. "Uh-oh. That looks like emotional baggage."

Rosie squints. "Please tell me that's a rolling cooler full of sauvignon blanc."

I drag the suitcase inside and let it fall beside the chair with a heavy thud. "I wish. It's just my entire life. Again."

Ginny's eyes widen. "You and Beckett?"

I nod, exhaustion pulsing behind my eyes. "Had a fight."

Rosie puts down her cards. "Like a we-need-a-day-to-cool-off fight or a grab-your-shit-and-don't-look-back fight?"

I sink into the chair beside her bed. "Well, I'm here, aren't I? It'd say it was more a door-slamming, tire-squealing, emotional-explosion fight."

They both go quiet.

Rosie finally breaks the silence. "Where are you going to go?"

"I don't know yet," I tell her. "I haven't figured it out."

There's a beat of stillness before Ginny clears her throat. "I'm staying in the caretaker's house on our family vineyard. It's empty, weirdly haunted, and smells like mothballs, but it's got a bed, hot water, and a roof. You can stay with me."

I blink at her. "Really?"

She shrugs. "Sure. It's not exactly luxury, but I've had worse roommates. I've filled the guest room with boxes I don't want to look at, but you can have the couch until I get it cleaned up."

Rosie gives her a look. "There's a catch. There's always a catch."

Ginny smirks and points a finger at me. "Avoid my grandmother like she's the plague. No eye contact. No sudden movements. And whatever you do, don't breathe a word about you working in the Paradise Hill tasting room. If she finds out, I'll be excommunicated from the family. Or worse, she'll make me work in the fields."

That gets a laugh out of me. "Got it. Grandmother equals danger. I'll stay invisible."

"Excellent," Ginny says. "You're officially qualified."

Relief floods through me so fast it makes me dizzy. *A place to go.* A place where I won't have to explain myself or keep pretending everything's fine.

My phone pings.

I reach for it, hope flaring to life inside me before I can stop it. *Beckett?*

I tap the screen.

Julia: Where are you?

My heart sinks like it's been dropped into a bucket of ice water.

"It's Julia," I mutter. "She cornered me at work and wants to meet tonight. She's asking where I am."

Rosie groans and throws her head back against the pillow. "Oh, no. What does she want?"

Ginny frowns. "Wait—Julia as in Alex and Simon's sister?"

"Yeah," I say, still staring at the screen like I can will it into changing. "She said she wanted to get together to catch up, and I—I don't know—I told her I'd meet her later to get rid of her because Zach was on a tirade. She came to my work."

Rosie sits up straighter. "She's as bad as her brothers. Whatever she wants, stay the hell away."

"She could be doing an errand for Simon and Alex," Ginny offers, and the goose bumps rise on my arm. "Desperate people do dangerous things."

They're right. I know they're right. But the part of me still wants to understand her. Wants to get to the bottom of whatever twisted mess this is.

"I think it's a bad idea," Rosie says, voice firm. "Plus, the three of us are hanging tonight. You don't have time for her."

I nod slowly. "Okay."

Ginny starts reshuffling the cards, and I really look at Rosie for the first time since I came in.

Her face is thinner. Her skin dull. The shadows beneath her eyes are darker than usual. Even her hands, usually full of restless energy, sit still in her lap.

She's getting worse.

And there's nothing I can do.

Suddenly, all my problems feel smaller. I reach over and squeeze her hand.

The nurse pops her head in. "Ladies, it's time to wrap up.

We've got vitals checks and quiet hours."

Ginny stands and leans over to hug Rosie. "I'll swing by tomorrow, okay? Try not to hustle the night nurses at poker."

"No promises," Rosie says, managing a grin.

I hug her tightly, holding on. "Hang in there. Hurry up and get that new heart."

"I'm working on it," she whispers. "But you need to take care of yours too."

I swallow the lump in my throat and follow Ginny out.

Outside, the air is cool and smells faintly of wet pavement. Ginny throws my suitcase into the trunk of her car like it's nothing. We slide into the seats, and for a moment, neither of us says anything.

She starts the car, and we steer down the road that winds out of town, streetlights giving way to the darker countryside. I lean my head against the passenger window and let my eyes close.

"Thanks for this," I murmur.

"You don't have to thank me. Just don't hog the hot water, and remember, no eye contact with Eleanor."

A smile tugs at my lips.

As the lights of Paradise fade behind us and the quiet stretches, I feel a little better. This will be just like old times.

Twenty-five

Beckett

I've been driving aimlessly for hours — back roads, long loops around the lake, streets I haven't taken since high school. My hands are on the wheel, but my mind is still in the hallway outside Sadie's room, listening to the slam of her door. Her voice still echoes in my head, sharp and shaky. Accusing. Hurt.

I was an ass.

She was already on edge after the cops showed up again, and I still pushed. I kept thinking, if she just tells them everything she knows, maybe we can get ahead of whatever this is. If Alex and Simon are tangled up in something dangerous — and let's be honest, they always are — we need the truth.

But Sadie shut down. She's made it clear she just wants to be done with that chapter of her life, and I'm sure she's worried about getting in trouble or making herself a target. Avoidance is a coping mechanism for her. I know that. Yet I didn't make it safe for her to do anything else.

At some point, I end up on the gravel road that leads to Ryker's place. My tires crunch over stones, the trees overhead casting shadows in the glow of my headlights. It's just past eight when I pull up. The porch light is on.

He's outside, sitting on the steps with a beer in hand, hoodie sleeves pushed to his elbows. His dog, Moose, is sprawled out at his feet. Ryker watches me get out of the truck like he's been expecting me.

"Rough day?" he asks.

"How'd you guess?"

I hold up a six-pack, and he jerks his chin toward the cooler beside him. I crack one open, take a long drink, and drop into the seat next to him.

"Let me guess," he says. "You pushed too hard, said the wrong thing, and now you need to do damage control."

"Something like that."

Ryker doesn't respond. He just waits. That's his thing. Doesn't offer advice until you've choked on your own mistakes.

"The cops came by this morning. They wanted to ask Sadie about someone. Showed her a photo."

He nods slowly. "Jonas?"

"Yeah, Officer Goodwin. I feel like she recognized the guy, but she didn't say so. Said she wasn't sure. Then she went to work and came home stressed, but I still pushed her. I told her she was hiding something, accused her of lying."

Ryker raises an eyebrow.

"She blew up. Said I was trying to control her, that I was just like every other man who's let her down. Then she slammed herself into the guest room, and I went for a drive."

Ryker exhales through his nose. "Damn."

"I wasn't trying to control her," I say. "I just wanted to protect her."

"Didn't feel like that to her, though."

196

"I thought she'd want to be honest. Help get ahead of whatever mess Alex dragged her into."

Ryker takes a slow sip of beer. "You thought safety meant answers. But for her? Safety probably looks like silence. Like shutting the door and drowning it out with music."

I blink. "She told you that?"

"No," he says. "But I know the type. You don't survive something terrible without learning to stay quiet and stay out of the way."

I stare out at the lake, the surface glassy in the moonlight.

"She's been through hell," I murmur.

"And you made it worse."

The words hit hard, though they're not mean, just honest.

"I didn't mean to."

"I know," he says. "But meaning doesn't undo impact. You want to fix it, you need to own it. No excuses. No speeches. Just start by showing up different."

I nod. "I told her she was a mess. That I was the one who kept everything together."

Ryker whistles under his breath. "You're lucky she didn't hit you with a frying pan."

"Don't think she didn't consider it."

We sit in silence a while. Moose lets out a low groan and stretches. Crickets hum in the distance.

"I want to fix this," I say. "Not just the fight. All of it. I gotta be ready before I go back home."

"Then do the work." Ryker leans back on his elbows. "But don't do it for the version of her you want. Do it for the version that's scared and scarred and still figuring out who she is."

I sigh. Damn him for being so wise.

"I thought I'd stop by Carrie's," I say after a beat. "Pick up that ridiculous chocolate cake she likes."

"The one with the edible glitter?"

"Yeah. I was thinking I'd just come home with it. No pressure, just cake — and an apology if she's willing to hear it."

Ryker grunts. "Not the worst plan. Carrie's probably

won't be open until tomorrow, though."

"Fine. Whatever." I roll my eyes. "All I'm saying is she smiled when she ate that cake. Laughed, even. I want to see that again."

He lifts his beer in a toast. "Then go earn it."

I take another drink. Hope hums under my skin, quiet but insistent. I might've screwed up. But I'm not done. Not yet.

I stay a little longer, drinking the last of my beer, breathing the cool night air, letting the lake and the vines remind me that some things grow slowly and some things only bloom if you tend to them with care.

I know something's wrong the second I walk in.

The house is too quiet. Still. Not the peaceful kind of quiet that means Sadie's curled up on the couch with a book or making something in the kitchen. This is the kind of quiet that presses against my ribs. The kind that makes the hair on the back of my neck stand up.

"Sadie?" My voice echoes back at me. No answer.

I check my phone out of habit. No missed calls. No texts. She usually lets me know if she's headed out. Sometimes a note on the counter with a crooked smiley face or a quick *went to see Rosie*. But there's nothing. Not a single damn thing. Maybe she's still angry? Still hiding in her room?

My stomach knots. I walk down the hall, calling her name, hoping for a response I know won't come. The door to her room is cracked open now, and when I push it wide, my stomach drops like a stone.

The bed is stripped bare. The soft pink comforter she had with her? Gone. Her shoes? Her hairbrush on the dresser? Her lotion on the nightstand? Her tornado of clothes? All of it — gone.

It doesn't just look like she left. It looks like she erased herself.

Panic rises in my throat.

I pull my phone out and call Sadie's number. It rings once, then goes straight to voicemail.

"Sadie, please," I say into the receiver. "Just...tell me you're okay. I don't know where you are or why you left, but I need to know you're safe. Call me back. Please."

I don't hang up right away. Like holding on a second longer might somehow make her answer. It doesn't.

I hang up, heart pounding and mind racing. I hit Rosie's number. She might know something — anything. It rings twice before a nurse answers.

"Hi, Dr. Beckett. Um, Rosie's sleeping right now," she says. "Can I take a message?"

I clench my jaw. "Is Sadie Callahan there? Or did she stop by earlier?"

"I'm not sure. She's not here now, but I just came on shift."

"Right. Okay. Thanks."

I hang up and stare at the screen. My fingers hover for a second before I try Sadie again. And again. Same result. I shoot off a text.

Me: Where are you?
Me: You don't have to talk. Just tell me you're okay.
Me: Please.

All of them stay marked as delivered. None of them show read.

I sit on the edge of the stripped bed, elbows on my knees, phone clutched in my hand. I try to think clearly, but everything is swirling. I don't know her other friends. I don't even know where she'd go. She kept her world so tightly wound, and I was just starting to get past those walls.

God, I'm such an idiot.

Then it hits me. She has my Jeep. I put a tracker dot in the glove box because I'm always forgetting where I park at the hospital. I open the app on my phone and check. The dot pings. It's still in the garage. I exhale, shutting my eyes. She didn't take the Jeep. Leaving it behind? That means she's serious. She's really gone.

I should've handled everything differently. I shouldn't have snapped at her. I shouldn't have pushed so hard when she already looked like she was drowning.

I rake a hand through my hair and lean back, staring at the ceiling like it might drop answers. But all I can hear is silence and the sharp, suffocating beat of regret pulsing behind my ribs.

I don't know where she is.

I don't know what she's thinking.

And worst of all, I don't know if she's safe.

Eventually, I force myself to get up and move, but I don't know where I'm going. I end up in the kitchen, pacing in slow, tight circles like a caged animal.

I need to talk to someone, someone who knows Sadie, someone who might understand her better than I do.

I scroll through my contacts until I find Caleb. My thumb hovers over the button as I do the math of the time change between here and London. It's early in the morning there. He should be at work.

I press the button and it rings. Once. Twice. Then again.

"Mate! Look at this. Beckett Paradise actually remembered I exist," Caleb says when he answers, laughing. There's noise in the background—muffled chatter and a car horn. "Hold on, let me get into my office."

I wait, chewing the inside of my cheek until the noise fades.

"All right," he says after a moment. "What's up? You don't usually call this early unless something's on fire or you broke a bone. Wait, is Sadie okay?"

I hesitate, swallowing the lump forming in my throat. "Has she called you?"

He's quiet for a beat too long. "Today? No. Why?"

"She's gone, Caleb." The words come out raw. "I came

home and…she'd packed up everything. Her room's empty. She didn't leave a note. No call. Nothing."

I hear him exhale sharply. "Damn. Have you tried Rosie?"

"Yeah, but she's asleep. Nurse didn't know anything. And Sadie's not answering. I've called and texted. No response."

"Shit," Caleb mutters, all traces of humor gone now. "What happened?"

I rub my eyes, feeling it all crash back down. "The police came to ask about Alex and Simon this morning. She didn't tell them everything, and I knew it. Later, I pushed her on it. I said things I shouldn't have. She shut down. I got pissed. I left the house to cool off, and when I came back she was gone."

"You think she left because of that?"

"I don't know." My voice cracks on the last word. "I don't know anything right now."

"I'll call her," he says quietly. "She might answer if she sees it's me."

"I was hoping she'd told you where she was going."

"She hasn't said anything to me," Caleb replies. "But…she's done this before. When things get overwhelming, she runs. That's what she did after I went back to school. She packed a bag and left your parents' in the middle of the night. Took me two weeks to find her that time."

My grip tightens around the phone. "Do you think she'd go back to Alex?"

"I bloody well hope not." His voice hardens.

"I'll go by Alex's place and check." I exhale slowly. "It's getting late, but I might drive by. Just to see."

"Don't be stupid, Beck. If he's dangerous—"

"I won't do anything reckless," I say, lying through my teeth. "I just need to know she's not there. Or that she is."

"Text me the address. I'll keep track of you."

"Thanks," I say quietly. "And if she calls you…"

"You'll be the first to know." He pauses. "You care about her, don't you?"

I stare at the window, where her reflection should be,

curled up with a blanket and tea. "Yeah. I do."

"Then find her. And this time, don't let her walk away."

I nod even though he can't see me. "I'll try."

I hang up and immediately text Caleb, giving him the address, just in case. Then I grab my keys and head out the door, the silence of the house chasing me all the way to the car.

Twenty-six

Beckett

B y the time I make it across town, the sky is ink black and the night is thick with shadows. The roads are quiet, and every traffic light seems to blink red just long enough to drive me mad.

The Tremblays' auto shop sits at the edge of town, where the pavement starts to crack and streetlights flicker like they're giving up. I pull onto the gravel shoulder across the street and kill the engine. The garage is dark, closed for the night. Nothing but the distant hum of bugs dancing around the neon sign that reads *Tremblay's Auto & Lube*.

But it's not the garage I'm interested in. It's the house beside it—if you can call it that. I hate that this used to be Sadie's life, and that she tried to hide it from me. The idea of her being back here turns my stomach.

I grip the steering wheel until my knuckles pop. I shouldn't be here. I know that. It's late. I'm uninvited. And this guy — Alex — he's not exactly stable. But if there's even a chance Sadie's inside, I have to know.

I shoot off a text to Tarryn. She's much closer than Caleb is.

Me: If you don't hear from me, I'm at the house next to the Tremblays' garage. I'll text when I leave.

Then I get out of the car, gravel crunching under my boots. I climb the creaking porch steps and hesitate. The door is chipped and splintered. A small sticker on the window says *Beware of Dog*, but the only sound I hear is the tinny roar of a crowd from the TV inside.

It sounds like hockey. My brow furrows. Hockey? In July?

I shake it off and knock. Once. Twice. Nothing.

I raise my hand and pound harder.

After a few seconds, I hear something crash inside, then a muffled voice swearing. The door swings open violently, and Alex Tremblay stands in front of me, shirtless and disheveled, with a beer can in one hand and bloodshot eyes that don't quite focus.

His pupils are too wide. His lips twitch like he's trying to decide whether to laugh or lunge. He smells like alcohol, weed, and something more chemical, something sharp and toxic that clings to his skin.

"Well, look who it is," he slurs, leaning on the doorframe. "The doctor. Sadie's new little watchdog."

I steel myself. "Is she here?"

He squints. "Sadie? You think she'd be here?" He lets out a harsh, humorless laugh and takes a long drink. "Nah. I don't keep strays anymore."

My jaw tightens. "I'm not here to fight with you. I just want to know if she's safe."

He lowers the can, and his face twists. "If I knew where

she was, you think I'd be getting drunk watching reruns of the Stanley Cup?" He jerks his hand toward the flickering TV behind him. "She took off. Like she always does. Unstable bitch."

I ignore the insult. "You said she took something?"

His gaze snaps to mine, suddenly sharper. "That's none of your damn business."

I take a slow breath. "If you're threatening her—"

"I didn't say I'd do anything," he cuts in. "But if I see her again, she better be ready to pay me back."

"For what?"

He steps forward until he's in my space. "You deaf, doc? I said it's none of your business. What she did—what she took—that's between me and her."

I hold his stare. He doesn't blink.

My pulse hammers in my throat, but I refuse to back down. "She's not coming back, Alex. And if I find out you laid a hand on her, I'll make sure the police know everything. They're already looking into you and your brother."

His mouth twitches again—half snarl, half smirk. "Yeah? Well, tell the cops they better be faster than me."

I've heard enough.

I back away slowly, not turning around until I'm off the porch and halfway to my car. I get in, lock the doors, and sit in the dark, forcing myself to breathe through my fury.

She's not there. At least there's that.

My phone buzzes.

Tarryn: You alive? Or do I need to send the cavalry?

Me: Alive. On my way. Be there soon.

I toss the phone on the passenger seat, shift into gear, and peel away from the curb. Outside, the night feels pitch black—no moon, no stars, just endless dark.

And somewhere in all of it…Sadie's out there.

Alone?

Running?

By the time I pull up to Tarryn's place, I feel like I've been driving for hours, though it's only been twenty minutes. Her porch light comes on as I kill the engine. The front door opens before I even reach the steps.

Tarryn stands barefoot in joggers and one of Dad's old football sweaters, her arms crossed tightly. Her expression is sharp enough to cut glass.

"You look like hell," she says as I step into the glow of the porch light.

"Feel like it," I mutter, brushing past her and into the living room.

The scent of woodsmoke lingers in the air. The house is warm, and I suddenly feel like I can't breathe. I sink into the armchair across from her worn leather couch and rake a hand through my hair. "She's gone," I announce.

She doesn't ask who. She doesn't need to.

Instead, she walks over to the kitchen, pulls two waters from the fridge, and cracks them both open before handing me one. I take it but don't drink.

"What happened?" she asks, folding one leg underneath her on the couch.

I stare at the floor. "We got in a fight, and I left. When I got home, she was gone. She'd packed up all her stuff and cleared out."

Tarryn doesn't speak, letting the silence fill the space until I force myself to go on.

"Everything was gone. I can't get a hold of her, so I called Caleb, and then I went by Alex's place."

"You think she went back to him?" she asks.

"No, but I wanted to be sure." I glance up at her. "She didn't seem to be there. He's drunk. Maybe high. Said she took something, and she's going to pay for it. But he wouldn't tell me what."

Tarryn's lips press into a thin line. "He's a coward. All the Tremblays are. And he knows how to manipulate her."

I nod. "I think she had a bad day at work. She was stressed when she came home, even before we argued."

She sets her water down and walks over to her desk. "Let's check the vineyard footage."

She powers up the screen and keys in a password. I get up and move behind her, leaning over her shoulder as she opens the security camera feed from today.

"Tell me what time she left for work?"

"Around ten," I say. "I remember she was heading in a little later because she wanted to drop something off for Rosie first."

Tarryn scrubs through the footage, fast-forwarding at 4x speed, her eyes moving from camera to camera — tasting room, front entrance, back office.

We watch Sadie bustle through the space. She moves fast, always two steps ahead, hair tied up, apron on. She's graceful in the way people are when they've done something a thousand times. Efficient. Capable.

"She's good," Tarryn murmurs. "Like, really good."

"She never stops," I say. "I think that's part of it. She doesn't know how to sit still."

Tarryn fast-forwards again, muttering, "Where the hell is Zach?" He wanders in and out but never seems to be working.

Ten minutes later, we get the answer to Sadie's bad day. At 12:43, the front door of the tasting room swings open and someone walks in. Sadie's body language shifts, her spine goes rigid, and her hand tightens around the glass she's holding.

"Wait." Tarryn slows the feed, rewinding until the figure comes into view.

"Oh, hell no," she breathes. "That's Julia Tremblay."

My stomach drops.

They watch each other, eventually talking a little as Julia gets a glass of wine.

We follow them on the hallway feed as Julia trails Sadie into the back office.

"There's no audio," I mutter.

"Doesn't matter," Tarryn says. "Look at Sadie's body language. She's not scared, not exactly. But she's holding herself like she's bracing for impact."

The footage shows them talking—Sadie standing stiff by the desk, Julia gesturing with a calm deliberateness that makes my skin crawl. Whatever she's saying, Sadie doesn't argue. She listens. Then, finally, she nods. Then Zach appears and points to the tasting room.

Moments later, Julia leaves.

Sadie exhales and disappears into the hallway.

"Sadie worked her ass off," Tarryn says. "Zach didn't lift a finger, except to find her when she took a break. Why am I paying him to do nothing?"

We fast-forward a little more. Tarryn swears under her breath as she watches Zach scroll on his phone while customers wait to be served.

"He left her alone to do everything," she mutters. "Typical."

I can barely focus on Zach. My mind's still stuck on Julia.

"Could Sadie have gone with her?"

"I don't think so. She left long before Sadie's shift was over," Tarryn says, clicking to the back parking lot camera. "But if Julia's involved, Sadie's in deeper than she let on."

"I shouldn't have left," I whisper.

"You didn't know," Tarryn says. "You couldn't have. Couples fight."

But that doesn't make the ache any less. I rise from the chair, my limbs heavy. "Thanks for looking."

"Where are you going?" she asks.

"To find her," I say.

I won't stop until I do.

Twenty-seven

Sadie

I wake with a start, my neck screaming from the awkward angle I must've slept in. The couch cushion is a crater under me, my legs dangling off the side. I blink into the soft morning light spilling through the curtains, dust motes dancing like slow sparks in the air.

For a second, I can't remember where I am.

Then it all rushes back—Beckett's face twisted with frustration, the hard edge in his voice, the way I stormed out without looking back. I pull the blanket tighter around me, even though it's warm in the room.

The quilt smells like lavender and something older, familiar. Like childhood summers or a forgotten book left open in the sun. It's comforting in a way that makes me want to cry.

"Hey," Ginny says, her voice floating from the hallway.

I lift my head as she walks in, her messy ponytail bobbing and her hands full — coffee for her, water for me. She's already dressed in jeans and a long-sleeve tee, the picture of someone who has her life together. I probably look like roadkill.

"How are you doing this morning?" she asks.

"Stiff," I mutter, trying to sit up. My spine cracks in protest. "And maybe a little embarrassed."

Ginny gives me a crooked smile and hands me the glass of water. "You were out cold last night. You looked like you needed sleep. I promise, I'll get the boxes off the bed so you can have that room."

"Thanks." I take a sip and glance around. Her place is small but cozy — plants in every window, books stacked in mismatched piles on the floor, and a worn armchair with a hand-knit throw.

I reach for my phone on the coffee table, but it's off. Dead. Just like I feel inside.

I find the charger and plug it into the wall socket. I wait for the screen to light up, dread already curling in my gut. I don't know what I'm expecting. Maybe nothing. Maybe everything.

"I've got to get in the shower and head out soon," Ginny says, tying her hair into a tighter knot. "But there's cereal, yogurt, and that really good French press coffee you like if you need it."

"Thanks," I murmur. I'm grateful — truly — but there's a numbness sitting beneath my skin, and I'm not sure how to break through it.

She watches me for a second longer, like she wants to say something else, but then she just nods and disappears back into the bedroom.

Alone again, I stare at the black screen of my phone, bracing myself for whatever's waiting when it finally powers on. After a moment it comes to life with a soft buzz, and the screen glows to full brightness. It's barely on when it starts ringing.

Zach.

My stomach drops. I look at the time.

Shit.

I'm twenty minutes late for my shift at the tasting room. I fumble with the screen and press answer, my voice tumbling out before he can say a word.

"Zach, I'm so sorry. My phone died, and I didn't hear my alarm. I'm on my way now."

There's a pause on the other end, and for a second I think he's going to let it go. That he'll say it's fine, he understands.

But he doesn't.

"Don't bother," he says flatly. "You're fired."

I sit up straighter. "Wait, what?"

"I need people I can depend on, Sadie. Not people who vanish and roll in late with excuses. It's unprofessional. I don't care what happened."

"You don't care —?" I press a hand to my forehead. "Zach, I've covered every weekend, every holiday. I worked a double shift when you bailed for your friend's bachelor party —"

"I'm not doing this," he cuts in. "You're done."

The line goes dead before I can say another word.

I lower the phone slowly. Fired. Just like that.

By him.

I've picked up after him, handled customers he ignored, stayed late to clean his messes, and he fires me? The guy spends more time scrolling on his phone than stocking shelves.

Rage sparks first — bright and fast. But it fades just as quickly, replaced by something heavier. Something like defeat.

I clutch the phone and lean back into the couch, blinking hard.

I walked out on Beckett last night. Didn't even wait for him to come home. I left him, and now, I've lost the one steady thing I had left. My job. My routine. The tiny slice of accomplishment that made me feel like I wasn't still hiding from everything I used to be.

I breathe in through my nose, slow and shaky.

Of course Zach wouldn't give me grace. Of course I'd screw this up too.

This is what I do — crack under pressure, run when it

matters, break things I try to build.

I close my eyes and let the silence swallow me for a moment, afraid of what I might find next when I open my messages.

The phone buzzes in my hand again.

Not a call this time. Just the flood of missed notifications finally syncing. And there it is — Beckett's name.

Over and over and over again.

Missed calls. Voicemails. Texts. One after another, a relentless stream of trying to reach me.

My throat tightens, and I draw my knees up, curling into the corner of the couch. I scroll without reading, just staring at the blur of his name on my screen. I could tap one. Just one. Hear his voice. Let myself feel something other than this hollow ache behind my ribs.

But I don't.

I can't.

If I listen to him, if I read what he said, I'll break. I'll want to go back. And going back means facing what I did. What I always do.

I run.

I didn't just leave his house. I left him. Nothing he said to me I didn't already know about myself. But I bolted with no explanation or warning. Just disappeared. And now, he's probably pacing around somewhere, hating himself, wondering what he did wrong.

But it wasn't him.

It's me. Always me.

I stare at the most recent message, time-stamped just a few minutes ago.

Beckett: Please, just let me know you're safe.

My thumb hovers over it. The screen starts to blur.

One quick tap and I could read them all. Instead, I press down until the little menu appears.

Delete All.

The screen goes blank. I hate myself a little more for it.

A new notification slides into place. Caleb. Of course.

He's probably talked to Beckett. I already know what it says. I don't even need to open it. It'll be something like, *Running doesn't fix things*, or *You owe him an explanation*, or *At least tell me where you are*. I suppose I don't want him to worry.

But I know if I call him, he'll scold me, like he used to do when I was alone and skipped school to avoid bad days. Though maybe then he'd tell Beckett I'm okay.

I tap into the message thread, but not on the new message. I scroll up through the old ones — memes, check-ins, that time he sent a video of a fox digging through a trash bin and said, *"Look, it's you at three a.m. in my kitchen."*

My heart twists. I miss him. Finally, I send a message.

Me: I left Beckett's and I'm staying with Ginny. I'll catch up with you later when I'm not so tired.

There. Hopefully that will take care of everything. I don't know how long I sit there, staring at nothing. Maybe five minutes. Maybe twenty. My eyes are gritty and dry, like I've already cried without realizing it.

Then I hear the soft shuffle of slippers on hardwood.

Ginny reappears, holding a mug in her hands. It's dark blue, chipped at the rim. One of her favorites. The scent of coffee cuts through the air — warm, nutty, comforting. She doesn't say anything as she sets it on the table beside me.

I glance up, and she offers a small, lopsided smile. "Brought you the good stuff," she says. "French roast with a splash of cream. I didn't make it weird this time."

"Thanks." My voice is hoarse, barely audible.

She sits on the edge of the armchair across from me and reaches into her hoodie pocket. "Also," she says, holding something out between two fingers, "this is yours now."

It's a key.

Simple brass. Smooth and cold in my palm when I take it.

"You can stay as long as you want," she says. "No expectations. No clock ticking. Just…rest, if that's what you need. I promise I'll get the boxes out of the guest room."

I nod, but my throat is too tight to say anything.

Ginny stands again, grabbing her travel mug from the counter. "I've got to head out. Inventory and prep for a tour this afternoon. But the place is yours. Eat something. Shower. Or just be. Whatever you need."

She walks toward the door, pausing with her hand on the knob. Then she looks back over her shoulder. "You're not alone, Sadie. Just in case you forgot."

The door closes behind her.

I stare at the key in my hand for a long time, the warmth from the coffee mug seeping into my skin. There's a knot in my chest that won't untangle, but maybe it's okay to sit still. Maybe I don't have to fix everything all at once.

I exhale, long and slow, and finally take a sip of coffee. There's a peace here that feels foreign. Like I'm borrowing someone else's life for a little while.

I'm not okay. Not even close. But for once, I'm not spiraling.

I don't need to have all the answers right now. I don't even need to make a big plan. I'll just do the next right thing.

And that means showing up for someone who matters to me.

I slide my phone into my pocket and force myself up from the couch. The blanket falls away, and the hardwood is cool under my bare feet. I stretch, working the stiffness out of my muscles. My body aches, but it's nothing compared to the heaviness I've been carrying around inside.

I head into the bathroom and splash cold water on my face. My reflection in the mirror is a mess — sleep-mussed hair, red-rimmed eyes, yesterday's mascara smudged beneath them. I barely recognize myself.

But I take a breath and nod at the stranger in the glass.

"I'm still here," I whisper. "That's something."

After I change into clean clothes, I write a note for Ginny on the back of an old receipt I find on the counter.

Thank you. For the key. For the quiet. For everything. I'll be back later.

I grab my bag, confirm my phone is in my pocket, and reach for the key, and head out the door.

Since I'm not going to work, today I'll hang with Rosie. I need the reminder that there are still good things in my life, good people who matter. And after that, I'll start looking for a job.

I don't know where I'll end up.

But I'm not running anymore.

Twenty-eight

Beckett

I didn't sleep last night. Not a damn minute.

When I left Tarryn's, I drove around looking until I couldn't keep my eyes open, but then I laid in bed, staring at the ceiling. When it was a reasonable hour, I reached out to Sadie again, asking if she could let me know she was safe.

Nothing in return.

But she has to come into work. She loves the job. Loves the people. Tarryn said she was on the schedule today, and that's enough to keep me upright. I'll go down to the tasting room and talk to her. I'll apologize. I'll grovel if I have to.

When the kettle screams, I shut it off and don't bother making the tea. I'm too wired. I throw on jeans, a T-shirt, and a hoodie, not caring that I look like hell. No shave. No shower. No appetite. Just this restless, hollow pain that only eases when I imagine seeing her again.

I'm halfway out the door when I double back and grab my keys off the counter.

I'm going to fix this.

Or at least try.

When I reach the vineyard, I park haphazardly, crooked across two spots, and jog to the entrance. I need to tell her I'm sorry and that I was out of line. That I didn't mean to make her feel small or questioned. That the way I came at her wasn't about her at all. It was about my own fear. About losing control. About failing her.

The bell above the door gives a lazy jingle as I enter. Inside, the place looks warm and ready for the day — glasses lined up on the bar, menus laid out, fresh-cut wildflowers on the hostess stand. But she's not here.

Zach is behind the bar, polishing glasses like he's actually doing something useful this morning. He looks up, eyebrows arching.

"Morning," I say tightly. "Is Sadie here?"

Zach snorts. "She quit."

I blink. "What?"

He shrugs, setting the glass down a little too hard. "Told me she was done. Walked out yesterday after her shift."

No. No way. "She quit?"

He leans on the bar, smug as hell. "Yep. Guess doing a half-ass job doesn't bring in enough tips, so working loses its charm."

I narrow my eyes. "You're the manager. You're supposed to help, not sit on your ass while she runs the floor."

He shrugs again. "Not my fault if she can't handle the job. Now, I'm going to hire a real sommelier. None of this amateur shit Tarryn foisted on me."

The muscles in my jaw clench so tight I might crack a molar. I don't have time for his power plays or his lazy-ass attitude. *What the hell happened here?* "She loved this job," I say, mostly to myself. "She wouldn't just walk away."

Zach wipes an invisible smear from the counter, feigning innocence. "Guess she didn't love it that much."

I take one last look around. In my bones, I don't believe she'd walk away from a job she loves because of me.

Unless she did.

I turn on my heel and walk out, the bell jangling behind me. My pulse hammers in my ears. Zach might have pushed her, but I'm the one who broke her trust.

I should've been the one to protect her.

I head straight to the vineyard offices. I find Tarryn behind her desk, one hand holding her cell to her ear while the other scrolls through a spreadsheet on her laptop. Her glasses are pushed up into her hair, and a legal pad sits on her lap, already half full. I knock lightly on the doorframe.

She waves me in and mutes her phone. "You still look like hell."

"Didn't sleep," I mutter, sinking into the chair across from her. "Busy morning?"

She exhales, switching to speaker and setting her phone down. "BC Liquor's trying to push up their fall release orders. I've got a call with our growers this afternoon, trying to nail down grape yields. Meeting with an equipment rep in an hour. Oh, and I'm reviewing Sadie's VIP Buyers proposal."

That gets my attention. "Sadie's what?"

She grabs a folder from her desk and slides it open. "She's been working on this quietly for a couple weeks. It's genius. She wants to create an exclusive tier for our highest-spending customers. Kind of a hybrid between a wine club and a luxury loyalty program."

Tarryn flips to the next page and reads, "Guaranteed access to limited and library wines. First look at unreleased vintages. Private barrel tastings. Concierge service for cellaring and shipping. Invitations to vineyard brunches and dinners with the family. Even custom labels and bottle storage onsite."

I sit back, eyebrows rising. "That is brilliant."

"I know." She chuckles and shakes her head. "I'm pissed I didn't think of it myself."

"What'd she want to call it?"

"She had a few names jotted down. Barrel Society. The Reserve List. Founder's Circle. Paradise Elite." Tarryn glances up at me. "She gets it, Beckett. The experience. The brand. She understands what people want before they even know they want it."

I rub a hand across my jaw, everything inside me tightening. I had no idea she was working on something like this. All over again, my gut tells me she didn't just quit.

"She's just as sharp as Caleb," I murmur.

Tarryn's lips twitch. "Maybe sharper."

I nod slowly.

She was building something here.

And now she's gone.

"I need to tell you something," I say, voice low.

Tarryn looks up from the proposal, her expression shifting from impressed to wary. "What is it?"

"She didn't just quit." I pause. "I'm sure Zach did something."

Her eyes widen. "Wait, what?"

"Zach didn't tell you? I came here to talk to her this morning, and he said she quit."

Tarryn leans back in her chair, crossing her arms. "Why would she quit?" She shakes her head. "We know why she quit. He's going to be sorry. Now, he's got to work."

"He seems to think a sommelier is what we need."

Tarryn's mouth presses into a tight line. "At a huge cost. I was thinking I'd send Sadie to get her certificate. I think she'd do well enough to become a master sommelier. So you didn't make any progress finding her? I need to talk to her."

"No." I pause. "I can't find her. Like I said, I came here to try to catch her at work."

Tarryn swears — loud and unfiltered — then scrubs a hand down her face. "Damn it, Beckett. I was just reviewing footage again from the tasting room yesterday. Do you know what I saw?"

I shake my head.

"After the incident with Julia and Zach, she ran eight tastings. *Eight*. Overlapping. And the dishwasher was down, so she was hand-rinsing glassware and hauling racks down to the restaurant. And Zach? He stood around like a lump, doing nothing but checking his phone and criticizing her timing."

The fury in her voice rises with each word. "I want to move Zach and give Sadie full control over customer experience," she continues. "She's ready for it — or she was. Hell, she was already doing the job without the title. She's creative, organized, and the guests love her."

Urgency rushes through me. "We need to find her."

"No shit," she snaps. "I'm sorry. I don't have time for this, and I'm not blaming you. That bullseye belongs right on Zach."

I don't argue. She's right.

"I don't care what drama's going on between you two, but I know Sadie," she says, more quietly now. "She wouldn't have left this job. Not unless Zach pushed her. Or something else made her feel like she didn't belong."

I stare at the grain of the desk between us. "I think I did that."

Tarryn doesn't speak for a moment. "You might have helped. But if Zach shoved her out, I'll take care of it. You handle your part."

I nod once, swallowing hard.

"She's not the type to leave something she loves," she adds. "But she is the type to walk away if she thinks she's not wanted."

That stabs me right in the heart.

I step out of Tarryn's office, the heavy wooden door closing behind me. The hallway feels cold. I walk past the framed photos on the wall — snapshots of harvests, winemaker dinners, staff toasts over barrels. Sadie would've belonged here. She did belong here.

And I set her up to be pushed out. My phone buzzes with a text.

Caleb: Heard from Sadie. She said she's staying with Ginny? Can that be right? I'll be up for a while if you want to discuss.

Okay, so she's safe, I suppose. But she doesn't want to talk to me. Outside, I lean against the railing on the porch. Rows of vines stretch out across the hill, neat and ordered, yet I feel anything but.

I keep going back to the look on Sadie's face. She'd been exhausted, cornered, and I just pushed her harder. Instead of offering comfort, I cut her off at the knees.

Because I was scared.

Not of her. Not of what she might have said or done. But scared that if I let myself believe in her, really trust her, and I was wrong…I'd lose everything.

And now I've lost her anyway.

I look down at my phone, thumb hovering. I need to talk to her, not Caleb. But there's no point in calling. She won't answer. And as much as I want to, I'm not going to ask Rosemary about this again. It's not professional. I can't risk making her uncomfortable. I've already crossed a line I told myself I wouldn't as her doctor.

I scroll. Past Caleb. Past work contacts. Then I pause on Ginny's name.

Sadie mentioned reconnecting with her recently, so staying with her makes sense. They lived together once before. I tap to message before I can second-guess it.

Me: Hey, it's Beckett Paradise. Do you know how to reach Sadie? I need to find her. Please.

I stare at the screen for a few seconds before sliding the phone back into my pocket. My hand runs down my face. I need a plan. I need to fix this.

And if I can't?

I at least need to tell her she mattered. That she was right to want more. That she didn't imagine the way I looked at her. The way I felt when she walked into a room. That it meant something. All of it did. And I hope it still does.

Twenty-nine

Sadie

The hospital room is quiet except for the soft hum of machines and the occasional beep of Rosie's monitor. Morning sunlight filters through the blinds, casting narrow strips of gold across her blanket. She's pale today. Not just tired but washed out, like someone drained the color from her skin overnight. The kind of pale that constricts around my heart.

I try not to react. If she sees fear on my face, she'll make a joke to brush it away, and I'll pretend I'm not scared. We've been doing that dance for days now.

We're playing checkers, or at least pretending to. Her fingers tremble when she moves a red piece. It takes her two tries to settle it on the square, and I act like I don't notice. I let her take one of mine, even though I could've jumped her a move earlier.

She looks up at me and smirks, weak but knowing. "Don't go easy on me just because I look like death."

My stomach clenches, but I play along. "You don't look like death. Maybe like you need a nap and a mimosa."

She chuckles. "Maybe two. And pancakes. God, I miss pancakes."

The room smells like antiseptic and overripe lilies from a wilting bouquet in the corner. I hate how flowers always smell like grief in hospitals.

I move my piece, though I've lost track of who's winning. I'm not really here for the game.

"I didn't tell you this last night..." I pick at a loose thread on my jeans. "The police came by to ask about Alex yesterday, and apparently I have a tell. When we talked about it later, Beckett said he knew I hadn't told them everything. He said I wasn't being honest, implied that I was still protecting Alex." I look up. "But I'm not. I just— I'm trying to get away from that situation. I don't want to start talking to the police and inadvertently involve myself more. And if Alex were to trace the information back to me? That could be dangerous." I sigh. "Anyway, Beckett doesn't seem to understand that at all. I don't think he trusts me."

Rosie nods slowly, like she understands something even I haven't figured out yet. "And so you left."

I nod. "I left because I realized he's like every man in my life. Tthey all want to control me."

The silence stretches between us, not quite comfortable this time. "I turned off my phone to clear my head, and so my alarm didn't go off. And Zach fired me for not showing up at my shift. I would have been less than an hour late, and we don't usually have customers until closer to noon, so I stock shelves. It's not like I couldn't have made up the time. Plus, yesterday the dishwasher went out and my calves hurt from climbing the back stairs to get our tasting glasses cleaned."

Her brows pull together. "Zach? That weasel. He's always been jealous of you. You worked hard and were much better at the job than he ever was. He only has a job there because his last name is Paradise."

That stings. Not because it's untrue, but because I didn't see it. I blink. "What?"

"You're good at that job, Sadie. People love you. You made that place better. I could tell by the way you talked about it. He couldn't stand it. He was just waiting for an excuse."

Something warm and bright unfurls inside me. I didn't think I wanted validation, but apparently, I did. Desperately. "And now," I say, my voice hitching, "I'm couch-surfing, unemployed, and single. So yeah, kind of a banner week."

Rosie shifts slowly and reaches across the board, her hand finding mine. Her fingers are cold, paper-thin. "Sadie, you deserve someone who shows up for you. Not someone who disappears when things get hard. And definitely not someone who makes you feel invisible."

She doesn't say Alex's name, but I hear it anyway. I always do.

"You think Beckett would've stuck around?" I whisper.

"I think he was trying," she says. "I think you didn't let him."

I look down at our hands. Hers seems so small next to mine. "I didn't mean to push him away. I just didn't want him to see how messed up things were. How messed up I am."

"You're not messed up," she says. "You're human. And scared. But you've got a good heart, Sadie. Don't waste it being scared."

I pull in a sharp breath. I want to argue. I want to say she's wrong. But I can't.

Rosie's face softens. "You're not allowed to talk yourself out of love because you're scared. Especially not the kind that really sees you."

My eyes sting. I look back at the checkerboard, but all I see is her — fragile, kind, fading.

"I hate that you're in here," I whisper. "I hate that I get to walk away from everything and you're stuck waiting for a heart."

Her smile is faint now, slow and sleepy. "We all wait for something, Sadie. Doesn't mean yours hurts less." She reaches for her cup of water, and her hand shakes. "We've talked about this before, but your parents loved you. Caleb loves you in his long-distance way. You deserve to love and be loved. Don't ever forget that."

Her voice drifts on the last words, and her eyes slip closed for a moment too long.

"Rosie?" I ask gently.

She opens her eyes with effort. "Sorry. Just tired."

"Maybe we should stop the game."

She nods.

The light outside has shifted, shadows stretching across the floor like they're reaching in. I sit there a moment longer, afraid to move. Afraid that if I do, I'll break whatever thread is still holding her here.

She squeezes my hand. Barely. But I feel it.

"You'll be okay," she says, eyes barely open. "Promise me you'll be okay."

I lean over, brushing her hair off her forehead with shaking fingers. "I'll be back tomorrow," I whisper. "Promise."

She exhales, soft and long. "Okay." She slips her lucky bracelet off her wrist. "Try to talk to Tarryn or someone else besides Zach at the winery. And you need to borrow this to bring you luck."

I hold up my hands. "You promised to wear this until you got a new heart."

"Sure. But you need a job *now*. Take it and go kick butt and bring it back to me."

It's not worth arguing with her. I take the bracelet and slip it on my wrist before I kiss her forehead. Her skin is cool. Fragile.

I stand, and I don't look back as I leave.

Because if I do, I won't be able to walk away.

I wish I could give her my heart. I would do anything to save her. I look up to a God I'm not sure is there and beg him to find her a heart. She is a beautiful person, inside and out, and she deserves to live somewhere outside of this stupid hospital.

Instead of dwelling on this, I'm going to find a job today. I don't know what happened at the tasting room, but I was good at the job there, and I see signs all the time about wineries looking to hire someone.

The air is warm and dusty by the time the rideshare drops me at the second winery parking lot, and I already know how this is going to go.

It's late afternoon, the sun hazy behind a veil of clouds, and everything around me smells like dry earth and distant fermenting grapes.

Fake it till you make it, right?

The Two Sisters tasting room is sleek and bright, with clean white counters and shiny rows of bottles lined up like soldiers. A curated playlist hums in the background, some soft acoustic set meant to make you sip slower and spend more. The woman behind the bar glances up from arranging a tray of polished glasses. Her expression is polite. Detached.

"Hi there," she says. "Looking to do a tasting?"

"Actually," I say, squaring my shoulders, "I'm interested in employment. I used to work at the tasting room at Paradise Hill. I've run large events, wine club logistics, private tastings. You name it."

She tilts her head, her smile tightening. "Do you have your sommelier certification?"

"No," I admit, trying to keep my voice light. "But I know my varietals, and I'm great with guests. I'd be happy to train into a more formal role."

She looks away—just for a second—but I can tell I've

already lost her.

"We're currently only hiring certified sommeliers, I'm afraid," she says. "But I can keep your information on file."

Of course. I hand her my resume anyway and thank her, though I know it'll go straight into the recycling bin the moment I leave. I call another rideshare, and it's the same driver when it arrives. She asks where to next. I explain, and she offers to wait for me at each vineyard. I'm so grateful.

I hit two more wineries. One manager greets me with a smile that fades the moment I say the word *employment.* The other lets me leave a resume, but her eyes skim over me like I'm invisible. I can practically hear her thinking, *Why are you bothering?*

At the last stop, a boutique winery off a gravel road lined with lavender, I get as far as the entry before a man in a golf shirt with a Bluetooth in his ear intercepts me.

"We're not hiring right now," he says without preamble, like he's done this a hundred times.

"I just wanted to leave my information," I say, holding out my resume.

He takes it reluctantly. His gaze narrows. "Wait…are you the girl who used to date one of the Paradise brothers?"

I blink, stunned. "Excuse me?"

He grins like we're sharing a joke. "I think I saw you in the paper at that big fundraiser. You were with what's his name? Beckett?"

It hits like a punch to the stomach. Not just the assumption, but the erasure of everything else I am. In his mind, I'm not a professional, not a manager, not even a decent candidate. Just some girl who used to date a Paradise.

I laugh it off, even though it stings. What else can I do? And I leave before I punch him.

Thirty

Sadie

By the time my faithful rideshare is driving me back toward Ginny's, the sun is low in the sky, casting long shadows across the fields. I did what I could. I showed up. I smiled. I tried.

And yet all I feel is defeat.

I miss the rhythm of Paradise Hill. I miss knowing the vintage before the cork even pops, knowing which couples will ask for the rosé flight and which want the reserve reds. I miss the way it felt to walk into work with purpose, like I belonged somewhere.

Now, I'm just floating.

And trying not to sink.

Ginny's place is quiet when I let myself in. The air smells like dust and whatever coffee she left in the French press for me this morning. It's cold and bitter now.

The couch looks smaller tonight. Or maybe I just feel bigger, heavier, like I'm carrying the weight of every decision I've made in the last forty-eight hours. I toss my purse on the coffee table and toe off my shoes, flexing my sore feet against the cool floor.

It's strange, the way something that felt like a safe haven yesterday can already feel cramped. I can't stretch out without knocking into something. There's no door to close, no corner to claim as mine. Just borrowed space. It's better than sleeping on the street, of course. And I'm not going to put any pressure on Ginny to clean out her guest room. A quick check tells me she hasn't yet.

I sit down with a sigh and reach for my bag, unzipping it slowly, not really sure what I'm doing. I tell myself I'm reorganizing, but really, I just want to feel in control of something. Anything.

I pull out a crumpled hoodie, a pair of jeans, a book I haven't touched since I moved out of Alex's, and then, there they are.

Alex's jeans. I didn't mean to pick them up when I left his place. I just scooped up everything in the room. Now, they're wadded and shoved in the bottom of my suitcase.

I hold them up by the waistband, the denim stiff from being worn and not washed. *What makes these so important?*

I sigh and decide to wash them, if only to get them out of my bag and out of my life. As I check the pockets — mostly out of habit — my fingers brush something hard, small, and plastic.

I pull it out slowly, like I'm unearthing a bug I don't want to touch.

A jump drive.

Unlabeled. Basic. The kind you buy in a three-pack at an office supply store.

What the hell, Alex?

I hold it between my fingers. It could be nothing. Or it could be the reason he and Simon have threatened me and accused me of taking something. Of stealing.

I set it on the coffee table like it's radioactive and go back to the laundry pile, trying to ignore it. But my eyes are drawn to it again and again, like it's whispering my name.

Eventually, I gather up the clothes and take them down the hall to the washer and dryer. The machine groans to life as I start the first load.

When I return, the jump drive still sits where I left it. I sit on the edge of the couch, staring at it.

It's ridiculous, really, how something so small can hold so much weight. It doesn't look like trouble. It looks like a school project or a forgotten set of family photos. Harmless. Nothing of consequence. Maybe it's his porn stash. I caught him more than once beating off to two guys with a girl. He always told me it was my fault. *Whatever.* I know better now.

But something about the drive feels wrong because Alex doesn't have a computer. After his laptop got stolen, he used his phone, and if he needed a desktop, they had one at the shop.

I reach for it, then pull my hand back.

Alex has been obsessed with something he lost. I'm guessing this is it.

And he wants it back badly.

I glance at my laptop.

I shouldn't look.

I tell myself that once, then again. But my curiosity is relentless, and ignoring the drive now feels more dangerous than knowing what's on it.

I set my laptop on the coffee table. The screen lights up when I open it, and I plug in the drive with slow, cautious fingers, half expecting sparks to fly.

It asks for a password. Alex uses the same password for everything. I type Password1234*, and it opens up. *What a moron.*

There is one folder with a single spreadsheet file titled *results_78-21.*

I hesitate.

What am I doing?

I click.

The spreadsheet opens, the cursor blinking in the first cell. Rows of data stretch out across the screen, dozens, maybe hundreds of entries.

At first, it's just a mess of code names, dates, dollar amounts, and strings of numbers that mean nothing to me.

Blinky | SF -3.5 | $200 | $190

TP | O 223.5 | $50

Vet | U 223.5 | $200

I frown as I scroll down. The names repeat—some regularly, some only once or twice. A few columns are highlighted in yellow. Others are bolded like someone was tracking patterns.

None of it makes sense. Is it a budget? A weird file from the shop?

I'm still puzzling when I hear the front door open.

"Sadie? You here?"

I tear my eyes away in time to smile at Ginny as she enters.

"Guess who texted me today?"

I take a wild guess. "God?"

She laughs. "Not so much."

"Beckett?"

She nods and walks her phone over. I read the message.

Beckett: Hey, it's Beckett Paradise. Do you know how to reach Sadie? I need to find her. Please.

I hand her back her phone.

"You okay?" she asks, setting her bag down on the kitchen counter.

"You didn't respond."

"I didn't know if you wanted him to know you're here."

"Zach fired me for being late. I'm sure Beckett wanted to tell me he recommended he move me along."

She makes a face. "You think he's so petty he asked for that?"

I shrug. I didn't think so, but it happened.

"That doesn't seem right, but I'll say whatever you tell me," Ginny says. "I can tell him to fuck off. Or come over and get you right now. Or I can just ignore it."

I look up. "You can tell him I'm at your place for now and I'm fine."

"That's it?"

I nod. "Thanks. And listen, I found something."

She raises a brow. "Define something."

I tap the jump drive where it's currently attached to my laptop. "This was in Alex's jeans. I think he thinks I stole it when I left."

Her face tightens. "And you're looking at it?"

"Yep," I admit. "Maybe I shouldn't. But after everything — and the way he's been acting — I just…I had to."

She doesn't scold me or offer an opinion. She just leans closer and gestures to the laptop. "What did you find?"

"I'm not sure."

I tilt the screen toward her. Ginny squints as she reads.

Blinky | SF -3.5 | $200 | $190

TP | O 223.5 | $50

Vet | U 223.5 | $200

"What am I looking at?"

"I don't know. It's all in some kind of code."

She looks at it. "There are over two thousand lines. I can't figure it out either." She holds up a bottle of cabernet. "I brought a bottle from the vineyard."

"Oh, that looks great."

Ginny opens the bottle and pours two generous glasses.

She returns to the couch, and we swap stories of our day. I tell her I'm worried about Rosie. She admits she is too. She says she stopped by this afternoon to see her and just missed Beckett doing his rounds.

"What did he tell her?"

Ginny shrugs. "Not much. Just that he'd like to see her increase her food intake. He's giving her fluids by IV."

"Did she tell him I'd been by earlier?"

She shakes her head. "He didn't ask, and as far as I know, she kept your secret."

I take a sip of my wine. *Caleb must have told him. That's good.* "I left resumes at several winery tasting rooms today. Everyone seems to want a certified sommelier."

"They're foolish to not want you."

"Thank you."

Ginny looks back at my computer screen.

I highlight a line in the spread sheet and copy it into a search engine. SF -3.5. O 223.5. U 223.5.

The results first give me something about kidney disease, but that doesn't seem a likely fit. Then I see the next line. The NFL Betting Pros website.

Maybe it's some kind of fantasy sports thing?

I open the website and see the team abbreviations — LAL, BOS, PHI — and something clicks.

Wait.

Lines.

Odds.

These aren't random numbers. They're bets. Big bets. Lots of them.

My breath catches.

I scroll faster now, the pattern revealing itself with each new row. The names are probably code for bettors. The numbers — wagers, spreads, over/under totals. It's all here. Names, amounts, odds, payouts. Organized. Tracked. Updated.

"That asshole. He left his gambling operation on a jump drive on the floor of our bedroom."

Ginny stares at the numbers. "Yes. It makes sense now."

But then my stomach sinks. Alex didn't make this. He couldn't have. This file is clean, methodical, too detailed for someone who can barely keep a doctor's appointment without forgetting where he parked. And this isn't just something he stumbled across. It's something he was involved in, likely working for someone else.

If this is what he's been trying to get back, if this is what he's been threatening me about, I might be in more trouble than I thought.

My heart pounds. The screen glows at me like a warning.

Ginny leans back against the couch and crosses her arms. "You think this is what he's been freaking out about?"

"It has to be."

We sit in silence for a beat.

"How do you think he's involved in it?" she finally asks.

"I don't know." My voice cracks. "He was hanging out with sketchy guys, and I figured he was up to no good. He couldn't have managed this by himself."

Ginny nods. "You need to take this seriously."

"I am."

"Then the next question is, what do you do with it?"

"I don't know."

"You could give it to the cops."

"The police already talked to me, and I didn't tell them the truth. If I turn this over, they'll want to know how I got it. What if they think I'm involved?"

"You're not."

"Yeah, but how do they know that?"

She's quiet for a moment, like she's weighing something. "What about Beckett?"

"I don't want him involved."

"What if he's your best option? He's been looking for you. And if nothing else, he's your brother's friend. He's smart. And he has resources. You don't have to do this alone."

I nod, eyes still on the spreadsheet. I feel like I've stepped onto a bridge in the dark, unsure how stable it is or if it even leads anywhere.

Ginny's voice softens. "This isn't some leftover love letter or a dumb prank. This is serious, Sadie. If someone realizes you have it..."

"I know." I close the laptop gently, my fingers trembling. "I don't think I can go back to pretending I don't."

She reaches out and squeezes my arm. "Good. Then we figure it out together."

Thirty-one

Beckett

I adjust Rosemary's oxygen flow and glance at her monitor again. Her heart rate's too low, O2 saturation isn't where I want it, and her skin's a shade paler than yesterday. It's subtle, but I see it.

She's slipping closer to the edge.

"You know," she says, her voice raspy but still laced with sass, "for a man with very nice hands, you sure have an aggressive bedside manner."

I huff a dry laugh. "Aggressive? Rosemary, I'm a dream. Ask anyone."

"I'd rather ask someone who hasn't had your fingers jammed under their ribcage looking for a liver," she says, eyes twinkling. "How's a girl supposed to flirt when her doctor looks like he's auditioning for the role of Grim Reaper?"

I chuckle despite myself. "If the Grim Reaper wore scrubs and had no social life, sure."

"Aw, don't say that. You've got some social life." She tilts her head, then lifts an eyebrow. "Or did Sadie take that with her when she moved out?"

I pause, caught mid-check of her IV line. *Damn.*

"Did she tell you?" I ask, trying not to let it sting. But it does.

"She mentioned it a few days ago. But I would have known."

"You think so?"

"The whole hospital is talking about it. You've been moodier than usual. They've figured it out."

"Aren't you Sherlock Holmes..."

She scoffs. "Don't need to be. I have eyes. And ears. And I live for hospital gossip. It's all I've got."

"Well, lucky for you, there is plenty of gossip in a hospital."

"I know. There's that nurse who was stealing morphine from the PCA pumps."

"Wow. You really are dialed in. What are they saying about my brothers?"

The corners of her mouth turn up. "They think Greyson's wife is already pregnant."

I turn and stare at her. They're newlyweds. That would be fast.

"And they're all a-twitter when Kingston comes to the hospital for surgeries. I guess there's a bulletin board somewhere covered in pictures taken with him. He's the best kind of celebrity, a local who became a billionaire with an invention he developed here in Paradise."

"Where is this bulletin board?" I can't imagine any place that could be hidden in this hospital. But if this exists, I want to get a picture of it so I can razz him.

"I'll never say. They don't repeat the good stuff if you have loose lips."

I chuckle. "What about Ryker?"

"They think he's fallen for someone, but they don't know who."

"What would make them think that?"

She sighs. "He jumps in and out of women's beds. He's a man whore. And suddenly, he's not playing anymore."

"Are you sure he didn't get a serious case of the clap?"

Rosemary laughs and then coughs. "You should do a comedy club."

"If you add that to your bucket list, I'll do it."

She smiles. "Consider it done. Promise me you won't give up on Sadie," she adds after a moment.

I sit on the edge of her bed and scrub my hand through my hair. "I screwed up. I pushed too hard. I accused her of keeping things from the police, and maybe she was, but I made it sound like she couldn't be trusted."

Rosemary hums, shifting against her pillows. "She's been through hell and back. You know that. Sometimes people don't talk because they're hiding something, and other times they don't talk because they're scared no one will believe them."

"I do believe her." I stare at the floor. "That's the worst part. I just…panicked. I wanted to protect her. Instead, I made her feel like she was dangerous to be around."

"Have you told her you love her?" Rosemary asks, one eye squinting as she watches me.

I blink. "No."

"Then there's still hope." She grins. "You Paradise men are all the same. Big hearts, tiny emotional toolkits."

"Hey, I have tools. I just haven't…read the instruction manual."

She chuckles, then coughs lightly and winces. I reach for the water cup, but she waves it off.

"That girl didn't leave because you said one wrong thing. She left because she's used to people walking away first. If you want her back, you've got to prove you're not one of them."

My heart squeezes. "I've tried to reach her. She's not

answering my calls. I even texted Ginny. Radio silence... But she's probably at Ginny's."

Rosemary's face changes, though she tries not to give anything away. "I'm guessing you're right. That means it's time to go old school. Knock on some doors. Be annoying. She's worth being annoying for."

I smirk. "Coming from you, that's a high compliment."

Rosemary grins. "Damn right. Now get out of here before you start crying and ruin my street cred with the nurses."

I rise, squeezing her hand. "Vitals are stable—for now. Don't do anything wild while I'm gone."

"Define wild."

"I'm not coming back to find you doing wheelies in the hallway in a wheelchair."

"I make no promises."

As I step out of the room, she calls after me. "Beckett?"

I turn.

"Don't let your pride cost you something that could be incredible."

I think about what Rosemary said for the rest of the day. By the time I get to the rec center for our Friday night pick-up game, my brothers are already running around, shirts damp, sneakers squeaking across the hardwood. Kingston passes to Greyson, who nails a clean layup.

"Nice of you to join us," Ryker calls as I jog in. "We figured you were either blowing us off because you'd reunited with Sadie and were having lots of sex or fell into a coma after writing Sadie's name in a notebook a hundred times."

"Or maybe," I mutter, grabbing a ball and dribbling it hard, "I had work to do."

Greyson checks my shoulder. "You're on my team. Let's go."

We set up, and I take the inbound pass. Ryker's guarding me, crouched low, eyes sharp.

"So, who's got you all serious?" he asks as I pivot.

I fake left, drive right, and take the lane. "No one."

He stays tight on me. "You're lying."

I bounce the ball to Greyson and cut toward the basket. "I'm dodging."

"Same thing."

Greyson finds me on the roll. I catch, go up strong, and slam the ball into the backboard. It circles the rim and drops in.

"Two," I say.

"Barely," Ryker mutters. "You've got the touch of a sledgehammer."

Kingston jogs past, grinning. "He's got the mood of a sledgehammer."

We reset. Ryker brings the ball down, showboating with a spin move that doesn't quite land.

"Ryker, I heard you're suddenly off the market." I fake a pass to Greyson. "I should ask who's got *you* all serious."

Greyson catches the ball and drives. "You're off the market?"

"Am not," Ryker insists as he catches the rebound. "Jeez. Have coffee with someone, and suddenly, we're in hot, passionate love?"

I stop short. "I didn't say love. You did."

He pounds the ball into the floor. "Whatever."

I look at Greyson and Kingston, and it's clear we've hit the nail on the head.

I steal the ball from Ryker, which is easier than usual.

"I don't think so." He lunges and strips it clean from me. "Still a free agent."

"You just said you had coffee," I call from midcourt. "You outed yourself."

He jogs backward, smirking. "Doesn't mean it was a

241

romantic coffee. Maybe it was networking."

"Right," Kingston says, eyeing him. "You network with dim lighting and dessert menus?"

Laughter breaks through the sweat.

Greyson steps behind the arc, dribbling. Everyone falls quiet as he sets up. It's his signature shot, and he never misses.

I watch his form and casually ask, "So when's Trinity due?"

The shot sails…and dies mid-air, hitting nothing but empty space.

"Airball!" Ryker shouts.

Greyson whips around. "How the hell do you know that?"

I shrug, wiping sweat from my brow. "Rosemary told me. Apparently, that made the hospital gossip mill."

"What?"

"The nurses talk. Also, there's a bulletin board someplace in the hospital covered in photos of Kingston in his scrubs. Ryker's off the market. Trinity's got a baby bump."

"We haven't told anyone," Greyson says, walking toward me. "We're waiting until she's twelve weeks. Haven't even told Mom and Dad yet. Don't repeat that."

"Then maybe don't get an ultrasound at the hospital," Ryker says, passing him the ball. "It's a little obvious."

"Please don't say anything," Greyson says. "Seriously."

"We won't," I say, catching my breath. "Mom and Dad are going to move into your condo after that gets out."

"That's what I'm afraid of." Greyson makes a shot from midcourt and hits the rim. "We live just down the hill from them. That's close enough."

The pace picks up. Sweat drips down my back. Kingston body-checks his way to the rim for a putback dunk, and we're tied again.

Greyson inbounds to me. I pivot and scan the court, about to pass when Ryker jogs past.

"So…Sadie's at Ginny's now?"

The ball slips. I fumble it. It bounces once, twice, and

Ryker's already snatched it and taken off.

"What did you say?" I call.

He doesn't answer. He just drives to the hoop and lays it in easy.

"Two more," he says, nodding like he just cracked some personal code.

Greyson claps me on the shoulder. "That looked painful."

Ryker tosses me the ball, eyebrows lifted. "You okay, Beckett?"

I nod, but it feels mechanical. "Fine."

He just watches me for a second. "You know, it sucks being the topic of hospital gossip…"

"Yeah," I mutter, gripping the ball. "It does."

"But it only happens when people care," he adds with a half-smile.

When we've finished beating each other up, my brothers head out for beers on the waterfront, and I beg off. It's seeming more and more like I need to make a stop at Ginny's. But I gotta get that cake, and I've missed my window at the bakery again.

When I get home, I drop my gym bag by the front door and move toward the kitchen, pausing as I pass the back windows. I look out at the pool shimmering in the early evening light.

And there it is. That ache.

Because all I can see is her—Sadie, bright and laughing, hair piled on top of her head, drops of water glittering on her skin as she stood in my pool wearing that ridiculous yellow bikini. The one that made her glow like sunshine. The one she called her "last clean option." The one that made me realize she wasn't a little fourteen year old anymore.

She brought light into this house—and a lot of mess—but now, it feels empty.

I pull out my phone and open the Paradise Grill app, tapping in a quick order—roasted chicken salad, dressing on the side, and an iced tea. I don't even have to think about it. Sadie thought all salad was rabbit food, but she loved to eat the croutons off the top.

I rub a hand over my face and sink onto the couch, propping my feet on the coffee table. The place is spotless. Everything is right where I left it. Not a disaster with a coffee mug on the counter. There isn't a single damn sign of her.

I'd give anything for her mess again—her shoes by the door, her hairbrush on the bathroom counter. That beat-up hoodie draped over the arm of the chair because she always ran cold at night. She used to leave little trails of herself everywhere she went. And now? Gone. Like she was never here.

Except I can feel her in every room.

I grab my phone again, scrolling to the text I sent Ginny. Still unanswered.

But I don't need a reply. Rosemary confirmed it. And Ryker did too. She's at Ginny's.

Cake or no cake, I can't sit in this house another night wishing I'd done something. I stand up and head for the stairs, peeling off my sweaty shirt as I go. A hot shower, dinner, and then I'm going over there.

Maybe she won't open the door and listen. And even if she does, there's always the chance she won't believe me.

But I need her to hear me. Even if it's just to get her to come back to the tasting room. Even if that's all she'll give me. Because I need her around. Not just in my house, but in my life. I'm not letting her walk away without a fight.

Then my pager goes off. *Shit.*

Thirty-two

Sadie

A sharp knock jars me awake.

I sit up, my heart thudding. It's just after five a.m. — too early for visitors. I look toward Ginny's room, and the light I left on for her is still glowing. She never came home last night.

Another knock, more urgent this time.

Ginny probably forgot her key. I pad barefoot across the floor and swing the cottage door wide. I don't even think to check the peephole, my mouth already forming a sarcastic, "Did you lose your—"

But it's not Ginny.

Beckett stands on the porch, looking like he's aged a decade. His eyes are bloodshot, his scrubs wrinkled, his hair a mess caused by tired hands and long hours.

My breath catches in my throat. "Beckett..." I choke, the apology on my lips. I left. I didn't even say goodbye. "I'm—"

"Sadie," he says. "I know we have a lot to talk about, but that's not why I'm here. I need to tell you something."

Something about his tone stops everything in me.

He doesn't ask to come in. He doesn't reach for me. "It's Rosie. Her heart gave out last night. I'm so sorry."

The world cracks open.

"No," I whisper, shaking my head like I can undo the words. "No, no, no..." My knees hit the hardwood floor, and a sound rips out of me that doesn't even sound human.

He's down beside me in an instant, gathering me into his arms. I clutch his shirt, his warmth, anything solid while my whole body convulses with grief. "She was fine," I gasp. "She was fine when I left. She was making jokes. She was gonna see the Eiffel Tower. We were going to swim with dolphins and have one of those ridiculous spa days with mud masks and cucumber water and—" I break, a fresh wave of tears knocking me down again.

Beckett holds me tighter.

I don't know how long I stay there, clinging to him. Maybe forever. Maybe only minutes.

Eventually, he shifts and lifts me to my feet. I'm not sure how I stand, but his arm stays around my waist, steadying me.

"Come sit down," he says, guiding me to the couch. I sink into the cushions, and he disappears for a moment before returning with a glass of water and a throw blanket from the armchair. He wraps it around my shoulders.

"She wanted to see a play on Broadway," I whisper, staring at nothing.

His jaw tightens. "I know. She told me."

"I was going to take her," I say. "We were going to go after she got the transplant. We were going to go to the Greek islands and drink wine and flirt with men who didn't speak a word of English."

He sits beside me, close but not touching. "She loved you,

Sadie. You were everything to her."

"I left," I whisper. "What if she woke up in the middle of the night and I wasn't there? What if she was scared?"

His hand covers mine. "She wasn't alone. I was there. She wasn't scared."

My eyes fill again, the tears falling silently this time. "I should've stayed at the hospital. I should've —"

"Stop." His voice is quiet but firm. "Don't do that to yourself."

Beckett shifts beside me and reaches into the pocket of his jacket. He pulls out a worn notebook — light purple with a faded sticker of a globe on the cover.

My heart races the second I see it.

"She told me a few weeks ago that she wanted you to have it," he says, holding it out to me.

My fingers twitch, but I don't reach for it right away. My eyes burn.

"She said it kept her hopeful," he adds. "And that you were the only person who believed she'd actually get to cross anything off it."

I take it slowly, like it might shatter in my hands. The cover is soft from wear. The corners are bent. Her name is scribbled inside the front, along with a tiny doodle of a heart. There's an envelope with my name on it.

But I can't open it. Not yet.

"I can't..." My voice cracks. "I'm sorry, I just...not right now."

Beckett nods. "You don't have to."

I set the notebook on the coffee table, like it's a sacred thing. I don't even look at it again.

We sit in silence for a moment.

"I always called her Rosemary," Beckett says. "Because it reminded me to keep things professional. Keep that boundary."

I glance over at him.

"She made it impossible, though," he says, eyes distant. "She didn't care if I was in a bad mood or if I told her she couldn't have salt. She'd still ask me about my day, or tell me I needed a vacation." He huffs a tired breath, somewhere between a laugh and a sigh.

I feel that wound in my heart again, softer this time. Not pain. Just understanding. Shared loss.

"She wasn't just a patient to me," he admits. "She was…a bright spot, a constant reminder that there's still joy in all of this."

I swallow hard. "She made me feel like I mattered."

"You did," he says. "You do."

I look down at my hands, then back at the notebook on the table. "It hurts so much."

"I know."

The tears keep pouring from my eyes, and my nose is running. But I don't care.

He doesn't say more, doesn't try to fix it or offer hollow comfort. He just sits beside me, quiet and steady.

And that keeps me from falling apart again.

"I'm going to do them," I say. "Every single one. For her."

Beckett nods.

"She gave me her lucky bracelet when I saw her yesterday," I whisper. "Said I needed the luck. It's like she knew."

"She probably did," he says. "Her heart was struggling, but I had hoped she'd have more time, that I could keep her going until we found her a new one."

I look over at him, this man I left, though it nearly gutted me. He looks wrecked — eyes raw, hands still trembling — but he's here. Holding me up when I can't do it alone.

"You didn't have to come," I say.

"I did," he replies. "I didn't want you to find out from anyone else."

"I was going to come see you today. To talk. I didn't mean to just disappear."

He nods. "I was going to come to talk to you last night until I got paged. We can talk later. Today's about her."

I close my eyes and let the grief wash over me again.

Beckett holds me tighter.

I feel him bury his face in my hair, hear the tremble in his breath, but he says nothing. What is there to say?

"I don't understand," I whisper as tears streak down my cheeks. "Why would God take someone like her? She was good. She made people feel like they mattered. She always had a smile no matter what."

He rubs slow circles on my back as I weep in his arms.

"She was the only one who stuck with me," I cry. "Through all of it — Alex, the move, everything — I don't know how to do this without her."

"You don't have to," he whispers. "You're not alone. I'll be here with you."

But Rosie's gone. And I don't know how to breathe in a world where she doesn't exist.

My eyes drift back to the notebook on the table. I don't touch it, but the weight of it is there. Her spirit. Her laugh.

"She once told me," I say, "that if she ever made it to Paris, the first thing she'd do was find the cheesiest souvenir shop and buy a keychain shaped like the Eiffel Tower."

Beckett lets out a soft laugh. "Of course she would."

"She said the tackier, the better. And that she'd bring me back a snow globe whether I wanted one or not." I can see it — Rosie clutching ridiculous trinkets with a smug grin on her face, daring anyone to call her on it. "She tried to give me her dessert once, just so I'd sit down and vent to her about you," I tell him.

Beckett arches a brow. "Oh really?"

"Yeah. She said I was holding it in like a backed-up drain, and I was about to burst."

His laugh is quiet but real. "Sounds like her."

"She saw everything," I whisper. "Even when I didn't want her to."

He nods, and I see something shift in his expression. Sadness, but also a kind of peace.

"I don't know what to do now," I admit. "I need her phone so I can find her mom."

He turns to face me. "I spoke to her mom before I left. She's hoping you'll step in and take care of the services because you know what she'd want."

I nod, and it's the first breath I take that doesn't burn. "She already arranged it all at her grandmother's diner."

I don't know what this means or where we go from here. But in this quiet, in this moment wrapped in grief and memory, I know one thing. I'm not ready to walk away from Beckett.

I lean my head back against the couch, my body heavy. I feel Beckett watching.

"I want to talk," he says, "really talk...when you're ready."

I nod. "Okay. Me too."

He doesn't press, just gives me a moment. I think he knows I'm barely holding the pieces together.

He shifts, elbows resting on his knees. "What are you doing for work?"

I swallow, staring at a tear-soaked corner of the blanket. "Still looking."

There's a long beat of silence.

"Tarryn's rolling out your VIP tasting strategy," he says. "She's calling it the Barrel Society, like you suggested, and giving you full credit for it."

My eyes blur again, the tears rising fast and uninvited. I bite my lip, trying to hold them back. "I really thought she'd like it. But I can't take too much credit. I looked at what other industries do for VIPs and pulled together ideas from them."

"Take the credit. You earned it. Trust me. Tarryn is impressed, and you deserve it."

The ache in my chest splinters wide. I don't even bother pretending I'm okay. "I lost everything," I whisper. "You. That job. My best friend."

He turns to me again. "Why did you quit?"

I shake my head. "I didn't."

His brow creases.

"I turned my phone off and overslept. When I talked to

Zach I told him I was on my way, he said I was fired. I thought it was because I'd moved out of your house. Or because Zach's a jerk..."

His lips press into a line. "You didn't quit?"

I shake my head. "No. I loved that job."

He scrubs a hand down his face, swears softly under his breath. "Zach told us you quit." He shakes his head. "I knew that wasn't right."

My gut clenches. *Zach is a jerk.* Damn him for making me doubt myself, doubt Beckett...

"It didn't make sense," he says after a moment. "But I thought maybe...after everything with us, and the way you left... But I shouldn't have believed him."

My throat tightens again, but it's not grief this time. It's frustration. Loss. Maybe a flicker of hope trying to squeeze through.

Beckett stands, looking down at me with that steady gaze. "Tarryn's going to call you," he says. "You'll get your job back."

And just like that, he's moving to the door.

I stand too quickly, blanket falling from my shoulders. "Beckett..."

He turns, waiting.

"Thank you."

He nods, his eyes softer now, less guarded. "Let me know when you want to get together for dinner."

I nod. And then he's gone.

I should feel better, a little hope burning like an ember in my heart. Maybe I'll get my job back. Beckett wants to talk. Maybe things aren't as permanently broken as they felt just hours ago.

But the moment I think of Zach, that hope wavers. He's petty. And now I've given him ammunition. If I return, what kind of backlash is waiting for me? Is it even worth it?

I sink into the couch, staring at the coffee table. At the notebook. Rosie's dreams. Her heart. I can't believe she's gone.

My hands shake as I pick it up and open the cover. The

envelope inside has my name written in her bubbly handwriting. I pull out the folded letter, the paper slightly creased, and read it through my tears.

Hey you,

If you're reading this, I'm not around anymore, and I'm sorry. I wanted more time, more chances to laugh and make you roll your eyes and drag you on ridiculous adventures.

But I need you to know something, Sadie. Every time you visited me, you lit up my day. You made me forget I was sick. You made me feel alive. Like I had a future, even if it wasn't promised.

You gave me that gift, and now I want to give you something back.

I want you to live this list. Really live it. Even the silly parts. Especially the silly parts. Take the trip. Dance in the rain. Buy the snow globe. And when you do, I want you to think of me and smile.

Don't settle in love. I know what you've been through. You deserve the big kind, the messy, all-in, heart-so-full-it-hurts kind. You find your soulmate and hang on. Don't let fear make the decisions.

And keep being you. Strong. Beautiful inside and out. Don't shrink yourself for anyone. Keep chasing your passions. Make something of that fire inside you.

I'll be watching, cheering you on. And when you're old and gray and finally get up here, I want stories, so many stories.

All my love, always,
Rosie

The tears come fast, but they don't knock me over this time. Instead, the emotion fills me like something warm. I press the letter to my chest, breathing in the comfort of her words, the promise of her hope, the fire of her love.

She believed in me.

I need to start believing in myself again too.

Even if the path back to the tasting room is rocky and Zach makes it hell, and even if nothing turns out like I planned, she left me a map. I'm going to follow it.

Thirty-three

Beckett

I take the curve out of Black Bear Vineyard and head toward the main road, gravel crunching beneath my tires. Leaving Sadie this morning felt like trying to remove myself from something vital, like air or blood. But she didn't ask me to stay. Just gave me that soft, tired smile and thanked me.

Rosie's death is still a punch to my gut. I spent half the night in the hospital waiting for a miracle that didn't come, then the other half trying to figure out how to tell Sadie. Watching her face crumple under the weight of that news... I'll never forget it.

And I won't add to her pain.

This isn't the time. Not while she's grieving, unraveling,

doubting everything she's ever known. I want her back—every cell in my body aches for her—but I'm not going to make her choose when her whole world is shifting beneath her feet.

Still, I'm not going to sit by while my asshole cousin plays games. Sadie gave everything she had to that job, and Tarryn needs her. She deserves to have it back.

My grip tightens on the wheel as I turn onto the gravel lane leading to the Paradise Hill offices. The rows of vines stretch out on either side, green and orderly, the lake glinting in the distance. The scent of wet earth and grape leaves drifts through the open window. Normally, it calms me. Today, it barely scratches the surface.

I park near the house and spot my father and Uncle Max standing at the edge of the vineyard. They're both squinting toward the rows, arms crossed, looking every bit like two aging kings surveying their kingdom. I brace myself. There's no way I'm getting to Tarryn without a detour through whatever family drama's already in progress.

"What brings you here this morning?" Dad says, straightening when he sees me.

"I need to catch up with Tarryn." I slam the car door and walk toward them. "What's going on?"

"We had a meeting early this morning with the irrigation consultant," Max says, not even bothering to hide his annoyance. "They didn't have good news for us."

"What did they say?" I ask.

"They're suggesting we replace the irrigation system we put in a few years ago on the western sloped vines."

"Why?" I remember this was a huge expense that we expected to not have to touch for a good fifteen to twenty years.

"The sun has been hard on the exposed sprinklers, and there's something better."

"What does Tarryn say?"

Max puts his hands in pockets. "We still run this place and make the decisions."

While technically true, she's really the person calling all

the shots around here. I mostly avoid rolling my eyes. "Okay then, next question. Does the irrigation guy sell what he's suggesting you replace it with?"

"Sure. He'd give us a good discount." Max looks at me as if I asked whether the sun was shining.

I nod. "I would check with Tarryn and see if the lines are breaking down. If they are, get the person who put them in to fix them. They must be under some sort of warranty. And, a smart person once told me — " I look straight at Dad. " — that you should always get a second opinion."

I step away. I need to get to Tarryn.

Dad raises a brow. "Something wrong?"

Everything is wrong. Rosie's gone. Sadie's broken. And Zach's out here smearing her name. But I rein it in, force a smile. "Just need to clear something up. It's about the tasting room."

Max snorts. "Shouldn't you be talking to Zach? He's the one who oversees the tasting room."

I want Zach canned. Kicked to the curb. There is no way I'd deal with him. "That's a good idea." I lie so I can move on.

Dad calls after me. "Don't go charging in there, guns blazing, Beckett. Tarryn's handling a lot this week."

I take the back steps two at a time and push through the side door that leads into the office wing. Tarryn's behind her desk, half-buried in spreadsheets and notes. She doesn't look up.

"Hold on," she says, raising her hand. "Elise already told me some yahoo is trying to convince us to rip out the irrigation system and install whatever overpriced crap he's selling. We'll get someone reputable to come out and give a second opinion. Grapes need water, not gimmicks, and you know how twitchy vineyards get when irrigation's on the line."

She looks up as I drop into the chair across from her, letting out a heavy exhale.

She studies me for a beat. "Good heavens. What is it now? Still Sadie?"

"We lost Rosie Kennedy last night."

Tarryn's head jerks back like I punched her. "What?"

"Her heart gave out. We did everything we could, but we couldn't get her a transplant in time."

She leans back slowly, her eyes going glassy. "Damn. Did you find Sadie? How's she taking the news?"

"I did find her, and about like you'd expect."

She shakes her head, blinking fast. "Rosie was in my grade, you know? That girl had a laugh that could stop traffic. She used to come to school in the wildest outfits — tutus and cowboy boots. No one ever teased her. She was too...bright. Her mama was who knows where. She was raised by her grandma — Dot. Ran that little diner by the fire station. Rosie was her entire world."

"Yeah," I say softly. "I remember Dot passed a few years back. The whole town was at her funeral."

"Yep, it was a full house." Tarryn scrubs a hand over her face. "Losing patients is part of your job. I get that. But I know Rosie meant something extra to you."

"She did. She reminded me of everything good. Everything we try to protect." I stare at the floor, my throat thick. "I keep thinking if I'd just pushed harder, pulled more strings...I could've gotten her moved up on the list. It wasn't enough."

"You know there was nothing you could do." Her voice is gentler now. "You're a damn good doctor, but you're still human."

"I know," I say, though the words scrape coming out. "But knowing it doesn't make it hurt any less."

We sit in the quiet for a few seconds. Tarryn watches me closely, waiting.

"I called Rosie's mom and then went to see Sadie. I didn't want to tell her over the phone."

Tarryn nods. "That was really kind of you."

I lean forward, elbows on my knees. "There's more. Sadie told me Zach fired her."

Tarryn's expression shifts in an instant, her features hardening. "What?"

"She didn't quit. Zach canned her. But he's telling

everyone she walked out."

Her eyes narrow. "He told Elise, the staff, Dad, and Uncle Max. He told all of us she quit. That fucking liar."

I nod. "And I think you need to see what the hell is going on before this turns into something bigger."

Tarryn crosses her arms, jaw tight. "That son of a —"

She doesn't finish. Doesn't have to.

Tarryn's already clicking around on her computer when I say, "We need to hit this from a different angle. If we go after Zach head-on, he'll cover his tracks. We need to let him sink himself."

She raises an eyebrow. "I'm listening."

"If he's claiming Sadie left on her own, let's watch what happens without her. He can't be enjoying his life these past few days."

"And what's your play?" she asks.

"Tell him he can hire the sommelier, but give him a budget the same as what you paid Sadie. Sommeliers cost at least twice as much, and she already knows our wines. But let's see what he can do."

Tarryn groans and drops her head into her hands. "They're not going to take that rate."

"I know. That's my point —"

"A certified sommelier," she interrupts, "wants to run wine programs in hotels or restaurants with five dollar signs beside their names, not stand in a vineyard tasting room answering bachelorette party questions about which rosé is cutest. And even if we find one who'll do it, they never sell. They talk, swirl, and educate on wines. But they don't move product. Not like Sadie."

I nod. She's right.

She swivels her monitor toward me. "Let's watch today. Saturdays are the busiest day of the week. Last weekend, with Sadie working, the tasting room hit over ten thousand dollars on both Saturday and Sunday."

That's a lot of money for the tasting room. "You're

underpaying Sadie."

She nods. "I was planning on giving her a raise."

She brings up the live feed of the tasting room. It's still early, and Kevin's easy to spot—tall, wiry, a bit frantic. Kevin Parks was Tarryn's first hire to work in the tasting room. He's a work in progress. He's talking to a group, gesturing with his whole body. Meanwhile, another group walks in behind him and is completely ignored.

Kevin bounces from one end of the counter to the other like a pinball, trying to be everywhere at once, and failing. One woman waits five minutes before giving up and walking out. Two couples browse the merch table and then leave without tasting. Zach doesn't make a single appearance.

"There," Tarryn says, pointing at the screen. "You see that? That's money walking out the door unsold. That's people with wallets full of wine money who left because no one made a connection."

I exhale, jaw clenched. "And it's only ten thirty."

Tarryn taps her keyboard and pulls up another tab. "The numbers will back it up. Friday sales were down over fifty percent from the same Friday last month. And we have higher foot traffic this time of year." She turns to me, arms crossed. "You want to bite Zach? This is how we do it. We let the numbers talk. We gather the data. But I don't want to wait a few weeks and lose all the summer traffic. I'll find what I need to make a move that sticks."

"And until then, can you pay Sadie for the time off Zach so helpfully gave her and maybe also next week so she can take care of Rosie's stuff?" I suggest. "I feel like that will keep her from looking for a new job. Then she can come back and take over the tasting room. We should have all the evidence we need, and I would hate to lose her to a competitor."

Tarryn nods. "I think we can do that."

"She's living with Ginny, and I can see the Dempseys hiring her out of spite."

Tarryn grimaces. "Agreed. You can tell her she wasn't

fired and to call me when she's ready to come back to work."

I nod.

"Meanwhile, we'll give Zach enough rope," she says with a cool smile, "to hang himself."

The office door opens behind me, and I spot movement in the reflection of Tarryn's monitor. Without missing a beat, she clicks the tab closed.

"Hey," Zach says as he strolls in, clipboard in hand and smug written all over his face. "My dad said you were having an issue with the tasting room?"

Of course he did.

I force a casual shrug. "Yeah, I used that as an excuse so I wouldn't get roped into another hour of irrigation talk."

Zach visibly relaxes. His shoulders drop and the easy smirk returns. "God, I hear you. He's been obsessed with the west quadrant for a week."

Tarryn leans back in her chair, arms folded like she's sizing him up. "What brings you in so early?"

"I've got an interview," he says, flipping the clipboard to show off a résumé. "Replacement for Sadie."

Just the sound of her name out of his mouth makes my stomach tighten.

"I know we talked about it," Zach continues, "but we really need a certified sommelier in that role. Someone dependable. Professional. Knows their stuff inside and out."

Tarryn gives a slow, diplomatic nod. "It's your domain. But make sure you stay within budget."

Zach waves a hand like it's already done. "Of course."

"Especially if we end up replacing irrigation on the west side," she adds. "That'll bite into the discretionary fund. We have no room beyond what we paid Sadie."

Zach freezes. His smile falters. "Wait, seriously? I'd rather we pull back on the wine knick-knacks," he says. "That stuff doesn't even move."

Tarryn shrugs. "It actually brings in the highest return margin per square foot. Talk to our suppliers. If the sommelier can't work for that, we can't hire one. We'll have to keep looking."

Zach deflates, then forces another tight smile. "Right. Got it. I'll figure it out."

They chat for a few more minutes — small talk, staffing, a mention of a new rosé label he wants to test — and then he heads out. As soon as the door shuts behind him, I glance at Tarryn. She's already clicking the camera feed back open.

"You notice how fast he got here?" I ask.

She smirks. "Max calls, and he bolts down here. And now…"

She scans the screen, finding the tasting room feed. Zach's already outside, phone to his ear, pacing in front of the barrels.

"Maybe we should put him in charge of the irrigation project," I say. "At least then we know it'll never get done."

Tarryn laughs under her breath. "Don't tempt me."

I stand, stretch, and glance at the clock. "You going to family dinner tomorrow night?"

She tilts her head. "Of course. Free meal. You?"

I shake mine. "I don't know yet. I'm on call at midnight, and as of now, I've been up almost thirty hours. If I don't get horizontal soon, I'll pass out standing. I can't make any decisions right now."

"Then go sleep," she says, waving me off. "We've got this."

I nod, already dragging my body toward the door.

The ride home is a blur. I don't remember the turns or the lights or even putting the Jeep in park. I just stumble inside, go straight to the bedroom, draw the blackout curtains, and collapse on the bed. Before I shut my eyes, I somehow remember to text Sadie the good news.

Me: I just spoke to Tarryn, and she wants you back. Take another week of paid bereavement leave — and you'll also be paid for the week you've been off — and let her know when you're ready to return.

Then, after two days of chaos, everything goes quiet.

Thirty-four

Sadie

My phone buzzes on the nightstand.

I almost don't check it. I've been staring at the same water ring on the coffee table for the last hour, lost in a fog of sadness and regret. But the screen lights up again, and Beckett's name flashes across the top.

I scan his text and blink. Then blink again.

A breath catches in my throat as I read it three more times.

He talked to Tarryn for me. He fought for me. After everything I did, — after I walked away from him, got fired, from all of it, he still went out of his way to make this happen. They're going to pay me for the week I've missed and for next week as well.

I press my palm over my heart like it'll stop my heart from bursting wide open. I don't deserve this kindness. But God, I needed it.

The door rattles, and I look up just as Ginny tiptoes in, barefoot and wearing the same clothes she had on last night. Her hair is a tousled mess, and she smells faintly of bourbon and stale perfume. She pauses when she sees me, slumped on the couch, puffy-eyed, the bucket-list notebook clutched in my lap.

Her smile drops instantly. "Sadie?"

I don't even try to hold it in. "Rosie passed away last night."

Ginny crosses the room in two strides, crashing down beside me and wrapping her arms around me. "No—no, no, no." Her voice cracks. "Oh God, I'm so sorry."

I bury my face in her shoulder, and we cry together. It's messy and wet and loud, but it feels good to know I'm not drowning alone.

Finally, she asks, "How did you find out?"

"Beckett came by this morning."

She lets out a shaky breath. "How was he?"

"Wrecked," I whisper. "Trying to hide it, but it was written all over him."

Ginny nods. "I'm so glad he found you to tell you. I can't believe she's gone." She wipes under her eyes. "At least I got to apologize to Rosie. I never should've taken off the way I did."

"She forgave you. You have to know that."

"We shouldn't have had to say goodbye," she snaps, voice tight. "She was Rosie. She deserved more than this broken system that couldn't find her a damn heart."

I nod, pressing the notebook into her hands. "She gave me this. Her bucket list."

Ginny flips it open, and we fall quiet as we read the scrawled notes in Rosie's bubbly handwriting.

"Disneyland," she reads. "Drive through Tuscany. Kiss someone under the Eiffel Tower. See the pyramids. God, she wanted to live."

"It's not fair," I whisper.

Ginny shuts the notebook. "So what now?"

I take a deep breath. "I'm going to do them. Every last one. Even if it takes me my whole life."

She smiles through her tears, eyes still glassy. "I'm coming with you."

I let out a watery laugh. "You sure? It's going to involve a lot of weird foods and foreign toilets."

"I'm in," she says without hesitation.

"Okay, but…first things first. Why are you doing the walk of shame?"

She flops back and grins like the cat that got the cream. "Because I had a night."

My eyebrows shoot up. "Do I know the knight?"

Ginny looks suddenly interested in the bucket-list notebook again. "Mmm…maybe."

"Oh no, no way," I say, sitting up. "You're not sliding past this one. Spill."

She shrugs, her cheeks going a little pink. "We've known each other since we were younger. I always had a thing for him, but he was older. I've run into him a few times, and there was some chemistry, and then last night I was out with my cousin after work at Micro Bar and Bites. We played pool, darts…talked. It was fun."

"Fun that ended in sex?"

"Incredible sex," she corrects with a dreamy sigh. "But don't get excited. The timing is off. I just ended my engagement, and he's… Well, let's say he's not exactly known for being into relationships. So we're aligned. No strings, no stress."

I narrow my eyes. "You're being suspiciously vague."

She stands, stretching. "It was one night. A good night. Let's leave it there."

Before I can press her, my phone rings. *Caleb.*

Ginny lifts a brow. "Duty calls. I'm going to shower and get to work. I'll have the guest room picked up tonight, promise." She waves and disappears down the hall.

I press the phone to my ear. "Hey, you."

"Hey." Caleb's voice is warm and familiar, and hearing it

brings a rush of emotions to the surface. "You moved out of Beckett's? How are you doing?"

"I'm okay," I say, then pause. "Actually...no. Rosie passed away last night."

There's silence on the line. A beat. Then a soft, stunned, "Shit, Sadie. I'm so sorry."

"Yeah." My throat tightens again. "Beckett came by this morning to tell me. He gave me her bucket-list notebook."

"Her bucket list?" His voice cracks just a little.

"We were going to do it together. All these crazy, beautiful things she dreamed about. I'm going to do them for her. Every single one."

He exhales hard. "You've got a free place to stay when you get to London."

I smile. "Thank you. I mean that."

"Where are you staying now?" he asks after a moment. "You said with Ginny? I didn't think she was in town."

"She's back," I tell him. "We're at the cottage on Black Bear Vineyard."

He groans. "God, every memory I have of the two of you ends with me getting a call from someone because you were in trouble."

"We've matured," I say, though I laugh. "Mostly."

He pauses, then asks softly, "What about Alex? Is he in the picture at all?"

I can't tell him about the threats and the drama. He's too far away, and I don't want him to worry. "He's been quiet."

"I would feel so much better if you were still living in Beckett's guest room. You know I don't like you hanging around the Dempseys."

I roll my eyes, but only because he can't see me. "Your view of the Dempseys is shaded by the Paradises. We are not a member of either family, and it's really not much of an issue anymore."

He snorts. "Let me know when you pull your head out of the sand."

"I love my job at Paradise Hill, and Beckett knows I'm living here."

"Okay, I'll drop it, but I'll always be worried about your safety."

"Thank you. It's good to know that."

"I also worry about Beckett. How is he taking Rosie's loss?"

"He's strong," I say. "Too strong, maybe."

Caleb sighs. "He takes losing a patient hard. Like, really hard. Doesn't show it to anyone, but it eats him up."

I hate hearing that.

"I know you're figuring stuff out," he adds, "but if you could mend things with him...I'd feel a whole lot better knowing you were safe. And I'm sure he could use a friend right now as well."

He has no idea what *safe* looked like when I was doing mattress aerobics with Beckett and not staying alone in his guest room, but I don't want to go there. "I'm fine. Really. Ginny's letting me stay here for now. It's peaceful."

"You don't want to talk about Beckett, do you?"

"Not really," I admit. "Tell me about you. Are you seeing anyone?"

He clears his throat. "I met someone. She's nice. But it's nothing serious."

"Are you getting naked together?"

"Sadie!" He barks out a laugh. "I don't know that I feel comfortable answering that."

I grin. "I'll take that as a yes. Just be kind. And honest. Okay?"

"I will," he promises.

We talk a little longer before he says, "I'm due for a vacation."

"Come home," I say immediately. "I miss you."

"I'll think about it."

"Bring the new girlfriend."

He laughs. "You're insufferable."

"That's why you love me."

He chuckles again, and we say our goodbyes. When the call ends, I set my phone down and curl my legs under me on the couch.

I miss him. I miss Rosie. But my grief feels manageable. There's a lot happening in my world, yet now I don't feel quite so lost.

Thirty-five

Beckett

On Sunday evening, the phone rings as I'm speeding down the two-lane road that leads to the Paradise vineyard. I glance at the screen — Mom. Of course.

I answer. "Hey, I'm coming, I swear."

"You're late, Beckett." Her voice is calm, and I hear the teasing under it. "What's your excuse this time?"

"My double bypass turned into a triple," I explain. "I'm just now hitting the gravel. Should be there in two minutes."

There's a pause and then she laughs. "I can see the dust cloud from the kitchen window. You always drive like a man on fire."

I chuckle, shaking my head. "See you in a sec."

I hang up and dust flies behind me like smoke. As I get

closer to the house, the low whirring of rotor blades cuts through the air. Kingston's chopper is landing across the yard, the wind whipping the grapevines nearby.

He steps out in all black, like he just walked out of a GQ spread.

I roll my eyes. "Let me guess," I say once I've parked, "Mom called you too?"

"Of course she did." Kingston grins. "Just like the old days. Only now it's not the PA system in the house. It's my cell blowing up."

We both laugh, heading toward the front door.

"So, why are you late?" I ask.

"Meetings in Vancouver," he says, brushing invisible lint off his jacket. "The traffic to the helipad from downtown was brutal this afternoon."

"Meetings, huh?" I glance at his neck and grin. "Is that a hickey?"

He tugs his collar higher. "No."

"It so is."

He grumbles under his breath, but he's holding back a smile.

We step into the house, and I'm engulfed in the scent of garlic, basil, tomatoes, and cheese. "Lasagna night," I murmur.

I'm grateful for this ritual. It's the same as when we were growing up. Except now we're grown, with lives that pull us all in different directions. But Sunday dinner still brings us back.

I pause in the hallway, watching Kingston head into the kitchen to greet Mom. I take one more breath in and let it out slowly. Family makes it all worth it.

Tarryn barrels into me like she hasn't seen me in a year instead of since yesterday, wrapping her arms tight around my middle. "You're here!" she beams, her long hair swinging. "You made it!"

I chuckle and ruffle her hair like I did when we were kids. "I always make it. Eventually."

She gives me a look. "You're late."

"Double bypass turned into a triple. What can I say?"

Her grin widens, and I know something's up. Tarryn always lights up when she has a plan cooking. "You look happy," I say, raising a brow. "This about Zach? You finally gonna can his—"

Before I can finish, Zach strolls into the living room, a bouquet of flowers in his hand.

"For you, auntie," he says with a smarmy smile, offering them to our mom like he's on *The Bachelor*.

Tarryn mutters, "Kiss up."

I grin. "Brown noser."

We exchange a look and crack up. But then my eyes drift over Zach's shoulder—and land on her.

Sadie. She's across the room, laughing at something Ryker just said. He's leaning in close, way too close. The guy's got that cocky smirk he pulls when he's turning on the charm, and I don't like it one bit. Ryker may be my brother, but if he thinks he's gonna slide in and take my girl, I will introduce him to my knuckles.

I catch Sadie's eye. She sees me and straightens, her laughter faltering. There's something shy in her expression, like she's not sure if she should come over.

Then she does.

She walks toward me, hips swaying in that way that always messes with my head. When she reaches me, her arms go around my neck for a quick, warm hug. I don't hesitate to wrap mine around her waist, pulling her a little closer.

She leans up and whispers, "Your mother insisted. She wouldn't take no for an answer."

I nod and murmur, "That sounds like her."

Sadie smiles, and for a second, everything feels right.

"Dinner!" Mom calls. "Get in here before it gets cold!"

We file into the dining room. Sadie slips into the chair beside me, and I catch Zach doing a double take like someone just slapped him with a wet sock. His smile drops, and he awkwardly shifts in his seat across the table.

Tarryn catches it too. She nudges me and smirks, mouthing, "*This is going to be good.*"

Damn right it is.

Everyone settles around the long farmhouse table. The lasagna trays are steaming, garlic bread stacked high, and a massive Caesar salad fills a wooden bowl in the center. Mom's real china is out. That means this is important.

In addition to me and Tarryn, my brothers, and our parents, Trinity's tucked in beside Greyson, her smile as sweet as ever. Zach sits two seats down from me, still eyeing Sadie like he swallowed a lemon. Uncle Max is seated beside him, trying to act like he belongs here more than any of us.

Dad clears his throat, bowing his head. The rest of us follow. "Thank you, Lord, for this beautiful meal, for Vicky's hard work in preparing it. Amen."

"Oh, stop it," Mom says, with a shake of her head. "You know very well I didn't make it."

Dad grins. "I know, I know. But I figured I'd wink and keep your secret."

He does just that—winks at her. And damn if Mom doesn't blush like she's twenty again.

"I work full time, Trace," she scolds lightly. "I don't have time to make a giant dinner like this from scratch. And don't you start filling these boys' heads with those kinds of expectations."

Greyson lifts his glass of water. "Don't worry, Mom. I know better."

Trinity, all soft curls and wide eyes, turns to him. "Really? Because I made you osso bucco last night. With chocolate soufflé."

Greyson grins, biting back a laugh. "Ohhh. That's what that was supposed to be."

Trinity gasps. "The carrots were a little mushy, and the soufflé slightly collapsed."

Mom narrows her eyes at Greyson. "That is not the way to appreciate your wife's cooking."

"He did appreciate it," Trinity cuts in sweetly, then adds

with a glint in her eye, "but it seems the appreciation may not be extending to tonight."

There's a moment of silence. Then Greyson raises his hand dramatically. "It was the best meal I've ever had. I'm sorry, Mom. I had to say it."

The entire table bursts out laughing. Even Dad leans back and wipes his eyes, shaking with laughter.

Once the chuckles calm down, Dad lifts his glass. "I just want to say how lucky we are to be here. All of us. Healthy. Happy. Together. That's what matters."

We raise our glasses. "Here, here," echoes around the table.

Mom leans forward with that warm smile she saves for guests she actually likes. "I'm so glad you were able to join us tonight."

Sadie returns the smile, a little shy but graceful as always. "Thank you for having me. It smells amazing."

Everyone digs in, the sound of forks scraping lasagna and clinking glasses filling the air. It's cozy.

Mom dabs her lips with her napkin and looks back at Sadie. "How's Caleb doing? Does he have any plans to move home?"

Sadie swallows a bite and nods. "We talked yesterday. He's good. Busy as always, and...I think he might have a girlfriend."

Mom's eyes light up like someone plugged her in. "Really? Caleb?" She practically claps. "Oh, that would be lovely. You know, I never used to be into matchmaking, but these days..."

Tarryn catches my eye across the table, and we try not to laugh. Mom's been on a mission lately to pair us off like she's casting a Hallmark movie.

Mom turns her attention next to Zach. "And how are things in the tasting room?"

He straightens in his chair like he's been waiting for this. "Fantastic. We just hired a certified third-level sommelier."

The room quiets a bit. Tarryn cocks her head and frowns. "Third-level? That usually comes with a six-figure salary. We don't have that to spend."

Zach doesn't flinch. "Dad and I talked it over," he says, tipping his chin toward Uncle Max. "We agreed that the value she'll bring is immeasurable. I'll find a way to make it in my budget."

I glance at Tarryn. Yep, she's seething. Her fingers tighten around her fork, and I can almost see the fire in her eyes. Zach makes everything so hard.

Dad, who usually stays out of these things unless the house is on fire, looks over at Max and Zach. His voice is calm but sharp around the edges. "Why exactly do we need someone that expensive in the tasting room?"

Zach launches into a long, overly rehearsed speech about wine education, enhancing customer experience, international reputation, blah blah blah.

Max adds, "The vineyard can more than afford it. Zach made a compelling argument. I supported the hire."

Dad nods slowly, but his jaw tightens. "And what was the budget you were given?"

Zach shifts in his chair. "Well—"

Tarryn cuts in. "The capital outlay for the new pinot vines has already eaten a huge chunk of profit this year."

Max crosses his arms. "Replacing those vines wasn't my idea."

Tarryn sits up straighter, voice rising. "Because you didn't want to deal with it! The vines were over a hundred years old, Max. After the smoke from the fire two years ago and last year's late freeze, they were nearly dead. If we'd waited like you wanted, we'd still be out the money *and* behind on harvest."

Dad raises his hand, palm out. "Enough."

The room goes still.

He looks at Max, then Zach, then Tarryn. "Office. Nine a.m. Tomorrow."

Even Ryker stops chewing for a second.

Dad doesn't say much when he's mad. But when his jaw locks like that, you know he means business. And from the look he just gave Max and Zach, I'm guessing he's on Tarryn's side.

The silence hangs thick, until Sadie clears her throat gently and offers a soft smile. "I wanted to let everyone know...Rosie Kennedy's funeral is Friday afternoon. We're holding it at Dot's Diner. Just like she planned."

That cools the air a bit.

"She arranged it all before she passed," Sadie continues. "She wanted it to be a party, not a sad goodbye. Her favorite local band will be there. There'll be barbecue, cold beer, and probably a few stories too colorful to repeat. Everyone in Paradise is welcome."

Mom reaches over and squeezes her hand. "That sounds exactly like Rosie. We'll be there."

"Wouldn't miss it," Greyson says.

I glance at Sadie, and pride swells. The way she carries herself, even in the middle of all this family drama... She's got more grace than anyone.

And she's going to be mine.

The rest of dinner is quieter after the fireworks Zach created. Eventually, the lasagna plates are picked clean, the salad's gone, and even the garlic bread basket looks sad and empty. Everyone settles into the soft murmur of dessert and decaf, and it's almost quiet enough to hear forks crack the golden tops of Mom's crème brûlée. It's perfect—crisp sugar, smooth custard.

When his plate is clean, Greyson pushes back from the table and stretches. "We've got early mornings," he says, glancing at Trinity.

She nods and stands, brushing her dress smooth. "Long day tomorrow."

Sadie rises too. "Since I'm not working right now, I can help clean up."

Mom waves her hand in dismissal. "Sweetheart, don't even think about it. I have a housekeeper who'll be here at dawn to load the dishwasher. That's really all that needs to be done."

Sadie laughs, seeming a little unsure, but she doesn't push back.

I step up beside her. "I'll walk you out," I say.

She hesitates. "Only if I can at least carry some dishes to the kitchen first."

I nod, ready to grab a few myself, but I hear my name.

"Beck," Tarryn calls, already halfway to the far corner of the room. Ryker's right behind her, motioning for me to follow.

I glance at Sadie. She gives me a nod, already stacking plates with Mom. I hate leaving her like this, but Tarryn's face is tight with frustration, and I know better than to let that stew too long.

I follow them to the corner, tucked away from the rest of the noise. Tarryn's already venting, arms crossed, voice low but fierce.

"What Zach did was a slap in the face. I gave him a clear budget. We can't afford a fancy sommelier."

Ryker nods. "Total power move."

"If Dad sides with them tomorrow," she says, eyes flashing, "it's going to feel like he's cutting me off at the knees again. Just like every time Uncle Max stirs up trouble."

"I don't think he will," I say quietly. "Dad looked pissed. He called them into that meeting tomorrow morning without even blinking. That's not neutral ground. That's backing you."

Ryker claps a hand on her shoulder. "He's right. I think Zach and Max are toast."

Tarryn exhales, just a little. "Still...I need to be ready."

Ryker nods. "Then go in with numbers. What a third-level sommelier costs, what the tasting room would have to make to justify that, and the capital expenditure for the pinot vines. Line it all up. Then make the case for bringing Sadie back."

"Yeah," Ryker says. "The tasting room was packed when she was working. She's local, charming, and doesn't cost six figures. Plus, bring her VIP strategy to the table. Show them your full vision."

I nod. "You're more than ready for this. Don't lose sleep over it."

But I see it in her eyes. She already has and maybe will again. Dad's always said he supports her, but there were times in the past when he folded to keep peace with Max. I know it still stings.

Out of the corner of my eye, I catch movement. Sadie's got her bag slung over her shoulder, and she's quietly slipping toward the door.

I shoot Tarryn a parting smile. "You've got this."

And then I'm off, moving quickly. "Sadie!" I call as I jog through the entryway.

She pauses at the front door, her hand on the knob. "Hey," she says.

I catch up, a little breathless. "You were going to leave without saying goodbye?"

Her smile wavers. "I figured you were busy."

"Not too busy for you." I open the door for her. "How are you getting home?"

"I was going to call a rideshare."

"I'll give you a ride," I say as we step out into the night, and I usher her toward my car.

We walk side by side under the soft glow of the porch lights, the gravel crunching beneath our feet. I want to reach out and take her hand—feel that spark, that warmth—but I stop myself. I don't want to push. Not tonight.

"I'll be there Friday," I say quietly. "For Rosie's funeral."

Sadie looks over at me. "Thank you. I'd love that. She'd love that."

I nod, swallowing around the lump in my throat. "What've you been doing lately? Until you go back to work, I mean."

She shrugs. "I guess I need to start looking again. After what Zach said tonight, it sounds like the job's gone."

"Don't," I tell her. "Just hold off. They're meeting in the morning, and I've got a good feeling about it. I think things will go the way Tarryn's hoping."

Sadie nods but says nothing. Her silence isn't cold. It's careful.

"I miss you," I say, letting the words land in the space between us.

She looks up at me, eyes wide and full of feeling. "I miss you too."

We stop when we reach my car. She turns, and before I lose my nerve, I step in close and kiss her.

It's slow. Lingering. Like I'm trying to tell her everything I haven't said. She doesn't pull away. She melts into it, and for a second, it feels like we're right back where we were...before everything fell apart.

When we break, she stays close, breath warm against my cheek.

"Come back to my place," I say. "Stay the night."

She stills. "Beckett..." Her voice is soft. "We broke up because you didn't trust me."

I nod guiltily. "I know. That was a mistake. A big one. And if you just want to talk tonight, that's fine. I don't care what we do. I just... I want to be with you."

She studies me for a long second. Then slowly, she nods. "Okay," she says. "Life's too short. Let's go."

Thirty-six

Sadie

I look out the window as Beckett drives. That kiss curled my toes—and scrambled my brain enough for me to agree to go back to his place, but after the week I've had, I could use some of Beckett's attention.

His hand reaches for mine, and it's as if all my nerves shift to excitement. When we pull into his garage, he turns to me again. "We can stop anytime."

I lean in and our lips touch. The kiss deepens, and suddenly, nothing else matters, only the warmth of his mouth and the roughness of his stubble against my skin. My heart races, and I search his eyes for any hint of uncertainty, but all I see is fierce determination.

"Sadie..." he murmurs, sending shivers down my spine.

"Let's just enjoy tonight," I whisper, feeling bold.

His expression softens. He comes around to open the car door for me, and as we step inside his house, a rush of familiarity envelops me. The scent of cedarwood and something uniquely him fills the air. Beckett leads me to his living room, where soft light dances across the walls, casting a warm glow that makes everything feel more intimate.

"Can I get you something to drink?" he asks, still watching me as though gauging my comfort level.

"No, I'm fine."

He steps closer. "I've missed you."

"Show me how much."

His hands move up to the knot at the top of my halter and in a quick movement, the front of my dress falls. My nipples pebble. His fingers graze my skin, igniting a fire. Heat rushes to my cheeks as I catch a glimpse of his desire. I push back against my swirling thoughts of caution and consequences, allowing instinct to take the lead.

He takes a step closer, our bodies just an inch apart. "Are you really ready for this?"

My breath hitches but I nod once more, spurred on by the need to feel wanted again. "What is our lesson tonight, professor?"

He looks at me a moment, but then decides to play along. "Well, we know you can deep throat my cock without issue, and we know you are very responsive." He unzips the back of my dress, and it drops to the floor.

I stand before him in plain cotton underwear, somehow not feeling self-conscious at all.

"Let's see how wet you are." He shimmies my panties down and slides his fingers between my thighs. He circles my clit, and I hold on to his shoulder to keep from falling as I arch into his touch. I am wetter than I thought possible, the evidence of my desire coating his fingertips. Beckett smirks as he puts his wet fingers in my mouth and I lick them clean.

"I knew you'd be ready for me." His words fan the flames of arousal, and I whimper in anticipation. He envelops me in his arms, kissing a trail down my neck.

"Beckett…" The sensation sends ripples through me.

He tilts my chin up so our eyes lock. His gaze is intense, searching for answers in the depths of my soul. Then his hands are on me, and my body answers like it always does — hungry, aching, desperate to feel connected again. But connection isn't the same as closeness, not really. We haven't said the things that matter.

We haven't talked about the pain, or the silence, or how he hurt me. We haven't talked about how I disappeared.

Yet here I am, letting him back in — no boundaries, no words. This doesn't move us forward. It just presses pause on all the broken pieces we keep stepping over.

I do want more than that. But right now, I'm not strong enough to say it out loud. His fingers move back to my swollen clit, and it erases everything going on in my head.

"Don't stop," I breathe, my heart pounding with fear and exhilaration.

His smile widens as he guides me to the couch, his hands steadying my waist. "Tonight you're mine," he replies, and his breath hitches when I grasp his shirt, pulling him closer until there's no space left between us.

I reach for his belt. "If I'm naked, you should be too."

His belt slips through my fingers as I unfasten it, the metallic sound echoing in the quiet room, and his pants fall to the floor. I feel his breath quicken.

"Sadie…" I can sense the battle he's fighting within, torn between the desire to take charge and respect for my pace. But tonight, I want him to let go, to surrender to the heat building between us.

I push him back onto the couch, straddling him, reveling in the power of this moment. Our issues fade to a memory in the recesses of my mind because all that matters now is this electrifying connection. His hands find their way to my hips, guiding me as I grind against him.

"You're incredible," he murmurs, his eyes darkening with

hunger. I smile. He knows just what to say to light up something inside me.

"Just wait," I whisper as I slide down his body, my fingers brushing over his skin. He's already hard for me, and the sight sends a wave of warmth flooding through my core.

"So now what are you going to do?" he asks.

I take my time, trailing my lips over his skin. "We need a condom."

"There's one in my pants pocket."

I reach in, my fingers brushing against the soft fabric of his boxers before I find the foil packet.

"Should we take this to the bedroom?"

His question hangs in the air, and I can feel the weight of my choice. But every doubt I had earlier evaporates in the molten heat of this moment. "Right here," I breathe, feeling bolder than ever. "I want you right here."

I tear open the condom wrapper and roll it on. The sight of him, fully exposed and utterly vulnerable before me, heightens every nerve ending in my body. Beckett's breath catches as I take him in my hand, exploring every inch while maintaining eye contact, a silent challenge that only serves to stoke the flames between us.

"Sadie…" he warns, his jaw clenched tight as I continue to tease him. "You're going to make it hard for me to be gentle."

"Good," I reply, thrilled at this new dynamic. A rush of power tingles in my fingertips as I settle back on his lap, positioning myself above him. I sink down and he fills me completely. Every cell in my body is alive.

In a sudden surge of boldness, I take the initiative. I guide his hand up to my breast, reveling in the way his fingers cup me, his thumb grazing over my hardened nipple. I can feel him respond to the pleasure coursing between us. It's intoxicating, this dance of give and take.

I lean closer, capturing his bottom lip between my teeth, pulling him into a deeper kiss, tasting the sweetness of his mouth and the heat of his desire. He groans against me, and I smile at the sound. *I have this strong man completely captivated.*

I can feel his heartbeat thrumming as I push my body against his, craving more of that undeniable chemistry we share. Our breath mingles, two hearts racing in time.

He grips my waist firmly, guiding me as I sink deeper. "God, you're so tight," he groans through gritted teeth, his eyes squeezing shut for a second as if he's trying to hold back.

A smirk tugs at my lips. "Let's see how far we can go," I challenge playfully, pulling back to catch his gaze. I roll my hips. "I think this lesson should be how to ride you."

Beckett's gaze darkens with desire as I settle myself over him, our bodies fitting together as if we were crafted to match. "Is that so?" he replies. There's a challenge in his eyes, a spark that stokes the fire within me even more. I arch my back, swaying my hips to test the waters and gauge his reaction. The way his breath changes tells me I'm on the right track.

I lean forward, pressing my palms against his chest for balance. "Just sit back and enjoy the show," I whisper as I move against him.

"You have no idea how beautiful you are," he murmurs, his eyes tracing over every inch of me.

"And you don't know how good this feels," I reply, savoring the way his touch sends electric pulses through my body. Each gentle thrust deepens the connection between us, and the world outside fades entirely into oblivion.

His grip tightens as I increase the pace. With each roll of my hips, I feel power surging through me, an exhilarating rush that mixes with an aching need for more. He pushes his hips up to meet mine.

"You're incredible."

I shift my weight, building a rhythm that sends delightful shivers through me. His breathing grows heavier, punctuated by soft grunts of pleasure that make my heart race.

"More," he urges. "Show me more."

A thrill shoots through me at his encouragement, and I lean forward again to capture his lips as I grind against him.

"Beckett..." His name escapes me like a prayer. My fingers tangle in his hair as I pull him closer, feeling the hard lines of his body beneath me.

"I want to feel you—everywhere," he murmurs against my lips before trailing kisses down my neck. The sensation drives me wild, sending pleasure skittering through me.

"You will," I promise, reveling in the power of his need.

I shift my weight again, pushing him deeper into the couch as a low growl escapes his throat. I quicken my pace, riding him with fervor, lost in the rhythm we've created.

"God," he breathes. "You're driving me insane."

"Let's see how crazy we can get," I challenge, rolling my hips again, feeling him stiffen beneath me. The sensation sends waves of pleasure crashing over me.

"Just like that," he urges, his voice thick with lust as I pick up the pace. My skin flushes at the sound of his approval. Seems this is what we both needed.

Every thrust brings us closer to the edge, our bodies moving in sync, and I can feel the tension building until it becomes almost unbearable. Beckett's breathing quickens, sharp gasps mingling with my own.

"Don't stop," he begs.

I can feel the heat pooling in my belly, a delicious ache that promises release if only I maintain this rhythm. "I'm close." The words spill from my lips.

"I want you to feel everything," he replies, grasping my waist. "Let go."

As his words echo, my body responds and I spiral closer to bliss.

"I've got you," he adds, and with that simple promise, I find myself tumbling into an abyss of pleasure.

My body convulses around him ecstasy crashes over me. I ride the waves of bliss, and Beckett groans beneath me. In that moment, I know we've crossed a threshold, one that binds us in a way I never anticipated.

Beckett pulls me close as I come down from my high. And

I collapse against his chest, panting as I catch my breath. For a fleeting moment, the world feels perfect.

"That was…incredible," he murmurs, his fingers tracing patterns on my back.

I glance up at him through my lashes. "Yeah," I breathe, unable to suppress the grin spreading across my face. "I didn't think you had it in you."

He chuckles softly, brushing a strand of hair behind my ear. "Oh trust me, there's more where that came from." His gaze darkens with mischief, and I laugh at how effortlessly he shifts from vulnerability to playful arrogance.

He rolls me off him, my body still humming from my climax. "Let's continue this in my bed."

He pulls me up and leads me to his room. My mind clears just enough to remember everything at stake. I can't fall back into old patterns. Being naked together just gets us back to where we were before.

After Beckett falls asleep, I'll get a rideshare home, I tell myself. We have to do things differently this time.

Thirty-seven

Beckett

I wake to cold sheets and a sinking feeling. Sadie's side of the bed is empty, the imprint of her body already fading. No note. No sound or movement in the house. Just silence.

I drag a hand through my hair and stare at the ceiling, cursing myself.

We needed to talk before we fell in bed and let our hormones talk for us. That gets us nowhere. I had one chance to peel back the layers, to say the hard things. And instead, I let the pull of her skin, her scent, the way she moaned my name, take over.

I wanted her so badly, I forgot everything else.

Grabbing my phone, I type out a message.

Me: Thank you for last night. It meant more than I can put into words. But we need to talk, Sadie. We're not done. Not by a long shot.

I stare at the screen, waiting for the typing dots to appear. They don't.

With a bitter breath, I toss the phone on the bed and tug on my running shoes. I need air. Space. Punishment, maybe.

The path along Black Bear Lake is quiet this early. My feet pound the trail, keeping pace with the whirlwind of my thoughts.

I let my body burn, trying to outrun the guilt crawling up my spine. I let my damn libido steer the wheel, and now, I'm left chasing a woman who's slipping through my fingers.

Again.

When my run is over, I head for the shower. The hot water pounds against my shoulders, but it doesn't do a damn thing to wash away the memories.

Sadie's soft moans still echo in my head. The way her nails scraped down my back, the way she arched into me like she needed it just as badly.

It was incredible. But it wasn't healing. And it wasn't clarity.

And I owe Caleb the truth. That's part of this process.

I brace my hands against the tile and hang my head. He's my best friend. I'm sleeping with his little sister. That's a line you don't cross without owning it.

She's not just some fling. She never was.

Still, the coward in me whispers that if she's already walked away, if she doesn't want more, what's the point in detonating everything with Caleb?

That voice makes me sick. I still need to come clean. If there's any hope of salvaging this, I need to get ahead of it.

I step out, towel off, and run a hand through my damp hair just as my phone chirps. My pulse jumps.

Please let it be her.

I grab the phone.

Not her.
It's my brothers in our group chat.

Kingston: Should we go in and stand with Tarryn?

Ryker: Full schedule. At the clinic all day.

Greyson: Emergency shift. Can't step away.

I type fast.

Me: I'll go.

Kingston: Already on my way.

I dress quickly, grab my keys, and head out. As I drive, I try to push Sadie out of my mind to focus on Tarryn and her confrontation. Not that Sadie isn't part of that too. The route up the back side of the estate is steeped in old oak trees and winding gravel. I spot Kingston's helicopter cresting the hill ahead of me, speeding like he's got something to prove.

I meet him at the helipad. We both climb out at the same time.

He gives me a long look. "You have a rough night?" he asks.

I slam the door shut. "You could say that."

He raises a brow.

I shake my head. "Not getting into it."

Kingston doesn't push, and I'm grateful. We walk up the steps toward the house. But before we reach the door, Mom steps out and holds up a hand, her chin lifted like a general calling off the troops. "Tarryn doesn't need your help."

Kingston doesn't even blink. He strides past her into the kitchen and heads straight for the espresso machine like this is any other Saturday morning. "You sure?" he says, fiddling with the portafilter. "Dad has a habit of siding with Max. And if he's not careful, the vineyard's going to end up in Zach's hands."

Mom smiles, but there's steel behind it. "He understands that. And he knows Max and Zach went too far."

I cross my arms, my mind still raw from last night, my gut burning with regret — and anger. "Zach fired Sadie," I say, voice tight. "Then told everyone she quit."

Mom shakes her head, disappointment in her eyes. "He knows," she says quietly. "Your father met with Tarryn this morning. He knows what Zach's been doing. And he knows she's got proof he's been skimming from the till."

I take a slow breath, letting that settle. So he knows. That should make me feel better, but it doesn't. Not really.

"What's he thinking?" Kingston asks, pressing the brew button.

Mom shrugs. "I think he's giving Max and Zach enough rope to hang themselves. Let them dig their own graves. He's tired. He loved working with his brother, but it's not the same anymore. Your father's ready to retire, and he wants Max to do the same." She sighs, softer now. "But Max won't walk away unless he thinks Zach has a future here. And your father's done waiting for him to realize that isn't going to happen."

I shift on my feet, heart still thudding. Dad's playing the long game, and that's what I should've done with Sadie last night instead of chasing something I hadn't earned back yet.

Kingston hands me a shot of espresso without asking. I take it and stare out the window toward the vines, wondering how many people we're going to lose before this thing rights itself.

After another minute, Kingston gets his espresso, and we follow Mom out to the long, cushioned bench that runs along the back deck. It's peaceful, or at least it seems that way, considering what's brewing beneath the surface.

Kingston leans back, stretches out his legs, and glances toward the office. "How long do you think this meeting's going to go?"

Mom sips her coffee, then checks her watch with a frown.

"Your dad was pretty upset. I think this could be a long one."

I cross my arms and lean against the deck railing, feeling the warm breeze. Dad doesn't get upset easily. But when someone's crossed a line so clearly, so blatantly, there's no going back. Today might be the day he finally draws the line in ink.

Kingston tips his head toward me. "You good?"

I nod, but it's a lie.

Mom doesn't even look at me when she speaks. "It was great to see Sadie last night. I've always liked the two of you together."

Kingston grins behind his espresso.

I rub the back of my neck, bracing for where this is going. "We're not...together."

Mom just hums, unbothered. "Still, I like you two together. You mellow each other out."

Mellow? That's generous. Last night was anything but mellow. It was raw and desperate and tangled in everything we haven't said.

I don't know what to tell Mom. So I don't tell her anything.

Thankfully, Kingston shifts the conversation. "So what's your plan? You going to retire and hand the practice over to Ryker?"

She smiles, a little wistful. "I'm more ready than Ryker would like. But I'll stick around until he says he's good to take it on. It's tough. I've been there since before most of you could walk. I know everyone's stories, their losses, their wins. Ryker's still getting to know all that."

"But he'll get there," I say.

She nods. "Of course he will."

The sound of a door slamming snaps all of our heads toward the offices. Zach storms out, fists clenched, mouth tight, eyes straight ahead as he marches to his truck.

Kingston takes a slow sip of his espresso. "Looks like Tarryn won this round."

A smirk pulls at my lips. "Good." I feel a little release of tension.

Not long after, the back door opens again and Dad steps out. He spots us and raises an eyebrow, like we've shown up uninvited in his backyard. "Well," he says, walking over. "Didn't expect to see you two here."

"We were here to support Tarryn," Kingston says. "Whether she needed us or not."

Dad nods, the corners of his mouth twitching like he might smile. "Well, you've both lost half the morning sitting around. Plenty of chores to be done."

I chuckle. "Thought you'd never ask."

Kingston finishes the last of his espresso and stands. "Let's get to work."

And just like that, we fall into the rhythm we've known our whole lives—sun, sweat, and dirt. But this time, there's a quiet understanding that things are shifting. Maybe we're finally on the right side of that change.

By late morning, my shirt's clinging to my back, and my fingers are stained green from pinching off excess vine growth. It's quiet out here, the kind of quiet that lets your mind wander. Mine keeps drifting to Sadie.

These vines need attention—hands-on, deliberate care. We prune so the grapes can thrive, concentrate all that energy where it matters most. I wonder what could happen if I gave Sadie that kind of attention...rather than just hoping she'd grow around me.

Kingston's off near the hives, his sleeves rolled up as he pulls frames, checking on the bees and siphoning honey. The little bastards are crucial, pollinating the fruit trees and flowers that end up in the flavor bouquet of every damn bottle we sell. Funny how something so small makes such a big difference.

The crunch of gravel behind me has me straightening, brushing the sweat from my brow. I turn just as Tarryn wraps her arms around me in a full-body hug.

"Hey," she says, beaming up at me. "Thank you. I mean it. I really appreciate you being here."

"Always," I say.

Kingston strolls over, wiping his hands on a rag. "So? What happened?"

Tarryn lets out a huff. "Zach showed up over an hour late."

I glance at Kingston. "You think that was on purpose?"

"Oh, absolutely. Dad started the meeting without him, asked Max when he's planning to retire. Max dodged, of course. Said he's still got pep in his step."

Kingston snorts. "Margolin hasn't dragged him on that river cruise she's always talking about?"

Tarryn smirks. "Dad asked about that too. Max said it's not time yet. But Dad pushed hard, told him to set a retirement date, suggested the end of this year."

I whistle low. "He's serious."

"Yeah," she says. "But Max didn't commit. That's when Zach finally showed up, no sommelier résumé, nothing. Dad sent him back to get it. Took another half hour."

Kingston shakes his head. "Classic."

"We finally sit down," she goes on, "and Dad asks me why I think hiring a sommelier is a bad idea. I lay it all out. She's too expensive, she's not focused on sales, and we don't have the money. Zach insisted we do, so I reminded him that what we have is our emergency cushion. What happens if another fire sweeps the valley? He insisted she would pay for herself, and I asked how he could guarantee that."

She pauses to sip from the bottle of water I offer her before continuing.

"I told them she doesn't know our wines. Zach said knowledge of our wines will come easy to someone with a third-degree sommelier certificate. But then I pulled out the numbers — Sadie's VIP proposal, her conversion rates. She's outperforming everyone. If we're going to spend money, I suggested we promote her."

I clench my jaw. "Did you tell him you knew he fired her rather than the BS he was promoting that she quit?"

"I didn't have to. Dad stepped in and told him Sadie said

she was fired — for being late. Zach looked at Max, hoping he'd bail him out. But Max stayed out of it. Probably knew Dad would push him out too if he didn't."

"And?" Kingston asks.

"Max backed Dad. Said the timing wasn't right for a new hire. We're sticking with Sadie. Dad then suggested maybe Zach needed a break from the tasting room and is moving him to a cellar-hand role."

My eyes widen. A cellar hand cleans and sanitizes tanks, barrels, equipment, and floors. It's real scut work.

Kingston laughs. "That's what that douchebag deserves."

Tarryn nods, letting out a long breath. "Dad and I had a talk after. He told me he supports me, even if he doesn't always show it."

I glance toward the tasting room. "Are you worried about retribution?"

"Maybe," Tarryn says. "But as long as I know Dad has my back, I'll be fine. And the best part is that Dad agreed with me. Sadie is the new tasting room manager."

Yes! Inside, I'm pumping my fists. "That's great news."

"Sadie is going to kill it," Kingston says.

We hug Tarryn again, congratulating her on the win.

"I need to confirm all that with Sadie after her leave, of course. But for now, I didn't sleep last night," she admits. "So I'm going to take the rest of the day off, start again early tomorrow."

We wave goodbye, and as she walks away, Kingston and I decide to finish up with the chores portion of our day. A little while later, we say our goodbyes and head back toward his chopper and my car.

Just as I open my door, he glances over.

"You know," he says quietly, "Mom's right. Sadie's good for you."

I exhale. "I know. But it takes two. And right now…I'm not sure she's there."

He nods. "I've been there," he says.

That stops me. A rare sliver of the past he never talks

about. I don't ask, but I don't forget it either.

We go our separate ways, and I barely resist the pull to drive straight to Ginny's cottage. But instead, I get an idea.

At home, I wander through my place, snapping pictures.

The pool first. It looks empty without her lying in that bright yellow bikini.

The kitchen counter where she stole bites of my dinner.

The guest room door, still closed, still confirming her absence.

I send the photos one by one, each with a message.

Me: You made this place feel like home.

Me: I miss you.

Me: I know you're focused on Rosie's service right now, but when that's done, let's have dinner. Just to talk. I want to do this right.

I hit send. And wait. There's still no reply.
Not yet.

Thirty-eight

Sadie

I don't want to do this. The thought's been circling in my head since I opened my eyes this morning, and it's only gotten louder. I've been sitting on the edge of my bed for what feels like hours, staring at the floor, trying to convince myself to move. Shower. Dress. Breathe.

It's been four days since I snuck out on Beckett. but who's counting? I spent the week working with Tom Callahan, Dot's old business partner, to prepare for Rosie's funeral, which is today. And I'm trying so hard to ignore my need to be with Beckett. If I'm going to do it differently this time, I have to move slowly. And right now, Rosie deserves the bulk of my attention anyway.

Ginny finally nudges me into the shower and hands me a soft black dress. Her gentle presence is the only reason I'm not still curled under my comforter. But none of this feels real.

I don't want to say goodbye.

After I'm dressed, a sharp knock at the front door startles me. My heart skips before it plummets. I already know who it is.

When I open the door, Beckett's there. He doesn't speak or ask how I'm doing, just wraps me in his arms like he knows I'm breaking. I let out a shaky breath. For a moment, I let myself lean into him, anchor myself in the quiet strength of his embrace.

"I'm with you," he murmurs into my hair. "Today, and whenever you need."

Something tight and painful clenches within me. I nod, even though I'm not sure I believe I can do this.

He takes my hand and leads me outside to where Ginny's waiting. We ride in silence, everyone seemingly lost in thought. But Beckett's hand never lets go of mine. He keeps squeezing gently, reminding me I'm not alone.

When we pull up to the diner, my stomach turns. The parking lot is full, and the space decorated like a party — balloons, string lights, flowers. Laughter drifts in the air, blending with music Rosie would've loved.

I helped plan it, but still, I'm not ready for this.

This isn't how grief is supposed to look. It feels too loud, too bright, too alive. I don't want to celebrate. I want to scream. I want Rosie back.

Beckett comes around and opens my door as Ginny climbs out on the other side and walks ahead to greet someone. But I stay where I am, rooted to the spot.

Then I see it — easels lining the sidewalk, stretching into the parking lot. Giant poster-sized photos of Rosie. Laughing. Dancing. Hugging people. And in so many of them, I'm right beside her.

My breath catches.

Tom must've done this. Each photo is like a punch to the heart. Memories flood back — Rosie at the booth in the corner drinking her black coffee, Rosie sneaking me pie when I worked the early shift, Rosie wrapping her arms around me at my parents' funeral.

I press a hand to my mouth. "I can't..." I whisper, my throat closing.

Beckett's there again, steady, his palm warm on my back. "You don't have to do anything except walk in. That's it. One step at a time."

I nod, eyes burning. *One step at a time.*

I take a shaky breath and finally step out of the car, my legs like lead. Beckett stays close, his hand at the small of my back. I scan the crowd and spot Tom before he spots me, — but it only takes him a second.

His face crumples. He abandons the conversation he's in and makes a beeline toward me, moving faster than I've ever seen him.

"Sadie," he says, voice thick with emotion as he pulls me into a hug. He's always been like an extra uncle — gruff but kind. Right now, he's shaking. "I—I didn't know if this was too much," he mumbles against my hair. "But I think... I think this is what she would've wanted."

I nod into his shoulder, trying not to cry. "It is," I whisper. "It's perfect."

When he lets me go, I take in the entire scene again with fresh eyes. Laughter. Music. The smell of grilled cheese and cinnamon rolls. And then I see it — Rosie's favorite thing in the world.

A s'mores bar.

A long strip of flame runs down a table lined with skewers, graham crackers, chocolate bars, and fat marshmallows. My throat tightens, but a laugh slips out.

"She would've loved this," I say. And that's what matters.

I grab a skewer and stab a marshmallow. Beckett follows and hands me a milk chocolate bar and a graham cracker slab. I step up to the fire and don't hesitate, sticking the marshmallow right in until it catches fire and blazes bright.

"Perfect," I murmur as I blow it out. Charred and gooey, exactly how Rosie liked it.

As I assemble the s'more, something catches my eye. I do a doubletake.

It's a photo of Rosie and Beckett, propped on an easel near the diner's entrance. She's hugging him from the side, her head tilted back in a laugh, his arm slung loosely around her shoulder, smiling. Really smiling. It's a moment I hadn't seen before. I always knew he was more than just her doctor.

Heat rushes through me. For a moment, I want to be mad at him. I want to scream that he didn't save her. That he didn't get her the heart she needed. Why is he here and she isn't?

But when I look over at him, he's staring at the same photo. His lips press into a tight line, and I watch as he swipes a tear from his cheek.

Just like that, my anger fizzles. Because he did everything he could, and he loved her too.

Maybe not the same way I did, but enough that this feels awful.

I reach for his hand again, and this time, I'm the one who squeezes.

The s'more is sticky on my fingers and sweet on my tongue, but it barely registers. Beckett and I step away from the crowd, around the side of the diner where it's quieter. We're part of the event, but on our terms. I can't take too much of it at once, can't entirely immerse myself in the experience.

The party runs into the evening as more friends, neighbors, and people who knew Rosie arrive.

"I didn't expect this to be so hard," I admit, wrapping my arms around myself. "Though I guess I should have known it would be."

Beckett doesn't respond right away. Instead, he watches me carefully, like he's giving me space to say whatever I need to say.

"I really appreciated all your texts this week," I tell him. "Every one of them made me feel a little less alone. I'm sorry I didn't respond."

Beckett shifts closer, his hand brushing mine. "I meant

every word. I just...didn't want to crowd you."

"You didn't," I whisper.

He clears his throat. "I know this isn't the right time. You're grieving. This is about Rosie. But I need to say it anyway."

I look over at him, my heartbeat pulsing in my ears.

"I want you in my life," he says, eyes locked on mine. "I spoke to Caleb."

That pulls a startled breath from me. "You what?"

He winces. "Yeah. It took a half hour of yelling, a few creative insults, and I'm pretty sure he questioned my entire existence, but he's okay with us together, if that's something you're interested in."

I laugh, though I'm not sure if it's relief or disbelief. "I don't know if that makes me happy or deeply unsettled."

Beckett grins. "Maybe both?"

"Maybe."

He steps closer, his expression softening. "I didn't know I was seeing the world in black and white until you came into my life and filled it with color. Everything's just...*more* when I'm with you."

That's when the tears come. I don't even try to stop them.

"I want to do Rosie's list with you," he says. "Every single thing. Wherever you go, I want to go."

I blink at him. "Ginny might want to come too."

"I don't care," he says. "As long as I get to be with you."

Emotion catches in my throat. "Beckett..." I reach up and kiss him, soft, full of everything I don't have words for. His hands cradle my waist, his forehead resting against mine when we part.

Just then, I hear voices approaching, and I instinctively step back. Beckett's parents are walking toward us, smiling warmly.

I wipe my eyes, feeling suddenly awkward, but Vicky pulls me into a hug.

"I'm so sorry for your loss," she says. "I know this must be difficult, even if it is a fantastic party." She smiles. When I nod and thank her she adds, "And we're so glad you two are here together. I just want you to know…we see how he is with you, Sadie."

I glance at Beckett, who looks slightly sheepish.

"He's lighter. Happier. It's like we've got our son back."

Warmth spreads through my veins. Maybe this is what Rosie meant in her letter about not settling, about finding someone who brings joy and meaning into your life.

Maybe I already have.

The event stretches on, blurring into a haze of hugs, memories, and too many tears. Eventually, I'm able to go inside and greet people I haven't seen in years — old classmates from high school, couples Rosie used to serve coffee to every Sunday morning, neighbors, teachers, people from all over town. Some hug me like no time has passed. Some just offer a kind look and a nod, as if they know words would be more than I can handle.

Everyone is saying the same things to each other.

"She was a light."

"She made this town feel like home."

"There was no one like Rosie."

And they're right. Every time someone shares a story, I try to hold it close, as if I'm collecting tiny pieces of her. But it gets harder and harder to stay upright. Eventually the weight of it all becomes more than I can bear.

I cry until my throat is raw. Until my eyes sting. Until I think I'll break in half if one more person says how much they miss her.

But then, something shifts.

Someone starts laughing, remembering the time Rosie danced in the middle of Main Street during the Christmas parade, wearing reindeer antlers and dragging me along. Someone else chimes in with the time she convinced the mayor to name a Milkshake Day in the city charter.

A few more stories bubble up. Each one brighter, louder.

She wasn't just kind. She was hilarious, vibrant, and perpetually happy.

Gradually, the mood changes.

The tears are still there, but now there's laughter mixed in. Heads thrown back. Smiles tugging at tear-streaked faces. It's like the whole town decided—without speaking—that grief wouldn't be the only thing we remember Rosie with.

I step back, needing a breath, and that's when I feel an arm slide around my waist.

Tarryn.

She's in a soft blue dress and has sunglasses perched on her head. She pulls me into a side hug. "Rosie was lucky," she says, "to have you as such a devoted friend."

My throat tightens again, but this time the tears don't come. I just nod, grateful.

Thirty-nine

Sadie

Most of the crowd has trickled away, their laughter and stories fading like the last notes of a favorite song. What started as a gut-wrenching day somehow became something beautiful. Rosie would've liked that, and in the end, I did too.

I've talked to just about everyone. Shared memories. Thanked them for coming. Smiled until my cheeks ached. Cried more than I wanted to. But now it's quieting down.

Tom and I stand near the front of the diner, saying goodbye to the last few guests. His hand rests on my shoulder as we exchange soft words with an older couple from down the street. His smile is tired but proud. "She would've loved this," he murmurs again. I nod. We've said it at least a dozen times, but it's still true.

I turn to survey the scene, and I feel her presence before I see her.

Julia Tremblay.

She's cutting across the parking lot with heels that click against the pavement like a countdown. "Sadie," she says smoothly, stopping in front of me. Her glossy lips twist into a polite smile. "I just wanted to say, I'm sorry you didn't make it to our happy hour date."

She says it like we're old friends and like this isn't someone's memorial.

"I had a last-minute emergency," I say, my voice saccharine. "I'm sorry I wasn't able to get there." *Lies, lies, lies.*

"Life happens." Her eyes narrow, just slightly. "Alex and Simon...they need what you took."

My spine straightens, but I smile like she's just told a funny story. "I have no idea what you're talking about."

She steps closer, and her tone shifts—lower, sharper. "Come on, Sadie. You're not fooling anyone. Paradise is a small town. You don't want Alex and Simon as enemies."

My heart pounds, but I don't flinch. I've had enough today. I tilt my head, cool and calm. "All I took were the things I brought with me when I moved in. Nothing more."

Her smile tightens. "Sure." She leans in, her breath brushing my cheek. "Just remember who you're dealing with."

Before I can respond, Beckett's arm slides around my waist. His presence is like armor—warm and solid.

"Julia." He greets her with an easy smile. "I didn't know you were close to Rosie."

"Oh, we weren't exactly close," she says with a dazzling grin, flipping the switch like only someone practiced in manipulation can. "But she was such a bright light. Always smiling. It's such a loss."

Beckett nods. "She was a wonderful patient and a good friend. We're going to miss her."

"I imagine the whole town will," Julia replies.

"How's business these days?" Beckett asks.

"Well, business is always shifting here, retirees coming and going. Keeps the real estate market active."

Beckett chuckles politely. "No kidding."

"Oh, I see someone I should talk to before they leave." With a little wave, Julia strolls off like she didn't just threaten me.

Beckett watches her go, then turns to me, his brow furrowed. "Are you okay?"

I give him a nod. But inside, I'm rattled.

Julia being here means Alex and Simon are still watching, still wanting that flash drive from me.

Right now, that's the least of my worries. I'm emotionally spent, my body aching from the physical toll of my grief. Beckett walks me to his car, opens the passenger door for me, and then slides behind the wheel. For a moment, we sit in silence. Just breathing.

"Where to?" he asks quietly, glancing over at me.

"I need to go to Ginny's."

He nods and starts the car. As he pulls out of the lot, he reaches across the console and takes my hand. The warmth of his fingers against mine eases the unrest still churning inside me.

As we get closer, I stare out the window at the vineyards and trees, gathering my courage. I know I need to tell him. I've known since I figured out what Alex and Simon were looking for. But the words don't come. I need to tell Beckett because hopefully he can help. But if he doesn't believe me, the police won't either.

It isn't until we're driving through the gates of Black Bear Vineyard that I finally speak.

"I found something," I say, barely above a whisper.

He glances at me. "Yeah?"

I nod. "When I left Alex, I scooped up my stuff so fast I didn't even realize I'd grabbed a pair of his jeans. At your place I tossed them aside and didn't think about them."

Beckett reaches for me. "Is that what he's so anxious about? A pair of jeans? Are they some designer or something?"

I look out the window as we cross the bridge, watching the lake below. "When I got to Ginny's, I realized there was something in the pocket."

Beckett turns and makes his way toward the cottage. "What was it? Drugs?"

"No. A flash drive."

We pull into Ginny's gravel driveway, and as he parks, I reach into my bag and pull the drive from its hiding place.

Beckett eyes it warily. "What does it have on it? Blackmail pictures?"

Before I can answer, Evelyn Dempsey, Ginny's grandmother, stops her big Mercedes at the end of the driveway. Even from this distance, I can tell she's not happy we're here. If she had lasers in her eyes, we'd be dead right now.

After a moment, we watch Evelyn drive on and climb the hill to the main house.

"I'm afraid to leave my car here," Beckett says, half-joking.

I crack a smile. "She's the only Dempsey you should be afraid of. She's terrifying."

He chuckles. "So true. It's rumored that her husband didn't actually leave her. He's buried by the house."

I shake my head as we go inside the cottage. Then I plop on the couch, plug the flash drive into my laptop, and pull up the files. Beckett leans over my shoulder as lines of spreadsheets and coded names fill the screen.

He frowns. "What am I looking at?"

"Sports betting," I explain. "But not just game results or casual bets. It's names, amounts, payouts, debt-collection schedules. This isn't someone's hobby. This is a business."

He straightens, his expression darkening. "Why would Alex have this?"

"I think he and Simon are either running a gambling ring...or working for someone who is."

Beckett runs a hand over his face. "Jesus."

"I didn't know I had it. I swear," I whisper, unease creeping in. "I found it when I was doing laundry a few days ago."

Beckett nods, pulls out his phone, and finds a contact. "I'm calling Derrick Bond. He's a good lawyer. Smart. Grew up here. He'll handle it." He holds his phone to his ear. "Derek, it's Beckett Paradise. Can you meet me at the Black Bear Vineyard cottage?"

I stare at him, and the corners of his mouth turn up.

"No. It doesn't have anything to do with the Dempseys," he says. "But I need your help. Maybe instead we meet at my house?" After a pause, he adds, "Okay, thanks."

He ends the call and turns to me. His voice is firm, calm, and terrifyingly clear. "You need to pack your stuff."

"What?" I blink.

"You can't stay here, Sadie. People are following you. Alex and Simon could know you're here, which means Ginny's not safe either. You're coming back to my house."

Fear slices through me. "If I go to the police, they'll know I lied before. I said I didn't know anything. I mean, I didn't know this then, but what if they think I was protecting the Tremblays?"

"They won't," he says, gripping my shoulders gently. "Because you weren't. Derrick's going to help us."

I nod, heart pounding. This is real now. No more denial. No more avoiding it. But Beckett believes me, and that gives me courage.

As we gather my things, I text Ginny.

Me: Hey. I'm going to stay at Beckett's for a while. Can you go stay with your brother? Please? Will explain later, but it's safer.

Ten minutes later, we're on the road again, my suitcase in the backseat and Beckett's hand in mine. I don't know what's coming next—but I know I trust him. And he trusts me.

When we get to his place, Beckett sets my suitcase in the living room. He doesn't move right away, just stands there with his back to me, hands on his hips like he's bracing himself. Then he turns. "I don't want to make the same mistake twice."

I shift my weight, unsure where this is going. "What mistake?"

"Rushing," he says. "Pushing when I should've slowed down. I know things between us moved fast, and I... I didn't give you space to catch your breath."

I fold my arms, but it's not defense. It's to hold myself together, because my heart pulls in too many directions at once. "You didn't push me," I tell him.

He gives me a look, sad and a little stubborn. "Maybe not on purpose. But I should've paid more attention. To how you were feeling. To what you needed."

He takes a step closer. Then another. Not reaching for me. Just closing the space. "I'm not going to rush anything this time. We don't have to figure everything out tonight. Or tomorrow. And we definitely don't have to go *there* again until you want to."

"I do want to," I say. "Eventually."

His eyes meet mine, steady, warm. "Then I'll wait," he says. "As long as it takes."

"Thank you," I whisper.

He nods but doesn't touch me. Not really. Just lets his pinky brush against mine. "Promise you'll tell me when you're ready," he says.

I nod, my fingers curling around his. "I will."

"In the meantime, I still want you close," he says. "I need to be near you."

When I nod, Beckett carries my suitcase straight to his bedroom.

I set my laptop on the kitchen island and boot it up, fingers trembling slightly as the screen brightens. The flash drive is already plugged in when the doorbell rings.

Derrick Bond walks in wearing jeans, a navy button-down, and the tired look of someone who's been cleaning up other people's messes since high school. He greets Beckett with a quick handshake, then turns to me. "Sadie, good to see you. I'm sorry about Rosie. We stopped by the diner, and that was exactly what she would have wanted."

I blush. "Thank you."

"So what did you and the Dempseys get into this time?"

"It's actually not the Dempseys. I promise." I take him through how I left Alex, grabbed what I could, and weeks later found the drive tucked in a pocket of his jeans. I explain how they've been harassing me about taking something, and I believe it's this.

"Let's see what we're working with."

I show him the files, the names, the coded bets. He leans in, nodding slowly. "You weren't kidding. This is organized, methodical...and stupidly sloppy to leave in a pocket."

"Sloppy's kind of Alex's thing," I mutter.

"Okay, let's get Jonas and Elijah here, and we'll give it to them. I'll do all the talking. They'll probably have questions for you."

A chill runs through me. "What if they don't believe me?"

"Did you know about the sports betting before you left Alex?"

"I'd heard him say he put money on a game, but I always thought it was a bet with a friend. I have no idea how he got this drive or if it even belongs to them."

He nods. "That's very believable."

Beckett makes the call to the police, and we chat politely while we wait for them to arrive.

It doesn't take long before the knock comes. Beckett opens the door for officers Goodwin and Fallwell, both dressed in plain clothes but carrying the weight of authority in the way they move. They nod to Derrick, then to me, their expressions serious but...a little excited?

Derrick tells them everything, and they listen carefully, glancing over at me. They don't interrupt.

When Derrick's done, Elijah steps forward and grins, eyes locked on the screen. "That's the smoking gun we've been looking for."

Beckett lets out a slow breath beside me. I hadn't realized how tense he was.

I clear my throat. "There's more. Julia Tremblay approached me after the memorial today and delivered what I'd call a threat. She said I shouldn't make enemies out of Alex and Simon. She also thinks I took something from them."

Jonas and Elijah trade a look, one of those cop silent-communication things that makes my skin prickle.

"Did you know she was involved?" I ask.

Jonas shakes his head. "We knew the family had some money floating around that didn't make sense, but not her."

Derrick crosses his arms, his tone firm. "Sadie only just figured this out. When she left Alex, she didn't know she had the drive. That's a critical piece. She didn't lie or withhold information. She didn't know."

Elijah opens another file. "Sadie, I need you to take a look at some surveillance photos. See if anyone stands out."

He flips through a few images on his tablet, and I pause on one. This isn't the same guy they showed me before. He's scarier. My stomach twists. "Him. I've seen him. He was at Alex's once. I thought he was just one of his buddies."

Derrick steps closer. "How dangerous is he?"

Jonas's jaw ticks. "That's Pierre Bouchard. We believe Alex and Simon are enforcers. This guy? He's part of the Rizzuto crime family based in Calgary. They run illegal betting rings, money laundering, and some low-level trafficking. But if Alex had this drive, it means he's more involved than we thought. And this…" He gestures to the computer. "This is a big break."

I grip the counter to steady myself. "So what now?"

"We'll assign a car out front," Elijah says. "And you'll have an escort—visible and invisible—for at least a few weeks. We're treating this as a potential threat. Until we wrap this up, you're not going anywhere alone."

I nod, surprised by the overwhelming relief that floods through me. I hadn't really acknowledged how much this was weighing on me. Leaving Alex and losing Rosie were awful enough. I've been waiting for the other shoe to drop.

But now, the police are on my side. Beckett is standing right here with me. Ginny is back in my life. I don't feel so alone.

"Thank you," I whisper. "Really."

Jonas smiles. "You did the right thing. And we're going to make sure you're safe."

I nod and thank them until the door closes behind the last of them, and silence settles over the house. My nerves are frayed, my brain is fried, and my heart is still hammering from everything that's happened.

I turn around and Beckett's already there, pulling me into his arms like he's been waiting to do it. I bury my face in his chest and breathe him in—warmth, comfort, safety.

"I'm glad you're back," he whispers into my hair.

I close my eyes and press closer, holding on like the world might try to take him from me too.

"I need to say something," he murmurs.

I tilt my head back to look up at him.

"I'm sorry," he says, voice quiet but sure. "I didn't believe in you. I didn't communicate effectively. I let my fear screw things up. And that's on me."

Tears well up again. "I'm sorry too," I whisper. "I ran. I didn't fight for us. I didn't trust that you'd see the real me and stay."

He brushes his thumb along my cheek. "Sadie..."

"I didn't want you to see how messed up I am," I admit. "How I panic and spiral and make dumb decisions when I'm scared."

"No one's perfect," he says gently. "And I love you. No matter what."

I blink, stunned. "Wait. Did you just say you love me?"

He grins. "You think I would've called Caleb and confessed to wanting to be with you and messing up our friendship if I didn't love you?"

A laugh bubbles out of me—half joy, half disbelief. I throw my arms around him and hold on tight. "I love you too," I whisper against his neck.

He presses a kiss to the side of my head, then takes my hand.

"Come on," he says softly. "Let's go to bed."

We climb into his bed like it's the most natural thing in the world. No expectations. No tension. Just us. He pulls me against him and wraps his arms around me, his chest to my back, his breath warm on my neck.

And I feel safe.

He falls asleep first, holding me like he'll never let go.

And maybe he won't.

Forty

Sadie

I wake to Beckett's hand trailing slow circles across my hip. His breath is warm against my shoulder, his chest pressed along my back, and it takes all of two seconds for me to melt completely.

There are no words. Just heat and skin and quiet need that builds with every brush of his fingers. He kisses the back of my neck, and I turn to face him, threading my hands into his hair as he pulls me closer. Everything feels right. Like we fit. Like there's nowhere else either of us is meant to be.

His touch ignites a fire as he leans closer, his breath warm against my ear. "You okay?" he whispers, concern flickering behind his smoldering gaze like a soft glow.

I nod, though a part of me wonders if I really am. The thrill of our connection is undeniable, yet shadows hang over me, remnants of betrayal and fear. But I can't let that overshadow the future. Not when Beckett makes me feel alive in ways I thought were lost.

"Sadie," he murmurs again, and there's an intensity in his voice that pulls me back to him. My heart swells as I take in the contours of his face, the way his jawline sharpens in the low light of the room.

Each kiss deepens our connection, igniting warmth that chases away the cold remnants of my past. Beckett's hands roam, mapping every curve and contour as though he were committing me to memory.

As he positions himself above me, our eyes lock, and I feel the world outside fade into nothingness. Every inch of him feels like a promise fulfilled, a fantasy I never dared dream would come true. His lips find mine again, soft yet insistent, coaxing me into a rhythm.

Beckett takes his time, savoring each moment as if we have all the hours in the world. He moves slowly, deliberately, letting intensity build between us, our breaths mingling in the air. I arch against him, eager for more, craving the way he fills me, a sensation that eclipses every doubt lingering in my mind.

He shifts his weight, and I gasp at the delicious friction between us. My body rises to meet him as we move in sync. With each thrust, Beckett gazes into my eyes, searching for permission, for understanding, like he knows this isn't just about desire but about healing too. And despite everything, the way he holds me makes me feel safe. Completely seen.

When it's over, we lie tangled in the sheets, limbs wrapped together, hearts pounding. We stay like that for most of the morning and into the afternoon, making coffee, sharing leftovers, reading bits of the news aloud. It's easy. Like we've done this a hundred times before.

Toward the end of the day, I slip out to the porch and call Caleb.

He picks up on the first ring. "Hey, Sadie. What's going on?"

"I just wanted to check in," I tell him, drawing my legs up. "Let you know I've moved back in with Beckett."

Silence. "If he hasn't treated you right, I swear to God, I'll be on the next flight out to kill him."

A laugh escapes me before I can stop it. "He's treated me better than I thought I deserved."

"You deserve everything," Caleb growls.

"He's nothing like anyone I've dated. He's...very good for me."

"Yeah?"

I smile. "To put it simply, he loves me for who I am."

There's a beat of silence. "You deserve that and more. I'm sorry I disappeared after Mom and Dad died. I—"

"Caleb, you were hurting too. I know that. We're okay."

"So...when are you coming to visit?" he asks, his voice warmer.

"Soon," I say. "I miss you."

"I miss you too. And just so we're clear—no eloping. If you're getting married, I'm going to be there. Tux and all."

I snort. "We are so far away from that."

Caleb chuckles. "Maybe. But I've known Beckett since he was three, and I've never heard him talk about a girl like this."

I hang up a minute later and just sit there, laughing to myself. Marriage? Caleb is way, way ahead of himself.

Then Beckett appears with a cappuccino in hand and a stupidly proud grin on his face. "There's a heart in the foam," he says, holding it out like it's a piece of art.

I look down. Sure enough—a perfect heart. "You trying to impress me?" I tease.

"It working?"

I take a sip and smile. "A little."

"The pool's perfect right now," he says. "Want to jump in before it gets too hot?"

"There's no such thing," I tell him.

He lifts a brow. "Are you going to argue with everything I say?"

I give him a cheeky grin. "Only when you're wrong, which is all the time."

His mouth crashes onto mine, and I yelp as he lifts me right out of my seat.

"Beckett! My phone—!"

It clatters to the deck as he carries me, laughing and squirming, toward the pool. One giant step and we're airborne.

We hit the water in a splash that drenches the pool deck. My sundress clings to my skin, and I come up sputtering and gasping between laughter and outrage.

"I was going to wear this to dinner at your parents' tonight!"

"There's plenty of time for it to dry," he says with a shrug. "Besides, I kind of like the idea of skinny dipping."

I push my wet hair out of my face. "There are way too many eyes for that."

"Not out here."

"Maybe not," I say, climbing out. "But the police are parked in the front yard. And there's someone stationed in the back." Nonetheless, I peel off the soaked dress and hang it on a chair in the sun. And just to spite him, I strut across the deck completely naked.

He's still in the water, watching me with that open-mouthed, half-awestruck stare that makes me feel powerful.

Until someone behind me clears his throat.

"Miss Calloway," an officer says, stepping onto the patio and averting his eyes. "Apologies. We didn't mean to startle you. Alex and Simon appear to be headed this way. We need you both to go inside."

I blink. "Okay. Sure. No problem."

Beckett is already out of the pool, grabbing a towel and wrapping it around me. His fingers graze my hip, and he leans close, his voice low. "Still think there's no such thing as too hot?"

"Shut up," I mutter, blushing, and let him lead me inside.

And just like that, the quiet safety of the day cracks open.

By the time I finish putting on dry clothes and twisting my

wet hair into a ponytail, Beckett and Elijah are in the living room, standing by the front windows. They're talking in low voices, serious and focused. Elijah's arms are crossed, and Beckett's jaw is tight.

I step into the room, trying to stay calm, but the energy in the air is electric, like we're standing on the edge of a storm.

Beckett turns the second he sees me and crosses the room in a few quick strides, cupping my face with both hands.

"You're going to do great," he says.

"What am I going to do?" I ask. My stomach is doing somersaults. I move to the window and glance outside. Two figures are approaching from the lake path, taking their time, heads down, like they're just out for a stroll. But I know better. One of them is Alex. I can tell by the way he moves, casual but coiled tight, like he's five seconds away from snapping. "They're coming from the lake," I say, voice barely above a whisper.

Elijah joins me at the window, his tone clipped. "We've got eyes on the property line. Officers in plain clothes, unmarked cars. You won't be alone."

He turns slightly, speaking just to me now. "We've got someone on the inside. The guy in Calgary's getting desperate. There's been pressure on Alex and Simon to deliver. They need that jump drive."

My mouth goes dry.

Elijah's radio crackles softly. He steps away, pressing the button to listen. He nods once, then looks back at me, all business.

"They're here."

He strides toward the kitchen but pauses at the threshold. "Sadie," he says. "Just do what they say. Don't challenge them. Don't push. As soon as they ask for the drive, that's our signal. We'll take care of the rest."

I stare at him, frozen for a second. "What if they —"

"You're safe," he says, firm and final. "I swear, we're not going to let anything happen to you."

Beckett takes my hand and gives it a squeeze. "You've got this."

I nod again, though I'm still not sure. My heart is pounding. My palms are damp. Every cell in my body is screaming at me to run.

But I don't.

Because this ends now.

And I'm not the scared girl who left in the middle of the night anymore.

Everyone disappears, leaving me in the hallway. After a moment, the house feels different. I feel it in my bones. The air changes, growing heavier, tighter, like the whole house is holding its breath. I turn around slowly, and there they are.

Alex and Simon. Standing in Beckett's living room.

How did they get in? My blood runs cold.

Alex's eyes find mine, dark and unreadable. Simon stands just behind him, arms crossed, lips curled in a sneer. They don't look angry. They look calm. And that's worse.

"You were sleeping with him before you left, weren't you?" Alex asks.

"No," I say, my voice steady even though my heart is thrashing inside my chest. "I wasn't."

"Really?" he presses. "You just happened to shack up with Rosie's doctor?"

"I came here because Beckett is Caleb's best friend," I tell him. "I needed a place to stay for a while."

Alex's jaw ticks. "You took something when you left."

"Like I've told you, I took the things that were mine," I reply, placing a chair between us. My hands are shaking, but I curl them into fists and plant my feet. *Just keep them talking.*

Simon's eyes narrow. "Bullshit. You know exactly what you took."

"I don't," I say. "I packed clothes. A few of my art supplies. That's it."

Simon storms forward. Before I can move, his hand snaps across my face.

The pain is blinding. My cheek stings, hot and sharp, and for a second, I can't breathe. "What the hell do you want?" I gasp, forcing the words out. I grip the chair in front of me to stay upright and nod toward the coffee table, where a folded pair of jeans rests. "Those are yours. That's all I have."

Alex steps over and rifles through them. His hands plunge into both pockets. He pulls them inside out, shakes them.

"Nothing," he mutters, turning to Simon. "They're empty."

"What are you looking for?" I ask, hoping I sound more irritated than afraid.

Alex turns back to me, eyes flat. "The jump drive. We want the drive."

I blink slowly. Let the silence stretch. Then I furrow my brow. "Oh," I say, lifting my chin. "That? I gave it to the police."

A beat of silence.

Then chaos.

The front door bursts open. Officers pour into the room from every direction, guns drawn, voices raised. It's like the entire Paradise police department materializes at once. Jonas, Elijah, and a half dozen others swarm.

Simon doesn't even have time to turn around before he's tackled to the ground, his arms wrenched behind his back. Alex shouts something I don't understand, but he's down a second later, cuffed and face-first on the hardwood.

I stumble back, heart hammering, one hand still pressed to my cheek.

Beckett hugs me and removes my hand to look at my face where Simon slapped me.

"I'm okay," I assure him.

Jonas glances at me as he reads Simon his rights. "You good?"

I nod, swallowing hard. "Yeah."

Elijah crosses the room and urges me back. "It's over," he says. "You did everything right."

I look at the two men who once held power over me now sprawled on the floor in handcuffs and feel the most unexpected thing of all—freedom—real, trembling, gut-deep.

Alex is still shouting, even as he's pinned to the floor. "You stupid bitch! You have no idea what you've done! You think this ends here? You don't know the hell you've just brought down on yourself and everyone you care about!"

The words hit like bullets, but they don't sink in. Not this time.

Beckett moves before I can react, shielding me from Alex's venom. His arms wrap around me. I feel his heartbeat against my cheek, steady and strong. "That's enough," he says, voice cold. "You should be worried about yourself."

Alex snarls, but the officers tighten their grip on him. Simon tries to twist around, but Elijah presses a knee to his back.

"You can scream all you want," Elijah says calmly. "But here's the truth. You're done. We've got enough evidence to bury you both. And even if you cooperate with Calgary and the federal police, you're still looking at serious time."

Simon swears under his breath. Alex stops yelling, but the hatred in his eyes is worse than anything he could say. I hold Beckett tighter and don't look away.

Let him see. I'm not afraid. Not anymore.

The weight I've been dragging around for months—the fear, the secrets, the shame—it finally lifts. My lungs expand, and I can actually breathe again. My legs are still trembling, but it's from adrenaline now, not helplessness.

I glance up at Beckett. "You're safe now," he whispers. "They can't touch you."

And for the first time since I walked out Alex's front door, I know he's right.

Forty-one

Beckett

I look around the dinner table and feel something I've been pursuing for years wash over me — peace. Not the kind that comes and goes depending on what's happening around me, but the kind that roots deep. The kind that tells me I don't need to keep reaching for what's next because this, right here, is enough.

Kingston and Greyson are across from me, deep in conversation about the Vancouver Canadians, our minor league baseball team. They're tossing around dates, talking about maybe heading into VanCity for a weekend game. I hear Greyson say something about grabbing a hotel and making a little trip out of it.

Trinity leans in, teasing Kingston. "Are you bringing a date?" she asks, lifting her glass with a knowing smile.

Kingston shrugs, trying to play it cool. "I've got a friend in Vancouver who might join us."

Mom's eyes catch the light, and I can see it, the sparkle she always gets when one of us drops a hint about something new. Something hopeful.

On the other side of the table, Tarryn and Ryker are locked in a heated debate over the last dinner roll. They're polling the entire table to figure out who had two when both of them swear they only had one. It's childish and ridiculous—and so perfectly them.

Mom gets up and comes back with the bread bag from the kitchen, laughing as she sets it down. "I'm sorry, I didn't put enough on the table."

Tarryn grins like a wolf, snatches two rolls from the bag, and dares Ryker to say a word. He opens his mouth, then wisely shuts it.

I stand, heart beating a little faster. "Hey," I say, clearing my throat. Everyone quiets down and turns to me.

"I just wanted to let you know that Sadie and I are officially together."

There's a beat of silence, and then Mom gasps, her hand flying to her heart like she's been waiting for this moment her whole life. "Oh, honey," she says, getting up and circling the table to throw her arms around Sadie. "I'm so thrilled. Welcome to the family, sweetheart."

Sadie beams, and I can tell she's holding back tears. My heart swells. I've finally arrived exactly where I'm supposed to be.

Dad lifts his glass. "To Beckett and Sadie. May your hearts always beat as one."

The family raises their glasses. I catch Sadie's eye, and she's smiling at me like I'm everything she's ever wanted.

Tarryn leans forward, chin resting on her hand, eyes sharp. "So...what was the commotion at your house this morning? All the sirens and police lit up the entire hillside."

Sadie gives me a quick glance before turning to the table.

"Alex and Simon Tremblay broke in. They were angry, convinced I took something when I left Alex. The police think they're tied to a pretty nasty sports-betting ring, and it looks like extortion and violence were part of the deal. Seems like both men will be spending time in jail."

Her voice stays calm, but her hand slips into mine under the table. She squeezes, and when I look at her, I see it, the quiet strength in her gaze, but also the affection. "I was scared," she says, her voice soft. "Really scared. But Beckett was there, and I don't know what I would've done without him."

Mom wipes her eyes like she's trying to play it off, and Dad reaches for the wine to top off everyone's glasses.

Ryker, always the one to cut the tension, raises a brow. "Are the police going to start going after people who, you know, placed bets through them?"

Mom turns toward him, her eyebrows rising. "Ryker, is your name on that list?"

He shrugs, guilty as hell. "It may be. But only once."

Sadie grins. "They seemed way more focused on the extortion and violence side of things. Not so much the casual bettors."

"The guys at the top are the ones in real trouble," I confirm.

Tarryn gives Sadie a look. "Did you know what they were doing?"

Sadie shakes her head. "They didn't include me in anything. I didn't know anything until I found a jump drive in a pair of Alex's jeans that I took by mistake when I moved out."

Ryker's eyes widen. "Wait, you found a jump drive?"

She nods. "Yeah, and from what the cops said, it had nicknames and initials instead of real names for the bettors. So, Ryker, if you only bet once, you're probably okay."

He laughs, lifting his glass. "It was the NFL Super Bowl. I lost bad. Swore off betting and stuck to medicine. Heartbreak is safer than gambling."

We all laugh, and the tension breaks, rippling around the

table like a wave of relief. For a moment, I sit back and breathe it all in — my family, Sadie at my side, laughter in the air, and peace in my heart.

This is what I've been running toward my whole life. And I've finally caught it.

The stars are out by the time we say goodnight. Hugs linger longer than usual. Mom holds Sadie tight. Dad clasps my shoulder like he's proud of the man I've become.

Tarryn and Trinity hug Sadie. "We have another sister," they tell her.

My brothers are full of teasing and grins, but there's warmth in their eyes.

Sadie slides into the passenger seat, her hand finding mine as I start the car. We don't say much on the drive home. We don't need to. The windows are down, the breeze is cool against my arm, and my heart is full.

When we pull into the driveway, the porch light casts a golden glow over the front of the house. I kill the engine, and for a second, we just sit there, looking at each other.

"You good?" I ask quietly.

She nods. "Better than good."

We don't make it very far once we're inside.

The door has barely shut behind us before I press her back against it, my mouth finding hers in a kiss filled with relief, love, and need. She melts into me like she's been waiting all night for this. Maybe we both have.

Clothes fall away as we move to the bedroom. The room feels different now. It's not just mine anymore. It's ours. She pulls me down, her hands in my hair, her breath catching as I move over her, under her, around her.

We take our time.

I memorize every sound she makes, every sigh, every whisper of my name. Her fingers grip my back, her thighs tighten around my waist, and everything in me sharpens with how much I want her. Need her. Love her.

I reach for the drawer, but she stops me. "I'm on the pill if you want to go without a condom. And I was tested after I moved out of Alex's."

Heat rushes through me, and I hesitate for just a moment. "Sadie..." I start, but she silences me with a kiss that ignites something primal within. "I'm clean." I open her legs and find her wet center. She's always so needy for me.

"Yes," she breathes, her lips parted, inviting me back.

She props herself up on her elbows, and I spread her wide and dive in.

I'm lost in her, in the taste of her skin and the way she responds to my every touch. It's as if I've been given a map to a land I never knew existed, and now that I've found it, I have to explore every inch. The way her body arches against me, the soft gasps that escape her lips. They pull me deeper into her world.

"Beckett," she whispers, her voice trembling with need.

I look up at her, and the sight of her flushed cheeks, those wide, dark eyes filled with something between desire and vulnerability, twists my heart in ways I never anticipated. "Just tell me if it's too much," I murmur.

Her hands weave through my hair, guiding me with a gentle urgency. "Don't stop," she breathes.

I dive back into her warmth and lose myself again, drowning in the sensations of our bodies colliding. There's vulnerability in her eyes, which pulls at my instincts to protect and cherish. I understand what's behind her, and all I want is to help her move forward.

I feel her body tense, the sweet contraction of her muscles against my tongue igniting an inferno within me. Her climax is a quiet explosion, a shattering of the walls she's built around her heart.

I pull back slightly to witness the expression on her face. She looks at me as if I've unlocked some hidden treasure inside her, and that fills me with a heady mix of pride and desire.

"God," she gasps, collapsing against the sheets, breathless and radiant. "What are you doing to me?"

The corners of my mouth lift in a smile I can't contain.

"Just giving you what you deserve." I press a soft kiss to her forehead.

This is only the beginning of our story, and I never want it to end.

She looks up at me, eyes wide and glassy, lips parted. "Thank you for loving me," she whispers.

My heart kicks against my ribs. "Always and forever."

Later, still tangled in sheets, I pull her close and press a kiss to her shoulder. She hums, already half-asleep, her body curved into mine like we were made to fit.

I close my eyes and breathe her in. I have everything I want right here.

Sadie

Tarryn pours the last of the iced tea into her glass and leans back in her chair, scanning the printout between us.

"Can you believe this?" she says, shaking her head with a smile. "We're at over a thousand platinum-level VIPs in just three months."

I grin, stabbing the last of my salad with my fork. "Honestly? Yes. It's an amazing product, and people are thrilled to have access. Personalized notes, private tastings, early access... People feel like they're part of something exclusive. Thank you for allowing me to do this."

Tarryn waves off the compliment like she always does, but her eyes sparkle with pride. "Your idea was a no brainer. You were made for this."

My cheeks warm. I'm still getting used to the idea of being part of something like this, something that feels like it's growing into more than just a job.

"I've been thinking about your suggestion," Tarryn continues, tapping her pen on the edge of the table. "I spoke to the owner of that vineyard in Oregon — Cascade Bluffs. They're so popular now, they're selling futures ten years out. People are locking in cases before the wine is even bottled."

I blink. "That's wild."

"Right?" she says. "But I think you're right. We could do something like that. A special reserve — just for VIPs — maybe from this year's harvest. Bottle it separately, make it exclusive."

I sit up a little straighter. "That could work. But do we have enough yield?"

She flips through the binder and pulls up the current projections. "Cab is solid. Merlot's a little tight. And pinot..." She exhales. "The new vines just aren't mature yet."

"They're still producing, though," I say, thinking it through. "Just...not a lot."

"Exactly," she says. "But maybe that's the point. Small batch, high value. Could add to the mystique."

I nod, wheels turning. "We'd have to be careful. Pinot's finicky, and the profile's still developing. But it could be brilliant. Make that scarcity work for us..."

We sit in silence for a beat, picturing it — sleek bottles, a private release, maybe even a tasting event to go with it.

"I'll run the numbers again," Tarryn says, scribbling notes. "If we time it right, we could open the futures list next spring."

I reach for my glass, my pulse picking up in that way it does when something feels big. Exciting. "I think it's worth exploring," I tell her. "Let's make it happen."

She grins across the table. "I was hoping you'd say that."

And just like that, we're off again, building something bold, one idea at a time.

Tarryn gathers up the last of the papers and stacks them neatly in her binder. I slide my plate aside and take the last sip of tea before she looks up at me with a smile.

"So," she says, tilting her head, "you ready for your vacation?"

I smile so wide it actually hurts a little. "Almost. As soon as Beckett finishes his rounds, we're heading to the airport. We're on the four o'clock shuttle to Vancouver."

"Straight to Caleb's?"

"Yep," I nod. "And I finally get to meet Kate. He hasn't stopped talking about her."

Tarryn grins. "Do you think it's serious?"

"I do," I say. "He's super excited. Honestly, I haven't heard him this happy since...maybe ever. I wouldn't be surprised if they get married."

Her eyebrows shoot up. "Wow. Big changes all around."

I glance out the window for a second, watching the breeze ripple through the vineyard. "Yeah," I whisper. "Six months ago, I felt like all I had was Rosie. No job, no future, no place to go. I never imagined any of this."

Tarryn stands and circles the table to pull me into a hug. "Just remember," she says against my ear, "you picked us. I was born into this chaos. You chose it."

I blink back tears as I hug her tighter. "I'd choose it again. Every time."

"Okay, okay, before we get too weepy..." She steps back and pats my arm. "You're only gone two weeks."

I nod. "I'm heading back to the tasting room. I've got a few last things to wrap up before leaving everything in Eric's hands."

"How's he doing?"

"Honestly?" I smirk. "With a little guidance, a lot better than I expected. He's sharp. Listens well. I think he might actually be ready."

She laughs. "See? You're a good teacher."

I laugh. "With a guide like you? I had no other choice."

We say goodbye with promises to text before my flight. As I watch her walk off toward the vineyard, clipboard in hand, I feel a sense of purpose settle over me.

Not long ago, I was drifting. Now, I'm anchored — by love and a life and family I never saw coming.

I can't wait to see where life takes me next.

Despite all I have to do, I linger at the table for a few more minutes after Tarryn's gone, enjoying the afternoon. The hum of bees floats through the open window, and a light breeze rustles the grapevines outside. I feel like I belong.

And this trip? It's more than a vacation. It's the next chapter, a reunion with my brother I haven't seen in so long, a celebration of love with Beckett, and a chance to honor Rosie in the best way I know how — by living and ticking off things to do in London from her bucket list.

As I finally get going, I sling my bag over my shoulder and take one last look at the vineyard bathed in sunlight. It takes me just a few minutes to finalize everything with Eric in the tasting room, and then I'm on my way.

I pull into the driveway just as Beckett's coming down the front steps, suitcase in one hand, travel bag slung over his shoulder. He grins when he sees me, that easy, warm smile that never fails to make my heart stutter. "You ready?" he calls as I climb from the Jeep.

"More than ready." I shut the door and walk toward him. "Tarryn and I just wrapped up the VIP planning, and I've handed the reins of the tasting room to Eric while I'm gone."

He raises a brow. "Think he'll survive?"

I laugh. "Tarryn and Trinity will be there to back him up if he needs it, but I don't think he will."

Beckett meets me halfway and hooks an arm around my waist, pulling me in for a quick kiss. It's soft but full of promise. "You look good," he murmurs against my temple. "Relaxed."

"I feel good," I say. "Like I'm finally standing on solid ground."

He nods. "Then let's get you on a plane so we can go show your brother."

I smile up at him. "Let's make some memories."

The sliding doors part, and a rush of cool London air hits my face, waking me up just a little, though my body's still screaming that it's the middle of the night. I didn't sleep more than an hour on the nine-hour flight, and jet lag is already setting in. What should be my bedtime is bright-and-early morning here.

The sky is a soft gray-blue, the kind of muted light that feels foreign and elegant all at once. Car horns echo in the distance, and there's a faint smell of something roasting mixed with history and the promise of adventure. I'm excited to see my brother and explore places I've never been.

Beckett slips his hand into mine as we exit customs, both of us scanning the crowd. Then I spot him.

Caleb is standing by the rail, waving, looking more relaxed than I've ever seen him. He grins, and next to him is a stunning woman with long dark hair, high cheekbones, and a megawatt smile. The second our eyes meet, she lights up.

"Sadie!" she says, pulling me into an enthusiastic hug. "I'm Katy. It's so good to finally meet you!"

She has a magnetic energy, the kind that draws people in—confident, open, full of warmth. Her smile reminds me of sunshine, even on this gray London morning. I like her instantly, and that doesn't happen often.

"It's great to meet you too."

Katy laughs, still holding on to my arms. "Okay, so I have to admit something. For the longest time, I thought you were Caleb's ex-girlfriend."

My eyes widen. "Seriously?"

"Even after I saw a photo," she says, waving a hand in the air. "You two have this whole same-eyes thing going on, but you don't really look alike. I was suspicious."

I grin. "That's fair. I look like our mom. Caleb's more like

Dad. But I promise, we're siblings. No drama."

"Thank goodness," Beckett mutters under his breath, and I elbow him playfully.

We pile into the back of a black cab, and Caleb gives the driver an address. The guy confirms it's in Notting Hill and pulls into traffic like he's late for something.

"You look great," Caleb says, turning toward me. "Beckett treating you well?"

I glance over at Beckett and smile, letting my head rest on his shoulder. "Very well."

Katy beams at us. "So what's on the agenda for your trip?"

I reach into my bag and carefully pull out Rosie's notebook. "My best friend, Rosie, passed away a few months ago," I say, flipping it open gently. "She'd been in the hospital for a while, and we talked about all the places we were going to go once she got better. She would scour the internet for all the great things to see and do and paste them into her bucket list. When she died, she left me the book and asked me to do them for her. So I'm checking them off."

I hand the notebook to Katy, who takes it reverently and starts flipping through. She scans the pages, her fingers brushing over Rosie's loopy handwriting, the glued-in photos and folded maps. She takes her time, pausing at the little notes Rosie and I scribbled in the margins. A map of Edinburgh with three stars, a restaurant receipt taped next to a photo of Big Ben, a quote written in purple ink: "Life's too short to play small."

"This is incredible," she murmurs. "There's so much here. Museums, restaurants, little villages I've never even heard of. You're going to be traveling for years."

I smile and take the book back, holding it close. "That was the idea. Rosie wanted to live big, and she wanted me to do it for both of us. Poor Beckett is going to be dragged along for the ride."

He kisses my head. "And I'll love every minute of it."

Katy reaches across the seat and squeezes my hand. "We better make sure this trip counts."

I nod. As the drive continues, Caleb and Beckett catch up

on some of the gossip from home, and I get to know Katy better. She grew up in London. Her mother is a doctor for the NHS, and her father is a banker. She has four sisters. She's adorable, and I can see why Caleb loves her so much.

When we arrive at our destination, the cabbie helps us unload the luggage, and then I stand staring up at the charming brick building. It's tall and narrow, with ivy crawling up one side and white-trimmed windows that practically glow in the morning light.

Caleb unlocks the door and leads us up a narrow staircase, and the moment we step inside his flat, I stop cold. "Oh my God," I breathe. "This is stunning."

The space is a perfect mix of modern and cozy—high ceilings, exposed beams, soft lighting, plants in every corner, and framed prints on the walls that look like they were curated by a designer.

I turn to Katy, my eyebrows raised. "Please tell me you had a hand in this."

She grins. "That's actually how we met. I was hired to redecorate his place. And well, one thing led to another."

I laugh. "So this was a very successful project."

"Exactly," she says, linking her arm through mine. "Come on, let me show you around."

Caleb and Beckett disappear down the hall, and I let Katy guide me through the space, every room more charming than the last. There's a rooftop patio with twinkle lights, a kitchen that looks like it belongs in a magazine, and a bedroom that somehow manages to be both masculine and full of soft touches.

"It's absolutely perfect," I say, stepping into the guest room where our bags have already been dropped off. "You've nailed his taste so well. And this is much better than his mattress on the floor."

She laughs. "That was so uni."

"How long have you been together?"

She smirks. "About a year," she says. "I only moved in a few months ago. I'd say it's serious." Her voice softens. "Would

332

you be open to having a sister?"

I look at her, this funny, kind, beautiful woman who makes my brother happy in a way I haven't seen in a long time.

"I'd love it," I say with a smile.

Katy hugs me like we've known each other for years. When she pulls back, her eyes are sparkling. "Okay, now your turn. How serious are you and Beckett?"

I grin. "He'd get married tomorrow if I'd let him."

Her eyebrows shoot up. "Really?"

"Yeah. We've known each other a long time, and somehow, it all just fits. It was a little rough at the beginning, but now, there's no drama, no games. Just a lot of love and a deep, steady kind of certainty. It feels easy. And right."

She lets out a happy sigh. "That's exactly how it is with me and Caleb. He's already talking about moving to Paradise once he's done here."

I snort. "Oh, you're in for a shock. Do not agree to go without a good bribe."

Katy laughs. "Noted. But I'll have fun having you as a sister to gang up on him when needed."

"That's a great idea," I say.

Perhaps the future isn't just something I'm chasing for Rosie. It's something I'm excited to step into for me.

London is dazzling. Every corner is steeped in history, and it all feels surreal.

Caleb and Katy spend the entire first day with us playing tour guide—Big Ben, Westminster Abbey, the British Museum. We walk until my legs ache and I'm running purely on adrenaline and espresso. But the highlight? Katy's friend, who works at Buckingham Palace, gives us a private tour since the

King isn't in residence.

We step into one of the grand salons and I whisper, "Someone actually calls this home?"

Katy laughs. "Can you imagine waking up here every morning? I'd get lost before breakfast."

"I wouldn't even make it to the bathroom without a map," I say, spinning in a slow circle, my eyes wide.

In early evening, Caleb and Katy guide us to the South Bank docks, and before I know it, they're hugging us goodbye and waving as they step back into the London twilight. "We booked you something special," Katy calls over her shoulder as they go.

I turn to Beckett, and he grins. "A dinner cruise."

The boat is sleek and elegant, lights strung overhead, a soft breeze in my hair as we pull away from the dock. London unfurls around us. We pass under bridges, spot the towering London Eye, and glide past the Tower of London, its stone walls glowing gold in the light.

"It's incredible," I say, leaning against the railing. "What do you think?"

Beckett's standing close beside me, and his hand slips easily into mine. "I'm having a great time," he says. "But I'd have a great time anywhere, as long as it's with you."

My heart blooms.

He turns toward me, his expression serious, his thumb brushing over my knuckles. "You've changed my life, Sadie. Completely. I wouldn't have it any other way."

I blink at him as the boat rocks gently beneath our feet. Then he reaches into his jacket pocket, and my breath catches.

"I talked to Caleb," he says, stepping back just slightly. "I asked if he'd be okay with me asking you to marry me."

My hand flies to my mouth.

"He said it wasn't up to him," Beckett continues, "but he gave me his blessing. That's all I needed to hear. Because there's no one else I want by my side. I want to explore every last page of that bucket list with you — and create a new one together. Our own."

Then he's kneeling, right here on the open-air deck with the lights of London shimmering on the water around us.

He opens a small, light blue box, revealing the most beautiful ring I've ever seen.

"Sadie Calloway," he says, voice thick with emotion, "will you marry me?"

I can't stop the tears. They're falling before I can speak, my heart so full it's hard to breathe.

"Yes," I choke out, then louder—clear, so there's no mistaking it. "Yes. Always and forever."

He slides the ring onto my finger, and it fits like it was always meant to be there. When he rises, I throw my arms around him, holding tight as the boat sails on and the city sparkles behind us.

This moment is everything.

Rosie, you'd be so happy.

Six months ago, I landed on Beckett's doorstep, soaking wet, with my hastily packed suitcase. I didn't have a job or a plan. I had no idea who I was without the weight of what I'd survived.

And now here I am—engaged, loved, using my gifts and building a life that feels like mine. With great friends like Ginny and Trinity. Like Rosie always knew I could.

The lights of the city shimmer like stars in the river, and Beckett's arms tighten around me. Love brought me back to life, and now, I get to live it, one unforgettable moment at a time.

Authors note: I hope you enjoyed reading *Dr. Beckett.* I cried for weeks as I wrote about Rosie and her bucket list. If you want to see one of the trips, check out this bonus content for a PDF copy you can read on any computer at https://bookhip.com/HXTLXRK.

Thank you so much for reading Dr. Beckett! I hope you fell for Beckett and Sadie the way I did, through every sharp word, soft moment, and second chance they didn't see coming. Their story means the world to me, and I'm so grateful you came along for the ride. Up next is Dr. Ryker, and let's just say things are about to get even more complicated (and a whole lot hotter) when Ryker Paradise falls hard for the one woman he's not supposed to want...

Dr. Ryker Sneak Peek

Unedited — so it's bound to be changed a little bit.

Ginny

I'm three rounds in my darts game and my aim is getting better, which is either proof I'm finally relaxing or that I've crossed the invisible line between buzzed and dumb.

The dart lands just shy of the bullseye. I smirk, turning toward my friend Kara Bishop — except Kara is no longer on the barstool beside me. She's across the room, giggling in the arms of Jonas Goodwin, one of Paradise's finest.

Figures. One flash of a badge and a square jaw and she's reenacting a scene from a country music video.

I sigh and wave off the bartender when he glances my way. "Water," I call. "Heavy on the ice, light on the judgment."

I don't do drama. And I definitely don't do Paradise men. That's a rule I've stuck to since I moved back, and I have the self-respect to keep it. Mostly.

I just need to sober up before I order a rideshare. It's late, but not too late, and Mikey's is tame tonight. A few locals at the bar. The usual town gossip brewing over pitchers of cheap beer.

Then he walks in.

Ryker Paradise.

The door doesn't creak, but it might as well. He's got that kind of presence — like the room takes a collective breath, unsure whether to be annoyed or impressed.

He's tall, confident—and unfairly hot. His dark hair is a little tousled, his jawline looks like it's never heard of insecurity, and his smile is the kind that gets women pregnant.

I turn back to the dartboard and pretend I didn't notice.

He's not for me. Too smooth. Too pretty. Too... Paradise.

Besides, I've already made one impulsive choice tonight. I don't need a second.

"You're either aiming for the bullseye or trying to kill someone. Should I duck?"

His voice is behind me—low, teasing. I curse inwardly as I feel the corner of my mouth twitch.

I let the next dart fly. It hits a solid red ring. "Depends. You planning on making yourself a target?"

He steps closer. I can smell him now—clean soap, something warm like cedar. He's wearing a Henley that hugs his arms in all the wrong ways. Or right ways, depending on the level of alcohol in my system.

"Only if you promise to go easy on me."

I glance at him. Big mistake. His eyes are a stormy blue and completely amused.

"Ryker Paradise," I say, like his name is a warning.

"Ginny Dempsey," he replies, just as smug. "I was starting to think you were avoiding me."

Of course I was. Everyone knows what happens when a Dempsey gets tangled up with a Paradise. Drama. Scandal. Reputations ruined. And I'm fresh out of patience for small-town headlines with my name in them.

I arch a brow. "Starting to think? You're slower than I thought."

He laughs—deep, warm, and way too charming.

I turn back to the board and toss another dart. This one misses. Damn it.

"You know," he says, stepping beside me, "we could make this interesting. Loser buys the winner a drink."

"I've had enough drinks for one night."

The corner of his mouth turns up. "Then how about a bet?"

There it is. That Paradise grin.

And despite every reason not to, despite the warning bells clanging in my head louder than the bar's jukebox, I feel my mouth move.

"You're on."

He grins like he's already won. "All right then. Closest to the bullseye."

I hand him a dart. "Try not to embarrass yourself. You Paradise boys already do that enough."

He laughs again, but there's a flicker of heat behind it. I've poked the bear.

Ryker takes his time. Lines up. Throws. It lands just outside the center.

"Not bad," I say, ignoring the flip in my stomach. "But not great either."

He shrugs. "Mediocrity looks good on me."

I step up and throw without overthinking. The dart lands—just outside his mark.

"Damn."

He raises a brow. "Looks like you're buying the first round of whatever we're betting."

"I thought it wasn't a drink wager."

"It wasn't." He steps closer. "But I'm open to suggestions."

The way he says it sends a shiver down my spine. Not dirty. Not innocent either.

"Are you always this cocky?"

He grins. "Only when I know I'm right."

"Right about what?"

His eyes flick to mine, steady and smug. "That you've been watching me since the moment I walked in."

I scoff, but the heat crawling up my neck betrays me.

"It's okay," he says, softer now. "I've been watching you too."My laugh comes out sharper than I intend. "You think very highly of yourself."

"No," he says, quieter. "I just pay attention."

Something about the way he says it pulls me in. I've spent so long brushing off attention that feels performative or possessive. But this? This feels different. Like he's seeing me — really seeing me.

I hate it.

I love it.

"You're not my type," I blurt. He's the kind of guy I've spent years avoiding. The kind that burns bright, then burns out. I've had enough ashes in my life. But damn it, there's something about him that makes me want to throw logic out the window and chase the fire anyway.

His mouth tips into a smirk. "What is your type?"

"Safe. Boring. Uncomplicated."

He steps closer. "Good thing I'm none of those things."

I exhale, low and shaky. I should walk away. Call my ride. Go home and eat a cold grilled cheese sandwich and forget any of this ever happened.

But I don't.

Because Ryker is heat and pressure and chaos. And maybe I need a little chaos tonight.

"I'm not sleeping with you," I say, even though part of me already knows I'm lying.

His eyes darken just a little. "Then let's play another round."

"Darts?"

He leans in, close enough that I feel the warmth of his breath against my cheek. "Flirting."

I should stop this. I should care that he's a Paradise, and I'm a Dempsey, and this whole thing has "town scandal" written all over it.

But I toss the dart anyway. It lands a fraction closer to the bullseye than last time. I smile, but I don't turn around. I know he's still behind me — I can feel him.

"Not bad," Ryker murmurs. His voice is low, like he's

impressed. Or turned on. Maybe both.

I straighten, my skin tight with awareness. "Are we still playing, or just pretending it's about darts?"

His chuckle is warm. Dangerous. "That depends. Are we still pretending you're not interested?"

I finally face him. "You want honesty?"

"Always."

I take a step closer. So does he.

"I think you're insanely attractive," I say, watching his pupils dilate just enough to catch it. "But you're also trouble. You've probably slept with half the single women in this bar."

He lifts a shoulder. "Exaggeration. Maybe a third."

That earns him a snort. "See? Trouble."

"Maybe," he says, voice dropping. "But the good kind."

He's close now. Too close. And the part of me that usually pulls away isn't moving.

"You're not what I need," I whisper.

"No," he agrees, eyes fixed on mine. "But maybe I'm what you want."

God help me, he's not wrong.

His gaze drops to my mouth, then lifts again. He doesn't move, doesn't touch me. He's waiting—for permission or for me to run.

I do neither.

"I don't do messy," I say.

He nods. "Then we'll keep it clean."

I arch a brow. "Doubt it."

"Dirty can be fun too," he says with a grin that should be illegal. "If you trust the person you're getting dirty with."

The air between us snaps taut. My pulse hammers. My mouth is dry.

"Say it," he murmurs.

"Say what?"

"That you want me."

I should walk away. I want to walk away. But his voice is gravel and heat, and my body's not listening to my brain.

I lean in, close enough that our noses nearly touch. "What happens if I do?"

He smiles. Slow. Dangerous. "Then I stop waiting."

Ryker's stands before me hiding me from the crowd at the bar. His hand slides up my thigh. "Are you wearing panties?"

I laugh, tossing my head back. "Wouldn't you like to know?"

His hand slides under my skirt, fingers finding the heat through my panties. "You're so wet for me."

I shut my eyes for a minute and let him take me away and his fingers are like magic.

"What do you want?"

"You," I whisper.

He pulls back from me and reaches for my hand. I look around and no one is watch us. He drags me back to the private party room that has a pool table.

The door shuts behind us, and he locks it. I don't want to think about how he knows this, instead I want to see if he's half the man I've made him out to be.

He leans down and his lips touch mine and it's fire.

The kiss ignites something deep within me, an urgency that pulses in time with the rhythm of my racing heart. His hands frame my face, firm and possessive, as if he's claiming me in this dimly lit haven away from prying eyes. I melt against him, surrendering to the heat that envelops us. My brain tells me this is a giant mistake but my body can't get enough.

"Tell me what you want," he breathes against my lips, his voice low and electric.

"I want..." My words falter as his thumb grazes my cheek, a simple yet intimate touch that sends shivers down my spine. "I want you to fuck me. I don't want a relationship with you. I don't want a repeat."

His smile is feral, predatory. "Then let's make it unforgettable."

With that, he spins me around, pressing me against the cool felt of the pool table. It's a stark contrast against the warmth radiating from his body as he steps closer, trapping me between him and the table. I can feel his breath on my neck, each exhale a promise of what's to come.

He's standing too close. His voice too soft, too sure. Everything about him is temptation wrapped in trouble, and I should walk away.

But I don't.

I look up at him, eyes locked. "You're not what I need."

"No," he says, his voice like smoke and slow jazz. "But I might be what you want."

His confidence makes me want to push him away — and pull him closer. I've made rules for myself, drawn lines I swore I wouldn't cross.

But something about Ryker makes me want to break every single one.

He brushes a strand of hair from my face, fingers lingering just long enough to make my skin buzz. "Tell me to stop," he murmurs. "And I will."

I swallow hard. My brain screams yes. My body says nothing at all.

Instead, I step in — into his space, into this moment, into everything I should avoid.

"Don't stop."

His mouth crashes into mine, and everything after that is heat and chaos.

"Do you like playing games?" he asks, his voice thick with anticipation.

"Only when I know I'm going to win," I reply, casting him a challenging glance over my shoulder.

He laughs softly, a sound that reverberates through the air like a promise. "Oh, I intend to ensure you enjoy every second of this one."

His hands roam along my sides, exploring every curve as if he's mapping out territory. I arch into his touch, craving more of that delicious friction. Just as I think I have him figured out, he pulls back slightly.

"Are you ready?" he asks, eyes focused intensely on mine, daring me to say no.

I nod, a heady mix of nerves and thrill coursing through me. "More than ready." The words tumble out, laced with a challenge that echoes in the charged air between us.

In an instant, he's on me again, lips crashing onto mine, urgency transforming every kiss into something raw and primal. His hands find the hem of my skirt, fingers inching up my thigh with teasing deliberation, and I gasp, heat pooling low in my belly. He pulls away just long enough to lock eyes with me, the intensity of his gaze sending sparks dancing along my skin.

In one hard snap, he pulls my thong off and puts it in his pocket. He pushes me back on the pool table as his fingers dive into my sweat heat.

I gasp, the sensation electrifying as he explores with deliberate precision. The room fades away — the music, laughter, everything blurs into the background until it's just him and me, lost in this moment of raw desire.

"Is this what you wanted?" he murmurs, his voice low and rough against my ear, as if he knows exactly how to unravel me. My fingers scramble for purchase on the edge of the pool table, grounding myself amidst the spiraling pleasure that threatens to consume me.

"Yes," I manage to breathe out, the word a desperate plea woven with longing. "Don't stop."

He smirks, a devilish glint in his eyes. "Oh, I won't." And with that promise hanging heavy in the air, he plunges deeper, creating sensations that make my head spin.

I can feel the tension building inside me like a coiled spring, ready to snap. Every brush of his fingertips is a challenge to my resolve, a reminder that I had said no attachments — only this wild escape.

"Look at you," he whispers as if reading my thoughts. "So ready to let go."

His fingers move faster now, coaxing soft gasps and moans from my lips. The world outside this room becomes irrelevant. Nothing exists but us and the electric pulse of our bodies colliding in fervor.

"Come all over my fingers so I can lick you clean."

The command sends a jolt of heat surging through me, igniting a wildfire. My body responds instinctively, surrendering to the crescendo building within. "Ryker," I breathe, the name escaping my lips like a prayer, both a plea and an invitation.

I bite my lip to stifle the moans pooling at the back of my throat, but it's futile. Sounds escape me as pleasure unfurls within—raw and unfiltered, echoing against the walls of our secret sanctuary. I arch my back, granting him access to every part of me he desires.

"Just like that," he breathes, his breath hot against my skin. "You're so beautiful when you're lost in it."

Something inside me shatters—fragments of restraint dissolving as I plunge headfirst into ecstasy. My body quakes under the force of it as waves crash over me. I'm swept away by a current that's impossible to fight.

He watches me closely, those blue eyes glimmering with triumph as I spiral further into this intoxicating release. The world outside ceases to exist.

With one last deep thrust of his fingers, I come undone— my body convulsing around him as every nerve ignites in bliss. But he doesn't stop there, he bends down and his tongue laps up my climax and sucks my clit.

The sensation is electric, a jolt of fire igniting every inch of my skin. I grip the edge of the pool table, my body trembling as he devours me, his mouth working magic that has me teetering on the brink of another wave. My breath is ragged, punctuated by soft cries that spill from my lips against my will.

"Ryker," I gasp, feeling the heat rise in the pit of my stomach once more. "Please…"

He pauses just long enough to look up at me, eyes dark and filled with a primal hunger. "Please what?" he taunts, reapplying pressure with his tongue that sends shockwaves through my core.

"Don't stop," I manage to plead, every syllable laced with desperation. "I need —"

But before I can finish, he dives back in with a fervor that steals my breath away. His tongue dances with expert precision, coaxing me toward an edge I didn't know could exist. I arch further into him, losing myself completely in the sensations that ripple through my body like wildfire.

I can feel the heat pooling deeper within me again, building and tightening, threatening to spill over into something fierce and consuming. His fingers find my thighs, holding me steady as if he knows this ride is going to be wild.

"Look at you," he murmurs against my skin, sending a shiver coursing through me. "So beautiful when you're like this."

The words wrap around me like a silken thread weaving deeper into this web of lust we've created.

He lifts me off and undoes his belt buckle. Holy shit his cock is huge. He pulls a condom out of his pocket and rolls it down his cock. "Now get ready for me to really rock your world."

He pulls me down from the table and bends me over. He begins to push in and it's tight.

I gasp at the sensation — every inch of him stretching me, filling me in a way I never knew I craved. My body instinctively adjusts, welcoming his intrusion as my breath hitches in my throat. There's no hesitation, no second-guessing. This is what I wanted — the raw connection forged in the flickering shadows of our impulsive desires.

"Damn, you feel incredible," he growls, his voice a low rumble that sends delicious shivers down my spine. He grips my hips tightly, anchoring me to him as he thrusts deeper, his rhythm both commanding and electrifying. Each movement sends ripples of pleasure coursing through me, igniting like a live wire.

"Ryker," I moan, the name slipping past my lips as if it were a sacred incantation.

He responds with an intensity that fuels the fire building inside me. "That's it. Let go for me." His thrusts become more insistent, harder, and the sound of skin meeting skin reverberates around us like a primal heartbeat. I can feel the weight of his body against mine, a beautiful balance of control and abandon wrapping around us both.

My vision blurs as each thrust sends me spiraling further into bliss. The world outside fades into nothingness. It's just the two of us trapped in this wild moment where time feels suspended. Each push ignites something deep within — the tension coiling tighter and tighter until it becomes unbearable.

"God, that was good," he murmurs as he leans over to press hot kisses along my neck, between breaths filled with desperation. "Shall we take this back to your place?"

"Can't. I have a friend staying with me."

"How about my place?"

His hands find my breast and he pulls and plays with my nipples. I can't think when he does that.

"Okay, that fine."

What the hell am I doing?

He tucks himself away with a wicked grin and reaches for my hand. "Let's get out of here. Your car's safe, but you're not — at least not with me."

I should stop. I should say no.

But instead, I let him lead me out the back door — straight into trouble.

Available in October 2025 Preorder/Download **on Amazon**.

Thank you

This book was brought to you by...

Early-morning writing sprints, way too many cups of coffee, lot's Earl Grey tea, and plot twists that even surprised me.

It was powered by dog-eared notebooks, deleted paragraphs, and that one perfect line that made it all worth it.

It was saved by:

Readers who leave reviews, share my books, and send the kind of messages that make me teary-eyed (in the best way). You're the reason these stories keep going.

My husband, who's read every book, listened to every meltdown, and still shows up with snacks and encouragement like it's his full-time job. You are my muse, my anchor, and my favorite plot twist.

My boys, who smile politely when I talk about "Mommy's kissy books" and pretend not to be horrified. Your quiet support means more than you'll ever know.

Jessica Royer Oken, my brilliant developmental editor, who takes my chaos and turns it into something cohesive and sparkly. You're a magician with a red pen.

Courtnay, Linda, Iris, Nancy, and Diana, the superhero proofreaders who spot every rogue comma, missing word, and sneaky typo before the world ever sees a page.

This book was also brought to you by doubt, perseverance, and the kind of stubborn hope that refuses to quit.

Thank you for being part of the journey.

With all my love,
Gracie

Books by Grace Maxwell

Men of Mercy

Doctor of the Heart (Paisley & Davis)
Doctor of Women (Nadine & Michael)
Doctor of Sports (Eliza & Steve)
Doctor of Beauty (Laine & Jack)
Men of Mercy Box Set

Mercy Medical Emergency

Doctor Delight (Tori & Griffin)
Doctor Bossy (Amelia & Kent)
Doctor Rebel (Lucy & Chance)
Doctor Enemy (Ava & Roman)
Previously released as *A Doctor for Valentines* **in "Love is in the Air, Vol 3"**
Doctor Tyrant (Hailey & Christian)
Mercy Medical Emergency Box Set

Brothers Paradise

Dr. Greyson (Trinity & Greyson)
Dr. Beckett (Sadie & Beckett)
Dr. Ryker (Ginny & Ryker)